W9-CDZ-872

True love is worth fighting for....

"Virginia Henley writes the kind of
book you simply can't stop reading."
—BERTRICE SMALL

Unmasked

Virginia Henley

A SIGNET BOOK

SIGNET
Published by New American Library, a division of
Penguin Group (USA) Inc., 375 Hudson Street,
New York, New York 10014, USA
Penguin Group (Canada), 90 Eglinton Avenue East, Suite 700, Toronto,
Ontario M4P 2Y3, Canada (a division of Pearson Penguin Canada Inc.)
Penguin Books Ltd., 80 Strand, London WC2R 0RL, England
Penguin Ireland, 25 St. Stephen's Green, Dublin 2,
Ireland (a division of Penguin Books Ltd.)
Penguin Group (Australia), 250 Camberwell Road, Camberwell, Victoria 3124,
Australia (a division of Pearson Australia Group Pty. Ltd.)
Penguin Books India Pvt. Ltd., 11 Community Centre, Panchsheel Park,
New Delhi - 110 017, India
Penguin Group (NZ), cnr Airborne and Rosedale Roads, Albany,
Auckland 1310, New Zealand (a division of Pearson New Zealand Ltd.)
Penguin Books (South Africa) (Pty.) Ltd., 24 Sturdee Avenue,
Rosebank, Johannesburg 2196, South Africa

Penguin Books Ltd., Registered Offices:
80 Strand, London WC2R 0RL, England

First published by Signet, an imprint of New American Library,
a division of Penguin Group (USA) Inc.

First Printing, September 2005
10 9 8 7 6 5 4 3 2 1

Copyright © Virginia Henley, 2005
All rights reserved

 REGISTERED TRADEMARK—MARCA REGISTRADA

Printed in the United States of America

This one is for my friends:
the Loopies, the Ladies of Louisiana,
the RT gang, and last but assuredly
not least my RWA sisters.

Prologue

Nottingham Castle
Summer 1644

$\mathcal{R}$obert Montgomery stood tall and proud in the castle's solar, looking down with interest at the small female beside him. Red gold tendrils peeped out from beneath her white lace headdress, and her dark lashes were modestly lowered to her cheeks. In the candlelight she reminded him of an image he'd recently seen in a painting. *She has the face of an angel!* He glanced at his father, Alex Greysteel Montgomery, Earl of Eglinton, and allowed most of his resentment to dissolve. A month ago when he'd been informed of his betrothal to Elizabeth Cavendish, he'd balked at the idea, but his father had been adamant.

"Do you not realize how high in the pecking order this girl is? Her father, William, is Viscount Mansfield of Nottingham, Baron Ogle, Baron Cavendish of Bolsover and Earl of Newcastle. He's also cousin to the Earl of Devonshire, who is considered equal to royalty. Fact is they've more money than the Royal Stuarts. If we turn down this match, it would toss away a dowry and estate of twenty thousand pounds."

Robert knew immediately there was little chance of that. Greysteel Montgomery was an authoritarian widower who ruled his own roost. Since Robert had no mother to fight his battles, he'd voiced his own protest. "I warrant that thirteen is too young to be betrothed, sir."

"Not when Mistress Cavendish is only seven. A six-year age difference is perfect! There's a possibility she may inherit Bolsover Castle someday. It's a good match for them too. A Montgomery is as good as a Cavendish! Our Worksop holdings adjoin their properties, and Newcastle inherited his mother's Ogle land, which runs parallel with ours in Northumberland. That is what has prompted this offer. The king has summoned his nobles to Nottingham to plan war strategy. We can have the betrothal ceremony there and kill two crows with one stone."

Lady Cavendish looked at her small daughter with love. *I'm so relieved to get her settled. Robert Montgomery is such a noble, upright young man that I shall have no fear for Elizabeth's future if something should happen to me.* She made a surreptitious sign of the cross. She knew her health was not robust—last winter she had almost died from pneumonia.

She glanced at her husband, William, who smiled his encouragement. She knew he doted on the child and wanted only the best for her. She looked at the Earl of Eglinton. *He's dark and dominant, but he exudes strength.* Her glance moved to the younger Greysteel, who stood beside her daughter. *He's cut from the same cloth. Elizabeth will have need of his strength.*

The future bride stood deep in thought, remembering the shocked look on her mother's face when she had insisted, "I can't be betrothed to Montgomery! I am going to marry Charles!"

"That is impossible, Elizabeth. Charles will be King of England someday. He must marry a lady with royal blood because she will become the queen. Montgomery is noble and strong. I vow he will protect you and always keep you safe, my darling."

Robert watched Nottingham Castle's chaplain step forward to perform the brief betrothal ceremony. He gave his consent gravely and then the chaplain put the question to Elizabeth. Before she answered, she raised her lashes and gave him a look of appraisal that made him feel somehow inadequate. He clenched his jaw and stared a challenge into eyes that were deep green. He straightened his shoulders, knowing they were broad and well muscled for his age, and when his betrothed lowered her lashes in what seemed meek acquiescence, his confidence returned.

The legal documents were duly signed and Lady Cavendish whisked her daughter off to bed with a protective arm about her, leaving the men to more important matters of war and whiskey.

The adolescent males riding through the acres of Nottingham Castle suddenly challenged one another to an impromptu race. Mounted on a massive bay gelding, swarthy Charles Stuart easily took the lead. The prince's startling physical maturity belied his fourteen years, making his twelve-year-old brother, James, and the Villiers brothers look like boys. Only Robert Montgomery, called Greysteel after his father, was a worthy challenger. Mounted on his sleek grey hunter, he pulled alongside Charles, and the young men exchanged a quick grin, acknowledging admiration for each other's horsemanship, as they left the rest to eat their dust.

From out of nowhere, a small black mare streaked past them, flying on the wind. Astride was a female who looked far too young to even approach a horse, let alone ride one.

"Who the devil is that?" Greysteel demanded in outrage.

Prince Charles grinned ruefully. "Lizzy Cavendish, the Earl of Newcastle's youngest and your betrothed, I'm afraid. My governor is the finest horseman in England and she's had the benefit of his instruction since before she could walk."

Greysteel's thunderous brows lifted. "Her mount carries no weight—that's why it streaked past as if we were stopped."

The girl's brother, Henry Cavendish, caught up with the prince and Montgomery. "She's an imp of Satan, a throwback to our great-grandmother Bess Hardwick. Father has spoiled her rotten. Frizzy Lizzy does and says whatever she pleases. She has most shocking manners, but Father laughs and encourages her."

As the young men slowed to a canter, Charles spoke quietly. "You cannot criticize your father to me, Henry. When I display shocking manners he laughs and encourages me too." The prince's father, King Charles, was a cold, remote, rigid man who believed in his *divine right* and would be obeyed at all costs. Courtly William Cavendish, Earl of Newcastle, had become Charles's savior six years ago when he'd been appointed to the governorship of the royal heir. "He taught me equestrian skills, swordsmanship, and believes I shouldn't be overstudious or too devout, for which I shall be eternally grateful." The earl also had taught Charles to speak courtly French, educated him to be gracious to his subjects and taught him that, to ladies especially, he could never be too civil or obliging.

When the young males reached the stables, they dismounted, happy to mingle with the Royalist soldiers crowding the courtyard, rather than enter Nottingham Castle, where the king's loyal nobles had been summoned to discuss strategy for the Civil War that was dividing England. Charles and Greysteel, far more interested in the soldiers' weapons than their uniforms, lusted to be in the men's places, ready to do battle for their country.

King Charles had dismissed Parliament over a decade ago and ruled with royal absolutism. The Stuart king and queen took part in High Church rituals, which both Protestants and Puritans viewed as dangerously papist. Angry Scots objected to a new English prayer book and signed a Covenant binding them to Presbyterianism, wholly at odds with the Anglican Church.

"Allow me to introduce my father's cousin Colonel Charles Cavendish," Henry said with pride.

"I understand you recruited all these men." *And*

paid for them yourself! Charles could not hide his admiration.

"It wasn't difficult, Your Highness. They volunteered."

"Oh, please call me Charles, Colonel. Your magnificent sword was acquired on your travels to Cairo, no doubt."

The Cavalier officer smiled. "Come out onto the lawn and I'll let you try it."

Charles arched a brow at Greysteel, who nodded eagerly. "If you'll furnish my friend Montgomery with a sword, I accept with pleasure, Colonel Cavendish."

Lizzy marched into the castle hall oblivious of her muddy riding boots and trailing damp skirts. Her red gold curls were a tangle from her wild ride. She deftly sidestepped her governess and gazed up with interest at the men gathered about her father. "Have you decided on your strategy to whip the enemy yet?"

As the gathering of men, which included His Royal Highness King Charles, Prince Rupert of the Rhine, the Earl of Saint Albans, the Earl of Eglinton and her noble relative the Earl of Devonshire, stared down in consternation, her mother stepped forward with an apology on her lips. "Forgive this intrusion, gentlemen. I'm afraid Elizabeth is a throwback."

Her father, the Earl of Newcastle, laughed and pointed to the portrait of his grandmother Bess Hardwick, which decorated the mantel above the great fireplace.

"I'm not a throwback!" The precocious child stamped her foot adamantly and glared daggers at the men. "A throwback is a little fish that's not worth keeping."

"Elizabeth, it is because you have an uncanny resemblance both in appearance and manner to your great-grandmother that we call you a throwback." He directed her gaze to the portrait. "There, do you see the likeness?"

The onlookers didn't have long to wait for her reaction. "How could you, Father? She's old and ugly! I'd rather be a little fish than a cod's head like her!"

The Earl of Devonshire glanced at the portrait. "Grandmother was a termagant and by the sound of things you haven't fallen far from the tree, Elizabeth."

"Don't call me Elizabeth. I hate it! Mother, Grandmamma and Great-grandmamma all had that horrid name. I've decided I shall have a beautiful name."

"That's enough, Lizzy." Glancing apprehensively at the grim-faced Earl of Eglinton, her mother took her by the hand and put her in the care of the hovering governess with a speaking look that said, *Try to control her.*

Maude clamped a firm hand to her charge's shoulder and led her away. The moment they were alone she pinched her cruelly. "Upstairs to your room, Lady Lizzy."

Tears sprang to Lizzy's eyes as she wrenched herself away from Maude. "To hell with my room—I shall go and find Charles."

She ran out into the garden and when she saw the sword fight on the lawn, the pinch was forgotten. She joined the group of watching boys, her emerald eyes alight with excitement. "Bravo, Charles! Beat the scurvy dog to his knees and slice him to ribbons!"

Colonel Cavendish reprimanded her. " 'Tis disrespectful to call the prince by his first name."

"Rubbish! I don't disrespect him. I love him."

She watched with disappointment as the two dark youths fought to a draw and saluted each other with respect. "Charles, why didn't you skewer him?"

Robert was stunned. Surely it was his betrothed's duty to champion him. *The little devil's spawn makes no bones about her preference for Prince Charles.*

"I'm afraid skewering him is not so easy, Lady Elizabeth. I have the longer reach, but Greysteel has the greater staying power. It's the breadth of his shoulders, I warrant."

"What sort of silly name is *Greysteel?*" she challenged.

Robert fought an impulse to smack her. "You are the rudest little girl I have ever encountered." His anger ticked up a notch when the hellion looked pleased.

Henry agreed. "Her manners are shocking—I warned you."

"Not soon enough," Greysteel said succinctly.

"Do you call yourself Greysteel because your eyes are grey and you ride a grey horse?"

"No, Elizabeth—"

She butted in, "I no longer answer to *Elizabeth.*" She stared down at a hybrid rose with dark crimson velvet petals. "I have decided my name shall be *Velvet.*"

Greysteel Montgomery mocked her by laughing out loud.

Velvet's eyes narrowed. She balled up her fists, wanting to jab him in his solar plexus and knock him into the fishpond, but she didn't quite dare. He looked capable of beating her. "If you can call yourself Greysteel, I can call myself Velvet!"

"She's spoiled and insufferable," Montgomery declared. "She needs to have her arse tanned."

Charles smiled indulgently. "I think she is enchanting. She's not only beautiful; she says exactly what she thinks. A decade from now she will be a heartbreaker." He plucked the rose and presented it to her with a gallant bow. "I think *Velvet* an enchanting name. It suits you well, mistress."

Greysteel looked at the prince as if he were a lunatic. "She's been indulged to such a degree she's ruined for life."

Charles's eyes twinkled. "You too express your opinions with frankness. I like that. I detest fawners and flatterers above all things."

A shot rang out and the young males instantly lost all interest in the little redhead and tore pell-mell back to the soldiers, who were having target practice with the new firearms they had been issued. With envious eyes Charles and Greysteel watched the men load and fire, and each decided that before the day was over he would have his own pistol.

The following day, William Cavendish, Earl of Newcastle, rode out alone with Prince Charles. "The king has given me the command of the royal forces in the north."

"At your own expense, my lord," Charles said shrewdly.

The earl waved that aside. "The Parliamentarians have demanded that the vast armory at Hull be transferred to the Tower of London. Naturally, His Majesty has refused and my immediate mission will be to secure that arsenal."

"I want to come with you, my lord," Charles said eagerly.

"Alas, no, Your Highness. I reluctantly pass your governorship to Lord Jermyn, Earl of Saint Albans."

"I'm taller than most recruits and as strong," he protested.

Newcastle, who understood the prince's hunger to do his part, held up his hand. "We are in sore need of arms, men and money. You are to go on a progress through Radnorshire, North Wales and Cheshire. Your popularity will draw recruits like a magnet. Each of us must go where he is most effective."

"You are ever the diplomat, my lord. I suppose I must accede with grace, but *damnation*, I'd like to see battle!"

"My cousin Charles has been put in charge of Nottingham and Lincolnshire and will ride with Prince Rupert's cavalry."

"I thank you both for so generously offering your services and your fortunes to the Crown. It is most selfless of you."

The following day, Prince Charles, his brother James and the Villiers boys were leaving for Raglan with Lord Jermyn. Robert Montgomery was returning home to Worksop, where his father, the earl, was to recruit his own army. The two dark young men who had become friends said their good-byes in the castle courtyard.

"Good-bye, Greysteel. I hope we meet again soon."

"Godspeed, Charles. I hope our armies have a speedy victory." They grinned at one another with the confidence of youth, and Greysteel lowered his voice.

"I hope it lasts long enough that you and I can ride into battle."

"My own thought, exactly," Charles agreed confidentially.

High above them at her chamber window, Velvet Cavendish watched her betrothed and Prince Charles depart. The thought of war secretly terrified her. To banish her overwhelming fear she stuck out her chin and shouted, "It's not fair! I want to go to war! Why did I have to be born a girl?"

Chapter One

*C*aptain Greysteel Montgomery came instantly alert the moment he awoke. War had sharpened his senses so that he knew immediately where he was, where his men were and whether danger threatened. He was a disciplinarian who demanded obedience and handled his men with total authority. He had a stark, dark countenance and fierce grey eyes, which could burn holes into any soldier who didn't give his all. Those who'd served under him in battle swore his name came from having guts of steel.

He had joined the army at fifteen, fighting in his father's regiment until he'd been promoted to captain at twenty. Hardened by war, he had seen too much violence, blood and death in his twenty-six years. He had fought many battles, tasting victory in some and bitter defeat in others, like Dunbar and Worcester.

After the Parliamentarians had executed King Charles, Greysteel had sworn an oath to help restore the Crown of England to its rightful heir, his friend Charles II. Now only a few pockets of Royalist fighters remained. Most had decided it was a lost cause and accepted Cromwell's rule to preserve their funds. His own father had decided that the Montgomery estates were more important than profitless loyalty to an exiled king.

The men Greysteel now commanded had been recruited in Northumberland. They were young, reckless fighters and his greatest challenge was not leading them in battle, but controlling them when they were not engaged in combat. They were waiting, close to the Scottish Border, for an invasion force to land that Charles Stuart had gathered in Europe.

Greysteel rolled up his blanket, impervious to the hard ground he'd slept on, and shattered the predawn silence.

"A new day! Up and at it!" His voice rumbled like low thunder over his sleeping men, who roused instantly, removed their clothes and began racing to the river, making a deadly challenge of who'd reach the water first. As he stripped, Greysteel did a count of naked bodies before he started to run. He wasn't the first to submerge, but he was first to reach the far bank of the river and start back.

Later, after the horses were watered and his men were wolfing down their first meal of the day, he moved among them, selecting half a dozen for guard duty.

"I know it seems like our wait is endless, but when the Royalist mercenary forces arrive, our orders are to cross the Border with them to strengthen the Scots' revolt. If you see anyone, friend or foe, sound the alarm loud and clear."

Greysteel knew his pubescent warriors' abundant sexual energy must be harnessed and channeled into activities that kept them at their physical peak without being lethal as they played a waiting game. Hunting, wrestling, racing and boulder throwing were favorite rough exercises. "Choose teams to practice close combat. Gashes and bloody noses are expected, but I will tolerate no more broken bones," he warned sternly.

The exercise had been under way only long enough to get the men's blood high when the guard shouted, "Royalist soldiers!" Greysteel tore up the lookout hill to view for himself what was afoot. He saw a great force of mounted men closing in on them, and knew his guard had made a terrible mistake. He recognized General Monck's Coldstream Guards. Monck was Cromwell's military commander in Scotland.

"Enemy upon us! Mount up! Prepare to attack!"

Some of his young soldiers tried to flee and were cut down by the forces that now surrounded them. Greysteel fought back furiously but saw that his men, greatly outnumbered, were receiving more wounds than they inflicted. He knew the young devils would all die if he didn't put a stop to it. Though it almost choked him, he thundered out an order. "Surrender!"

Saint-Germain, France

Velvet Cavendish lay in her bed dreaming. A rebellious feeling rose up inside her and threatened to explode as she listened to her governess.

"A lady does not laugh out loud. It shows a lack of

breeding and moreover, it is downright vulgar. A lady merely smiles."

Velvet laughed and woke herself up. It took only a moment for her to realize where she was. A sigh of regret escaped her lips as she realized that luxuries such as governesses were long gone.

Her father's days of glory, when the late King Charles had given him command of the royal forces in the north, had not lasted long. The Earl of Newcastle had failed in his siege of Hull and his troops in Lincolnshire were destroyed by Cromwell. When Prince Rupert, in command of the Royalist Cavalry at Marston Moor, suffered defeat, King Charles lost the north to Parliament. Newcastle had fled with his family to France, where they had stayed at the opulent French Court of Versailles for a time, but for the past dozen years had lived at the impoverished English Court of Saint-Germain with the other exiles.

"Though I'll be a woman of twenty next week, my clothes are those of a young girl." Velvet looked down at her ankles, which were no longer covered by the gown she'd donned. *I'll let the hem down, but that won't solve the tightness across my breasts.* She felt guilty about needing clothes when her mother hadn't had a new gown in a decade.

Sadness clouded Velvet's thoughts. Her mother grew thinner and looked more wan by the week. She was wasting away. She had a chronic cough and was often racked by spasms. "I'll take breakfast with Mother and make sure she eats." Velvet picked up an astrology book to take along. *When she has her* sieste *this afternoon I shall go outside and watch for Father. Surely he will return from the coast today.*

*   *   *

Bruges, Belgium

Charles Stuart, held fast by Morpheus, was in the midst of a sensual dream. He'd been in so many beds in his years in exile, the females all blurred together. Except the first. The lady had seduced him and he often had a recurring dream about her.

Charles lifted heavy lids and smiled uxoriously. The soft breasts cushioned upon his chest made his cock stir. His hands came up to caress a pair of lush bottom cheeks. "Bonjour, my beautiful lady, I am yours to command."

The Duchesse de Chatillon traced the prince's long nose and sensual lips with a fingertip. "You are insatiable."

The corner of his mouth went up. "I am eighteen."

"That explains everything . . . that and your Medici blood." She shivered. "Your Italianate swarthiness excites me."

"My lovely liar—I know what excites you." He lifted her onto his rigid weapon and drove it home. When he was sheathed to the hilt, and her cries of pleasure filled the air, he rolled her beneath him and rode her until the curtains of the bed billowed from their gyrations.

Sated, she reclined and watched him dress. Her hooded eyes showed the triumph she felt over being bedded by a royal prince. Her seduction had succeeded where all her rivals' had failed.

Though Charles's clothes were immaculate, his shirt boasted no fine lace and the cuffs of his brocade coat were frayed. He combed his fingers through his long black lovelocks to rid them of tangles and reached for his hat. "Tonight, ma belle?"

"Ah, non. I think it politic that I reconcile with my husband. The Duc de Chatillon returns today."

Charles bowed gallantly. He felt used and slightly more cynical than he had yesterday, if that was possible.

Charles awoke with a start. He was alone, the shabby chamber was small, and the fire had burned to cold ash. "Lord God, I hardly knew what cynical was at eighteen." Since then, it seemed everyone in his life had tried to use him and many had succeeded. His efforts to return his father to the throne had ended in miserable failure. Parliament had executed his father, and for nine years Charles had been a king without a country.

He had seized every opportunity to regain his Crown, even sailing to Scotland to lead the Covenant army Argyll had raised. He fought battles from the Border all the way to Worcester, where Cromwell defeated him with an army of thirty thousand paid for by a heavy burden of taxes imposed on the people of England.

Charles, barely escaping with his life, found that neither France nor Holland would have him back. His small Court now lived in Bruges, Belgium, territory owned by Spain. In order to survive he had learned to vacillate, prevaricate and make his decisions in the secret recesses of his own mind. He had learned to his cost that the advice his courtiers gave was often to their own advantage.

He slipped from the bed and donned a darned linen shirt and breeches. He knelt at the hearth to kindle a fire and then put a few coals on it. He sat down at the table and pushed aside the bills; his debts were insupportable. His fists clenched in angry frustration as he reread the letter from King Philip of Spain. Charles had gathered a force of Irish and Scots Royalists, and Spain had promised to supply ships and money for an invasion that would regain his Crown. Now Spain had reneged, claiming its treasury was depleted from its war with France.

Charles thought of all the loyal Royalist forces scattered about the Border, waiting to join an invasion that would never come. As a soldier and as a king, he felt his heart bleed for them.

An aide brought him bread and cheese on a plain trencher. He had not tasted meat in a fortnight. Charles smiled and thanked the man graciously. He would not allow his rage to spill out.

"I love you." Velvet Cavendish tucked her mother into bed and then read to her from their favorite book of astrology until she fell asleep. She closed it softly and left the bedroom.

Speaking to her mother's servingwoman, she said, "Emma, I promised to visit Princess Minette today. Mother seems comfortable. If she starts to cough, give her the medicine. I'll be back in an hour." Then Velvet hurried through the corridors of Saint-Germain Palace, where the Royalist exiles lived. She went outside and stood at the gate, searching the road for an approaching horseman. When there was no sign of her father, she went back inside and made her way to the queen's apartments.

"Velvet! How lovely to see you." The dark eyes of Henriette-Anne, affectionately called Minette, lit up with delight.

Velvet kissed the young girl's cheek and felt a stab of pity for the dark princess whose thin shoulders were uneven. The poverty she had lived in all her life was pitiable. Her mother, Queen Henrietta Maria, resolved to maintain the Royalist cause at any price, had sacrificed her guards, maids of honor, carriages and horses. She had been unable to restore her husband to the Crown, but now pinned all her hopes on her son, England's rightful king. Minette's clothes were shabby, her luxuries nonexistent. The princess lived a life of hardship and humility, which few royals had ever endured.

Minette drew her to a window seat and took out a letter.

"Is that from Charles . . . I mean, His Majesty?"

"Yes, but it's an old one. I like to keep it with me. Tell me about him, Velvet. I haven't seen him for five years."

It was a familiar ritual between them. "Charles was the most gallant gentleman I ever met." Velvet's thoughts flew back to the last conversation she'd had with him, when she was fifteen and he'd come to Saint-Germain to visit his mother.

"Velvet! You are surely the most beautiful lady in France."

Her heart beat wildly. "Your Highness, you honor me."

He quickly raised her from her curtsy. "Let's not be formal, Velvet. Please call me Charles."

She smiled and curiosity got the better of her. "Do you miss the French Court?" Velvet knew he lived in an austere apartment at the Louvre, and could hardly believe he preferred the grime of Paris to the opulence of Versailles.

"Truthfully, no. In the beginning, since my mother was

sister to a King of France, I was naive enough to believe we would be guests. Eventually, it dawned on me that we were refugees—as are all the Royalist exiles," he added with regret.

"It's untenable," Velvet declared. "How do you endure it?"

"Nay, it is much harder for you. Your family had all its estates confiscated. Remaining loyal to the king cost your father everything."

"I blush to think how spoiled I was when we lived in England. At Nottingham Castle, Bolsover and Welbeck Abbey I had scores of servants to care for me, dozens of horses to ride and countless pretty dresses, all of which I took completely for granted."

"A lady should be spoiled. My heart is heavy that you have no luxuries, but truth to tell, I'm relieved that you're no longer at the decadent French Court. It is an unfit place for an innocent young lady to grow up."

A bubble of laughter escaped Velvet's lips as she recalled the lessons she'd learned from the courtesans who denuded their bodies of pubic hair and rouged their nipples. She suspected they had taught him a lot more than they had her. She'd heard stories of his numerous liaisons, and tried not to be jealous.

"Leaving Versailles was good for me too. It allowed me to study in Paris. I was voracious to learn shipping and fortification and the technicalities of navigation."

"When part of the Parliamentary fleet mutinied to Holland, it was so brave of you to lead the ships against the enemy to save your father's throne. Blockading London from the Thames must have been so exciting!" Her eyes shone with loving admiration.

"You mustn't make a hero of me, my dear. All my at-

tempts to secure the English throne have ended in dismal failure."

Velvet's mind came back to the present and she covered Minette's hand. "Charles will never give up! It is written in the stars that one day he *will* be restored to the throne of England and we shall all go home and live happily ever after."

Minette took a brush from her pocket. "Will you do my hair and make me some pretty ringlets like yours, Velvet?"

"Of course." The pair spent a happy hour talking of the dogs and horses they would have when they returned to England. Then Lady Margaret Lucas, one of the few remaining noble ladies who tended the queen, came in and put an end to the visit.

"Good-bye, Velvet. Will you come tomorrow?" Minette begged.

"I think not, Henriette," Lady Margaret said coldly. "You spend too much time with Mistress Cavendish."

Velvet knew the woman did not like her. A cutting retort sprang to her lips, but she bit it back and smiled at her young friend. "Perhaps not tomorrow, but soon," she promised.

When Velvet left the queen's apartments, she decided to go outside again to look for her father. Before she got to the front entrance, she saw him striding toward her.

"Who's the most beautiful girl in the world?"

Her father's voice made her heart lift. "I'm so glad you are back!" Happily, she walked beside him. She knew he'd ridden to the coast to meet a mail packet from England. "I hope your journey was successful."

With satisfaction he patted the saddlebag he carried. "Most successful, Velvet. Fortune, at last, is smiling upon us."

When they entered their apartment, Emma stood wringing her hands as tears streamed down her face. "Oh, Lord Newcastle—"

Fear gripped Velvet as she saw the blood on Emma's apron. She rushed to her mother's bedchamber, dreading what she would find, as the sobbing Emma blurted out her story.

"The countess had a coughing spasm. . . . Then she hemorrhaged. My dear lord, there was nothing I could do—"

Velvet stared down in horror at her mother's pale face, and the blood on the coverlet. *No, no, please God, no! She cannot be dead. . . . Father said that Fortune was smiling upon us!*

Chapter Two

*G*reysteel Montgomery paced the small cell like a caged wolf. He and his men were imprisoned in the impregnable Castle of Berwick, garrisoned by General George Monck and his troops. Today, as he had done for a week, Monck came to observe him.

Greysteel gripped the bars. "Allow my men to go free, General. They are no threat. They only obeyed my orders."

Monck, who was built like a bull through his chest and thick neck, stared at Montgomery with bulbous, shrewd eyes. He saw a man who was hardened beyond his years by war, and whose Achilles' heel was the responsibility he shouldered for the men who served him.

"Such dogged determination. You repeat yourself every day. Why do you think of your men's welfare rather than your own?"

"They are young, boisterous, used to physical activity. Captivity will be a slow death to them. If you release them, I vow, they will go back to their farms in Northumberland."

"I will gladly release them"—Monck paused, holding out the carrot—"if you will change sides and fight for me."

Greysteel's mouth firmed. "I will never fight for Cromwell. I am a Royalist."

"Did you know that I too was once a Royalist?"

"You are a *turncoat?*" Greysteel's voice dripped contempt.

Monck ignored the taunt. "I was a prisoner in the Tower of London. Two years felt like a lifetime. Then I was given the choice between rotting in prison or joining the Parliamentarians and fighting rebels in Ireland. I took the latter."

Montgomery's piercing grey eyes stared into Monck's. *In your heart of hearts, you must hate Cromwell.* "I only know of your Scottish service, General. You recruited the Coldstream Guards, a great fighting force who are a credit to you."

"Then join us, Montgomery."

Greysteel shook his head. "My loyalty is pledged to Charles."

Over the harsh winter months, whenever Monck returned from Edinburgh, he continued the exchanges with Captain Montgomery, extending the offer and being refused. The meager rations and the cold were not the hardest part for Greysteel to tolerate. It was the close confinement that was far more difficult to bear, and the thought of his young soldiers being caged up nearly drove Montgomery to the edge of his endurance.

One morning he heard from the guard that one of his men had hanged himself. Greysteel was immediately covered with guilt and blamed himself for the boy's death. The next time Monck came to Berwick, Montgomery was ready to relent.

"General, extend the choice to my men. If they agree to join you in exchange for their freedom, I make no objection."

"And you will lead them?"

Greysteel was incredulous. "Nay, General. How can you ask? You know I am pledged to Charles Stuart."

"Without your men behind bars, I have no leverage with you."

Two days later a guard unlocked Montgomery's cell, shackled his wrists and delivered him to Monck's office. Greysteel, wary as a wolf scenting a trap, remained silent in hope that the general would play his hand first.

Monck came from behind his desk, peered out the door as if to make sure they would not be overheard, then removed the manacles. "I have been testing you for months."

Greysteel held his silence.

"You have passed the test." Monck took his seat behind the desk. "The test of unswerving loyalty."

For my men's sake, you have no idea how close I've come the last two days to giving in to you. With difficulty, Montgomery forced himself to stand at ease with his arms behind his back.

"I have need of an agent."

Greysteel remained silent. *You are wasting your time.*

"I believe you would make a good secret agent." When he saw Montgomery shake his head, Monck held up his hand. "I will release your young men back across the Border."

Greysteel hesitated. "An agent?"

"You will not work for Cromwell; you will work for me. I hear many rumors—that the people are sick and tired of living under a Protectorate, that they have grown resentful, caught between a military regime and religious fanatics. On the other hand, I hear the English love him so much, they want him to be king. Yet another rumor says that Cromwell is in ill health. I need someone to take the pulse of England and report the truth. I could trust a man with your noble sense of honor."

You needed to make sure I'd remain loyal to Charles Stuart! "You hold the power here in Scotland. Are you saying that under certain circumstances you would put that power behind restoring the monarchy?" A faint glimmer of hope rekindled.

Monck remained silent for a full minute. "I am saying no such thing. I am a cautious man. That is how I maintain a position of power. I need ears and eyes in London. I pledge to you the release of your men. You pledge to me the truth."

"Married?" Velvet, who had been numb with grief all winter, was jolted out of her sorrow by her father's announcement.

"Fortunately you are already acquainted. The noble Lady Margaret Lucas became my countess yesterday."

Velvet recoiled. "How could you replace my mother with a new wife so soon? And why Margaret Lucas, a bluestocking lady-in-waiting, half your age?"

"Velvet, that is unkind. We will all benefit from this union. Lady Margaret is a young lady of means and it was she who suggested that I appeal to our family in England for funds. With the money Devonshire sent me, I have leased us a lovely house in Antwerp, closer to where King Charles resides. Promise me you will do your utmost to make Lady Margaret happy?"

Velvet nodded, her numbness replaced by heartache. The thought of seeing Charles again was the only glimmer of hope in what she viewed as an intolerable situation.

The stylish house in Antwerp had once belonged to the famed artist Rubens. It had all the luxuries, including servants, a carriage house and riding horses. Lady Margaret spent her time writing plays and encouraged her new husband to compile his equine wisdom into a book on horsemanship.

From the moment they moved in, the new countess was critical of her stepdaughter. Each day when Velvet came downstairs, Lady Margaret made a point of voicing her disapproval.

"Your clothes are a disgrace. Why did you choose drab grey for your new gown? You have no appreciation that your father is an earl and has provided you with this lovely home. You show little respect for me, the plays that I write or the literary guests we entertain. All you care about is galloping your horse like a madwoman, allowing that untidy red hair to fly about." She smiled with malice. "I shall ask your father to curtail your riding, Elizabeth."

Velvet had held her tongue week after week, struggling to keep her promise to her father. Now, however, the threat of taking her horse away, coupled with Margaret's calling her Elizabeth, made Velvet lose control.

"I chose drab grey because I am in mourning for my mother. I cannot show respect because I *have* no respect for you, or the appalling plays you write. I would show more appreciation for this lovely home if my father had provided it for my mother, rather than depriving her for over a decade."

"You wicked creature! Your father's English lands were confiscated and his losses total a million pounds in the Royalist cause."

Velvet narrowed emerald eyes. "You have a great interest in money—be sure to keep track of every penny. At your shameful suggestion Father got money from the Devonshires, who saved their estates by making a pact with the king's enemies!"

"I am not without wealth," Lady Margaret said regally. "Some of my own money goes into the upkeep of this house."

"If you had wealth, how could you have allowed Her Highness the Queen and Princess Minette to live in abject poverty?"

"Enough, Elizabeth!"

Velvet raised her chin. "I've had more than enough, Margaret." She turned on her heel and ran back upstairs to her room. Impulsively, she stuffed brush and comb and other toilet articles into a saddlebag and flung on her cloak. She knew exactly where she would go.

The two-hour ride to Bruges gave Velvet ample time to cool her temper. When she saw that the entire town was a sprawling military camp filled with rough English and Irish mercenary soldiers, she realized she should not have come. She was shocked at the dress and familiar behavior of the women she saw mingling with the men. *These must be camp followers!*

A soldier grabbed her reins. "Lookin' fer company, luv?"

"I am looking for King Charles. Let me pass, sir!"

He laughed. "You an' all the other bawds. Fear not, he'll get around to you—in the meantime, come an' ride my cockhorse."

Velvet cried out in alarm and raised her riding crop. A cavalry officer came to her rescue. "What's the trouble here?"

"I'm the Earl of Newcastle's daughter. Would you take me to His Majesty the King, sir?"

His eyes widened. "I serve under the Duke of York with your brother, Henry. He'd have a fit if he knew you were here."

He escorted her to a stone building and turned her over to a member of the King's Court. "I'll stable your horse, my lady."

Used to escorting females to the king, the courtier asked discreetly, "Are you expected, milady?"

Fearing she'd be turned away, she said, "Of course I am."

He knocked and opened the door, and she stepped into the room.

The man behind the black oak table rose to his full six feet and bowed. His dark eyes roamed over the lovely young creature before him, missing no finest detail. His brows lifted. "Velvet? Can this exquisite young lady possibly be the urchin who always outrode me?" He hugged her tightly and kissed her cheek. "Your father didn't tell me you accompanied him today."

Her wild pleasure turned to dismay. "Father's here?"

Charles grasped the situation. "He's gone to visit Henry. Before he returns, why don't you tell me what's wrong?" He sat her down in a worn leather chair and brought her a footstool. "I am sorry over the loss of your mother, Velvet. She was always exceedingly kind to me. I understand how you must miss her."

"It seems that I'm the only one! Father has already taken another wife—that bluestocking Lady Margaret Lucas, who was lady-in-waiting to the queen. I don't understand!"

Charles sat down beside her and took her hand. He searched her face with his brown melancholy eyes. A quick calculation told him that she was now twenty. He realized her innocence had been overprotected, yet he knew she had a quick intelligence and an innate shrewdness, which could someday match his.

"Your father is a dashing nobleman in his middle years. Women have always thrown themselves at him. His military forays ended in defeat, so it was important that his conquest of a woman end in victory. Can you understand that?"

"Yes." *Now that you have explained so bluntly, I understand your need for so many conquests.* "But why does she hate me?"

His mouth curved in a lazy, charming smile. "Your youth and incredible beauty are a threat to her, Velvet."

"Lady Margaret pressed Father to accept money from his cousin Devonshire, I'm ashamed to tell you. They made a pact with that devil Cromwell to keep their estates intact!"

"My dear, there is no shame in that. It was a brilliant political move. Your father's branch of the Cavendishes was able to throw its wealth into the Royalist cause only if the Earls of Devonshire preserved their vast domain, wealth and possessions for the future."

"You don't hate the Devonshires for dealing with Cromwell?"

"It was the expedient thing to do. The old countess and the queen are friends. They write often. One must learn to do the expedient thing in order to survive, Velvet. Odds fish, my best friend, George Villiers, just deserted me. No sooner did he arrive in England than he married General Fairfax's daughter."

"Why would the Duke of Buckingham marry the daughter of a Roundhead general?" she asked in outrage.

Charles smiled. "Expedience, Velvet. She is an heiress. I am casting about for my own royal heiress."

Her heart constricted. "You would marry without love?"

"Little innocent! I cannot afford the luxury of love. Look about you. I have begged, stolen or borrowed money for every stick of furniture, every candle, every mouthful of food. I have no money to pay the soldiers, and no money or ships for the invasion I promised my faithful Royalist soldiers waiting in vain since last year for my landing on the Scottish Border."

"Your problems are untenable. I am ashamed that I came to burden you with my complaints, Your Majesty."

"I want there to be no *Majesties* between us, Velvet. I want only friendship. Try to cope with your problems and I shall do the same. With a little expedience, we shall muddle through."

A knock interrupted them. It was Newcastle, beside himself with fury that his willful daughter had followed him to Bruges.

"William, I forbid you to be fierce with Mistress

Cavendish. I call you to task for not including her in your visit." He looked at Velvet and allowed one eyelid to close in a slow wink.

Oh, Charles, I do love you! Velvet, deciding upon expedience, lowered her lashes and presented a meek face to her father.

The long ride home gave the earl and his daughter a chance to talk to each other. Velvet held nothing back; she told her father her true feelings about Margaret Lucas.

"Velvet, my dear, I've tended to think of you as a child, but now I realize you are a lady grown who does not need the ministrations of a stepmother. I've selfishly thought only of my needs and not yours. Two grown women cannot be happy in one household, I fear. It is unfair to both."

"I've tried to hold my tongue for months, but the truth is that Margaret doesn't like me and resents sharing you with me."

"She is a new bride. You will understand these things when you are a wife. At your age you *should* be married and have your own household. Living in exile has robbed you of these things."

Velvet blushed. She was extremely sensitive about reaching the age of twenty without being married. She harbored a fear of being left on the shelf—a spinster forever.

"Would you like to return to England, Velvet?"

"I have dreamed of going back to England for years."

"I shall write to the Devonshires and make the

arrangements. We shall get you back across the Channel in no time."

Velvet was reluctant to live with the other branch of the family when they had chosen Cromwell over Charles, but at least she would be living in England and she and Margaret would not be at each other's throats. With great daring she found the courage to voice a thought she'd kept hidden deep, and never spoken aloud before. "What about my betrothal?"

Newcastle rubbed the back of his neck. "I wouldn't count on it, Velvet. Circumstances have changed considerably over the years we've lived in exile. The Earl of Eglinton will not be eager for his heir to take a wife without a substantial dowry."

Deeply stung, she tossed her head. "Nor am I eager to wed Eglinton's heir. I am delighted the betrothal is null and void. I don't even remember the callow youth," she lied.

"Of course, should King Charles be restored to the throne and we get back our confiscated estates, I have no doubt your union would once again become most desirable to Eglinton."

Velvet lifted her chin. "That will be too bad. I wouldn't have his son for a husband if he were the last man alive!"

When the awaited letter arrived, it wasn't from the Earl of Devonshire or his wife, but from his mother, the Dowager Countess of Devonshire. William read it to his daughter:

> *My Dearest Newcastle:*
> *It is with anticipated delight that I invite your daugh-*

ter, Velvet Cavendish, to come and make her home with
me. It is my great honor to correspond with my dear
friend Queen Henrietta Maria, and know from her letters
the hardship of life in exile.

On my advice, my son, Devonshire, does not reside at
Chatsworth. (Far too ostentatious in a Commonwealth.)
He now lives at Latimers in Buckinghamshire.

Tired of my cutoff life in the country at Oldcoates, I
have recently moved back to my late husband's house in
Bishopsgate, London. Velvet's company will be most wel-
come, I do assure you, until such time as you return to
your own estates.

My felicitations on your union with the noble Lady
Margaret.

Christian Bruce Cavendish, Dowager Countess of
Devonshire.

"I don't remember her," Velvet said blankly.

"Christian Bruce is the daughter of the late Scottish
lord Kinloss. She'll be about sixty now." Newcastle did
not tell his daughter that the dowager wielded her
great power with an iron hand and had certainly always had his cousin Devonshire under her dominant
thumb. "I expect she will be lonely rattling about in a
house in London and would benefit from your company."

A house in London sounded like heaven to Velvet.
"Thank you, Father. I have decided to take the dowager up on her offer."

Chapter Three

*G*reysteel Montgomery was given permission to speak to his men on the eve of their release. He found them thinner and quietly subdued, as if their cocky spirits had been knocked out of them.

"I have bargained with General Monck for your freedom on the condition that you do not take up arms again. Our Royalist force is disbanded and you are free to return home to Northumberland. You served me well and I thank you."

His lieutenant said quietly, "Nay, sir, we thank you for whatever sacrifice you made so we wouldn't rot in prison."

The gratitude in their eyes made him glad he'd made the pact with Monck regardless of whether it was morally right or wrong.

The following day, before he left Berwick, George Monck handed him a ciphered code using numbers to represent names and places. "Commit this to memory; then burn it." Monck gave him a written pass in case he was stopped by the military. "There are spies everywhere, so it is best not to use a false name. As heir to the Earl of Eglinton, who made his peace long ago with the English Protectorate, you should not be under suspicion in London. Cromwell's official residence is Whitehall. I shall leave it to your ingenuity to gain access." Monck returned his sword and pistol. "I want regular reports."

"Whom will I use as courier, General?"

"When you get to London, my man will contact you."

Greysteel crossed the Border and rode directly south to Montgomery Hall, in Nottinghamshire. He was relieved that he was free to set his own course of action and his own timetable. Monck's only stipulation was that he report regularly.

Greysteel hadn't seen his father since he'd retired from the Royalist army six years ago. Though the earl was still curt and abrasive, his son was surprised to see how much he'd aged.

"Damned glad to see you've come to your senses. Fighting wars is a thankless business. No profit in it."

Greysteel neither confirmed nor denied that he was finished with the Royalist cause. He kept his own counsel.

The earl grudgingly modified his authoritative manner. He could see that young Greysteel was an authority unto himself. "It is time you eased my load with the estate business."

"I can see you have tripled the sheep flocks."

"Sheep—or rather, *wool* is money, especially on the London Wool Exchange. I don't enjoy traveling back and forth anymore. If you have a nose for business, you could act as our agent."

"Agent?" His grey eyes flickered with irony and

then it was gone. "Since the business end is all conducted in London, it would benefit us to establish a permanent office there."

His father nodded, immediately seeing the merits. "It would cut out the cost of using middlemen as brokers."

"I will have to go and familiarize myself with the capital. I'll rent a small house and set up an office."

"If you can find a good piece of property with a manor house on the outskirts of London, I recommend that you buy it."

"That's exactly what I had in mind. Land always increases in value. A London property would be a sound investment."

"Our banking is done with a goldsmith in the Temple by the name of Samuel Lawson. I'll give you a draft so you may draw whatever you need. The spring shearing is finished and the wool has been shipped to a warehouse we rent at Paul's Wharfe on Thames Street. That will allow you time to get the best price."

"Tonight I'll go over the account books with your steward."

"The books will tell you we're in excellent financial shape."

"By the way, is the Derbyshire land my mother entailed to me still leased for grazing? I'm sure it would bring a higher income if we leased the mineral rights. I should consult with the Earl of Devonshire about his coal contracts."

"Devonshire's mother controls the purse strings in that family. She obtained full legal guardianship over the heir's inheritances when her husband died. She's the one to advise you. The dowager countess recently moved from her Oldcoates property to the city. I still owe her for a few hundred sheep I bought when she left. You should pay a call on her in London and settle the account. It doesn't hurt to have connections." With a look of guilt the earl lifted a decanter of whiskey and poured them each a drink. "Damn Puritans consider every act of comfort a sin! London has been ruined with religious fanatics."

Velvet, accompanied by Emma, disembarked from the small trading vessel, which had brought them across an extremely rough Channel. She stood on the London dock trying to exude confidence but felt her optimism ebbing away as she eyed a black cloud. She looked about for shelter and found none; then her fears were fulfilled by a downpour of summer rain.

When it stopped, a somberly dressed man of middle years approached. "Excuse me, mistress. I am looking for the Earl of Newcastle's daughter, who was supposed to arrive on this vessel today. Do you know anything of the lady's whereabouts?"

"I am she," Velvet said with a rush of relief.

The man gave her a doubtful look. "Are you sure?"

Velvet's self-esteem plummeted, yet she knew she must convince the lofty servant. "Yes, I am Mistress Cavendish and this is my traveling companion. Did the Dowager Countess of Devonshire send you?"

He recovered his aplomb. "She did indeed. The carriage is waiting over yonder. Where is your luggage, my lady?"

Velvet blushed as she indicated the single bag at her feet.

The coach driver bowed politely and picked up the bag. "My name is Davis. Kindly follow me, ladies."

The carriage departed the docks and eventually left the dilapidated area behind. Velvet gazed with curiosity at the bustling streets of London. She tried not to think of her upcoming meeting with the wealthy countess after the reception she had received from the servant. The buildings and residences they drove past became more imposing and she glanced nervously at Emma, who sat clutching her bundle. *I shouldn't have come!*

They came to the London Wall and the carriage left the city through the Bishops Gate. Here, the large houses had their own gardens. They drove up a long driveway and stopped before a great mansion. With resolution, Velvet went up the steps and was about to knock when the door was opened by a manservant. She stepped into a black-and-white marble reception hall and came face-to-face with the Dowager Countess of Devonshire. As they stared at each other, Velvet's knees began to tremble.

"What a radiant woman you have become!" The rail-thin countess, with iron grey hair, had a faint Scottish accent.

Velvet feared she looked like a drowned rat and the dowager was mocking her, and her hand flew to her hair. With relief, she realized that in the carriage it had dried into a mass of tight curls. Belatedly, Velvet remembered to curtsy.

"None of that." The countess tapped her ebony stick on the floor. "My own hair used to be red, but nothing like your glorious golden shade. I am delighted you are here."

Velvet's voice quavered. "Thank you, Countess—"

"I'm the dowager—you will call me Christian. Who's this?"

"This is Emma, who was kind enough to travel with me."

The countess pointed her stick at her coachman. "Take Emma into the kitchen and tell Cook to give her a good hot meal." She waited until they left, then told Velvet, "The woman is constantly trying to fatten me up. Emma will divert her."

Velvet smiled as some of her apprehension and preconceived notions melted away. *The dowager is a delight!*

A few hours later, after a warm bath, Velvet sat propped in bed and pushed away the dinner tray. "Everything was delicious. I couldn't eat another morsel."

"Tomorrow, my sewing women will start on your new wardrobe. Well, actually, you will need two wardrobes."

"Two?" Velvet tried not to feel overwhelmed. The elegant chamber she had been given was the last word in luxury, from its polished silver mirrors to its satin bed hangings.

"Yes, darling. London is not the pleasurable place it once was. It has been transformed into a Puritan society, all piety and no wit. Attending church thrice weekly is the highlight of a drab existence. The Velvet Cavendish we present to the outside world will wear plain and sober garments. Simple dresses in dark brown or dull grey, with white collar and cuffs, will be worn beneath modest cloaks and sheer linen caps. But of course it will be a facade. When you are at home you may go mad with a little color. Oh, nothing low-cut or overtly feminine, God forbid," Christian said with exquisite sarcasm, "but perhaps slippers with rosettes, rather than sensible square-toed shoes with those infernal buckles! Ah, good, I've made you laugh."

"It feels good to laugh. Though when I was a child, my governess taught me that it showed a lack of breeding."

Christian hooted. "When you were a child, you were so willful, your governess could teach you nothing."

"You remember me!" Velvet was aghast.

"You were so deliciously precocious, how could I forget? You came by it honestly enough—your great-grandmother was Bess Hardwick. Now, *there* was a woman, but that's another story for another time. Now, where was I?"

"You were telling me that London is puritanical."

"Exactly. Just remember that everything is considered a sin and anything enjoyable is forbidden. They still allow sex, but not for pleasure—there must be no joy in the act. Oh, I've made you blush. You must get used to my irreverence, darling—I have a flagrant fondness for it."

Montgomery's first stop in London was at the goldsmith's in the Temple, where he presented the draft and opened an account in his own name. He decided to find out how Samuel Lawson felt about the way London was being governed.

"Is business good, Mr. Lawson?"

"My business as moneylender thrives. Alas, that means that London and the country are drowning in debt above their eyes. The people are doubly angry—not only are they ruled by the military, but they are being forced to pay for it."

"You believe the ordinary people have grown resentful of the military regime and long for a quiet life?"

"The old form of government was better," Lawson murmured.

Lord Montgomery walked all about the city, familiarizing himself with the streets and districts, looking for the best place to open an office. He decided on Salisbury Court, where he rented a narrow house with an office on the ground floor and furnished rooms above. It even had a stable nearby to care for his horse. It was conveniently located, not far from the Temple and within a short distance of the Thames at Blackfriars.

Next he went to the barber. Long lovelocks hinted at Royalist sympathies, yet he refused to get his hair cropped in the ugly *Roundhead* style. He compromised by having it shortened and clubbed back neatly with a black ribbon.

Montgomery, needing a new wardrobe, observed the fashions. Men's clothing seemed to fall into three categories, with Parliamentarian army uniforms predominating. The other extreme was the severely plain, sober costume of the Puritan fanatic with square leather shoes and black steeple hat.

He visited the law courts and the wool exchange and decided to dress like the professional class. He ordered a black suit and a dark grey, whose jackets were shorn of all trimming. The breeches that came to the knee were worn with tall riding boots. His shirts boasted no lace, but had plain cambric neckbands.

He kept his ears open wherever he went and heard rumors of so many plots against Cromwell's life, he reasoned some of them must be true. He also heard gossip that the Protector was in failing health. *I have certainly used my ears. Now I will use my eyes. I shall go to Whitehall and see for myself.*

He went for a ride along the Strand to observe the layout of Whitehall. The area around the Old Savoy Palace was thick with soldiers and he realized he would never get past the guards.

Before he returned to Salisbury Court, he stopped at a secondhand shop on Cheapside. For the sum of six shillings, he bought a military uniform that had belonged to a Parliamentarian lieutenant. He searched through a box of brass buttons and paraphernalia until he found a captain's insignia. That night before he retired Robert patiently stitched on the new badges.

In the morning when he put on the enemy uniform, he did not feel like a traitor. Instead, he felt a mild exhilaration at the challenge that lay before him. *The uniform is sadly lacking when compared with a Cavalier uniform, but I think it will pass muster.* He fastened on his own sword, saluted his image in the mirror and walked down to the Thames.

The watercraft going upriver had few early-morning passengers. He got off at the Old Palace Water Stairs and walked briskly along the path that led to Whitehall Palace. He gave the guard on gate duty a piercing stare, which prompted the soldier to straighten his shoulders and salute the captain.

Without hesitation, Montgomery strode into the palace grounds as if he knew exactly where he was going. When he passed knots of Parliamentarian soldiers, he nodded curtly and moved on. He entered Whitehall with other uniformed men and made his way to the kitchens by following his nose. It was a busy place filled with cooks, cooks' helpers and scullery boys. The clattering noise of pots, pans and crockery made it necessary for the kitchen workers to shout above the din. He spied a plump woman in a striped apron. She was sitting at a table eating her breakfast.

He winked at her. "May I share your table, madam?"

She beamed. "And anythin' else ye fancy, luv!" Her glance openly admired his broad shoulders. "What are ye doin' in the kitchens, Captain?"

He bent toward her in a confidential manner. "Inspecting."

Her mouth dropped open. "The cooks? The food?"

He put his finger to his lips. "A certain high authority has voiced suspicions."

"So that's why Old Noll's food trays come back untouched. He thinks we're poisoning him!"

"Softly, my dear—I have found no evidence of anything untoward in my investigation so far."

She pressed her lips together in consternation. "I should think not. Here, let me get ye some food that I was in charge of cookin' this morning. Ye can taste it yerself."

She jumped up and came back in no time with a

trencher piled with gammon ham, eggs and kidneys. "Tuck into that."

Robert enjoyed his breakfast. *I must remember to hire a cook.* "My compliments, ma'am, this is excellent. Perhaps he sends his food back because it's cold by the time it gets to him."

"Well, he is way up on the third floor, but Sergeant Bromley always keeps his food warm with silver covers."

"I shall go and have a word with him. Remember, not a hint to anyone. This is between you and me."

Montgomery made his way into the adjoining kitchen and filled a jug with boiling water. Then he carried it up to the third floor of Whitehall. He looked along the corridor and saw a door that was guarded by a soldier. On the floor against the wall was a tray with silver covers. Montgomery stopped at the door, looked down and shook his head sadly. "Couldn't eat again?"

"Same every day, Cap'n."

Suddenly the door opened. Without missing a beat, Montgomery spoke. "Sergeant Bromley, to save you a journey to the kitchens, one of the cooks prevailed upon me to bring you hot water."

"Thanks." Bromley took the jug and motioned his head to someone inside. "He's bilious again."

"Would you like me to go for a physician, Sergeant?"

Bromley shook his head. "He's seen 'em all. He's at prayer at the moment—spends hours on his knees. I have to go—I think he's callin' me." The sergeant shut the door.

"Is there a garderobe on this floor?" Robert asked the guard.

He pointed the way. "At the end of the corridor."

Montgomery walked to the end of the hallway, turned and sat down on the staircase to wait. He wanted to get a good look at Oliver Cromwell. *Sooner or later, nature is bound to call.*

In about an hour, Montgomery's patience paid off. As he heard someone come down the corridor, he stood up and stepped into the shadow of the stairs. Light from the hall window illuminated a man whom Montgomery recognized as Cromwell. His tall figure was stooped and his pallor was a sickly yellow as if he was jaundiced. It was his eyes, however, that gave Greysteel pause. He'd seen the look before, in battle on the faces of deeply religious men who had convinced themselves they were the chosen instruments of God. Cromwell's eyes burned with a fanatic light like those of a man on his last mission who knew he was going to die.

That night, at his desk in his new office, Montgomery sat for a long time, trying to bring himself to write the report to General George Monck as he had agreed. No matter how he rationalized it, it went deeply against the grain to help the enemy in any way. In the end he reached for a quill and put down on paper his honest view of what he'd heard and seen in London. When he finished, he reread the letter. "My words are slanted against the Parliamentarian government, but if such a report makes Monck unhappy, he shouldn't have chosen a Royalist for his agent."

Greysteel felt an urge to write to Charles and tell him that Cromwell was ill. He wanted him to know that the people of London were sick and tired of the military dictatorship and some spoke of monarchy in a favorable light. He decided to wait until he knew more. The last thing he wanted to do was give the king false hope.

"If I write reports to both, I will be acting as a double agent." His jaw hardened. Being a double agent was no more palatable to him than being Monck's agent. He melted the sealing wax on the letter and locked it in his desk drawer.

Velvet looked at her reflection in the mirror. Though most females would have thought the dress of plain grey cambric with starched white collar and cuffs extremely plain, she was most grateful that it was new and fitted her perfectly.

She picked up the silver hairbrush and fashioned her unruly red gold hair into neat ringlets and pinned on a sheer linen cap. She hurried downstairs to take breakfast with Christian.

"Good morning, darling, you look lovely." *Oh, dear, you look like a little milkmaid rather than an aristocratic Cavendish. Your years of penniless exile robbed you of your confidence. I must build up your self-esteem and try to restore some of that delicious precocious attitude you displayed as a child.*

She watched Velvet eat, bemused that she seemed to relish plain bread and honey. "My dear, you have the most radiant complexion. Your skin is translucent and seems to glow from the inside. What is your secret?"

Velvet flushed, pleased at the compliment. "I use cold water. Mother told me about using glycerin distilled with rose water when she was a girl. I wish I had some."

Her wants are so simple. "Well, we have glycerin and the garden is filled with summer roses. Go out and gather some."

"Oh, thank you." She wiped her mouth and folded her napkin.

Christian watched her through the back windows of the breakfast room. *Odsbodikins, you'd think I'd given her the crown jewels.*

Montgomery had learned the Dowager Countess of Devonshire was living at her grand house in Bishopsgate, the one where her late husband had entertained royalty on a lavish scale. He turned his horse over to a groom at the carriage house and went up the front steps. He presented his card to the butler.

"I'm here to see the Devonshire steward on business, but first I'd like to pay my respects to the dowager countess if she is receiving."

"Very good. This way, my lord." The butler showed him into the library and in less than two minutes the dowager appeared.

She gave her visitor a quick appraisal and liked what she saw. The gentleman had a commanding presence, which set him apart. She glanced at his card. "Lord Montgomery?"

"My father is Alexander, Earl of Eglinton. I'm here to pay your steward for some sheep we recently acquired from you."

"Ah, Robert, you were a captain with the Royalist army." *I have a flagrant fondness for military gentlemen.*

Velvet came into the library, her head bent over a

flower basket. "Christian, it is such a pity that these lovely cream roses have specks of soot on—" She looked up and saw the dowager had a male visitor. "Oh, I beg your pardon. . . ." Her voice trailed off as she stared. The man had a military bearing with a ramrod straight back and broad muscular shoulders. His face was dark, hard and lean, and his grey eyes were so compellingly direct, a shudder ran down her back. He was the most powerfully attractive male she had ever seen and her physical response to him was immediate and profound.

Robert took one look at the female and felt as if time stood still. His heart too stopped beating momentarily and then began to thud. The young lady before him in the simple gown, carrying a profusion of cream roses, was a vision of sweet innocence. She had the face of an angel; he'd never seen anyone as lovely.

"Velvet, darling, this is Captain Robert Montgomery—"

His dark brows drew together. "Velvet?"

Her green eyes widened. "Greysteel?"

Chapter Four

"*O*f course!" Christian's face lit up as she realized why his name was so familiar. "Greysteel Montgomery is your betrothed!"

Velvet's cheeks turned crimson. "He is no such thing!"

"It was so long ago. You were only about seven— perhaps you have forgotten," Christian suggested.

"Yes, I have forgotten." *No, I never forgot. That was the day I decided to name myself Velvet and realized I was in love with Charles. Your first glance told me you wanted to beat me. You were forced to betroth me because of my family's wealth, and you hated me for it. Now that the wealth is gone and you don't wish to be reminded of the betrothal, you still hate me.*

"Perhaps you *have* forgotten, Mistress Cavendish. I was a thirteen-year-old youth. My looks have changed considerably."

Velvet stared at him haughtily, desperately trying to mask her physical response to him. Though there was no trace of youthfulness left in the dark, hard countenance, she could never forget the mesmerizing grey eyes, which had the ability to look into her mind and read all her secrets. Moreover, the arrogant devil knew she hadn't forgotten him.

"I'm sure the Earl of Eglinton considers the betrothal null and void, as does my own father, after all these years."

"It matters little what they consider." Greysteel set his jaw. "It is I who will decide about our betrothal."

"You must be mad!" She defied him.

Her words stung him. She had made it plain she hadn't wanted him then, and she didn't want him now. *Set yourself against me and you will lose; your objections only make me more determined.*

"My lord, do forgive Velvet. She doesn't mean to be rude."

"Of course she does. She'd like to run me through with my own sword, but she doesn't quite dare."

"You read my thoughts exactly, sir," Velvet said sweetly.

Christian eyed the pair of antagonists with relish. The sexual sparks between them heated the air. "Lord Montgomery, may I suggest that you come to dinner Wednesday night? Perhaps you two can settle your differences—or continue your duel. Either would be vastly entertaining, I warrant."

"I would consider it an honor, my lady."

"An undeserved honor," Velvet murmured with disdain.

A discreet tap on the library door interrupted them. As the steward entered, Velvet took the opportunity to escape.

"Here is Mr. Burke, my valued steward. This gentleman is Robert Greysteel Montgomery, the Earl of Eglinton's son, who fought with the Royalist army."

"I am honored, sir. We are indebted to your loyal service."

"Indeed we are," Christian agreed. "Though I make sure my family conforms with the law under Cromwell's rule, I am a Royalist sympathizer and keep in touch with the Stuarts."

Greysteel glanced at Burke. "My lady, I admire your sentiments but hope you are aware of the danger involved."

"I assure you the people I entrust with my communications are reliable and cautious. Well, I shall leave you in the capable hands of Mr. Burke. I bid you *adieu* until Wednesday."

Montgomery settled the account for the sheep and gave Mr. Burke his card. "I've opened an office in Salisbury Court."

"A good location, convenient to the Temple and the river. It is a pleasure to do business with you, Lord Montgomery."

"I don't wish to seem presumptuous, Mr. Burke, but I'd appreciate some advice. I have been thinking about leasing the mineral rights to some land I own in Derbyshire."

"By all means. Her ladyship has coal contracts on quite a few acres in Derbyshire. I'll give you some names of companies that will be eager to do business with you."

Christian went in search of Velvet and found her in the kitchen, meticulously washing the smudges of soot from the roses. "Leave the flowers, darling, and come and talk with me."

Reluctantly, Velvet followed the countess to her favorite sitting room and took a chair by the window.

"Greysteel Montgomery is a most compelling man. He is heir to wealth, estates and an earldom. Is it his devilish dark, hard looks that repel you?"

"Oh, no," Velvet denied quickly. *His physical attraction is so powerful it almost overwhelmed me.*

"Then I am at a loss. Why did you reject him?"

"When Father proposed sending me to England, I asked him about my betrothal. He explained that because my circumstances had changed considerably, the Earl of Eglinton would not be eager for his heir to take a wife who was without a substantial dowry." Velvet's cheeks warmed with humiliation.

"Greysteel Montgomery is his own man, I warrant . . . doesn't give a tinker's damn what his father thinks. He may very well consider that your betrothal is still legal and binding."

Velvet's blush deepened. "Don't you see? He knows of your wealth and, because I am living with you, thinks my circumstances have changed. I will be twenty-one on my next birthday—past the ideal age for marriage. Montgomery has no personal interest in me and I have too much intelligence to believe otherwise."

"Didn't you see the way he looked at you? Why, he almost devoured you. Velvet, no man ever looked at me that way. Would you like to hear my story?"

Velvet nodded shyly.

"My father was Edward Bruce, Scottish Baron of Kinloss. As a reward for helping James Stuart attain the throne of England, the king promised him an alliance with a rich and rising English house. The king himself added ten thousand pounds to my dowry and arranged for me to marry the Earl of Devonshire's son. I was twelve years old. William was eighteen and madly in love with Margaret Chatterton, a young household serving girl he had seduced. William adamantly refused to marry a twelve-year-old.

"Pressure was brought to bear and he finally agreed on condition he be allowed to keep his freedom and Mistress Chatterton. He left me with his family in Derbyshire and didn't return until I was old enough to bear him a son and heir. With that accomplished, he returned to King James's dissolute Court, where he lived the life of a brawler, a spendthrift and a rake.

"When James Stuart died and his son Charles became king, the licentious Court was purged of its catamites, and immorality was frowned upon. Suddenly, I became the valued wife and chatelaine as William lavishly entertained the new king and queen. That's when Queen Henrietta Maria and I became friends.

"By the time his father died, William had borrowed so much against his inheritance that he was deeply in debt. His solution was to sell valuable Cavendish land. *Fate* intervened to prevent him from doing such a reckless thing. My husband died of *excessive indulgence* and left me to pay the bills."

"Whatever did you do?" Velvet asked in a whisper.

"I closed up this house, stopped the lavish entertainments, dismissed an army of servants and gradually cleared up the debts. The lawsuits brought against me were settled in my favor, thanks to the queen. I shall be forever in her debt."

"You were such a young widow. Why did you never remarry?"

"Now we come to the point of my story. If any man had looked at me the way Montgomery looked at you today, I would have grabbed him in a minute. Unfortunately, no man ever did. Velvet, you seem unaware of your devastating attraction. Few women are gifted with that indefinable essence that is irresistible to the male of the species. Your great-grandmother Bess Hardwick had it. She married four husbands and had each one wrapped around her fingers."

"Four husbands?"

Christian nodded. "By the time she was thirty-five." She took a leather-bound book from a cabinet. "Here is one of her journals I found at Oatlands. I think you should have it."

"Thank you . . . I will treasure it."

Christian patted her hand. "Far more important to read it, darling, preferably before Wednesday."

As Velvet readied herself for bed she couldn't get the things Christian had told her out of her mind. Her husband had brought her nothing but unhappiness and humiliation. *Men cannot be trusted. They are never satisfied. Not only do they insist their wives bring a noble name and a substantial dowry to the marriage; they demand utter faithfulness as well. They don't apply this standard to themselves, of course. Men consider it their God-given right to keep a mistress outside their marriage.*

Velvet thought of her father. She had revered him all her life and had been convinced he loved his wife and family with his whole heart. When he quickly remarried, her illusions had been shattered. Her father had betrayed her mother. It was obvious that he had been having a liaison with Margaret Lucas while his wife was alive. *Women are fools to trust men.*

Velvet climbed into bed and began to read Bess Hardwick's journal. She caught her breath over some of the audacious things her great-grandmother had written. After two hours, she set the book aside. She was beginning to see Bess in a new light. Here was a woman who set her own rules. She took control of her life and the men around her, rather than allowing them to have the upper hand.

Velvet thought about Greysteel Montgomery. Unbidden, he had appeared in her dreams for years, yet the flesh and blood man he had become far exceeded her dream version. *Does he truly find me attractive or does he have an ulterior motive?* She knew he was dominant and liked to be in control. *Perhaps he is determined to become my husband simply to thwart our fathers.* Deep inside, she didn't want this to be true. She wanted Montgomery to lose his heart to her.

If I could make him want me for myself, would I marry him? The thought made her shiver deliciously and she realized how vulnerable she was to the dark, attractive devil. To protect herself Velvet lifted her chin and declared aloud, "It would be a marriage without love—Charles Stuart owns my heart."

She remembered what Charles had said: *Little innocent! I cannot afford the luxury of love.* She thought of Bess's surefire advice for enslaving a man: *All you have to do is keep him off-balance by luring him with one hand while rejecting him with the other!* Velvet smiled a secret smile.

Montgomery had a successful business day. At the London Wool Exchange he sold half the spring shearing at a higher rate per pound than the Montgomerys had ever received before. The price of wool was going up and he gambled that next week he'd get an even better price for the bales, which were stored in the warehouse.

Tuesday he visited Samuel Lawson at the Temple and, on the goldsmith's advice, bought some shares of the Bermudas Company, a New World venture. He returned to his office to write a letter to his father and a business report to their steward.

Shortly after he finished, he had a visitor. The man, no older than himself, had a weathered complexion, a wiry build and sharp eyes. *Here is my courier from General Monck.*

"Montgomery? Pleased to meet you, sir. A mutual acquaintance suggested I might be of service to you."

Greysteel detected a twang in his voice, but it didn't sound Scottish. "Of service to me?"

"I specialize in communication."

There was no way Montgomery would turn over the letter until he had proof that he was the expected courier. "Does this mutual acquaintance have a name, sir?"

"Mr. Burke, though I'd deny it under torture," the young man said with a grin. "Royalists need to be cautious."

Montgomery, caught slightly off guard, suddenly recognized the accent. "You are from the Isle of Jersey?" He knew that Carteret, the governor of Jersey, was a staunch Royalist.

"Seaman Spencer, quartermaster of the frigate *Proud Eagle,* anchored at Blackfriars. There's usually a Carteret vessel somewhere in the Thames ready to make a swift run across the Channel with a confidential communication."

Montgomery grinned. "When they're not stalking a Dutch merchantman or sinking one of Cromwell's fleet! I thank you for your offer, Spencer. I may avail myself of your services."

"We sail on the midnight tide, tomorrow night."

That same night, after dark, Monck's man arrived. He wore the military uniform of a Parliamentarian and presented a letter authorizing him to act as courier. There was no signature, but the letter bore the official seal of the City of Edinburgh.

Montgomery unlocked the desk drawer and took out the sealed letter. Reasoning that the courier was not privy to the cipher, he wrote *General George Monck* beside the sealing wax, then handed it over. After the courier left, he locked the door and put out the light. As he sat in the dark, he thought long and hard about writing to Charles Stuart. With resolution he made his decision. *Tomorrow midnight—I don't have much time.*

On Wednesday morning, Greysteel made another visit to the secondhand shop. In the afternoon he leased the mineral rights to half of his Derbyshire property at five times the amount he could get for grazing rights. The contract included a clause that the lease be renegotiated whenever the price of coal went up. Pleased with himself, he returned home to bathe and change before he went to dinner in Bishopsgate.

Montgomery was filled with eager anticipation at the thought of seeing Velvet Cavendish again. He was convinced that Destiny was smiling upon him. Fate had not only returned her to London but had also arranged for their paths to cross.

He had thought of her many times since the day of their betrothal, of course, when he'd been convinced her angelic face masked an imp of Satan. By the time he had risen to the rank of captain, in charge of young army recruits, he had become quite knowledgeable about human nature. Extreme bravado and cockiness were devices young males used to mask their fear and insecurity. It dawned on him, when Velvet insinuated herself into his dreams on a regular basis, that she used precocious behavior and willful defiance to cover a delicate and fragile vulnerability.

Montgomery knocked on the door of the Bishopsgate house promptly at six and stood waiting in the black-and-white marble reception hall while the butler went off to announce his arrival to the dowager countess.

Christian arrived in less than five minutes. He felt immediate disappointment that Velvet did not accompany her. As he and Lady Cavendish exchanged pleasantries, he tried to control the impatience that was building inside his chest. *Where is she? Surely she isn't refusing to dine with me?* Greysteel felt awkward holding the roses he'd brought and finally, reluctantly, good manners forced him to present them to the dowager.

"How lovely. Do come into the sitting room."

Montgomery followed her and sat in the chair she indicated. The moment he was seated, he shot to his feet again as Velvet entered the room. She was wearing a simple white dress and tonight she had left off her cap. He could not take his eyes from her glorious hair. He put his hands behind his back so he would not be tempted to touch her. "Mistress Cavendish."

Velvet was testing advice she'd read in Bess's journal: *I always keep a man waiting long enough to make him anxious, but never long enough to make him angry.* She felt she'd succeeded. Greysteel was staring at her hair as if mesmerized and she knew that Bess had been right again: *If left uncovered, my red hair holds a special fascination for men.*

Christian placed the two dozen roses in her arms. "I'm sure these flowers were meant for you, darling."

Velvet gazed down at the dark crimson blooms and was transported back to the garden at Nottingham Castle. The roses were the exact same color as the one that had inspired her to choose the name *Velvet.* She glanced up quickly and saw by the light in his intense grey eyes that he had chosen them deliberately to invoke the memory of that day.

"I'll put them in water." She knew she sounded breathless.

The moment she left the room, Greysteel missed her. The countess poured him a glass of wine and one for herself. Though it seemed an eon, Velvet returned shortly and it pleased him that she brought the roses back with her in a crystal vase.

"Would you like a glass of wine, Velvet?"

"Oh, no, thank you, my lady, I've never had wine."

Her words sent Greysteel's imagination soaring. *I'll warrant there are many things you've never tasted.*

"Have a little so we can toast the king," Christian tempted.

"Oh, yes, I would love to drink to Charles!"

She said the name *Charles* with such reverence, Greysteel's imagination dropped like a stone. *Bloody hell, you've been infatuated with the charming prince since you were a girl. It's time you outgrew such nonsense.* They drank to His Majesty's health; then dinner was announced and they carried their glasses into the elegantly appointed dining room. The countess chose to sit at the head of the table. Greysteel held her chair, then moved around to assist Velvet. As he gazed down at her, the swell of her high breasts quickened his blood, yet inexplicably he was pleased that her modest neckline covered her completely. *Her innocence is irresistible.* He quickly took his seat opposite her so he could gaze his fill.

Greysteel enjoyed the food, yet hadn't the least notion what was served. The countess kept the conversation lively and he responded to the topics of staffing his residence and how he found London after living in the country. He became reticent only when his army service came up. "Fighting a war is a necessary evil. It's never a pleasant subject for ladies."

The conversation moved on to safer ground and he found himself watching Velvet eat. She had a dainty appetite and when she licked her lips like a kitten, he found it arousing. He had the urge to go around the table, slide her into his lap and feed her. He felt himself harden. *What the hell is the matter with you, Montgomery? Control yourself!*

"I have arranged for a special dessert," Christian announced. "I'll just go and see if it's ready."

Greysteel immediately realized the countess was giving them an opportunity to be alone and he silently blessed her. He got up, moved around the table and sat down beside Velvet. "How is your first taste of wine affecting you?"

She lowered her gaze. "I could say it has no effect at all." She raised her lashes. "But your intense grey eyes have never left me tonight and you know that would be a lie."

"Yes." He felt the impact of her emerald eyes. "You feel warm and light-headed and slightly intoxicated."

"Yes. And you are sure it is more than the wine that is making me feel this way."

"Now you are reading my thoughts," he teased.

"Indeed I am. You too feel warm, light-headed and slightly intoxicated, though it is definitely not from the wine." She paused, luring him on before delivering the setdown. "It comes from your cocksure, high-handed opinion of yourself."

"Well, I'll be damned. I know another one of your secrets. Wine brings out that precocious hellion who lurks beneath your innocence, looking for a chance to escape."

"And I know one of your secrets." She dipped her finger into her wine and licked it. "You still want to tan my arse."

Christian returned with a tray. "I have a flagrant fondness for strawberries and cream." She watched Greysteel move away from Velvet and return to his chair. "I am so glad that you have decided to settle your differences."

"No, we haven't." The corners of Velvet's mouth lifted in a challenging smile. "We have decided to continue our duel."

As he watched her dip her strawberries in cream and then lick it off, he decided the dessert had been chosen to torture him. He almost groaned out loud.

Christian watched the byplay. *Either she read Bess's journal or she's ready to write one of her own!*

He lingered for almost an hour after dinner, wanting to stay, yet knowing he must leave. He did not want to go without restaking his claim. The future of England might be uncertain, but Greysteel was sure of one thing: He wanted Velvet Cavendish in his future and he was determined to have her. He stood, reluctantly. "Before I overstay my welcome—"

"You are welcome here any time," Christian assured him.

"You are extremely gracious, my lady. Velvet and I do have differences to settle. I consider us betrothed, but since she does not, I would like your permission to pay court to her."

"You have my permission and now I shall say good night and withdraw so that you may persuade Velvet to give hers."

When they were alone, he closed the distance between them.

Her head went back so she could look up at him. "I know almost nothing about you. I am not ready for courtship."

He lifted a red gold tendril, feeling its silken texture. Then he stroked her cheek with the backs of his fingers. "Shall I persuade you that you are?" He dipped his head and briefly touched his mouth to hers. Her lips parted in a gasp, as he had hoped, and this time he took full possession. Greysteel looked down at her in wonder. "You have never been kissed before!"

"Yes, I have! No, I haven't. . . . Damn you, Montgomery."

"Your innocence enchants me, Velvet."

Bess was right: The only thing more titillating to a man than experience is innocence.

"Did I persuade you?"

His voice had roughened and it thrilled her. "I'm not ready for courtship, but I'm ready for something," she said faintly. "Perhaps a long sword to keep you at arm's length."

"I am your man, whatever you desire."

"Is that a threat or a promise, Greysteel Montgomery?"

"It is both. You are a saucy baggage, Velvet Cavendish."

After he stabled his horse and paid the hostler for extra oats, it was after ten o'clock when Greysteel unlocked his door at Salisbury Court. Velvet was a delicious distraction and he knew he must put her out of his mind and focus his attention on the task ahead. The *Proud Eagle* would sail on the midnight tide.

Montgomery locked his desk drawer, put out the lights and left by the back door. Though time was short, he forced himself to walk slowly to make sure he wasn't being followed as he made his way down to Blackfriars and the Thames. He was thankful for the darkness and the fog, which blanketed the river. He did not see the riding lights of the vessel he sought until he was upon her. He heard the anchor chain being pulled up through the hawsehole and knew she was almost ready to slip her berth.

A sailor was removing a thick cable of rope from a stanchion. Montgomery asked to see Spencer, who appeared within seconds. The seaman drew close, then grinned. "I didn't recognize you. You have a letter for me?"

Greysteel shook his head. He pulled the thick collar of his seaman's rough coat, which he'd bought at the secondhand shop, close about his neck. "I have a passenger for you."

Chapter Five

*I*t was a straight one-night run from the mouth of the Thames Estuary to Ostend. The *Proud Eagle* sailed past the port and made anchor in a hidden bay farther up the coast at Blankenberge.

When Spencer led Montgomery from the ship and produced a pair of mounts, which would take them to Bruges, Greysteel knew the seaman from Jersey was an old hand at smuggling. It was less than seven miles to the sprawling military camp town where the exiled king had set up his headquarters. When the pair arrived at the stone building that housed Charles Stuart, everyone seemed to recognize Spencer and allowed him to enter. Finally they came to a door with a guard. Spencer gave a password, and like magic, they were ushered into the room.

The swarthy, six-foot man who rose to his feet was much thinner than Montgomery had expected, and far shabbier. The two men stared at each other for a long stretched-out minute, and then Charles's saturnine face broke into a smile. "Odds fish, it is you, Greysteel Montgomery. By the look of things, we are both reduced to paupers." The last time they had seen each other had been at the disastrous Battle of Worcester.

Spencer saw that the king knew the man, and silently withdrew.

"Your Majesty—you may not wish to hear what I have to say, but I feel compelled to say it."

"Truth is often unpalatable. That's why I hear it so seldom. My advisers, my courtiers, tell me what they wish me to believe and I have learned that most men are self-serving."

"I too am self-serving. I'm here to assuage my conscience."

"Conscience?" Laughter rolled from Charles's throat. "I forgot what conscience was by the time I was sixteen." He poured them each a drink and grimaced. "Holland gin, I'm afraid. Sit, drink and unburden yourself."

"Last autumn I captained young recruits from Northumberland. We were taken captive by George Monck's Coldstream Guards and imprisoned in Berwick."

Charles's face set in melancholy lines. "You were snared like coneys, waiting for my invasion force that never came."

"After a hellish winter, I made a pact with Monck to free my men across the Border. In return he wanted information about Cromwell and wanted the truth about how the people felt."

"And what is the truth, as you see it?"

"The people are sick and tired of military rule. Most feel that the country should be run by an elected government, not the Parliamentarian army. Many secretly long for a monarchy and there is even a rumor that they will ask Cromwell to be king."

"Your unvarnished truth holds little hope for me, my friend."

"You are wrong, Your Majesty. Cromwell is dying."

Charles sat forward, eagerly. "You have seen him?"

"I put on a Roundhead uniform and went to White-hall. He is stooped, jaundiced, and he cannot keep food down."

"Poisoned perhaps?" Charles suggested blandly.

So the rumors of plots against his life are true. "It is more than that, Your Majesty. Men may recover from poison. Cromwell will not recover from what is ailing him. The Protector has turned into a zealot, who believes he has been chosen as God's instrument to reform religion and turn England into the New Jerusalem. But the people have become fearful of the godly, and embittered by the reform he tries to impose. Cromwell is dying of fanaticism."

"What was in your report to George Monck?"

"He asked for the truth. I gave it to him."

"I wonder why he seeks the truth. What is his agenda?"

"There's more to George Monck than meets the eye. He is an excellent general and governs Scotland easily with his Coldstream Guards. Though there are fewer of them, they are a superior fighting force to England's Parliamentarian army."

"So if—when—Cromwell dies, Monck could hold the balance of power in his hands. Will it be enough to tip the scales?"

"In my opinion, yes. Monck was a Royalist who never took up arms against your father. When he was captured, Cromwell kept him in the Tower for two years. Given the choice of rotting there forever or fighting rebels in Ireland, he chose freedom."

"A man astute enough to choose expedience would do so again. He is well worth cultivating. We need Monck on our side."

"He is cautious, Your Majesty. He'd never commit openly."

Charles nodded thoughtfully. "I too have learned to be cautious. I think we should bring in Chancellor Hyde for his views. He has a shrewd head for policy and has learned to be closemouthed from necessity. I thank you for risking your neck to bring me this information. It will be safer to communicate by letter in future. In your reports to Monck, I know I can trust you to be selective."

"All summer it's been church on Friday, church on Sunday. I cannot stomach one more fire-and-brimstone sermon," Christian declared. "The Anglican service at St. Botolph's, Bishopsgate, used to be uplifting with traditional prayer and lovely music."

"Music is an instrument of the Devil," Velvet said with a straight face. "Only agonizing probing of the soul can bring one to a state of grace."

"Probing of the soul is pious claptrap. We need a change. Let's take the carriage and go shopping. We'll take Emma."

As the coach made its way to the New Exchange in the Strand, Velvet noticed Emma's face. "I thought you'd enjoy an outing."

"All these soldiers on the London streets frighten me."

"I believe that's their purpose. Protectorate indeed! It is rule by intimidation," the countess declared.

Velvet took Emma's hand. "We'll stay together."

As they walked through the mercantile stalls on the first floor of the Exchange, Velvet took an interest in everything. Christian, however, could not conceal her dissatisfaction. "These stalls were once filled with ribbons and fans. I have a flagrant fondness for fripperies and French fashions. All they have now are Puritan collars and woolen hose. There isn't a fan or a feather in sight. Ah, something has caught your eye, Velvet."

"Yes, I believe I see Greysteel Montgomery, up ahead. You didn't tell him we were coming, did you?"

"Of course not, darling. This is a happy coincidence."

They came up behind him as he was buying paper and sealing wax. He turned and saw them. "Ladies, such a pleasant surprise." His glance lingered on Velvet and he could not let her go without making an assignation to see her again. "I know that you ladies attend St. Botolph's. It would be my pleasure to escort you to church tomorrow evening."

Velvet looked appalled and Christian burst into laughter. "We've been twice this week, and been purged of our sins. We need a diversion, and I was thinking of taking Velvet for a drive in the country tomorrow. Though it's autumn, London's hot and oppressive. Why don't you come too, if you can get away?"

"We mustn't impose upon Mr. Montgomery," Velvet said coolly.

"I'd like nothing better than to explore the countryside," he insisted, determined to overrule her objection.

"Then it's settled. I have a small manor house and an estate at Roehampton along the river. The fresh country air will be like a tonic."

It is obvious to him that the countess is throwing us together. He thinks that with Christian on his side he has the upper hand. I must make sure that I am the one in control!

The following morning, as they drove along the river road with Montgomery riding along beside their carriage, Velvet's eyes were drawn again and again to the way Greysteel sat his mount. His straight back and military bearing, as well as the ease with which he handled his horse, fascinated her. She finally admitted that the dark, powerful male, who enjoyed being in control, was becoming more attractive to her every day.

This morning at Bishopsgate she had purposely kept him waiting, then apologized profusely when she finally arrived. "Do forgive me, my lord, I had no idea you were here yet."

He gave her an amused and tolerant look, which told her she was a little liar. She was deliberately demonstrating her indifference to him and he was determined not to let her see that her disdain affected him.

When they arrived at the Roehampton estate, Greysteel could tell Velvet was enchanted with the place. She looked at the house and the grounds with a hungry longing. She left the carriage with eager steps that carried her into the stables.

"Oh, Christian, you have riding horses! Roehampton is like paradise. Would you mind if I took a gallop?"

"Now, why do you suppose I brought you here? I'm sure I can entrust Montgomery to keep an eye on you. Off you go. Explore to your heart's content. There's a lake over there, somewhere. I shall go and have a word with the staff. Don't hurry—it will give them time to prepare some lunch for us."

Velvet grabbed a saddle, but Greysteel tried to take it from her. "Allow me to ready your mount."

She refused to let go. "I am perfectly capable of saddling my own horse, sir. Father taught me when I was a child."

"So long as you are with me, Velvet, you will never saddle your own mount. That is a man's job."

She stopped struggling, let him have the saddle and laughed. "You enjoy being in control, but I give you fair warning, Montgomery. You will never have the least control over me!"

As he saddled the black palfrey, his eyes never left her. When he was done, he closed the distance between them, placed firm hands at her waist and, deliberately lifting her high, set her in the saddle. "I shall, Velvet. Never, ever doubt it."

Without waiting for him, she trotted the palfrey from the stable and, the moment she was outside, gave the animal full rein. Each time Greysteel caught up with her, she raced ahead, throwing him a playful look that said, *Catch me if you can!*

For a while, Montgomery let her take the lead, content to watch how happy and carefree she was, galloping across the meadows, pretending to be the lady of the manor. It was easy to see that she was enchanted with the place, and Greysteel suddenly knew that he wanted Roehampton. *Velvet may be able to resist me, but the potent allure of this exquisite estate so close to London would capture her heart and hold her fast.*

A slight pressure of his knees brought his horse, Falcon, abreast of hers. "How about a race around the lake?"

She was off on the wind, laughter trailing behind her.

Greysteel let her lead until they were two-thirds of the way around; then swiftly, surely, he closed the distance between them. When their stirrups touched, he reached over and deftly plucked her from the saddle and set her before him.

Though she gasped from his audacity, her eyes were filled with joy and excitement at the reckless thing he had done.

He turned from the lake into a freshly mowed hayfield, which slowed his horse to a canter. He jumped to the ground and lifted his arms, knowing she'd take the chance. He rolled, cushioning her body from the impact, and they came to rest against a sheaf of hay.

Laughter made her lush breasts rise and fall as she gazed up at him. "A gentleman would have let me win!"

"I'm a *man*, Velvet. I've too much pride to let a female beat me at any game." He picked a straw from her disheveled hair.

If a man is smitten, he will find an excuse to touch you. Bess had also written: *If you want to be kissed, lick your lips.*

Velvet carefully touched the tip of her tongue to her top lip.

In a flash, Greysteel took possession of her soft mouth and groaned with the pleasure it brought him. His powerful arms went about her back and he held her captive with the tips of her breasts against the solid muscle of his chest. "Will you reconsider our betrothal, Velvet?"

"Montgomery, I am penniless. Without a dowry it is impossible—do you think I have no pride? When Charles is restored to the throne and I am an heiress, ask me again."

He was stunned. "When Charles is restored? Velvet, that could take another decade, or mayhap it will never happen!"

She flung herself at him in outrage and pummeled his chest. "You faithless swine! You must believe in him, you must! I will never lose faith in him. Not in a *hundred years.*"

She was fierce as a wildcat and though Greysteel realized her trust was completely unrealistic, he felt a sharp stab of envy at the deep devotion she felt for Charles Stuart.

"Forgive me. You were filled with joy, and I spoiled it."

She stood up and brushed off her skirt. "Of course you didn't. How could I suffer a moment's unhappiness in a magic place like Roehampton?"

"I'll get the horses—lunch will soon be ready."

She took the palfrey's bridle. "I shall walk down to the lake and look at the swans . . . perhaps make a wish. Will you tell Christian I wanted to be alone for a while?"

* * *

When Greysteel entered the manor house, he knew he would do his utmost to buy it. The polished oak floors, leaded windows and high beamed ceilings spoke of its Elizabethan origins. He searched out the countess. "Velvet is fascinated by Roehampton. She's still exploring. Why don't you put me to work?"

"If you could carry the table and chairs out to the terrace, we could dine alfresco. The flower borders are ablaze with yellow and bronze chrysanthemums—the first blooms of autumn."

Greysteel carried out the table, and the housekeeper set it with linen and silver. He brought out some cushioned chairs and he and the dowager countess sat down. "It is no secret that I would like Velvet to reconsider our betrothal."

Christian eyed him coyly. "Have you asked her again?"

"I have, but she resists me. She finds it easy to say no to me, I'm afraid. Now, if I had something to offer her that she could not resist, I believe I could change her mind."

"You are offering her marriage; what more could she ask? I am in favor of this match. I think you are exactly what Velvet needs. Is there something I can do to help persuade her?"

"You could sell me this manor house, my lady."

"Roehampton? Oh, dear, I am rather superstitious about selling land. It goes against my acquisitive instincts."

"Velvet has fallen head over heels in love with the property and the horses. She would thrive in a setting like this."

"Yes," Christian said slowly, "I can see its attraction

for a young woman who has had everything taken away from her. The security of having her own home would be a great incentive. But I'm afraid Roehampton isn't for sale. Don't be disappointed—there are only twelve acres that bring in no income whatsoever."

"I am not considering it for crops or profit. I think it would be perfect for Velvet and her future children."

"I admire a man who knows exactly what he wants and goes after it. But I advise you to look elsewhere. Ah, here comes the fair damsel now. Not a word of our conversation to Velvet. You mustn't get her hopes up when Roehampton is not for sale."

"Please don't say no—say you will think about it."

Christian spoke to Velvet. "The fresh air has put roses in your cheeks. Greysteel would like a row on the lake after lunch, but I'm sure he'd prefer your company to mine, darling."

"If I may have a tour of the manor house first, I will gladly go out on the lake."

After a lunch of lamb cutlets with fresh mint from the garden and a cheese soufflé, followed by a cream-filled apple tart, Christian took Velvet and Greysteel through the manor house. As they moved from room to room she watched Velvet's face for her reaction. When they explored the bedchambers and she saw the longing in her eyes as she looked from the upper windows, the countess saw that Velvet had fallen in love with Roehampton.

The autumn light was fading from the afternoon sky by the time they arrived back in the city. They parted company at Ludgate Hill, with Montgomery turning down toward Salisbury Court and the carriage proceeding on to Bishopsgate.

When the dowager countess arrived home she was surprised to learn that a visitor awaited her. The butler had barely uttered his name when the young man descended the grand staircase as if the mansion and everything in it belonged to him. "Surprise, surprise, Grandmother. I've come to banish your boredom."

"Cav? Is that you, my boy? Come to banish your own, I warrant." Christian turned to Velvet. "This is my grandson, Lord Will Cavendish. Selfish to the core, as only an eighteen-year-old can be."

The Earl of Devonshire's son was handsome in the extreme. His blue eyes and thick blond hair gave the impression of a youthful sweetness he did not possess. His glance slid over Velvet, taking note of her damp, bedraggled skirts and her muddied slippers. "Is this a new maid?"

Velvet flushed. "Please forgive my appearance, Lord Cavendish. We were in the country all day."

"No, Cav, this is not a new maid. Her nobility is quite on par with yours, dear boy. It gives me the greatest pleasure in the world to present Mistress Velvet Cavendish, who is a guest of mine—an *invited* guest, I might add, unlike someone else I could name. I must tell the butler to lock up the whiskey."

"You have a wicked wit, *grand-mère*, which is why I adore you."

"I am delighted to meet you, Lord Cavendish. Please excuse me. I must go up and change."

Once Velvet reached the security of her bedchamber, she was most reluctant to leave it again that night. Young "Cav" had made her feel distinctly self-conscious and she found herself wishing that he had never come. Since she wasn't the least hungry, she didn't want to go downstairs for dinner. Finally, she convinced herself that it was only good manners to allow Christian and her grandson to spend the evening alone together.

When Cav poured his grandmother a second glass of wine and carried it into her favorite sitting room, she suspected that he wanted something. She watched the play of candlelight on his golden hair. *He looks exactly like his grandfather. Let us hope and pray the resemblance is only physical.*

"You have no idea what a blessed relief it is to get away from Buckinghamshire. The slow pace of Latimers suits Father down to the bloody ground, but in truth the estate is no more than a glorified sheep farm."

"Don't disdain sheep, dear boy. Their wool provides you with all of life's luxuries."

"Ah, I do appreciate that, Grandmother, but it makes for a stultifying existence. I swear that the ennui I experience in Buckinghamshire will drive me mad if I stay there any longer."

"An eighteen-year-old shouldn't know the meaning of *ennui*."

"My own sentiment exactly! I shall be nineteen soon, a man in fact, and as such, I loathe and detest the idea of having to live with my parents. I need a home of my own, and not one in the wilds of Buckinghamshire. London is much more to my taste."

"I fail to see how living with your grandmother would be any less stultifying than living with your parents," she said dryly.

"Oh, no, I'm not talking about living here in Bishopsgate. Roehampton is the property I have in mind. Being just a couple of miles from London makes it an ideal home for a bachelor."

"Roehampton belongs to me," she reminded him.

"As does all Cavendish property. But shortly, you will pass it on to my father. Then in turn he will pass it on to me. Why should I have to wait, when Roehampton suits my purposes now?"

You think I'll die soon, but not soon enough, apparently.
"Did it never occur to you that I might wish to sell it?"

He laughed. "Grandmother, you cannot sell entailed property. It can only be inherited by your lineal descendants."

"I am most impressed that you know the law. It tells me that you haven't frittered away your entire eighteen years. It may come as a shock, but Roehampton is not entailed property."

He stared, speechless for a moment. "Then in theory you could give it straight to me, without Father getting it first?"

"In theory, yes, dear boy. In practice, not a chance."

"Why ever not?" he demanded aggressively.

"I have made arrangements to sell Roehampton to Greysteel Montgomery, heir to the Earl of Eglinton."

Chapter Six

*E*arly the next morning, a footman arrived at Salisbury Court with a letter from the dowager's steward, Mr. Burke, telling Montgomery that she had reconsidered his offer to purchase Roehampton. After assessing its vàlue, Lady Cavendish was asking one thousand pounds for the estate. If he wished the sale to be completed today and the deed registered in his name, he was to meet Burke and Lady Cavendish at the chambers of her lawyers, Benson and Wilcox, at the Inns of Court.

Greysteel was elated at her change of heart and in his opinion the price was reasonable. He wondered what had occurred to make her change her mind, but decided to act upon the offer immediately. He scribbled a note of acceptance, saying he'd be at the Inns of Court at two o'clock, and gave it to the footman.

Montgomery then went to the Temple and asked Samuel Lawson to make him out a draft for one thousand pounds.

"Do you want this taken from your account, my

lord, or do you wish to arrange a loan for the thousand?"

"I'm buying Roehampton property—what's your recommendation?"

"Under normal circumstances I would advise that you leave your capital intact and borrow the money. However, interest rates have shot sky-high and are climbing every day, so I do not recommend borrowing money at the moment."

"Then I shall heed your advice. Did the cost of the war with Holland cause the rates to rise?"

"Cromwell's treaty came too late. The navy failed to capture enough enemy ships to cover its costs. Spanish privateers ruined British trade." He lowered his voice confidentially. "The goldsmiths have done an accounting and we estimate the government is over two million pounds in debt to us and we have decided not to extend them any more credit. Once we inform the government, all will be thrown into chaos."

Montgomery took his money and returned to his office. He'd garnered enough information from the goldsmith to write yet another report to Monck about the government's state of affairs.

As well as being widely unpopular, the late Dutch war has been ruinously expensive to Cromwell's government. Despite the heavy taxation Cromwell imposed, there is a serious shortfall in revenue. The government is over two million pounds in debt, and its credit is virtually nonexistent. Bluntly put, arrears of pay in the army and navy will continue to mount steadily. Cromwell has kept this hidden but will soon have to call a session of Parliament to authorize a massive increase in taxes.

Montgomery sealed the letter and locked it in his desk drawer. Then he penned an almost identical letter to Charles Stuart, adding two paragraphs.

I urge Your Majesty and Chancellor Hyde to communicate directly with General George Monck. If Cromwell's army starts to desert for lack of pay, the Protector will no doubt order Monck to bring his Scottish force into England.

I feel it is worth the risk to make Monck an honorable offer. Make it more advantageous for him to join forces with you than with the fanatic Cromwell. If he refuses your overture, you have lost nothing. If he accepts or even plays for time, you will have taken a giant step toward regaining England's throne.

Montgomery sanded and sealed the letter. He would take it with him to the Inns of Court and prevail upon Mr. Burke to use his connections to get it across the Channel to Charles Stuart.

From her bedchamber window, Velvet was surprised to see the countess, accompanied by Mr. Burke, enter her carriage. "At lunch, Christian didn't mention she was going out," Velvet remarked to Emma. "While she's away, I think I'll try that recipe for apricot face cream which Bess wrote down in her journal." The Bishopsgate garden boasted an apricot tree that had produced a bountiful crop. "If the autumn weather suddenly turns cold, the fruit will drop to the ground and be wasted."

Velvet put on an apron to protect her dress and went out into the garden to gather some ripe apricots. She carried them into the stillroom and set them on the trestle table next to the flacon of glycerin and rose water she had made last week. The air was redolent with the fragrance of herbs that had been hung to dry and the lavender-scented beeswax candles that the kitchen maid had poured into molds yesterday. Velvet took a large wooden bowl and pestle from a shelf and then remembered that the recipe called for powdered starch. Since the laundry was next to the stillroom she took one step in that direction and was distracted by a shadow that fell across the doorway, blocking the sunlight. She saw immediately that it was Christian's grandson. "Good afternoon, Lord Cavendish."

"A good afternoon indeed." A grin spread across his handsome face as his warm glance roamed over her.

Velvet felt slightly uneasy. "If you are looking for your grandmother, my lord, she and Mr. Burke left in the carriage."

His grin widened as he drew closer. "Yes, I saw them leave." He picked up an apricot and bit into it. "Sweet and luscious." His eyes lingered on her mouth, dropped to her breasts and then lifted to meet hers. "Fruit, ripe for the plucking."

She realized he meant her as he popped the golden fruit into his mouth and grabbed her. When she opened her lips to scream, his mouth came down on hers and she tasted the apricot. Though she struggled frantically, he was stronger than she expected and she had to endure the kiss until he released her. The moment he did so, she jabbed her fist into his solar plexus and watched him swallow the fruit.

"Oh, my lord, surely you are aware that the pit of the apricot is deadly poison?" she asked with great concern.

Cav's hand flew to his throat. "I know the kernel inside a peach stone is poisonous—Christ, does the apricot also have lethal properties?" He ran outside and vomited into the grass.

Velvet slipped from the stillroom into the laundry, and then into the kitchen, where Cook and her assistants were preparing dinner and she knew she would be safe. She masked her agitation. "The guinea hens smell delicious. Would you show me how to make the special wine sauce that accompanies this dish?"

Velvet was relieved that Christian returned in the late afternoon. When she joined the dowager for dinner and saw that Cav was absent, she made up her mind to tell Lady Cavendish about the incident in the stillroom. Before she could speak, however, the young lord strolled into the dining room and took the chair next to hers.

"There you are, Cav. I trust you were able to entertain yourself while left to your own devices this afternoon?" Christian inquired.

"Yes, I can always find some little thing to amuse me."

The soup was served and Christian waited until the servant left the dining room. "You'll be nineteen soon. It's time we started thinking of a suitable match for you."

"I shan't be satisfied with just any heiress. Nothing less than a duke's daughter will be good enough for me."

"Since you've been blessed with title, wealth and exceptional looks, I warrant you'll have your pick, my boy."

He glanced sideways at Velvet and grinned when she blushed. Then he pressed his leg against hers and laughed when she flinched away from him.

When the guinea hens were served, Velvet passed the gravy boat to Christian. "I helped to make the wine sauce this afternoon. I hope you like it."

Cav drawled, "You are very wise to become domesticated. A woman of your age, without a dowry, is unlikely to marry well."

"Nonsense, a lady with Velvet's beauty and breeding will have many offers."

"Many offers indeed, but will any of them be for marriage?" Under cover of the table he slid his hand along her thigh.

Velvet picked up her fork and surreptitiously jabbed it into his hand. "Lord Cavendish has a remarkably droll wit for an eighteen-year-old boy." She saw his eyes narrow dangerously.

"I believe you are a match for him, my dear."

When dinner was over, Will Cavendish went off to visit his friend Henry Killigrew, who was attending nearby Gresham College, and Velvet followed the dowager countess into her favorite sitting room. She gathered her courage to broach the subject that was causing her a great deal of apprehension.

"Christian, I hate to carry tales, but when you were out this afternoon, Cav followed me to the stillroom and made unwelcome advances toward me."

"Advances?"

"He . . . he kissed me!"

Christian began to laugh. "Oh, how amusing! The dear boy has developed an infatuation for you."

"I didn't find it amusing. . . . He frightened me."

"Velvet, he's a boy! Surely you can handle a young man who is smitten with you. It's rather flattering, don't you think?"

"My lady, young Lord Cavendish is spoiled and not used to being denied what he wants."

"Precisely! A few setdowns from you will do him a world of good. I told you that you had an irresistible allure. Perhaps now you'll believe me, Velvet."

After the dowager countess retired, Velvet went into the library to get a book. When her eyes fell on the desk with its paper and writing utensils it reminded her that she should send a letter to Minette. She almost sat down; then her instincts told her she didn't want to be found here alone in the library when Cav returned. She picked up paper, ink and a quill box and carried them upstairs to her chamber.

Velvet wrote an amusing letter to her royal friend, telling her about her voyage across the Channel, the downpour that had drenched her when she arrived and her unnecessary apprehension about meeting the Dowager Countess of Devonshire. When she was finished, she decided to write a letter to her father. She picked up the penknife and cut a fresh quill. She had dashed off a note to Antwerp telling her father that she had arrived safely, but now wanted to thank him properly for allowing her to come home to England. She wondered if she should tell him that she was being courted by Robert Greysteel Montgomery. She smiled and knew she would keep the secret to herself for now.

When she finally got into bed, Velvet lay awake a long time thinking about Greysteel. She relived the hours they had spent together at Roehampton, and recalled the fragrant hay and the hardness of his body when he had held her captive against him and kissed her. He had the widest shoulders she had ever seen and she remembered every vivid detail of how his muscles had rippled when he'd rowed her across the lake.

Velvet drifted into a dream. She was back at Roehampton, watching a pair of swans glide toward her on the lake. When they got close she began to whisper to them. "I wish . . ."

"What do you wish, Velvet?" Greysteel's hands cupped her shoulders and drew her back against his powerful body.

"I wish I had someone to hold me, and love me, and keep me safe forever." She felt his hand on her hair and his hard thighs brush against her bottom. Suddenly, her body tensed, her eyes flew open, and she knew she was no longer dreaming. Someone was in bed with her, pressing against her, and she knew exactly who it was. She tried to scream, but his hand covered her mouth.

"Don't cry out. If we are caught in bed together, you will be labeled a whore. I'll say you lured me in here, hoping to become my mistress. Who do you think they'll believe?"

She could smell whiskey and guessed that he was drunk. She thought of the penknife on the writing desk and wished she had put it beneath her pillow. She lay still, her muscles tense, knowing she must escape from the lecherous young swine.

"If you promise to be quiet, I'll remove my hand."

Velvet nodded slowly and drew in a deep quivering breath as she felt him withdraw his fingers from her lips. She knew that if she attempted to scream for help, he would subdue her and hurt her. Instinctively, she knew that she must help herself. She lay motionless and counted to ten, then flung the covers aside and catapulted from the bed.

Uttering a foul curse, his cruel hands made a grab for her, catching hold of her nightgown and pulling her back to him.

She fought him, and as her hands came into contact with his flesh she learned that he was naked. *If he's naked, he's vulnerable!* She brought up her knee and caught him in the groin. She heard a gurgling sound and as he doubled over, she felt her nightgown tear. Suddenly she was free. She bolted from the chamber and didn't stop until she reached Emma's room.

She leaned back against the door to catch her breath.

"Is that you, Velvet?"

"Yes! May I sleep with you tonight, Emma?"

"Of course, my love. Did you have a bad dream?"

"Yes, it was a nightmare! No, no, don't light the candles, Emma. I'll be all right now." She wrapped her torn night rail about her and slipped into bed.

Gradually her trembling ceased, but her thoughts darted about frantically, searching for a way to solve her dilemma. She believed that Christian would laugh at her fears. Indeed, she had already done so. And if it came to taking sides, it would be natural for Lady Cavendish to choose her grandson over a penniless relative. He would be excused because he was drunk, but she knew that if she remained here, sooner or later the vile swine would catch her alone and force her to submit to him.

Vivid thoughts of her childhood came back to Velvet. Her earliest memories were lessons her father had drilled into her: *Never show fear; it is a contemptible sign of weakness.* She had soon learned to cover her fear with bravado. Timidity, anxiety, alarm and panic were other names for cowardice, according to her father. She was a Cavendish and pride must always take precedence over fright. He had laughed at her audacity and encouraged her to show defiance.

Only her mother had known of the vulnerability she hid beneath the surface of her bold facade. *When she sensed my dread of being betrothed she told me that Greysteel Montgomery's strength would keep me safe in the face of any peril.*

She thought of him now, and his powerful image eased her terror of the lewd young lout who had tried to ravish her. Velvet contemplated going to him in the morning. If she told Greysteel that Lord Cavendish had come to her bed, he would thrash him within an inch of his life. *No, no, if you tell him such a thing, he will never want you for his wife!*

Velvet knew it was time to become a woman, yet she vowed it would not be lecherous Lord Cavendish who initiated her. Though she had pledged her heart and soul to Charles Stuart, she knew that there was only one other man whose touch she could tolerate. *Perhaps I can tempt Greysteel into making love to me. . . . Perhaps he will still want to marry me. . . . Perhaps . . .*

When daylight arrived Velvet knew that she could not proceed with the plans she had made in the darkness. She had far too much pride to go running to Montgomery and give herself to him in return for his protection. She was determined, however, not to remain under the same roof as "Cav" for one more night and knew there was only one possible place where she could go.

Velvet made sure that Emma accompanied her back to her bedchamber while she bathed and dressed. Then she told her what had happened. "I need your help, Emma. I'm going to Roehampton until Christian's grandson returns home. Please pack me a bag and take it down to the carriage without anyone seeing you."

"I should come with you. A lady cannot travel alone without damaging her reputation."

"Thank you, Emma. It's very brave of you. It means deceiving the dowager countess, which is a thankless thing for me to do, but I shall leave a letter of explanation in her chamber and hope she understands."

Velvet penned her letter, waited until there were no servants about and slipped it into Christian's bedchamber. Then, as she had done every morning since she arrived, she went downstairs to take her breakfast with Lady Cavendish.

"I wrote to Minette last night. You kindly offered to send my letters with yours when you wrote to Queen Henrietta."

"Of course, darling. I'll write her today."

"Thank you." Velvet gathered her courage. "May I have the carriage to go to the Exchange, Christian? I need some ingredients to make face cream and I'd also like to start my own journal like the one my great-grandmother wrote."

"What a splendid idea. Just ask Mr. Burke to have Davis ready the carriage, and ask him to give you some money for your purchases. Your wants are so modest, Velvet. Why don't you buy yourself something pretty?"

"Thank you, Christian. You are too generous." Velvet was covered with guilt over the deception. *Please forgive me for lying to you!* Velvet rushed through breakfast and, when Emma appeared at the door, jumped up quickly. "I'm ready to go."

"I wish I could garner such enthusiasm for the Exchange," Christian declared. When she was alone her thoughts turned to Cav. "I wonder if the young lout managed to crawl home last night." She made her way upstairs and spoke to his valet.

"Yes, my lady. Lord Cavendish is still dead to the world. He seldom arises before ten."

"So I've noticed," she said dryly. She repaired to her bedchamber to change from her slippers and found Velvet's note.

> *I beg your forgiveness for deceiving you, but feel I must escape from your grandson's attentions. He came to my bed last night. He was both drunk and naked and his intentions were very clear. I know you think I should be capable of discouraging him, but I've had little experience in dealing with the opposite sex, and know I will be safe at Roehampton for a few days.*

The sound of carriage wheels on the driveway made Christian glance through the window. She saw Velvet and Emma hurry toward the coach and was about to open the window and call down to stop them. Instead, she glanced down at the letter and began to laugh. Velvet was jumping from the frying pan into the fire. "How very delicious. I couldn't have planned it better. She has no idea that Roehampton belongs to Greysteel Montgomery." Christian wiped away tears of mirth. "Velvet, I warrant that you are in for a delightful surprise. Your experience in dealing with the opposite sex is about to expand and will no doubt provide you with enough worldly wisdom to add a few naughty notes to your journal!"

Chapter Seven

*W*hen the carriage slowed to a crawl to enter the city gate, Velvet stuck her head out the window to speak to the driver. "We are not going to the Exchange, Davis. I want you to take us to Roehampton, please. The dowager countess knows about the change in plans." *At least she will when she reads my letter.*

Davis, quite used to the contrariness of the female gentry, drove along Bishopsgate and turned his horses onto Cannon Street, which widened into the Strand. He then took the road to Richmond until he arrived at Roehampton.

Velvet, luggage in hand, stepped from the coach and Emma followed. "Thank you so much, Davis." She hesitated. "I don't know when I will be returning to the London house."

"Very good, mistress. As soon as I've wet my whistle, I'll be on my way." Davis headed to the back kitchen door.

Emma eyed the Elizabethan manor house with apprehension. "Will we be made welcome?"

"Oh, of course. Bertha Clegg, the housekeeper-cook, is the most comfortable woman in the world. Her husband, Alfred, takes care of the horses and the grounds. It's the most charming house I've ever seen. I wish it were mine."

When no one answered the front door, Velvet opened it and went in without hesitation. "Mrs. Clegg? Bertha?" They found her in the kitchen, pouring ale for Davis.

"Welcome back, Mistress Cavendish. Is her ladyship here?"

"No, Bertha. Her grandson is visiting, so she stayed in London. I'm here for at least a week. This is Emma."

"I'll go right up and furbish a couple of bedchambers."

"No, no, we are quite capable of looking after ourselves."

Velvet led the way upstairs and chose a large chamber whose windows overlooked the lake. "Emma, the view is breathtaking. I love everything about this house. Which room will you have?"

"I should go to the servants' wing."

"What nonsense! There are six large bedchambers up here."

Emma chose a rear chamber over the kitchen. Beneath her window was an herb garden and another filled with every autumn vegetable from marrows to leeks. "I always took care of the kitchen gardens at Nottingham Castle," Emma said with nostalgia.

They found sheets and towels in the linen press and made up the beds. Then Velvet unpacked her bag and hung her clothes in the wardrobe. She changed into her dark green riding dress and pulled on her boots. "As you guessed, I'm off to the stables."

"Ask Mrs. Clegg if I can potter about the gardens, my love."

Velvet laughed. "To each his own. Horses for me . . . tansy and marrows for you. I believe there is a fruit orchard too."

At the stables, she greeted Mr. Clegg. "You'll be seeing a lot of me, Alfred. I'm visiting for at least a week and intend to ride every single day. I can saddle my own mare and promise to give her a rubdown when I'm finished."

"I know the animals couldn't be in better hands. Your father was the foremost horseman in England, I heard tell."

"And will be again when Charles returns to the throne!"

"Amen to that, Mistress Cavendish."

Velvet chose the same black palfrey she had ridden before. She tightened the girth. "Does this mare have a name, Alfred?"

"That's Raven. She's a little sweetheart."

"It suits her! She flies on the wind. Don't worry about me, Alfred—I'll be gone for a couple of hours, at least."

A short time later, he heard the clatter of hooves on the courtyard paving stones and thought Velvet had returned. He stepped from the stables to investigate and was surprised to see another visitor. Alfred recognized him immediately by the way he sat his horse. "Good day, Lord Montgomery."

"It is a good day, Mr. Clegg. Can you find an empty stall for Falcon? I have something to tell you and your wife that I hope won't inconvenience you in any way. I'm proud and happy to say that I am the new owner of Roehampton. I bought the estate from the Dowager Countess of Cavendish."

"That is a surprise. I had no notion she intended to sell."

"She didn't." Montgomery grinned. "I had a devil of a time persuading her. I'd appreciate your company while I break the news to Mrs. Clegg. Sometimes, women don't like surprises."

Alfred led Falcon into a stall. "This is a fine piece of horseflesh, my lord. Are you contemplating any staff changes?"

"None, Mr. Clegg. You are doing an admirable job here."

"Thank you, sir. Let's go and tell Bertha the news."

The two men entered through the front door but didn't find Mrs. Clegg until they went through to the kitchen.

"Another visitor! I love to cook, so I'll simply double up on my recipes." Bertha beamed.

"Lord Montgomery is not a visitor, my dear. He is the new owner. The dowager countess has sold Roehampton to him."

When Bertha's mouth fell open, Greysteel said quickly, "Once I saw the estate, I knew I had to have it. I beg that you remain as my housekeeper-cook, Mrs. Clegg."

"Indeed, your lordship, it is an honor to serve you. When Mistress Cavendish arrived, she never breathed a word!"

"Velvet is here?" Greysteel asked with surprise.

"Yes, my lord. Came an hour ago, and already went riding."

"She doesn't yet know that I have bought this estate."

"Oh, dear," Bertha declared, "that will be awkward for her."

"Not at all, Mrs. Clegg. Velvet is my betrothed. I'd like to tell her myself about Roehampton, if you don't mind."

A beatific look came over Bertha's face. "Oh, my, how romantic! I could tell that Mistress Cavendish had fallen in love with the manor house. So that's why you bought it—for her! Alfred and I will keep your secret, never fear, my lord."

Montgomery nodded his thanks. *Judas, am I that transparent?*

"After I put the bread in the oven, I'll ready your room."

"I am a military man, Mrs. Clegg, and pride myself on being self-sufficient. I shall take care of it myself." *I hadn't planned on staying overnight, but all that has suddenly changed!* He took the stairs two at a time. When he saw that Velvet had chosen a chamber facing the lake, he chose the bedroom that adjoined it. An intrusive thought shadowed his elation: *Perhaps Velvet has discovered that I bought Roehampton and it has miraculously changed her mind about our betrothal.* Greysteel questioned himself: *Isn't that the reason you bought the place?* He answered honestly: *Yes, but I would be considerably happier if she desired me more than Roehampton.* He chided himself for being a romantic fool. He had always been a realist; life was seldom romantic and in any case her first words would tell him whether or not she knew he owned the place.

Montgomery removed his coat and rolled up his shirtsleeves. After he made his bed, he went into Velvet's room and laid a fire, though he didn't light it. The autumn sun was shining brilliantly at the moment, but the September night would be cool. When he was done, he went for a walk on his own land.

Eventually he walked the perimeter of the lake. When he reached the far side, he spotted Velvet. He watched unnoticed, admiring the way she rode. Though she was a featherweight, she controlled her animal with ease. When she saw him she rode a direct path to him, and he felt a rush of pleasure at the way the breeze tumbled her glorious red gold hair about her shoulders.

Velvet reined in and walked her mount directly up to him. "What the devil are you doing here?" she demanded.

Greysteel's heart skipped a beat. *She doesn't know!*

"I was about to ask you the same thing," he countered.

"I—" She hesitated, searching for a plausible reason. "Christian's grandson is visiting her and I thought I'd give them some privacy by coming to Roehampton for a few days." She glared down at him. "Did she tell you I was here?"

He grinned up at her. "Why do you suspect such a thing?"

"Because she wants us to marry and is doing her damnedest to throw us together. It is highly improper for us to be here."

"Is it?" He held up his arms in invitation.

Velvet permitted him to lift her down and could not help being aware of his powerful muscles beneath the shirt. "Did you ask her permission to come here?"

He removed his hands from her waist and cupped her shoulders. "I must confess that I did not."

"Then you are trespassing," she accused, rather breathlessly, "and I suspect you are not in the habit of asking permission for anything you wish to do!"

"Your suspicions are correct, Velvet." To demonstrate, he lowered his head and covered her mouth with his. The kiss was not tentative; it was deliberate and sensually persuasive.

As his powerful arms drew her close, she became aware of how very tall and how dark he was. Her lashes swept down to her cheeks and a picture of Charles came full-blown to her. She melted against him and opened her lips in sweet invitation.

Greysteel's body responded instantly. His cock hardened and lengthened against her soft belly. When Velvet did not pull away, but nestled closer against him, it enticed him to explore further. His hands stroked down her back and came to rest intimately on her round bottom. He lifted her so that her woman's center rested against his hard length, and groaned at the throbbing torture.

Velvet's lashes flew up and he saw that her green eyes were dilated with pleasure and he knew she was experiencing her first delicious taste of arousal. She wet her lips with the tip of her tongue. "Put me down," she said breathlessly.

Instead, Greysteel traced her lips with his own tongue and it was Velvet's turn to groan. Then he set her feet to the ground and withdrew his arms. He masked his triumph when she swayed toward him with longing.

His kisses make my insides melt. Her inner voice warned: *It is Greysteel who is kissing you, not Charles!* Velvet replied, *I know, but the resemblance between them is uncanny.* Her inner voice mocked, *Velvet Cavendish, you don't even recall what Charles Stuart looks like at this moment.* "That's true," she whispered aloud.

"What is true, Velvet?"

She sighed deeply. "That I am shamefully ignorant."

He shook his head. "Enchantingly innocent," he corrected. He tore his gaze away from her and looked across the water. "This may be the last warm day we'll have this year. If only you knew how to swim, I'd invite you to join me in the lake."

"Of course I know how to swim!"

Ods feet, this is too easy. She swallows my bait like a little rainbow trout. "Velvet, is that the truth or bravado?"

"It's the truth! I can swim—not too far, but some."

"A pity you're not able to defy convention, throw caution to the wind and remove your clothes, as I'm about to do."

She knew he was challenging her to behave shamelessly, and it excited her. Her wicked juices compelled her to match him. With hands on hips, she declared triumphantly, "If you can call yourself Greysteel, I can call myself Velvet!"

He threw back his head and roared with laughter. "Come on, then. I'll race you." He removed his shirt, pulled off his boots and glanced over at her. While she was busy pulling her riding dress over her head, he threw off the rest of his clothes and waded into the water. He watched her sit down, pull off her boots and carefully remove her stockings. "You lose—I win!"

"It's not fair! Females wear more garments than males!"

"I always thought that was such a pity."

"You devil! I shall keep my petticoat on." She turned her back, removed her drawers, set them on top of her stockings and splashed into the water. "Oh, God help me, it's freezing cold!"

"Cold? Southern ponds are warm as bathwater. Don't you remember the icy feel of the lakes in Nottingham?"

"It was a long time ago, and little girls don't feel the cold like grown ladies do." She flung a handful of water at him.

He swam toward her. "You are still a little girl, Velvet." He took her hand and pulled her deeper. "I'm glad you haven't forgotten how to play. Don't ever grow up."

When she couldn't touch bottom, she grabbed his other hand. "I'm over my head, Greysteel."

In more ways than one, I hope. "Trust me to keep you safe."

She looked into his compelling grey eyes, saw his strength and his confidence and gave herself over to his keeping. He took control effortlessly, taking her into ever deeper water. She recalled something she'd said on their first visit here: *You enjoy being in control, but I give you fair warning, Greysteel. You will never have the least control over me!* He had replied: *I shall, Velvet. Never, ever doubt it.* She shivered at the thought of how easily he had lured her beyond her depth.

She glanced down at her floating breasts and when

she saw her nipples were erect like tiny spears and visible through her almost transparent petticoat, she blushed profusely. "You can let go now and I'll swim back."

He withdrew his hands from hers and glided beside her. They swam together for a few yards. When the water splashed into her face, she grabbed for him and slid her arms about his neck. Her eyes widened in accusation. "You are naked!"

"Guilty as charged, sweetheart."

"I am not your sweetheart," she protested breathlessly.

He stroked her glistening cheek with the backs of his fingers. "Shall I persuade you that you are?" He took possession of her lips and after the slightest hesitation she closed her eyes and yielded her mouth to him. As the entire length of their bodies touched beneath the water, she also yielded control to him.

His hands moved to cup her bottom. "Wrap your legs about me, Velvet." His voice roughened with arousal.

Slowly, with great daring, she opened her knees and straddled his narrow hips. She could feel his swollen sex cradled against her mons, with only the thin fabric of her petticoat between their naked bodies. She looked into his eyes and saw the raw need smoldering and smoky within their depths. Without a doubt she knew that this man found her physically alluring and for the first time in her life she felt like a desirable woman. Velvet opened her lips to him in wanton invitation and Greysteel took all she offered and then his hungry mouth demanded more.

She clung to him feeling deliciously boneless and

Greysteel, cradling her against him, walked slowly from the water. She unwrapped her legs and slid down his naked body until her toes touched the grass. Her lush breasts rose and fell as she took deep breaths to try to steady her wildly beating heart. "You . . . we must dress," she panted, and closed her eyes.

He stepped away from her and watched her turn blindly toward her clothes. He slipped on his breeches, picked up his shirt and advanced toward her as she stood in her soaking wet petticoat with her back toward him. He lifted the ends of her dripping hair and rubbed them with his shirt. Then he dried her neck, slid the petticoat down from her shoulders and gently dried her back. He dipped his head to kiss her ear and, at the same time, pulled down the wet garment from her breasts. He wrapped his damp shirt about her shoulders and pulled her back against him. "You are so lovely, you take my breath away."

Words from Bess's journal floated through her head. *Any man worth his salt can get a woman out of her clothes before she can say him nay!* Velvet gasped as his arms slid about her and he cupped her bare breasts with his powerful, calloused hands. "My great-grandmother warned me about men like you," she whispered.

"Bess Hardwick was a connoisseur of men."

"She certainly wasn't afraid of marriage," she murmured.

"Are you afraid of marriage, Velvet?"

"Yes . . . no. I don't know."

He turned her to face him and looked down into her lovely emerald eyes. "Are you afraid of me, Velvet?"

"Mayhap . . . I'm afraid of feeling passion for you,

yet more afraid of not feeling passion. Do you understand what I mean?"

"Lord God, it matters not. I can conjure enough passion for us both. Put on your riding dress before I lose all control."

They returned separately for propriety's sake. In the stables she unsaddled Raven, but Alfred insisted that he would give her palfrey a rubdown. "She drank from the lake and cropped quite a bit of grass." Velvet blushed at how long they had lingered out there, and retrieved the rolled-up wet petticoat from her saddlebags.

She went upstairs to remove her riding clothes and Emma came into her chamber.

"You missed lunch. I was starting to worry."

"Lunch?" She smiled a secret smile. "Never thought of it."

Greysteel tapped on her door and walked in. He was wearing a wet shirt. "Ladies, allow me to light the fire I set for you."

She watched him kneel and in less than thirty seconds he had an inviting fire blazing in the hearth. "Thank you, my lord, that is most thoughtful of you." Her eyes sparkled with delight as she watched him retreat. Velvet sat to remove her boots and roll off her damp stockings.

Emma's eyes were big as saucers. "Did he tell you?"

Velvet undid the buttons on her green bodice. "Tell me?"

"Did Lord Montgomery tell that he owns Roehampton?"

Her fingers stopped in midair. "Where did you hear such?"

"Mrs. Clegg—Bertha—told me that I could pick any of the vegetables in the garden that were ripe. I spent a delightful hour out there and when I returned to the kitchen, she was bursting to tell me that Lord Montgomery had arrived. 'Isn't it the most romantic thing you've ever heard?' she asked me. 'His lordship has bought Roehampton because his betrothed has fallen in love with the Elizabethan Manor.'"

"I find that difficult to believe." Velvet stood up and ran to the door. "But I shall soon find out."

She flung open his bedchamber door without knocking and walked in. She found Greysteel naked to the waist and saw that he had hung his shirt to dry before his own fire. She raised furious eyes to his and demanded, "Is it true?"

There was absolutely no point in his pretending he didn't understand what she was asking. Though he wished it were otherwise, someone had told her. He answered her question by asking another. "Do you want it to be true, Velvet?"

The question caught her off-balance. *Do I want him to own Roehampton?* "Did Christian Cavendish really sell it to you?"

"When we were here together, I did my utmost to persuade her. She refused, but miraculously changed her mind the next day."

"You devil! Why didn't you tell me?"

He looked down at her bare feet and felt her vulnerability. He took a step toward her. "Do you want the truth, Velvet?"

"Of course I want the truth. Men are so devious, I wonder if you are capable of the truth!"

"I bought the estate because I knew you had fallen

in love with it. I thought it would persuade you to marry me. I didn't tell you because suddenly I was jealous of the passion you felt for this house. I wanted to be sure you were attracted to me, Greysteel, not Lord Montgomery, owner of Roehampton."

Velvet's fury dissolved. She looked at his powerful naked muscles and blushed. "I think I gave ample proof of that." She curled her toes into the plush carpet. "I feel rather foolish, accusing you of trespassing when I am the one doing it."

He grinned. "I forgive you your trespasses."

Roehampton can be mine. All I have to do is marry him. Careful, Velvet . . . he hasn't asked you yet. Though she tried to banish them, Bess Hardwick's words insinuated themselves into her thoughts: *The most compelling reason to marry is property; the second is pregnancy. Love takes a distant third place.*

"I intended to return to London tonight, since it's so close, but once I learned you were here, wild horses couldn't drag me away. I long to play indulgent host, Velvet. Will you dine with me up here tonight, where we can banish the world?"

She caught her breath. *She who hesitates is lost. Cast the die quickly.* "I should like it above all things," she conceded.

He took her hand and lifted it to his lips, bestowing a gallant kiss. His eyes held a promise of what was to come.

Dear God, was it only last night that I wondered if I could tempt Greysteel into making love to me? "Until later, then."

Back in her room, Velvet flung open her wardrobe door and studied the dresses she'd brought. "It's true,

Emma. Lord Montgomery *is* the new owner of Roehampton."

"So I take it you are going to wed him?"

"Since we are betrothed, we are expected to marry."

Emma rolled her eyes. She had guessed that Velvet
couldn't resist the dark, dominant noble for long, despite her protests.

"Greysteel invited me to dine privately with him
tonight. I want to wear my most flattering gown."

"Did you go in the lake in your petticoat? I found it
wringing-wet. It's the only one you brought."

"I'll manage without," Velvet said, as if it were the
most natural thing in the world for her to go without
underclothes. Yet her cheeks turned pink at the consequences she imagined.

She deliberately plucked her most tempting dress
from the wardrobe. It was a delicate lavender silk creation. *Greysteel is planning to seduce me tonight, but God
help him, he is the one who will be seduced. I have a flagrant
fondness for Roehampton!*

Chapter Eight

Greysteel carried the dinner tray upstairs, which Mrs. Clegg had loaded down with mouthwatering food. Buttered marrow, glazed parsnips and crisp roasted potatoes accompanied a plump pheasant with chestnut dressing. The cook also had made them a trifle of light sponge cake, fruit, custard and thick clotted cream. A bottle of golden Canary wine was tucked beneath his arm.

He set all down on a small table he had carried up to his chamber earlier along with a pair of carved armchairs. Then he tapped on Velvet's door. "Dinner is here. Are you hungry?"

Velvet licked lips gone suddenly dry and studied her reflection in the mirror with an anxious eye. Without the fullness of a petticoat, the lavender silk outlined the contours of her body enticingly. She feared that she looked decidedly bold, yet knew it excited her to be daring. Heeding Bess's advice, she had purposely left her hair uncovered in a deliberate attempt to lure Greysteel to touch it. *A man lusts to taste that which he has touched. One taste and he won't be satisfied until he has devoured you whole!*

She opened the door and smiled. "Yes, I'm hungry. Are you?"

His glance roamed over her possessively. "Ravenous."

"The aroma of Bertha's food is tantalizing. I can't wait."

"Anticipation whets the appetite, and patience is a virtue."

"I have virtue aplenty, though I doubt you can claim any." She threw him a teasing look. "Lead on and I shall follow."

They were playing with words, choosing those that added titillation to the intimacy of dining alone together in his bedchamber. He led her inside, closed the door and watched as she moved to the fire.

"Your shirt dried quickly."

"You sound regretful. I can remove it, if you like."

She turned to face him. "Conceited devil." She watched avidly as his fingers undid the buttons. "Bold with it too."

As she stood before the fire, he could see the outline of her slender curves through the delicate silk. "And who's the bold little wench who left off her petticoat?"

"Blame yourself. You declared it a pity that females wear more garments than males. I'm attempting to be fair."

"I'll gladly accept the blame for your dishabille if it banishes your guilt tonight, Velvet. Come, let us eat." He pulled out a carved chair for her. "If I have my way, and I usually do, the food will be the prelude to a memorable encounter we will remember always."

She walked slowly to the chair he held. The way his intense grey eyes studied her made her feel beautiful. When she sat down he bent and dropped a kiss on top of her head, then caressed her hair with his hand. A small frisson of delight ran down her back, making her shiver. *The first touch of many!*

Greysteel took the chair opposite, lifted the silver cover and began to carve the game bird. He took her plate, served her with the choicest pieces, then handed it back and allowed her to choose the rest for herself.

Her first taste brought a rapturous look to her face. "We are so lucky to have such delicious food. Fare like this was unavailable when we lived in exile at Saint-Germain."

"I don't like to think of you being deprived, Velvet."

"Knowing we were sacrificing for Charles made it bearable. What about you? I warrant army fare was nothing like this."

"We seldom dined on pheasant stuffed with chestnuts," he admitted, but did not elaborate on how difficult it had been to feed his men. Watching Velvet eat gave him great pleasure. She had such dainty habits, yet at the same time relished her food with great delight. He poured two glasses of golden wine and felt her hand brush against his when she took one from him. He smiled into her eyes and offered a toast. "May you have everything you desire, tonight and always."

After a few sips, she set it down and ran the tip of her tongue over her lips. His imagination soared, mentally arousing him. When she dipped her finger into her wine and licked it, he became physically aroused. *Her gestures inflame my senses.*

They finished the main course and she helped herself to the trifle, relishing every mouthful. When Greysteel didn't take any, she said, "I love sweet desserts. Aren't you tempted?"

"Tempted beyond endurance," he acknowledged. He arose from his chair and moved around the table, and then he scooped her up and slid beneath her, so that she was sitting in his lap.

"That was rather impulsive of you," she said breathlessly.

"Not really. I planned the maneuver to coincide with dessert, knowing you would be distracted."

"Your courtship resembles a military campaign, Captain. You have besieged my defenses from the beginning."

"Hoping to avoid a battle," he said softly. "Once I have disarmed you, you will realize that resistance is futile."

She dipped her finger into the trifle dish and lifted the cream to his lips in blatant temptation. He succumbed to the bait and licked it. "I believe you just surrendered. The roles of captor and captive are now reversed." She wriggled her bottom into a more provocative position, which made his arousal throb, and slipped her hands inside his unbuttoned shirt.

"Would you plunder a defenseless prisoner?" he growled.

"Defenseless?" Her hands stroked the slabs of muscle on his hard chest. "I warrant you have a weapon hidden belowstairs." Velvet licked her lips and her fingertips circled his nipples.

He lowered his mouth until it was a mere fraction from hers. "You are the rudest little girl I have ever en-

countered." His lust ticked up a notch when she
looked inordinately pleased.

His lingering, seductive kiss stirred her desire. She
could feel the heat of his body seep through the fine
silk that covered her thighs, and thrilled with anticipation at what was to come. Greysteel left her in no
doubt that tonight he would make her a woman. As he
rose from the table, she slipped her arms about his
neck. She clung to him, hearing the thud of his heart
and deeply inhaling the intoxicating scent of his male
skin.

He let her slide down his body until her feet
touched the rug before the fire. He removed his shirt,
tossed it aside, then went down on his knees and
pulled her down before him. He threaded his fingers
through her curls. "The firelight turns your hair to
molten flame." He kissed her hungrily, then gently
pushed her back so that she reclined before him.

She gasped as his hand slid beneath the hem of her
gown and folded it back to reveal her stockings. Then
his hand inched its way up her leg to the intimate ex-
panse of skin above her garter. His fingers unfastened
the garter and he slowly drew off her stocking. "Have
you any idea how long I've wanted to do this?" He
raised her bare foot to his mouth and trailed kisses
across her dainty arch.

It was such a pretty gesture that Velvet felt as if her
insides were melting. She watched his bold hand slide
up her other leg and when he removed her stocking,
she felt the heat of the fire warming her bared skin.
The sensation of heated flesh was arousing and her
woman's scent was sensual.

He stretched his long length beside her and cupped

one of her breasts with his palm. The heat from his hand was scalding through the fine silk and she wondered what it would feel like without the impediment. As if he could read her mind, he unfastened her gown and slipped it from her shoulders, baring her lush breasts to his avid gaze and eager touch. His palm was rough, but amazingly this added to her pleasure. Her ruched nipples thrust up like tiny spears, luring his mouth to taste where his fingers had played. The hot sliding friction of his tongue sent threads of desire shooting down through her belly, and then lower into her woman's center.

Greysteel raised his head and looked into her eyes to gauge the effect of his wooing. Their emerald color had deepened to jade and they had become slumberous. He took possession of her mouth in a primal kiss that made her heart beat wildly. His hand stole beneath her skirt and his fingers stroked the soft flesh on the insides of her thighs. "Your skin feels like warm silk. I am insatiably curious. Are the curls on your mons red gold too? Don't tell me—let me guess," he teased. His fingers played among the tiny tendrils until she was blushing from his boldness, yet at the same time, she was panting with excitement at the new sensations his touch evoked.

"You cannot tell by touch alone."

"Of course I can. Black hair like my own is springy and coarse. Blond is superfine. Red curls, however, are rather saucy to the touch, exactly like their owner."

She caught her breath as he separated the tendrils and slipped the tip of his finger into her cleft. He traced the folds gently until their fevered dryness became moist.

"You have a tiny bud, just here." He stroked it, and when she gasped with pleasure, he slid his finger up inside her honeyed sheath. He felt it close possessively on him and he felt his pulse beating in his throat and his cock throbbing with anticipation. He circled her tiny bud with his thumb as his finger thrust in and out, slowly at first, then faster in a rhythm that matched the tempo of her quickened breathing.

The pleasurable sensations inside her increased in intensity, slowly building to a taut peak. She stopped breathing, wanting to hold the sensation forever; then her body arched as she experienced her first delicious little climax. It felt as if her bud unfurled into an exotic flower whose petals were drenched with dew.

He feathered kisses across her eyelids and temples. "How did that make you feel, Velvet?"

"Wicked," she whispered softly.

"Do you like feeling wicked, sweetheart?"

"I do," she confessed, with great daring and honesty.

"Then you are going to *love* the way this makes you feel." He took her hands and pulled her to her feet. "But first I want to see you unadorned, as God made you." He lifted the silk gown over her head and it fell in a pool at their feet. He gazed down at her naked beauty, enthralled by how delicate she looked.

He stroked her upthrust breasts with their proud pink crests, then slid his powerful hands down across her rib cage until they came to rest about her tiny waist. Then he sank slowly to his knees, trailing a fiery row of kisses down across her belly.

Velvet gazed down at his dark head in disbelief. What he was doing to her made her feel like a naked houri in paradise. His hands covered her bottom and pressed her forward for his mouth's ravishing. When Greysteel's lips touched her most intimate part she felt more wicked than she had ever felt in her life. Then his tongue plunged into her honeyed sheath, and the protest on her lips dissolved into a sigh of delight. His hungry mouth made her feel so excited she wanted to scream. Her fingers threaded through his long black hair, her head fell back, and a cry of rapture erupted from her throat.

His thrusting tongue brought a surging wave of sensation that made her feel drunk with its insistent, tantalizing rhythm. This time, when her climax came, it was more intense and her body shuddered with liquid tremors.

Greysteel stood, gathered her into his arms and kissed her deeply, knowing she would taste herself on his lips. He lifted her high against his heart and carried her before the mirror. "I want you to see how beautiful you are in your first passion." He lowered her feet to the carpet, and then cupped her shoulders to steady her from behind as he towered above her.

Their reflection made such an intimate picture that she flushed all over. Her skin glowed, rosy from arousal, and her eyes were languid from his love play. Her knees felt like water and she would have fallen if his hard body had not supported her. She arched back against him as his palms captured her breasts. His rigid phallus throbbed against her soft flesh and for the first time she realized that her beauty was irresistible to him. *He truly desires me. Perhaps I can make him love me.*

She met his ardent gaze in the mirror. "I want to see

you." She watched his reflection as he removed his breeches and undergarment. She saw his cock rise in rampant splendor, saw the heavy sac beneath, nestled in crisp black curls. His muscled thighs looked powerful as young tree trunks. She closed her eyes, willing her fear to leave her. Bravely, she swallowed her apprehension, and raised her eyes to his. "Take me to bed."

He picked her up and carried her across the chamber. As the head of his lance brushed against her bum, his blood surged and he cautioned himself that he must not lose control. Not yet. Velvet was still virgin. He must breach her hymen, giving her as little pain as possible. For that, he would need to curb his lust and exercise restraint.

He pulled back the covers and laid her upon the sheet. Then he lay down beside her, inviting her to explore him. The shadowed chamber was filled with the sensuous sounds of rustling covers, the whisper of sleek skin against skin, the gasp and moan of mouth against mouth, the slide of rough hands through silken hair, the vibration of hot breath upon fiery flesh. Erotic sounds, intimate sounds, love sounds.

Velvet lay in a wanton sprawl, almost incoherent with need, her hair a wild, disheveled tangle. When he moved between her thighs, he hung above her, allowing the head of his shaft to trace its teasing touch across her belly. He positioned the tip against her hot cleft. "Now, Velvet!"

His low, husky voice rumbled over her like thunder and she felt as if she had been struck by lightning as he plunged down swiftly, surely, taking her maidenhead in the ancient hymeneal rite of a first mating. Her cry shattered the night. She contracted so tightly upon his long, thick shaft that it was momentarily as painful for him as it was for her. He willed himself to remain motionless until she got used to the fullness.

As he held still, Velvet became aware that deep within they pulsated and throbbed against each other. Heat leaped between them, making her feverish with need. "Please, Greysteel!" Suddenly, she was welcoming him in an undulating rhythm that felt like hot, rippling silk. He wished it could last forever, but knew he must make it short and sweet for her sake. With potent, powerful thrusts he brought them to a swift climax, crying out hoarsely as he spent.

So that she would not have to bear his great weight, he rolled her on top of him, and cradled her in the dominant position, whispering love words as their sated and satisfied bodies softened. "I'm sorry I hurt you, sweetheart. There is pain only the first time." He lifted a red gold tress that drifted across his chest. "You enthrall me. Tell me that you feel the same, Velvet."

She thrilled at his choice of words. *Enthralled* meant charmed or held in slavery. "Yes, I feel spellbound." *You have magically transformed me into a sensual, beautiful woman.* She also felt extremely languorous and her heavy eyelids began to close. She snuggled against him, her lips touching his throat. She remembered her mother's words as she drifted into sleep: *Montgomery is noble and strong. I vow he will protect you and always keep you safe, my darling.* Velvet's hand brushed across his heart. "My darling," she murmured softly.

Greysteel held her tenderly, amazed at the way he felt. He realized that, until Velvet, there had always been something missing in his life. He had lived in a man's world without women. He didn't remember his mother, he had no sister, and he had never had a sweetheart. The females who'd accommodated him while he'd served in the army had been camp followers. He had never known a woman's warmth and tenderness. He had never known a woman's love. Velvet made him feel whole, complete. He had always ranged alone, suppressing the need for a companion, a soul mate. This woman—his woman—brought him comfort and solace, which he hadn't known he needed until tonight.

A wave of protectiveness rose up in him and as he tucked her head beneath his chin, he vowed to make her his wife.

In the morning, when Velvet awoke, she was aware that Greysteel was in bed with her before she raised her lashes. When she did, she found his intense grey eyes watching her.

"You didn't tell Christian that you were coming to Roehampton, did you, Velvet? If you had, she would have told you that she had sold the manor to me."

"No, I left her a letter instead," she confessed.

"The dowager countess will know that we have been together. Overnight. You are well compromised." The corners of his mouth lifted in a smile of elation. "You will have to marry me to avoid dishonor."

Relief washed over her that he intended marriage, and then she began to laugh. "You are still waging a military campaign. You speak as if you have me cornered, outflanked, and I have no alternative other than to surrender."

He reached out to stroke her cheek, a look of wariness in his eyes. "Do you surrender?"

Velvet's glance roamed over his muscular torso, and lifted to his dark unshaved jaw, assessing the powerful male before her. "Your weapons are indeed formidable." Her eyes dilated with pleasure. "Instead of your telling me that I must marry you, I would much prefer that you asked me."

"Sorry, sweetheart. I'm used to giving orders."

"And that makes you unbelievably attractive," she whispered.

It is Roehampton that makes me attractive to you. He pulled her into his arms. "Will you marry me, Velvet Cavendish?"

"I will, Greysteel Montgomery, and preferably before I see the dowager countess again."

"St. Bride's is the closest church to my house in Salisbury Court. We can be married there as soon as we return to London. This afternoon, if you like."

"Let's stay at Roehampton one more day?" she pleaded prettily. "I want us to go riding this morning and explore every acre of this heavenly place."

His hand rubbed the dark stubble on his chin and he warned, "I don't even have a razor with me, nor anything clean to wear."

"I don't mind." She pushed him back against the pillows and rose up over him. "I like you unshaven and naked."

He lifted his hand to stroke her cheek. "Your skin is so delicate and without a blemish. It looks like cream alabaster. My beard will scratch you."

"Mmm, do you promise?" she teased.

Though her invitation was blatant, Greysteel started his lovemaking very slowly, gently pushing her down and spreading her glorious hair across the pillow. He caressed every curve, every warm hollow of her body, with reverent hands. Then he spread her legs apart to examine every detail. He took each delicate layer of pink flesh, stroked, separated and kissed. His touch was as light as a butterfly wing.

An hour later she lay replete from the long drawn-out loving he had given her. *That was absolutely perfect.*

"Velvet, when I make love to you, it feels so right. I've never felt this way before." He traced a pattern of adoration on her face with his lips. "You are my angel love."

She stirred and stretched. "An angel who needs a bath."

"There's a hip bath in your chamber. I'll carry up hot water for you. Then we'll go riding."

He encountered Emma in the kitchen, taking breakfast with Bertha Clegg. "Good morning, ladies. I think you'll be happy to learn that Velvet has agreed to become my wife and we are going to make Roehampton our home. Since that means expanding the staff, would you consider coming to work for me, Emma?"

"I would be most happy to, Lord Montgomery. I much prefer the country to London. The soldiers in the city frighten me."

"Congratulations, my lord. Emma will be a godsend to me."

"Shall I take Mistress Cavendish a breakfast tray, sir?"

"Just bread and honey, Emma. We are going riding as soon as she has bathed. By the way, I've been a soldier for almost a dozen years."

Emma threw him an approving glance. "Oh, but

you're a Cavalier, my lord. It's the blasted Roundheads I fear."

Greysteel bowed gallantly to the ladies. Then he filled a large bucket with steaming hot water and took it with him.

As she cut the fresh-baked loaf, Bertha said, "This is so romantic, and it's not the first love match this Elizabethan manor has spawned. Legend has it that every unwed couple who sleeps under its rafters tumbles head over heels in love!"

"Mistress Cavendish has been betrothed to marry Lord Montgomery since she was seven," Emma pointed out.

"Yes, but how many couples whose marriages are arranged actually fall in love? It's Roehampton's romantic atmosphere."

Two hours later, Greysteel and Velvet rode from the village of Richmond, where he had made a few purchases including a razor. As they headed back to Roehampton, only a mile away, he pointed to the heavens. "Do you see that dark line across the sky? It means colder weather is moving in."

"Our lovely summer is ending," she lamented. "I know it is September, Greysteel, but I have no notion what the date is."

"Today is the third of September," he said quietly. "It is the anniversary of the Battle of Dunbar and of Worcester. They both fell on the same fateful date, a year apart."

"Charles fought at Worcester and had to flee for his life."

"Yes. The citizens of Shrewsbury closed its gates

against him, and Gloucester ignored his call to arms. He had twelve thousand men from the north and Scotland who'd been on the march for three weeks and they were exhausted by the time they arrived at Worcester. Charles said, 'It is a crown or a coffin for me.'"

"You were there?" Velvet asked in astonishment.

"I was," he said quietly. Large raindrops splashed his face. "We are about to get soaked. Let's ride!"

Since there was nothing they could do to avoid the drenching, they began to laugh at their plight. By the time they reached Roehampton's stables, their clothes were soaked and their hair was plastered against their heads. They tended their horses, then, hand in hand, ran to the house, grinning like children enjoying an escapade. They left puddles on the stairs as they ran up, and Greysteel knelt to build up the fire while Velvet brought towels from the linen press.

He helped her remove her green riding dress and petticoat and took delight in toweling her hair while she stood before him clad in only stockings and boots. Then he stripped off his own garments and set them to dry before the fire. "Nature is conspiring with me to get you out of your clothes."

They sobered momentarily when Emma tapped on their door. "I've brought lunch. . . . I'll just leave it out here."

"Thank you." Velvet's eyes sparkled with mischief. "One day soon, we really will make it down to the dining room."

While their clothes dried, the lovers took full advantage of their situation. When the rain stopped, in the early afternoon, Velvet threw open the window, then joined Greysteel to watch him shave. They heard a commotion of loud voices and moved to the window to see Alfred talking earnestly with a man on horseback.

"What's amiss?" Greysteel called down.

"Oliver Cromwell is *dead*, my lord!"

Chapter Nine

"Could such an amazing thing be true?" Velvet asked.

"Yes, it could very well be true." Greysteel pulled on his clothes and strode from the room.

Velvet slipped on her petticoat and went into her own chamber to find a dry gown. She took her blue linen from the wardrobe, found shoes and stockings to match and carried them to the other room. She ran the brush through her hair and was just about to put on the fresh gown when Greysteel returned.

"The news from Whitehall is spreading by word of mouth like wildfire. I have to return to London, Velvet."

"I'll pack immediately. Isn't this marvelous? Now Charles can return to England!" she exclaimed joyously.

"Velvet, sweetheart, it means no such thing. Old Noll has a son. Richard Cromwell is the logical successor to the office of Protectorate. You cannot just wave a magic wand and restore Charles Stuart to the throne of England."

Velvet looked so crestfallen that he took her into his arms and kissed her brow. "It is marvelous news, though, and unbelievable that it should happen on such a fateful day. Are you sure you want to come with me? I can see which way the wind blows, attend to my business and return in a couple of days."

"Of course I want to come. This is an historic event. Londoners will be agog with the news of Cromwell's death!"

"We'll have to ride, since we don't have a carriage. I promise to buy you one tomorrow."

"It's less than four miles. No distance at all to a Cavalier's lady." She dropped the blue gown onto the bed and donned her green riding dress once more, though it was still slightly damp. "I'll just pack a few things and have a word with Emma."

Within half an hour of hearing the momentous news, Velvet and Greysteel were in the saddle and on their way to London. In the city, crowds were gathering on street corners, and soldiers seemed to be everywhere, ready to stop trouble if it started.

When they arrived at Salisbury Court, Greysteel paid the hostler and made arrangements to stable the extra horse. Then he asked the stableboy to deliver a note telling the woman who did housekeeping for him that her services would be needed tomorrow.

Greysteel unlocked the front door of his tall house and ushered Velvet upstairs to the living quarters. "I don't have any live-in servants yet, sweetheart. You'd better keep on your cloak until I get the fires lit."

Velvet's curious glance roamed about the sitting

room. "It is remarkably neat and tidy for a man with no servants. I suppose that is your military training."

"The note I sent was to Mrs. Fletcher, who keeps house for me and does my washing."

Velvet watched him light the fire. When he went through to the bedchamber to light another, she hesitated at the doorway. "May I explore?"

"I have something I must attend to down in my office. Why don't you explore the house instead?" he teased. "You can explore me later." He drew her into his arms, gave her a lingering kiss and promised not to be long.

Montgomery's thoughts were at odds with his emotions. He knew he had to inform George Monck that Oliver Cromwell was dead. He would prefer that Charles receive the news first, but he could not be reticent about informing the general. Though both men would inevitably hear the news from other sources, Greysteel knew he had no choice but to write to Monck.

With determination, he set aside his feelings of guilt and disloyalty and sat down at his desk to write the letter. Greysteel put down the date, place and time of Cromwell's death. *Tomorrow, after I've had time to take London's pulse, I can add to the letter. The courier won't be here before tomorrow night; he always comes on Wednesday.*

Though Greysteel had discouraged Velvet from wishful thinking about Charles being restored to England's throne, he knew there was a remote possibility that this might be achieved if people of influence and power worked secretly to that end. The exiled king would be in the thoughts of many on this fateful day.

Most certainly George Monck will think of Charles Stuart when he learns that Cromwell is dead. Perhaps I can plant a seed that will take root. Montgomery hesitated, knowing if his letter fell into the wrong hands, he could be hanged for treason. His mouth set. With deliberation he redipped the quill and wrote:

> *The death of the Protector will inevitably give rise to speculation about the future. It places the country, and perhaps you yourself, at a crossroads. After the long night of Puritanism, will the people be ready for a change or will they strive to keep the status quo under leadership that may not be up to the task?*
>
> *The government is deeply in debt and the new Protector will have to call a session of Parliament to authorize a massive increase in taxation. At this point wide rifts will develop below the surface of national life. I sense a current of unrest, which will be difficult to contain if it grows stronger.*

Engrossed in his task, Montgomery was not immediately aware of Velvet's presence. When he glanced up and saw her he was momentarily nonplussed. He immediately flipped over the paper on which he'd been writing and set down the quill. "Whatever are you doing?" he asked curtly.

She was completely surprised by his reaction and his tone of voice. "I was curious to see your office."

He deliberately lightened his tone and erased the frown from between his brows. "Sweetheart, I assure you, there is nothing here of interest to a lady." Smoothly, he opened the top drawer, slipped in the letter and got up from his desk. He took her hand and drew her from the doorway into the room. "Well, as you can see, this is where I attend to business matters. This is my desk, these are the cabinets where I keep my papers filed, and this bookshelf holds vastly entertaining tomes pertaining to the wool exchange, mineral rights, London's warehouses and various shipping schedules." He led her over to the window and lifted the blind. "The view of London's grimy pavement, exhilarating as it is at first glance, soon begins to pall."

Velvet laughed. "I believe I can take a hint. It is clear you do not wish me to interfere in your business affairs."

"I would never consider your interest as *interference*," he assured her. "My business would simply bore you to death." He led her from the room and showed her the kitchen and the empty servants' quarters, which were located behind the office.

Who the devil were you writing to? You certainly didn't want me to see the letter! Velvet's thoughts chased each other. *Perhaps you were writing to your father about marrying me.*

As they went back upstairs, she felt his hand playfully caress her bottom, and it gave her courage to ask, "Will your father be angry that you are marrying a penniless wife?"

"Velvet, I am a man, not a boy. I'm sure he will respect my decision. Speaking of marriage, I think I'll walk over to St. Bride's Church before it gets dark, and make arrangements for a special license so that we can be married tomorrow. I have no intention of waiting three weeks while the banns are read."

"I packed my blue dress and matching slippers. Do you think that will be appropriate attire for a bride?"

"It will be perfect." He dropped a kiss on her bright

curls. "On the way back I'll stop at the cookshop on the corner of Tudor Street and get us some supper. I think you'll find a bottle of wine in that cabinet over there."

After Greysteel left, Velvet found the wine and set it on the table. She picked up her cloak and heard the chink of the two silver half crowns Mr. Burke had given her to buy something at the Exchange. *I'm not penniless after all!* The irreverent thought made her blush. She had nothing to bring to this marriage, yet miraculously Greysteel wanted her.

She carried her cloak through to the bedchamber. The fire lit up the cozy room and she turned back the covers of the bed to make it intimately inviting. She opened the wardrobe to hang up her cloak, when she saw something that gave her pause. She lifted the sleeve of the military uniform and stared in disbelief. *It's the uniform of a Roundhead!* She saw the captain's insignia and, recoiling in horror, dropped the sleeve.

She began to shiver and walked to the fire to warm her hands. In spite of the fire, she had suddenly gone cold all over. She put her hands to her temples in an effort to stop her wicked, suspicious thoughts. She picked up her cloak, retreated to the sitting room and sat down, staring into the flames of the fire as the late afternoon light faded and twilight gathered.

Velvet could not contain her errant thoughts. They strayed to the letter Greysteel had been writing and finally she gave in to temptation. She went downstairs to his office and tried to open the desk drawer. When she found it locked, her suspicions began to multiply. *Before he went out, he came back and locked the drawer!* Though she didn't want to believe that he was deceiving her, it was obvious he had secrets that he was concealing.

Her glance fell on a letter opener. She picked it up, carefully poked its tip into the keyhole and tried to unlock the drawer. When it didn't work, she began to jab in desperation. Finally, she broke the lock and was able to open the drawer.

Suddenly, Velvet was afraid of what she would find. She closed her eyes and whispered, "Please . . . no!" She gathered her courage and raised her lashes. The first thing she saw was an envelope sealed closed with wax. Her finger touched the seal and as she suspected, it was still slightly soft and warm. She could not bring herself to break the seal and read the letter, afraid that the contents would sicken her.

Beneath the envelope she found other letters. She scanned them looking for names but found only numbers in some sort of ciphered code. The letters were not signed, but one, authorizing the bearer to act as courier, bore the official seal of the City of Edinburgh. Velvet drew in a swift breath, her suspicions hardening into conviction. Then her hand closed on a piece of paper that condemned her lover absolutely.

This is a safe-conduct for Greysteel Montgomery, signed by General George Monck! Velvet knew that Monck commanded the Scottish army and had been appointed to govern Scotland by the hated Oliver Cromwell.

Her hand crushed the letter as her mind screamed denial. Then a strange, ominous calm settled over her and she tucked the damning paper into her bodice. As if in a trance, she went back upstairs and waited for Montgomery to return.

*   *   *

Greysteel took the stairs two at a time. He opened the door to the sitting room. "Velvet, why are you in the dark?"

"You have purposely kept me in the dark!"

He lit the lamp and stared at her, uncomprehending. He noted how pale she looked and saw that her eyes glittered with accusation. His gut knotted and his instincts told him to brace himself for her condemnation.

"You changed sides. . . . You are a *traitor*!" She flung the words like steel-tipped arrows and they found their mark.

"You filthy coward! You betrayed Charles, you betrayed your country, and you betrayed me!" She thrust the safe-conduct at him with a look of utter contempt.

His fierce grey eyes made his face look stark. She could not call him anything he had not called himself. It was weakness, pure and simple, that had made him an ally of General Monck. Greysteel could not excuse himself to the woman he wished to marry. At the moment he was covered with self-loathing. He would not add to his disgrace by explaining the circumstances like some pathetic supplicant begging for understanding and forgiveness. *Though my intentions were honorable, my actions were not. To claim that the end justifies the means is immoral.*

"How you could betray Charles is beyond my comprehension."

Jealousy flared up in him. "Velvet—"

"Don't touch me!" she cried, suddenly seeing him as dark, dominant and dangerous. Fear propelled her to action. She swept up her cloak and ran past him and down the stairs.

He bolted after her and grabbed her arm. "You cannot go out in the dark alone."

She raised her chin and hissed, "Take your hand from me, sir. It makes me feel *sick*. I shall be safer on the street than here alone with the Devil incarnate!"

He loosened his grip and watched bleakly as she ran from him. He walked after her, allowing some distance between them, but ready to sprint forward if aught threatened. She reached the corner and he watched her climb into a hackney coach. He stood silently, long after the carriage departed. Then finally, he walked back to his house with slow regretful steps.

He went into his office and lit a lamp. He looked down into the open drawer with its broken lock and was surprised to see the seals on the letter he had written to Monck were still intact. Ironically, if Velvet had read the letter, she may have realized he was trying to sway the general to throw his power behind Charles Stuart rather than Richard Cromwell.

Just one more day and we would have been married! He slammed the drawer closed with a curse. *You would not reveal your role to Velvet even if you were married. Especially not*, his inner voice prompted. *I would never involve my wife in anything that was dangerous or tainted with dishonor.* It dawned on him that perhaps it was fortunate that they were not married. *At least not yet— not until this matter is settled, once and for all.*

Velvet was painfully aware that she had nowhere else to go but Bishopsgate. She had left on a deceptive note and would now have to go, cap in hand, begging to be taken in and given refuge. When the hackney coach arrived at the house in Bishopsgate, Velvet gave the driver a silver half crown and did not wait for change. With trepidation she knocked on the door, uncertain what she would say to the Dowager Countess of Devonshire. She murmured a polite "thank you" to the manservant who opened the door, and hurried through the reception hall to the brightly lit sitting room.

Christian Cavendish came forward with hands outstretched in welcome. "Velvet, darling, I didn't believe the day could get any better, but here you are, proving me wrong!"

The warm reception made Velvet feel unworthy. "My lady, I humbly beg your pardon for deceiving you. It was a wicked and ungrateful thing to do after your generous hospitality."

"You left because of my grandson's lewd and lascivious behavior. I soon sent him packing, back to his father." Christian smiled coyly. "When I read your note and learned your true destination was Roehampton, I was vastly amused to think you were running straight to the arms of Greysteel. Dare I hope that you have an announcement to make?"

Velvet took a deep, steadying breath. "Yes. Lord Montgomery and I are no longer betrothed—we have severed our relationship. If you will let me come back, I will be forever in your debt."

"Oh, tush, my dear. Where else would you come after a lovers' quarrel? I'm sure it is nothing that cannot be straightened out. Everyone's emotions are bubbling over the surface on this momentous day. I have written to Queen Henrietta Maria. The royal family will be overjoyed at the news of Cromwell's death. Let us hope this will be the catalyst that sets in motion the restoration of our rightful king."

"My thoughts exactly. I hope with all my heart that Charles will return." *In spite of what that devil Montgomery says!* "Can we go and fetch Emma back from Roehampton tomorrow?"

"Yes, darling." She poured them wine. "Join me in a toast."

Velvet raised her glass. "Here's to His Majesty Charles Stuart, King of England, Ireland and Scotland!" She drained her glass and did not demur when Christian refilled it. They emptied the bottle, then climbed the staircase on unsteady legs.

After a sleepless night, Greysteel Montgomery arose before dawn. He spent the entire day riding about London. He visited every section of town, listening to what was being said by the wealthy, the poor and the working-class citizens. He spoke with Puritans, Quakers and Roundheads. He stopped at the Temple and spoke with the goldsmiths; he visited the markets and listened to the merchants. He traveled from Whitehall to London's docks. He talked with women and apprentices, churchmen and coach drivers, cookshop owners and watermen navigating the Thames.

Montgomery returned home and went into his office. He removed the sealed envelope from his desk drawer and weighed it in his hand. As he sat in deep thought, he was actually weighing his role in the scheme of things. Frustration roiled inside him. He was used to taking an active part, commanding and controlling men and events around him. Scribbling furtive notes was too passive an occupation to suit his temperament.

After he thought everything through, he made up his mind decisively, and put the letter in his pocket. *That is the last missive I shall write.* He took a blank sheet of paper, folded it and placed it inside a fresh envelope. Then he sealed it with wax and waited for the courier.

Chapter Ten

Edinburgh, Scotland

Greysteel Montgomery's intense grey eyes looked into the bulbous eyes of George Monck as the men sat facing each other across the general's solid oak desk.

Monck opened an envelope and took out a blank page. "The courier delivered this two days ago." He raised his eyebrows.

"Since this is my *last* report, I decided to deliver it myself." As Montgomery handed him the sealed letter, he noted that Monck showed no anger. *He is not masking his anger—his temper is imperturbable.* Greysteel watched him read the letter and saw that the general's expression did not change. *Unfortunately, his thought processes are impenetrable.*

"So. Cromwell is dead. How was the news received?"

Montgomery had always given Monck the unvarnished truth, and he did so now. "Not even the dogs wept."

Monck nodded. "Give me your assessment of his son Richard."

"He was quick to step into his father's shoes and become Protector, but if a man of Oliver Cromwell's iron resolve could not hold England together, the weak, ineffective son will see the country descend into chaos."

"Tumble-Down Dick," Monck murmured.

"Precisely." Montgomery had a great fear. Did General George Monck, who had the military experience, the power of office and the better-disciplined army, covet the exalted Protectorship for himself?

Monck's square hands rested on his desk. He steepled thick fingers and said blandly, "I shall cheerfully proclaim Richard Cromwell the new Protector in Scotland. We shall see how he performs—given enough rope."

You cheerfully want him to hang himself!

"You are the commander of the Protectorate forces in Scotland. If—when Richard Cromwell starts to falter, will you step in and shore him up?"

Monck was silent for a moment, then said, "The alternative would be to sweep him aside and make way for a new ruler."

Montgomery wanted a straight answer, yet he knew Monck was too cautious to give him one. "You have the power to seize the office of Protector, but the sole responsibility for the kingdom would then rest on your shoulders. There is a way for you to attain honor and security, along with power. In a restored monarchy, your reputation in arms would fit you to command all military forces. It is not inconceivable that you also could become a valued privy councillor. Worthy goals for a man who has reached the half-century mark."

"Though you acted as agent for me, your loyalty to Charles Stuart has never wavered."

"It has not."

"I suspect it was your advice that prompted Chancellor Hyde to send me a secret communiqué."

"Did you reply, General?"

"Give me credit for some acuity."

"I do. You're far too cautious to commit anything to paper. But if you would consider a verbal communication, I would act as go-between and carry your words directly to Charles Stuart."

"As I said, I shall *publicly* proclaim Richard Cromwell the new Protector in Scotland. At the same time I would *privately* urge those in exile to exercise extreme caution and do no sudden thing, if—when the new regime begins to collapse."

Montgomery caught the subtle nuance. "The public Monck will pay lip service to another Protectorate. Could the private Monck be open to the alternative of a restored monarchy?"

"I wouldn't go that far. Yet. I do believe that a return to a freely elected Parliamentary government is essential. Another military government is doomed to failure."

Though you're not ready to commit to Charles, I know you're not averse to a restored monarchy. Deep down you're a Royalist.

Monck's bulbous eyes stared into Montgomery's. "The Stuart Court could do itself some good if it moved from a conspicuously Roman Catholic city to one in a Protestant country."

"That is shrewd advice." *And so bloody obvious it should have occurred to all of us in the Stuart camp.* Greysteel got to his feet and held out his hand. When Monck readily shook his hand, Montgomery sensed they had an unspoken understanding. "I thank you for your time and your valuable advice, General."

Montgomery knew he had no time to waste. Once news reached Bruges, Belgium, that Richard Cromwell had been proclaimed Protector of Scotland as well as England, desperate Royalists could set in motion any number of rash uprisings.

Since Greysteel had stopped in Nottingham to visit his father on his journey to Edinburgh, he decided another stop was not necessary on his return to London. And within twenty-four hours of arriving at Salisbury Court, he crossed the English Channel, once again disguised in the rough garb of a seaman.

When Montgomery arrived at the town of Bruges, he found everyone at the exiled Court in hopeless despair. Charles alone displayed his usual stoic self-possession.

"Your Majesty, I come to give you firsthand knowledge of what is being done and said in London and the rest of England."

"I brace myself for your frankness. It will be a change from the reports of the fawners and flatterers."

"The funeral arrangements for Cromwell are ostentatiously royal. A wax effigy draped with black velvet was put on display in Somerset House. People lined up to see this out of curiosity. When the black was replaced with crimson and adorned with the scepter and crown, mud was thrown at the shield bearing Cromwell's escutcheon. He is to be buried in Westminster Abbey. Londoners love medieval pageantry, but I do not believe they will appreciate it being lavished upon the Protector. Now that Old Noll is dead, some, though not all, are whispering about *happy days approaching*."

"By that I take it they mean a restored monarchy. I would ask your personal insight regarding this matter."

"The time is not yet ripe. Any uprisings would be crushed."

The cynical lines on Charles's face deepened as he smiled. "I am too well schooled in adversity to make another abortive dash for my throne. If Richard Cromwell's Protectorate begins to falter, I might be tempted."

"Do not be tempted, Your Majesty. His Protectorate *will* falter and it will *fail*. This must be allowed to happen. He must be given enough rope."

"I sense you have more to tell me, Montgomery."

"I spoke with George Monck personally. After Cromwell's death I rode to Edinburgh to tell the general that I would no longer be his agent. He is well aware that I am your man, Sire. Though Monck has publicly proclaimed Richard Cromwell the Protector of Scotland, privately he expects him to fail. He referred to Cromwell's son as Tumble-Down Dick."

"The question is, does Monck aspire to the exalted position?"

"He has the power of arms to snatch it from Cromwell, but Monck is no longer a young man. Moreover he is aware of the heavy burden of such a position. Monck is far too shrewd to openly commit himself to restoring the monarchy, but he told me that he believes in a freely elected Parliament."

"The general never replied to Chancellor Hyde's overtures."

"He is too cautious for written replies. Any future overtures would have to be verbal. I will be your go-between."

Charles leaned forward. "What is his price?"

"Extremely high. Monck would insist on choosing the means to restore you without interference from your courtiers. Once you regained the throne, you would have to make him commander of all your forces. Perhaps even consider him for your Privy Council."

"I am prepared to offer more—a noble title and a pension."

"Will you guarantee it, Your Majesty?"

Charles's smile was sardonic. "I will guarantee the noble title. It will cost me nothing. The pension will be up to Parliament. I haven't a farthing to my name." He arose and leaned against the desk. "While I play a waiting game, I think my time would be well spent securing myself a wealthy wife."

"George Monck said something that I pass along to you. Advice that is as obvious as the nose on your face."

Amused, Charles stroked his large nose. "Indeed?"

"His exact words were 'The Stuart Court could do itself some good if it moved from a conspicuously Roman Catholic city to one in a Protestant country.' "

Charles looked favorably impressed. "That reveals his shrewdness. It also tells me he has thought a great deal about effecting a restoration." Charles smiled. "What will you ask of me, Greysteel Montgomery?"

"When you are crowned King of England, ask me again, Sire."

"Oh, the news is dreadful!" Velvet looked up from the evening paper she was reading. "Sir George Booth has been arrested."

All winter, Velvet and Christian Cavendish had eagerly consumed every bit of news they read in the papers or heard by word of mouth. Pockets of Royalist sympathizers across the country were constantly forming, but General John Lambert, head of England's Parliamentary army, was successful in arresting the leaders and seizing their caches of arms.

"I had every confidence that Booth would turn the tide when he gained control of Cheshire and Lancashire." Christian sat down before the fire as if the strength had gone out of her legs. "Royalist hopes have been dashed asunder once again."

Velvet scanned the newspaper, desperately searching for a scrap of positive news. "It says here that the London apprentices have started a petition expressing opposition to the overthrow of Parliament. When they get enough signatures, they intend to present it to the City authorities."

"Good for them! We shall go into town and sign it. The will of the people should carry some weight with our wretched excuse for a government." She stood up and stretched. "I ache all over. I'm off to bed, darling. I shall see you at breakfast."

Velvet sat staring into the flames of the fire. Everything seemed so hopeless. Richard Cromwell was proving such a weak leader that the army was gaining more political power every day. He had given in to all their demands so that they would quell the rapidly spreading unrest. Finally, Cromwell had surrendered his control of all military matters to General John Lambert. Velvet shuddered. *Roundhead soldiers patrol every street!*

She went to bed and when she finally succumbed to sleep, one man as usual dominated her dreams.

The dark, lean face of Greysteel Montgomery hovered above her as she floated in the lake at her beloved Roehampton. "I cannot touch bottom. . . . I am over my head!"

He reached for her. "Trust me to keep you safe, Velvet."

She clutched his hands and allowed him to draw her close. "You are naked!" Her outrage was a pretense. She had known he was naked all along. Beneath the water, she too was bare. It was all part of her planned seduction to attain Roehampton, the Elizabethan manor that she longed to possess. She had followed her great-grandmother's advice, and it was working like a charm.

When he carried her from the water and laid her down in the rustling tall grass that grew beside the lake, she smiled. "From the beginning your courtship has been like a military campaign. You believe you have won the battle, but I am the captor and you are my captive. Surrender your control to me."

His smoldering grey gaze swept over her. "Here is my sword."

She reached out to stroke his great weapon, and invited, "Sheath your sword, Greysteel!"

Velvet soon lost control as she surrendered to her lover's passion. She gave everything he demanded, willingly, eagerly, slavishly, and reveled in his mastery. He was dark, dominant and dangerous and she loved him with every fiber

*of her being. Her need for Roehampton paled beside her need
for Greysteel.*

*As the afternoon shadows lengthened they began to dress.
She looked up and suddenly became aware that Greysteel
was wearing a Parliamentary uniform. "You changed
sides. . . . You are a traitor!"*

"If you love me, it shouldn't matter."

*Velvet turned away and saw Charles. The king held out
his hand to her and murmured her name seductively. She
felt torn and looked back into Montgomery's intense grey
eyes. Velvet knew she had no choice. Charles had claimed her
heart while she was still a child. She turned and gave her
hand to the king.*

In the morning when she awoke, the vision of
Charles lingered in her memory. At first she refused to
acknowledge that she had also dreamed of Greysteel,
but as his image and his male scent persisted, Velvet
admitted he had been present. She told herself that she
had dreamed of him only because he owned her
beloved Roehampton. She insisted that her dream reflected reality. Between the two men, there was no contest. She would always choose Charles over that
traitorous devil Montgomery.

At breakfast, Velvet carried in the morning paper,
shocked at the revelations that the government was
two million pounds in debt. "Yesterday, Cromwell
called a session of Parliament. Senior officers in the
army demand that it be dissolved, and Cromwell has
refused."

"Much as I hate to agree with Cromwell, we must
always support Parliament. A military government
will trample every freedom. We shall go into town and
show our support!"

The dowager ordered the carriage for eleven o'clock, but when Velvet, dressed in warm cloak and boots, joined Christian in the reception hall, Mr. Burke informed them that Davis was repairing a coach wheel and their plans would have to be postponed.

"Delayed perhaps, but not postponed, Mr. Burke. Tell Davis to hurry. Get a couple of footmen to help him."

When the carriage had still not appeared at the front door by one o'clock, Christian again summoned Mr. Burke. "What is the problem?" She banged her ebony stick on the tiles. "Do you not realize that we are on a mission?"

"That is precisely the problem, my lady." Burke looked at Velvet, seeking her support. "Your mission would be courting danger. Ladies cannot expose themselves to crowds of people with inflamed tempers. There could be an outbreak of violence."

Velvet's chin went up and her eyes flashed defiance.

Christian drew herself up, standing tall and rigid. "Your dire warnings add impetus to our determination. See that the carriage is brought round immediately."

"Very good, my lady, but I insist upon accompanying you." Burke scribbled a quick note, then went to the carriage house and gave Davis careful instructions. He told the groom's son, who often rode on the back of the coach as tiger, to hop aboard and entrusted him with the message.

Christian, wearing her most elaborate hat with a defiant ostrich feather, declined Mr. Burke's help with a fierce glare as she stepped up into the carriage.

Velvet hid a smile and graciously accepted the steward's aid. As the coach entered London through the

Bishops Gate, excitement began to race through her at the thought of adventure. She noticed there were not many soldiers about and wondered why.

When the carriage slowed to climb Ludgate Hill, the young lad hopped down from his perch at the rear. Then Davis picked up speed again as they reached Fleet Street. Where it widened into the Strand, however, other coaches and groups of people milling about impeded their progress. Mounted soldiers were pushing their way through the crowds.

"We should turn back, Lady Cavendish," Burke said quietly.

"Retreat would be decidedly lily-livered. We shall press on to the House of Commons to show our support. Tell Davis to turn here and station the coach behind the Savoy Palace. We shall get out and walk from there."

With Mr. Burke close on their heels, Velvet and Christian, with the aid of her stick, pushed their way through Charing Cross and headed toward St. James's. It took over an hour to reach the palace grounds, which overflowed with thousands of raucous Londoners who had been rounded up by the military, calling for the overthrow of Parliament and for Richard Cromwell to resign.

"Mad buggers," Christian shouted in alarm as she and Velvet were swept along by a tide of humanity that was out of control. "How will we ever get to the houses of Parliament?"

"Parliament is dissolved, missus," a red-faced hooligan shouted. "Lambert's troops now occupy the house!"

"Good God!" Christian cried. "London is under military rule!"

A well-dressed, but frightened, man pushed Velvet aside. "The soldiers have looted the wine cellars at Whitehall!"

Suddenly, a shot rang out. Without hesitation, Mr. Burke elbowed two people aside, grabbed the dowager countess, wrapped his arm about her narrow shoulders and half dragged her out of the crowd. More shots were fired, and people began to screech and push frantically.

Velvet found herself alone, surrounded by rampaging lunatics. Mounted men in uniform were trampling the crowds. She saw a horse with an empty saddle. It was rearing, its hooves wildly pawing the air, as it screamed in fright. Velvet's first impulse was concern for the animal. She darted forward, unafraid of the flailing hooves, and grabbed its reins. She tried to calm the frantic horse as those about them fell back screeching and shouting in alarm.

"Velvet!" The deep, powerful voice rolled over her like thunder. Then she felt an arm like a steel band wrap around her waist. She was lifted into the air by the man who towered beside her as he mounted the terrified horse. He set her before him in the saddle. "Hang on!" he thundered as he concentrated on controlling the animal.

By dint of will, Greysteel Montgomery forced the horse to obey him and it charged forward as the crowd in its path parted. "Christ Almighty, Velvet, what the hell is the matter with you? Were you deliberately trying to get yourself killed?"

She looked at him in disbelief. *How did he know*

where I was? What on earth is he doing here in the midst of this unruly mob? Then she saw his uniform and recoiled. He was part of the detested Parliamentary military that was responsible for the chaos. In a blind fury, she smote his chest with her fists. "Put me down! We are enemies!"

He ignored the blows. "Where is your coach?" he demanded.

"You arrogant swine! You are wrong if you think you rescued me. I could have handled the horse," she panted.

"I don't question your ability with horses. I question your judgment in dashing headlong into danger, involving yourself in affairs that are best handled by men. Where is your carriage? I won't ask you again, Velvet."

"It's behind the Savoy Palace," she hissed. "I kept your shameful secret about being a Roundhead, but now Christian and Mr. Burke will see you for what you are!"

Greysteel turned the horse toward the river. There were hardly any people behind Suffolk House, so he spurred the animal across the lawn that sloped down to the Thames.

At York House, Velvet spied her chance to escape him. She slid down from the horse and began to run. In a flash he was out of the saddle and after her. He snatched her up like a piece of baggage and slung her over his shoulder, clamping one arm about her thighs, while he clung to the horse's reins with his other hand, effectively controlling both.

He strode forward with dogged determination until they arrived at the dowager's coach. Davis stood guard, whip in hand, while Mr. Burke plied Lady Cavendish with whiskey from his flask. "Stand aside," Greysteel directed Burke. When the steward complied, Montgomery tossed Velvet inside without ceremony.

"Thank God you found her!"

"God had nothing to do with it. Her flaming hair was like a beacon." He lowered his voice. "I'm heading north tomorrow."

Mr. Burke nodded. "All depends on your success, milord."

Edinburgh, Scotland

"London was in chaos when I left. General Lambert dissolved Parliament and took over the house. The army has roused the rabble against Richard Cromwell to force his resignation."

"The mob is not the people; what is the voice of the people?"

"Military government is anathema to the general population, not just the nobility and gentry. The people are vehemently opposed to the overthrow of Parliament. London's apprentices launched a petition and got twenty thousand signatures. They tried to present it at Guildhall the day I left, but were prevented by a troop of horse. Violence again broke out and people were shot. It is time for a decisive move on your part, General Monck."

"A return to Parliamentary government is essential. I will issue a letter condemning the actions of my fellow officers. My troops and I declare for the expelled members of Parliament."

"Will you also declare for a restored monarchy?"

"No. Not yet. When my letter arrives in London, General Lambert will rush his troops to the Scottish Border to oppose me. He will not be successful," Monck said calmly. "Tell me, how did Charles Stuart manage to move his Court to Breda in Protestant Holland without antagonizing Spain?"

"He simply told them he was visiting his sister Mary. He set up headquarters in Breda, and the Princess of Orange brought her entire Court from The Hague to visit Charles and her younger brothers." Montgomery leaned forward. "General, if you put your power behind Charles Stuart and he regains his throne, he is prepared to name you commander of all military forces."

"When I defeat England's General John Lambert, I *will* be the commander of all military forces."

Montgomery doggedly pushed aside his impatience and pressed on. "As well, Charles will honor you with a noble title."

"An earldom comes with estates, does it not?"

Montgomery's grey eyes intensified. "He offers a *dukedom*." Greysteel reached into his doublet. "Moreover, he has put the offer in writing and signed it." He proffered a sealed letter.

When Monck reached out and took it, Montgomery knew he had him. *You will not declare for Charles Stuart one moment before you are ready, you canny bastard, but declare for him you will!*

To save time, Montgomery boarded a Dutch merchant vessel in the Scottish port of Leith and reached Breda two days after the news arrived that Richard

Cromwell's Protectorate had ended. Charles immediately had a private meeting with Greysteel.

"My siblings are celebrating Cromwell's downfall, but without Parliament, England will suffer under military rule."

"Not for long, Sire. Monck has sent a dispatch to London condemning the actions of the English military. He knows this will bring General John Lambert and his army north. Monck is preparing his troops to cross the Border."

"Life has taught me there's many a slip 'twixt cup and lip."

"Monck will prevail."

"But will he call for a restoration of the monarchy?"

"When the time is right. I give you my word that when George Monck is ready, he *will* call for restoration, Your Majesty."

Charles looked skeptical. "When will he be ready, my friend?"

"When he arrives in London. I pledge my life on it, Sire."

Chapter Eleven

"Charles is coming home!" Velvet dropped the morning paper and did a pirouette. She smiled at a beaming Mr. Burke, then threw her arms about Christian and the two ladies did a little dance of happiness. "Oh, I knew as surely as spring follows the long, dark winter that Charles would be restored as England's rightful king. I never doubted it for one moment!"

"You were more steadfast in your belief than I, darling. I relegated mine to the realms of wishful thinking when dreaded General Monck marched across the Border from Scotland."

"The Roundheads deserted General Lambert when they found out there was no money to pay them. Then like cowardly turncoat dogs they joined Monck's army. I hate and despise them all!" Greysteel Montgomery was never far from Velvet's thoughts. *That devil joined Monck before any of the other cowards!*

"Monck arrived in London and became commander in chief of Parliament's forces. When he ordered the house to issue writs for an election, then dissolve, surely he knew a Royalist Parliament would be elected? He must be the stupidest man alive!"

"Or shrewd and cunning as a fox," Mr. Burke murmured.

"I shall have my Lion and Unicorn tapestry brought down from the attics along with the portraits of the Stuarts. Every Royalist can breathe easier, especially the landowners."

"Father and my brother, Henry, and all the other exiles will be coming home!" Velvet declared happily.

"My son, Devonshire, and his family will be able to move back to our ancestral home, Chatsworth. It is without doubt the most magnificent house in England. It was no easy matter keeping its ownership in the Cavendish family under Roundhead rule."

"The king will restore Nottingham and Bolsover Castles to my father, and my brother, Henry, will get Welbeck Abbey."

"I hope that doesn't mean you will go running off to Nottingham and other points north. The King's Court will be the perfect setting for beautiful ladies of noble birth."

"How could you think I would leave London at such an exciting time? The shops, the fashions, the customs, the people . . . all will be transformed."

"After a decade of Puritanism, Londoners will go mad!"

"Quite," Mr. Burke concurred. "The streets will still not be safe enough for ladies to venture out alone."

"Oh, please don't say that, Mr. Burke. We have been very good all winter, confining ourselves here at Bishopsgate since that dreadful night when we were caught in the rabble."

"We shall take your warning to heart, Mr. Burke, but I remind you that we have had enough of *Protectors!*"

Velvet pushed away the picture of Montgomery rushing to her rescue and forcing her to comply with him against her will.

"Never mind, darling, you and Emma put your winter confinement to very good use concocting face creams and cosmetics and herbal hair rinses. Such things will be in high demand at Court."

"The recipes are old-fashioned . . . copied from Bess's journal or remembered from things my mother invented, using herbs."

"London will be turned on its head. Everything fashionable will become déclassé . . . Everything old will be new. You'll see!"

"My only regret is that Minette won't be coming home!" Velvet had received a startling letter from her friend that she was going to France to be married to the young brother of Louis, King of France. It was a political marriage, which her mother had arranged. "Still, she will live in a palace and be surrounded by luxury, so I shall be happy for her." Velvet placed her hand over her racing heart. "Listen! All the church bells are ringing. Oh, I cannot wait to see Charles again!"

In his office at Salisbury Court, Montgomery picked up his newspaper and read the Declaration of Breda, which Charles Stuart had issued. Greysteel's mouth curved. *It is designed to reassure the nation and remind it of royal tradition.*

The Declaration stated that history was brought

about not by accident, but by the hand of Providence. The restoration of the king was not man-made, but an act of God. Faith, reconciliation and tradition would ensure civil order. Charles offered a free and general pardon to all the enemies of the house of Stuart, save those whom Parliament chose to except.

Greysteel laughed out loud at Charles's shrewdness in emphasizing Parliamentary authority. "He is courting the members of Parliament and makes no mention of the king's traditional prerogative powers." He laid the newspaper on his desk and pictured Charles greeting the Parliamentary commissioners when they arrived in Breda. "Ods feet, they will shit themselves when they see their king in rags and tatters!"

He heard the bell of St. Bride's Church begin to peal and he immediately thought about Velvet. "She will be ecstatically happy this morning." He crushed down his feelings of jealousy. It was a demon he must never acknowledge.

The post arrived and Greysteel opened a letter from his father. His brows drew together when he saw that their head steward had written it.

> *Lord Montgomery,*
> *I regret to inform you that the Earl of Eglinton suffered a fall from his horse while visiting one of the tenant farms. With the advent of the spring shearing almost upon us, your father urges that you return home with all possible speed.*

Greysteel saw that his father's signature, which he had scrawled at the bottom of the letter, was almost indecipherable. He packed immediately. Over the course of the winter he had traveled to Edinburgh numerous times on the exiled king's business. Now that Charles was going to be officially restored as England's rightful king and he and Monck were able to communicate without secrecy, Greysteel felt free to look after Montgomery affairs.

The Earl of Eglinton, propped in the massive four-poster, made no attempt to disguise his relief that his son had arrived.

"How are you feeling, Father?" *He looks vulnerable for the first time in his life.*

"Poorly!"

One side of the earl's mouth was drawn up, making him look as if he were smiling. Greysteel knew that he was not. His father made an effort to rise, then fell back in defeat because the limbs on his right side were paralyzed.

"What can I get you to make you feel better?"

"Sh-sheeing!"

Greysteel realized his speech had also been affected. "Shearing?" he guessed, knowing that business matters had always come first and foremost with Alex Greysteel Montgomery. He put a comforting hand on the earl's shoulder. "I'll oversee the shearing, Father. Rest easy."

"Will . . . will—"

"Will I what?" Greysteel prompted gently.

The earl shook his head in exasperation and with his steely eyes indicated a leather case on the bedside table.

Greysteel retrieved it and opened it up. Inside he found his father's last will and testament, along with many other legal papers, certificates and deeds. "I will keep them safe," he assured the bedridden man. "The steward is waiting for me. If you will rest, I will see to the Montgomery sheep."

During the next three days, Greysteel spent countless hours in the saddle, overseeing the shearing of thousands of precious Montgomery's sheep at more than a dozen tenant farms. No easy task when more than half of the ewes were lambing. By midnight on the fourth day, he had personally aided in the birth of almost five hundred lambs. He grinned at the steward. "My respect for Father's endurance has risen considerably."

"Aye, it's hard work and long hours in the spring." Montgomery stood up and stretched. "But most rewarding."

Though the hour was late, Greysteel looked in on his father and was relieved to find him asleep. He retired to his own bed and though he was physically tired, he was mentally wide-awake.

He reached for the leather case and drew out the documents. Among them was his baptismal certificate and when he saw that he had been named Robert Greysteel, he realized that it wasn't just a nickname. He looked at his parents' marriage certificate and saw that it was dated only two years before his mother had died. *Father has been without his wife for twenty-eight years.* Though Greysteel had no memory of his mother, he was convinced that if she had lived, the Earl of Eglinton would not have become such a rigid, irascible and difficult devil.

He picked up the betrothal contract signed by his father and Newcastle. It was a legal paper and, to

Greysteel, completely binding. He thought of Velvet and a tender smile curved his mouth. She was all he wanted in a woman and he was determined to make her his wife. Without her, he knew, his life would be incomplete. *God forbid that I turn into my father!*

He picked up the will and began to read. It confirmed what he already knew, that upon Alexander's death, he would automatically inherit the earldom. As well, his father bequeathed all Montgomery holdings to him. He went over the list of familiar properties, and then his brows drew together as he read a new addition at the bottom.

"Bolsover Castle!" Greysteel exclaimed aloud. "This has to be a mistake. Bolsover is owned by William Cavendish, Earl of Newcastle." Then he remembered that Velvet's father had had all his landholdings confiscated by Oliver Cromwell. "But Old Noll most certainly wouldn't bestow any of Newcastle's property on Father." Greysteel searched through the deeds and sure enough he found one for Bolsover Castle.

He read every word of the legal document and saw that Bolsover had been confiscated from Newcastle and granted to Charles Fleetwood, a Parliamentary general, for services rendered. Three years ago, Fleetwood had sold Bolsover Castle to Alexander Montgomery for the sum of five thousand pounds.

"Holy God, Father coveted every Cavendish acre and finally got his hands on Bolsover, one of their cherished possessions!"

Greysteel silently cursed. *This will put Charles in one hell of an awkward position. Newcastle will expect Bolsover Castle to be restored to him. That could be easily accomplished if a Roundhead enemy had possession, but even the king could not, nor would not, confiscate a deeded land-holding from a Royalist supporter and friend*. He thought of Velvet and groaned. He knew she would hate him for what his father had done.

He blew out the lamp and tried to sleep, but his active mind ran in circles with one thought chasing after another for hours. Finally, just before dawn, he fell into an exhausted sleep and began to dream.

Velvet thrust the document at him with a look of utter contempt. "You greedy swine, you covet anything that bears the Cavendish name!"

"The only thing I covet with a Cavendish name is you, Velvet."

"Liar!" She set her hands on her hips and lifted her chin. "You couldn't wait to get your hands on the manor at Roehampton. You had to have it because it was owned by Christian Cavendish!"

"I bought the Elizabethan manor because you fell in love with it. I wanted us to live there when we married."

"We will never be married, Montgomery!"

"We shall, Velvet. Never doubt it for one single moment."

"Dominant devil! You will never bend me to your will again."

"There is one sure way to make you beg to become my wife."

"By offering me Bolsover Castle?" she sneered.

"By getting you with child!" He reached out and pulled her forcefully into his arms.

Fear widened her emerald eyes. "You'd ravish me, Greysteel?"

"Aye! You purposely defy me and drive me to violence."

He crushed her mouth beneath his, forcing her submission.

He awoke, drenched with sweat, her female scent filling his nostrils, the feel of her warm flesh lingering on his body. He threw back the tangled covers and quit the bed with an oath.

He padded to the window and pushed open the shutters. The dawn sky was streaked with gold and red. *Even the heavens remind me of her. I would never hurt her—she's my angel love.*

Greysteel turned and saw the documents and deeds scattered on the carpet. He picked them all up and shoved them back into the leather case. "I will have this out with Father."

Greysteel paced the hallway until Stoke, his father's manservant, fed the irascible invalid his breakfast and changed his linen. Then Montgomery entered the bedchamber, pulled out the deed for Bolsover Castle and presented it to his father. "What on earth were you thinking when you acquired this prized possession that rightfully belongs to Newcastle?"

The earl grimaced. It was definitely not a smile; it was a sneer. "Montgomery . . . stands . . . higher."

Greysteel recalled how overjoyed his father had been when he learned his son had bought Roehampton from the dowager countess. Then Velvet's words from his dream echoed in his head and he realized that the earl had always coveted Cavendish holdings. "That was the reason you betrothed me to Newcastle's daughter!"

His father nodded vigorously.

"Don't you realize this will set not only Velvet but the entire Cavendish family against me?"

"No . . . marriage!" the earl shouted. His face turned dark red.

Greysteel stared at his father, trying to make sense of his words. Then understanding dawned. "You don't want me to marry a Cavendish because she would have a claim on Bolsover."

"P-promise!" his father demanded. The earl suddenly fell forward and his face turned purple as he gasped for air.

"Stoke!" Greysteel called the earl's manservant. "Fetch the doctor!" He gripped his father's shoulders and eased him back against his pillows. Then he pulled a chair to the bed and sat vigil. His father's breathing eased and the dark color drained from his face, but his eyes remained closed. He seemed to be sleeping peacefully, when suddenly his breathing stopped.

Greysteel jumped forward and pumped on his chest, trying to force breath back into him, but his father had slipped beyond help. When the doctor arrived, he pronounced the earl dead, wrote *apoplexy* on the certificate and offered his condolences.

Alone with his father's body, Greysteel was covered with guilt. *I killed him!* His inner voice taunted: *He's not the first man you've killed.* He argued: *That was different—that was in battle.* His inner voice asked: *Were you not battling your father?* The proof stared him in the face: *A battle to the death.* Montgomery squared his shoulders and accepted the blame.

The following day Greysteel stood beside his father's grave while the Montgomery tenant farmers paid their respects. The men shook his hand; their wives bobbed curtsies.

As he stared down at the mound of earth, Greysteel realized he was in deep mourning. He mourned a lifetime of abrasive relations and the cold distance his father had always kept between them. He mourned the warm love and acceptance for which he had strived so hard but never achieved. And he mourned the fact that matters could never be set right between them, for their time had all run out. He knew they could never be reconciled. His father's last request stood starkly between them. If he did not honor it, they would be enemies forever.

He moved to the left and knelt at his mother's grave. With his fingertips he traced her name, etched in the granite stone:

CATHERINE PAISLEY MONTGOMERY, COUNTESS OF EGLINTON, WIFE OF ALEXANDER GREYSTEEL MONTGOMERY, EARL OF EGLINTON.

"It doesn't even say *beloved* wife," he murmured. Greysteel realized that he was also mourning the loss of his mother. He'd always mourned her. His fingers touched the date, only months after his birth. *Perhaps I'm responsible for her death too.*

Montgomery saddled Falcon and rode for miles, climbing ever higher through the Pennines, though the sky looked threatening. There was a long, low rumble of thunder, followed by a drenching shower. Deep in thought, Greysteel was impervious to the weather. He urged his mount to the peak, then allowed it to rest while he sat motionless in the saddle.

Steadily the wind picked up and blew away the dark clouds. The green valley below, filled with ewes and their newborn lambs, was dappled with spring sunshine. The breathtaking view touched a chord in his soul. He filled his lungs with the crystal fresh air and felt the weight lift from his heart.

It's a new day, with a new king. It's like a rebirth. He vowed to look forward and embrace the future. *Perhaps it will be a golden age.* Strange that he and Charles had come into their titles together. *All things come at their appointed time.*

He leaned forward and rubbed Falcon's ears. "I'm a bloody earl who owns a Cavendish castle. That won't sit well with Velvet!"

That was a masterstroke of understatement. The weather I just encountered will be nothing to the thunder and lightning storm that will erupt once the little devil's spawn finds out.

Greysteel, determined to leave the past behind, urged Falcon to start down the mountain. He relished the challenge ahead.

Chapter Twelve

Breda, Holland

"*Y*our humble servant, madame." Charles Stuart's dark glance of appreciation swept over the display of ripe female breasts as he raised the lady before him from her deep curtsy.

"Nay, 'tis I who am looking forward to serving Your Majesty."

Charles raised his eyes to hers. He could have sworn she said *servicing Your Majesty.* Barbara Palmer had mahogany-colored hair, slanting, slumberous eyes and a sensual mouth that pouted provocatively. She and her husband, Roger Palmer, had joined the throng of Royalists who had rushed to Holland the moment they learned that the exiled king was to be restored to his throne.

It is most fortunate that the Parliamentary commissioners gifted me with a chest of sovereigns or I would be standing before you raggy-arsed rather than royally arrayed.

King Charles; James, Duke of York; Henry, Duke of Gloucester; and all the exiled courtiers were accompanying Princess Mary back to her own Royal Dutch Court at The Hague before they sailed home to England. More than seventy coaches pulled by Thoroughbred horses had been provided to carry the royal party and their visitors to the beautiful city.

Barbara Palmer, assigned to a carriage carrying Princess Mary's ladies-in-waiting, suddenly declared that her gown would be crushed because there was not enough room inside the coach.

King Charles gallantly offered his arm to the lady. "It would be my pleasure to have you ride with me. You may regale me with news of your cousin Buckingham. Though George deserted me, I still count him one of my dearest friends."

Barbara preened as she placed her hand on the king's arm and allowed him to lead her to the royal carriage at the head of the procession. She sat facing Charles and settled the folds of her expensive gown across the seat. "Your Majesty, why do you tolerate Buckingham?"

His sensual mouth curved. "His audacious wit amuses me."

"He's not the most audacious member of the Villiers clan." Barbara paused, licked her lips and added suggestively, "I am."

"Then I suspect that we too shall become *intimate* friends."

"Suspect? Your Majesty, I intend to convince you of it."

Their conversation became laced with sexual innuendo as the carriage began to roll. Barbara glanced at the mounted, uniformed guards who rode beside the king. She reached up and pulled down the leather window shade to half-mast. "The *affairs* of a monarch require a certain royal privacy."

Charles bent forward, took her hands and pulled her to the edge of the seat. "My dearest Barbara, I agree wholeheartedly." He set his mouth on hers and felt his cock begin to swell when she opened her lips, inviting his tongue to delve deep. There was absolutely nothing tentative about the kiss.

Barbara smiled with satisfaction. She had allowed him to make the first move. Now she felt free to take control. If she was right, Charles Stuart was a male with a large sexual appetite, one she intended to lead by his prodigious prick.

Her slumberous glance rested on his dark, saturnine face with its thick black eyebrows and pencil-thin mustache. She was close enough to see the deep lines of bitterness and irony that ran from his nose to his sensual mouth. She leaned forward and reached out her hand to touch the blue ribbon of the Garter on his chest. Then slowly, deliberately, her hand slid down his long coat, dipped beneath it and caressed the heavy bulge between his legs. Her fingers outlined the shape of his cock through the material and when she cupped him, she felt him grow longer and harder in her hand.

His black eyes glittered with arousal and when he made no protest, her busy fingers concentrated on freeing the royal member from his breeches. Liberated from the tight cloth, it sprang to attention like a ramrod. When she grasped him firmly, Charles drew in a sharp breath and went rigid.

His cock was so hot it scalded her hand. "You are on fire!"

"I do feel consumed."

"Shall I extinguish the flames?"

"Make haste lest we ignite the carriage and go up in smoke."

Barbara slid to her knees between his legs. "I serve at the pleasure of the king," she purred. Her fingers drew down his foreskin and the head of his cock jerked wildly in anticipation. She traced the tip of her tongue along the valley beneath the pulsing crown, imagining that it was engorged with the blue blood of royalty. Then she sucked it whole into her mouth, relishing its size, texture and salty taste.

She tightened her fingers around its thick base, squeezing and releasing in a rhythm that matched the pull of her lips and the swirl of her tongue. Barbara focused her full attention upon his male center, hoping to brand him with her unique erotic imprint for all time. Her other hand slid beneath his heavy sac. She had him by the balls, and never intended to let go.

Charles closed his eyes, bit his lip, then gave in and groaned with unadulterated pure pleasure. He threaded his long fingers through her hair, and held her captive, knowing that at any moment he would start to thrust. Unable to control himself longer, he began to buck powerfully, then stiffened and cried out hoarsely as he spent. He looked down, pleased and amazed she didn't withdraw her mouth from him until she had milked him.

Barbara licked her lips as she arose and settled herself back against the leather squabs of the seat. She watched with knowing slumberous eyes as he tucked himself back into his breeches. "I heard a rumor about the royal scepter and was prepared to swallow it whole."

"Christ, Barbara, you make me randy as my stallion!"

She chuckled, low in her throat. She had achieved her goal. Though she had brought him temporary release, she had aroused an insatiable lust in him that only she could satisfy. In return, His Majesty had empowered her with the omnipotence of a goddess.

In his magnificent Hague Palace suite, Charles Stuart spoke privately with James Butler, the Duke of Ormonde, who had been with him in exile from the beginning. He had entrusted Ormonde with secret marriage overtures to various royal princesses over the years, none of which had borne fruit. When Oliver Cromwell died, Ormonde had presented an offer of marriage from Charles to Princess Henriette Catherine of Orange, sister of the late king. The princess was most eager, but her mother had adamantly refused the offer when Cromwell's son was named Protector.

"Now that it is common knowledge that I'm to be restored to my throne, Princess Henriette's formidable mother may have miraculously changed her mind about her daughter's marriage."

"I have no doubt of it, Your Majesty. Especially now that we are here in The Hague in such close proximity."

"Be your charming self, Ormonde, but assure the lady there isn't the remotest chance in hell."

"With the greatest pleasure, Your Majesty."

"I have letters from the Portuguese ambassador, hinting at a union with the Princess of Braganza, and another from his Spanish rival, suggesting the daughter of the ruler of Parma." Charles handed Ormonde the letters. "Enter into negotiations with both and let them know, subtly of course, that we will take the highest bidder."

"I shall leave for Portugal immediately, Your Majesty."

"And I shall proceed to my audience to accept vows of undying loyalty while pretending I am blind to their self-interest."

When Ormonde departed, Charles checked his image in the mirror. His long, richly embroidered dark blue coat emphasized his height and amid the brilliant pastel shades and gaudy attire of his courtiers, he would appear both somber and sober, as he intended. The deep lines in his face and the grey hair at his temples added to his image of maturity.

A short time later, seated in the throne room, flanked by his royal brothers, Charles Stuart received the representatives who had gathered. The Dutch, no longer wishing to shun him, presented him with seventy thousand pounds, a service of gold plate and a great royal bed.

The English stepped forward next. John Grenville, Earl of Bath, representing the houses of Parliament, presented the king with fifty thousand pounds, and then he was given another ten thousand by the delegates from the City of London.

"I have always nourished a particular affection for the capital, the place of my birth," Charles said graciously. Then with great dignity and ceremony he knighted the delegates.

Next came a dozen or more private citizens with personal contributions of a thousand pounds each.

Roger Palmer, Barbara's husband, was the last in line. He seemed truly oblivious when Charles said gravely, "You have more title than many to my kindness."

The King listened cynically to the representatives of the Presbyterian Church. They begged him for tolerance, something that they had never extended to him, and then asked him directly to desist from using the Prayer Book. Charles's answer was directed to the larger audience of Englishmen listening.

"While I give you liberty, I will not have my own taken from me. I have always used that form of service, which I think the best in the world, and have never discontinued it in places where it is more disliked than I hope it is by you."

The ceremonies were concluded when His Majesty's chaplain brought forward a number of people suffering from scrofula, known as the King's Evil. The affliction supposedly could only be cured by the touch of the king's hand. In reality it was a shrewdly calculated move to show the monarch had divine powers.

A week later, the king and his royal party stepped aboard the newly named *Royal Charles* for their voyage to England. He was greeted by his general at sea, Sir Edward Montagu, who saluted with a round of the ship's cannon. Though a crowd of fifty thousand wellwishers gathered to watch him depart, Charles Stuart had never been so thankful to leave a place in his life. Many hours later, as he paced restlessly across the deck, eagerly searching for a glimpse of the Dover cliffs, he vowed only one thing: *an absolute commitment to his own survival as king.*

*   *   *

Velvet, elevated on a stool, surveyed her new gown of pale green silk in the mirror. "The full skirt is perfect, but I would like the bodice to be much tighter," Velvet told the dowager's sewing women. "Could you design it to lace up the back and come to a point at the front?"

Both Velvet and Christian Cavendish were caught up in a whirlwind of plans for King Charles's return to London, and fashionable new clothes were the first order of business.

"Your undergarment is all wrong for such a design, Mistress Cavendish," the head seamstress explained.

"Yes, I understand that. I want you to fashion me a new corset that fits high under the arms and lifts the breasts."

"What a splendid idea! Where did you get the notion for such a flattering style?" Christian inquired.

"To tell the truth, I got it from the French Court. Though I was very young, I realized their fashion sense was superb."

"Such a corset would allow you to bare your shoulders, which would be deliciously risqué!"

Velvet laughed. "The courtesans bared their *nipples*. They were rouged, of course," she added wickedly.

"Well, I doubt the Court of St. James will go that far, but I warrant anything will seem daring after the prudish Puritan fashions that were foisted upon us by Cromwell."

"Do you think that is where Charles will set up his Court?"

"It is where he had his household when he was a child, but I believe he will set up his Court at Whitehall. Most likely he will have apartments at St. James's Palace as well."

Christian scrutinized her own image. "I think this gown should have *passementeries*. I don't believe I can get away with *galants* at my age."

"What are *galants*?"

"They are bunches of ribbon loops that gentlemen may steal as favors. Silver would be most fetching on that pale green silk."

"We must have fans too. They are so pretty and feminine."

"I think perhaps I had better employ some extra sewing women," Christian told her head seamstress. "Velvet and I will need many gowns for Court, and of course splendorous coronation dresses. I believe I'd like something in royal purple."

"Because of my hair color, I'd like white and gold."

"That would be exquisite, darling, and most suitable for an unmarried young lady. A virginal facade is most alluring."

When Velvet blushed, Christian winked. "I did say *facade*!"

That evening the dowager countess opened up her jewel chest and invited Velvet to select a few pieces that struck her fancy. "You must develop a flagrant fondness for diamonds and rubies."

"I've never worn jewels in my life. You are so generous!"

"Nonsense. I shall drop a note to my daughter-in-law and tell her to fetch the Devonshire jewels. The Devonshires will be arriving any day. They are bound to take part in the Court festivities. Your great-grandmother Bess's jewels are in the collection. Elizabeth

Cecil, the present countess, isn't a showy female, by any standard. Never puts herself forward. Well, how could she? I've always had her firmly under my thumb. I'm the matriarch of the family."

"I suppose your grandson, Cav, will come too?"

"You suppose correctly, darling." She lifted a brow. "Do you think you can handle the young lecher?"

Velvet smiled a secret smile. "I'm certain of it."

Christian reached into her jewel cabinet. "Here's something to help you. This miniature dagger is called a bodkin. It's rather old-fashioned, but most effective, I warrant!"

In her own chamber, Velvet threw open the windows. Bonfires had lit up the night sky since the king's return had been announced, and Londoners were celebrating in the streets by cooking huge rump roasts and chestnuts. Inside she was bubbling with happiness. "You're coming home at last; you're coming home. I always knew this day would come. I never lost faith. Oh, Charles, I cannot wait to see you!"

When she drifted into sleep, once again she had a variation of the recurring dream. Greysteel Montgomery dominated it, and dominated her. When he made love to her, she pledged her heart to him and promised to marry him. Then she learned that he had betrayed her and betrayed the king. As always, she was forced to choose between him and Charles Stuart. And as always, Velvet chose the king.

Resplendent in rich, dark attire, brightened only by a red plume in his hat, Charles Stuart stepped ashore at Dover on a sunlit afternoon in May. *Home! And home is where I'll stay. I vow by Almighty God that I will never go roaming again!*

Charles fell to his knees on his native soil. "I thank God for this miraculous restoration!" He was acutely aware that to the masses awaiting his return, it would show humility and a submission to Providence. He wanted none to doubt he was the nation's legitimate king, sanctified by God.

As Charles arose from his knees, the cheers were so loud, they almost drowned out the gun salute from His Majesty's Navy. "God save the king! God save the king! God save the king!" He walked a direct path to the kneeling figure of General Monck.

"Your Majesty, I am deeply honored."

Charles raised him. "Nay, General, the honor is mine." He kissed him on both cheeks. "I thank you with all my heart."

Then the lord mayor, the bishops and many other dignitaries were presented to the king before he could retire to Dover Castle, where he was to spend the night.

Greysteel Montgomery, along with many devoted Royalists who were personal friends of Charles Stuart, had gathered at Dover Castle. He felt himself lucky to have secured a small chamber at the massive fortification and found himself already acquainted with the man in the next room. They emerged from their chambers and descended to the great hall.

"Well, I'll be damned. Montgomery, isn't it?" George Villiers stuck out his hand.

"Delighted to see you, Buckingham. I'm surprised

that you recognized me." Montgomery shook his hand warmly.

"It's the eyes—they skewer a fellow through the vitals and pin him to the wall. A rogue such as I must beware."

Greysteel grinned as it dawned on him that George had likely delivered his father-in-law, General Fairfax, into Charles's camp. "We are all rogues and vagabonds, I fear."

"I'm here to get a close look at the great man himself."

Montgomery, aware of the duke's famed irreverence, knew he didn't mean King Charles. "Monck—I'll introduce you to him. I'm sure the general will want a close look at you also."

"You know him?" Buckingham looked surprised.

"He took me prisoner once," Greysteel acknowledged.

Dover's great hall was crowded to the rafters. Sir George Carteret, governor of Jersey, had sailed in from the Channel Islands aboard the *Proud Eagle* and Montgomery knew most of the crew. The head of the Admiralty, Edward Montagu, who had captained the *Royal Charles* on the king's voyage, was there with his secretary, Samuel Pepys, and the crews of the two vessels were quick to make friends.

General Monck had brought a few hundred soldiers with him to guard the king, and many of them also crowded into the great hall, mingling with the royal servitors. As well as Charles's loyal friends from London, ships had been arriving all day, bringing the men who had been in exile with him and at the moment all these people milled about the hall anxiously awaiting the king's arrival. To a man they were hungry and thirsty.

When Charles entered the great hall, flanked by his royal brothers, he was immediately surrounded by well-wishers. The guards did their best to keep people back from him, but it was an impossible task to separate the gathered crowd from their restored monarch, especially when he too was eager to acknowledge their friendship and goodwill.

Slowly, stopping every few feet to greet another acquaintance, the king finally made his way to the dais and took his seat at the table that had been prepared for the royal banquet. George Monck was seated between King Charles and Chancellor Hyde, while Montagu was seated on the king's left, between James, Duke of York, and Henry, Duke of Gloucester.

Soon the goblets were filled and the great hall rang with royal toasts. "A health unto His Majesty," was a cry that was repeated over and over before the feast was done.

Charles's dark eyes met those of George Monck without subterfuge. "What truly made you decide to help me, General?"

The bulbous eyes looked directly into the king's. "I fought for your father at the siege of Nantwich. The Royalists lost and I was taken prisoner by the Parliamentarians. When I was starving in the Tower of London, your father sent me a gift of a hundred pounds." He shook his head. "I never forgot."

Without doubt, that was the best money my father ever spent.

Finally, Charles was allowed to retire to a hastily

prepared suite of rooms in the castle. And it was here that his faithful intimates were invited to join him privately.

Henry Jermyn, Earl of Saint Albans, and George Digby, Earl of Bristol, who'd been with Charles throughout his exile, filled goblets for those present.

Charles threw an arm about Buckingham's shoulder. "Odds fish, George, I actually missed you. Gives you an idea of how desperate I'd become."

"I knew you couldn't bear me having England to myself, Sire."

Charles thumped Greysteel's shoulder. "You know you have my undying gratitude. You deserve at least an earldom."

"I have one, Sire," Greysteel said quietly.

"My condolences on your father's passing," Charles said soberly. Then he looked at both men and a smile lit his saturnine features. "Eglinton and Buckingham—you are the best sort of friends a king could have. You already have noble titles and don't need them from me."

"Fear not, Sire, I'll soon think of something else I need."

"If I know you, George, you already have," Charles said laconically. He sipped his wine thoughtfully and addressed the dozen men in the room. "You know, the irony of my situation is not lost on me, gentlemen. Over the years, all my attempts to regain my Crown ended in bloodshed and defeat. Now I have been bloodlessly willed into power by the people declaring me their legitimate monarch. I've played no part in my own restoration."

"Not so, Sire," Greysteel disagreed. "Today is a culmination of all that has gone before—for you, for us, for England."

"The future is at hand, Sire. I suggest a spectacular entry into your capital," Buckingham advised.

"I will leave that to Digby, Jermyn, Hyde and my brothers, who have a wealth of ideas. Though four days from now I turn thirty—it would be satisfying to enter London on my birthday."

"That's simple enough to arrange, Sire," Greysteel declared. He counted on his fingers. "Overnight stops at Canterbury, Rochester, and Deptford will bring you to London on May twenty-ninth."

"We'd like your presence at Court unless you would like a commission in my army, Montgomery?"

"I have no such ambition, Sire. My fighting days are over."

"Would you consider organizing and heading my King's Guard?"

Greysteel was surprised. He'd expected nothing, and was not sure he wanted responsibility for the king's person, yet he didn't hesitate to accept the duty. "I am honored, Your Majesty."

Chapter Thirteen

"The preparations for the king's arrival are spectacular! I saw some of the tapestries being hung in the streets yesterday."

Velvet studied a pamphlet, which had been hastily printed, laying out the route that King Charles and his royal procession would take. "Charles will enter the city at Blackheath, and at St. George's Fields, the lord mayor and aldermen are to present him with the City Sword. It says that a hundred young girls in white with blue head scarves are to scatter flowers and herbs before his horse. I would so love to see that!"

"We cannot see everything, darling," Christian declared. "The procession will be hours long and that's why I accepted Lady Salisbury's invitation to view the spectacle from her newly opened house in the Strand. Mary Anne has always been a social climber, so we might as well take full advantage today."

Velvet looked around guiltily to make sure that Christian's daughter-in-law was not within earshot, since the Countess of Salisbury was her mother. "The

Countess of Devonshire will hear you," she whispered.

"Bless your heart, Velvet, Elizabeth knows ambition rules her mother. Why else would she have pushed her to marry my son, Devonshire? By the by, you look extremely fetching today."

"I chose forget-me-not blue as a symbolic gesture. I think I shall save my new white kid shoes for when we visit the palace."

The dowager pinned on her hat with its ostrich feather dyed rose pink to match her gown. "Do shout up to Elizabeth and tell her we are ready to leave, Velvet."

"I'm here, my lady." Elizabeth stepped quietly from the corner where she had been patiently waiting for an hour. Her beige satin gown had rendered her almost invisible.

"Such a biddable female," Christian said, smiling at her. Then she spun about and rolled her eyes at Velvet.

Poor lady. We have the same name: Elizabeth Cavendish. Thank heaven I had the audacity to change mine to Velvet!

"Oh, he's coming at last. I can see the procession!" Velvet cried, leaning far out over the Salisbury House stone balcony. All the way from Temple Bar to the Strand ladies stood at open windows and filled the balconies, ready to shower the king with flowers as he rode beneath them.

"How gallant! Charles is riding between his brothers. The Stuart princes have changed so much I hardly recognize them."

Velvet fastened her eyes on Charles and saw no one else. "His coat is so dark, I cannot tell its color, but the plume in his hat is blue, matching his blue ribbon of the Garter!"

She watched enthralled as he rode gravely. Then suddenly he would raise his eyes to the ladies in the windows and take off his hat in response to their cheers.

Velvet held her breath as he approached Salisbury House. All at once she could hold it in no longer. "Charles! Charles! Charles!" she cried. He lifted dark sparkling eyes to hers and she was certain that he saw her when he raised his hat and swept it across his heart in a gallant gesture. "Oh, he saw me, he saw me!" She picked up her fan and wafted it quickly to catch her breath.

"Look! There's Buckingham!" Christian cried. "My God, he's riding abreast of General George Monck! There's an odd pairing if ever I saw one! Ah, well, they say if you live long enough, you'll see everything."

Suddenly, Velvet's fan went still. She stared down at one of the mounted men and her mouth fell open. *Greysteel Montgomery! How can it be? You are a bloody traitor. What the hellfire are you doing in the king's procession?* She blinked her eyes and looked again. There was no mistaking the erect figure, who rode his horse like a centaur. He wore a rich, dark coat and a Cavalier's hat with a great sweeping plume, contrasting markedly with the gaudily dressed men about him.

"Look at the gilded coaches!" Lady Salisbury gushed. "I should love one of those."

Many of the king's gentlemen wore doublets of silver cloth. Scores of Stuart servants wore livery of purple or green and twenty thousand soldiers marched in the parade. Heralds made proclamations and trumpeters blared their horns as they marched past fountains, red with wine.

All was just a blur to Velvet. She could not get the vision of Greysteel Montgomery out of her thoughts. *I must warn Charles about him. He cannot know that he is a traitor!*

Since he was the highest ranking peer in England, Christian's son, William, the Earl of Devonshire, along with his son, Lord Will Cavendish, was part of a noble delegation awaiting King Charles's arrival at Whitehall. Together with the Earls of Bath, Arlington and Southampton, they would be called upon to help plan the coronation, and every noble present vied with one another for the chance of a lucrative post at Court.

It was late when Devonshire and his son arrived back at the house in Bishopsgate, but Christian had insisted that the ladies stay up to wait for them, so they could hear every last detail.

"One of the first things to be decided will be the Privy Council," Christian said. "Dare I hope that you have ambitions in that direction, William?"

"Not really, Mother. I'd be far happier back at Chatsworth. Cav here is going to join the Court, however."

Velvet was annoyed. She hoped to join the Court and didn't fancy tripping over young Lord Cav every day. She gave him a contemptuous glance. "But not as a privy councillor, I warrant."

Christian hid her amusement. "Court should be the ideal place to find a suitable wife, Cav, since you've set your sights on a duke's daughter." She turned again to her son. "Tell me, who were the men who arrived with the king?"

"Well, his brother James and Buckingham, of course. Then there was Chancellor Hyde, Henry Jermyn, George Digby, and that uncouth Scot, Lauderdale."

"They'll all be on the Privy Council along with that damned upstart Monck. The Duke of Ormonde is certain to be included also. Was he not there with His Majesty?"

"No, he's on a delicate mission regarding a suitable bride. I believe old Southampton is fishing for office and his son-in-law, Anthony Ashley, is politically ambitious in the extreme."

Velvet had stopped listening after the word *bride*. "Your Grace, did you learn where the Duke of Ormonde has gone?"

"Mmm, m'dear? Parma, Portugal . . . something with a *P*, and that reminds me—I'm off upstairs. Don't have the capacity anymore."

"Wait. . . . When may *we* go to Court?" Christian demanded.

"Next week—reception at Whitehall."

"Why the devil didn't you say so? Off you go, William."

The countess accompanied her husband upstairs and Christian followed her, leaving Velvet alone with young Lord Cav. Velvet did not hurry to catch up with them because it would reveal her fear. She was extremely wary but refused to panic.

"Well, cousin, I warrant you aspire to Court life since you are desperate for a husband," he drawled.

Her cool glance swept over him. "I am not your cousin. It is our fathers who are cousins."

He moved toward her. "A small distinction, surely?"

Velvet deliberately dropped her glance to his groin and smiled maliciously. "Yes, distinctly small."

His eyes narrowed. "You little bitch. Have a care at Court. Keep glancing over your shoulder—enemies will be everywhere."

She gave him a pitying glance of contempt. "If only you knew how *impotent* your threats seem to me." She swept from the room as if she were in complete control of the situation and congratulated herself on her performance.

The Presence Chamber at Whitehall overflowed with visitors, courtiers and nobles, most of whom had been invited. Posted at every palace entrance were guards selected by Greysteel Montgomery. He'd chosen from Cavalier officers who'd been in exile with Charles and served under the Duke of York.

Montgomery moved among the crowd, determined to become familiar with as many people as possible who had access to the king. Fortunately, he had a keen eye for connecting faces with names. He greeted Buckingham and his glance came to rest on the fair-haired lady who stood talking with him.

"Eglinton, this is my kinswoman, the Countess of Suffolk."

Montgomery bowed gallantly. "Your servant, Lady Suffolk."

"You may introduce me too, George."

Greysteel turned to see a voluptuous young beauty

appraising him from beneath slumberously lidded eyes.

"This is my wicked cousin, Barbara Palmer—a force to be reckoned with, as are all the Villierses. This is Eglinton."

Greysteel raised the hand she offered to his lips. "I prefer to be called Montgomery. I've only just come into my earldom."

"Strange, you don't look self-effacing. I've been told that you command the palace guard." Barbara tapped him with her fan. "We'll no doubt encounter each other from time to time."

Greysteel realized she was the young wife of Roger Palmer, a prosperous London businessman currying favor with the king. As he met the various people in the Presence Chamber, he was aware of where King Charles was at all times. From the tail of his eye he had seen the Dowager Countess of Devonshire arrive with her family and Velvet, and seen how warmly Charles greeted them.

Barbara Palmer touched his sleeve. "Who is that radiant young lady with His Majesty?"

As he looked across the chamber, he saw Charles slip his arm about Velvet and spirit her through a door. Greysteel felt the muscle in his jaw tick. He smiled down at Barbara. "That is Lady Elizabeth, the daughter of Newcastle, who was the king's governor. They've known each other since they were children." He realized he was trying to convince himself as much as Barbara Palmer that the encounter was innocent.

Barbara's interest was piqued. "Ah, yes, the noble Cavendish family. I'm told the dowager and her son, the Earl of Devonshire, are both wealthy as Croesus."

Buckingham took pleasure in admonishing her. "There are more important things than money, Barbara."

"Yes—power. A lesson you learned at an early age, George."

Velvet slipped her arms about the king's neck as he lifted her and swung her around. "Oh, Charles, welcome home! I knew this day would come. I never gave up hope."

Charles laughed and set her feet to the floor. "I grew old waiting. You must join the Court, Velvet. I intend to surround myself with beautiful ladies."

"Thank you, Sire. It will be my pleasure and honor."

"Has your father arrived back yet?" Charles asked.

"No. We expect him any day."

"I am eternally indebted to him and will never be able to repay what I owe him."

"Your friendship has repaid him a thousandfold, Sire."

"The moment he arrives, I want you to send me a note. We'd best return to the chamber, but we'll talk again soon."

When they entered the room, the king moved away from her and was swallowed by the crowd. *Damnation, I forgot to ask him about his marriage plans.* Velvet rejoined the dowager. "Charles asked me to join the Court." She sighed deeply. "He is so very tall."

"Velvet, you have stars in your eyes. Don't go falling in love with the king, darling."

She laughed. "Too late. That happened when I was seven."

"That was hero worship, not love, darling. I spy the

Countess of Suffolk over there. Come and I'll introduce you." Christian pushed through the crowd. "Lady Suffolk, how lovely to see you. May I present Mistress Velvet Cavendish, Newcastle's daughter?"

"So happy to meet you, my dear. This is my niece, Barbara Palmer, and of course you know Buckingham."

Ready to stir shit to banish his boredom, George drawled, "I knew Mistress Cavendish when her name was Elizabeth."

"You changed your name?" Lady Suffolk asked.

"Yes, I did. Over the years there have been a dozen with the name Elizabeth Cavendish. There is only one Velvet."

Barbara laughed. "A lady after my own heart. I am delighted to meet you, Velvet Cavendish—we redheads must stick together."

Christian scoffed, "I've never seen more dissimilar shades of hair in my life, though I concede you both have the wondrously translucent skin of redheads."

"We compliment each other." Barbara wafted her fan. "My husband, Roger, and I are entertaining Friday evening at our house in King Street. I shall send you both invitations in hope that you will fit us into your busy schedule."

Barbara's audacity appealed to Velvet, who was delighted to make a new friend. She spread her own fan. "Thank you. I shall look forward to it."

When Velvet and Christian were out of earshot, Barbara turned to Buckingham. "She's maddeningly pretty and extremely young."

"Actually, she's older than you are, Barbara."

"Really? And she's still unwed?"

"Betrothed to Greysteel Montgomery when she was a child, but she's lived in exile until recently."

Barbara's inquisitive glance roamed over the crowd, searching for a glimpse of the tall, dark Montgomery, whom she'd met earlier. Finally, she spotted him and watched avidly as he encountered his betrothed.

When Velvet came face-to-face with Greysteel Montgomery, it was so totally unexpected, she gasped. Determined to crush down any sexual attraction she felt, she drew her lips back and hissed through her teeth, "How dare you? How dare you show your traitorous face at the king's reception?"

Montgomery's dark face turned hard. "King Charles is my friend, Velvet, just as he is yours."

Her chin went up and she trembled with anger. "Then he must be in ignorance of your betrayal."

"Velvet, you are drawing every eye. Don't cause a scene."

Her eyes narrowed. "Hell and furies! Don't issue your orders to me, Montgomery. I promise you the king will remain in ignorance no longer. Then we shall see who causes a scene." She turned from him furiously and hurried away as if she could not bear to remain in his presence a moment longer.

Barbara smiled slyly. "I believe I shall invite the Earl of Eglinton for Friday's entertainment. Perhaps we'll have fireworks."

When Velvet found the dowager and the other Devonshires, they were conversing with a man in uniform. "Henry! I had no idea you were here in London," Velvet cried. She threw her arms about her brother, and then held him at arm's length so she could observe him from head to foot.

"I returned with my regiment, commanded by the Duke of York. Technically, I'm still in the army until my official discharge. Once the king returns Welbeck to me, I'll go north immediately."

The Earl of Devonshire clapped Henry on the back. "A man after my own heart. We can't wait to get back to Chatsworth and begin restoring it to its former glory."

"You're fortunate that I made sure Chatsworth never left the family, William. I warrant it will take an order of Parliament before the king can return Welbeck to you, Henry."

"Welbeck rightfully belongs to my brother, just as Nottingham and Bolsover Castles belong to Father!" Velvet protested.

"I'm sure His Majesty will sort everything out, darling. In the meanwhile, Henry, you are welcome at Bishopsgate anytime."

"Thank you, Lady Cavendish. Ah, there's the Duke of York. I must have a word with him before petitioners surround him once again. Excuse me, ladies— Devonshire."

Velvet followed him with her eyes as he moved across the chamber to join the king's brother James. She was chagrined to see Montgomery standing beside James. She bit her lip, desperately hoping they would not speak of her.

Henry greeted James, and then shook Greysteel's hand. "Good to see you again, Montgomery. You managed to avoid marriage with the little devil's spawn all these years, but I doubt you'll manage it much longer, old man."

"Especially now he's Earl of Eglinton," James declared.

Montgomery grimaced good-naturedly. "I concede to the inevitable." *If only my earldom could tempt her into marriage.*

Henry laughed. "I look forward to having you as my brother-in-law, Eglinton."

I very much doubt that, Henry, once you learn that I am the new owner of Bolsover Castle!

The following day, the Earl and Countess of Newcastle arrived at Bishopsgate. They had sailed from Rotterdam on a ship that brought them all the way to the Port of London.

Velvet was overjoyed to see her father again and had made up her mind to treat his wife, Margaret Lucas, with respect.

The family celebrated their reunion at a lavish dinner that Christian had arranged and it wasn't until almost bedtime that Velvet had her father to herself for a few minutes.

"I wish you had been here to see His Majesty's entrance into London. It was spectacular and the people were delirious with happiness."

"I shall be on the front row at his coronation, never fear. When I was sailing up the Thames and saw the smoke of London, it never looked more wondrous in my eyes."

"When we were at Whitehall yesterday, Charles bade me send him a note the moment you arrived."

"Ah, the dear boy likely has some great post of state

in mind for me. I shall be torn between London and Nottingham, but know where my duty lies."

"I saw Henry yesterday at Whitehall. He looks wonderful and cannot wait to return to Welbeck."

"I shall see him soon. No doubt His Majesty will summon me to Whitehall immediately. Christian tells me you have been invited to join the Royal Court. I warrant you will be the most beautiful lady to grace Whitehall, Velvet."

She kissed him. "It's a fairy tale!"

Chapter Fourteen

"*I*t's a nightmare!" King Charles threw down his pen and indicated the mountain of parchments, scrolls, property rolls and journals scattered across the long refectory table.

The king, Chancellor Hyde, and Jermyn, Earl of Saint Albans, along with four clerks, were trying to sort out which properties had been confiscated from prominent Royalists and given by Cromwell to Parliamentarians. "I have every intention to restore the confiscated estates of those who remained loyal, but odds fish, it is easier said than done."

Charles ran his fingers through his long black hair, now peppered with grey. "Sadly, properties that Royalists were forced to sell for taxes and other debts cannot be restored because there are simply too many of them."

Chancellor Hyde nodded. "Estates that were confiscated must be restored, but any who come forward with *proof of purchase* should be confirmed as owning the property."

"Are we all agreed?" asked the king.

"Aye, Your Majesty," the men chorused.

Charles took up a paper and thrust it at Hyde. "Here's another nightmare! This list Monck gave me of men he deems worthy to serve on my Privy Council consists of forty Presbyterians and rebels and exactly two Royalists! Damnation, this poses difficulties. The general wields considerable power and I'm bound to have him on my council, but I won't have these other men under any circumstances. I'm afraid he is in for a disappointment."

"I'll handle it, Your Majesty." Hyde took the list from him. "It is my political task to form the royal administration."

"You're a born diplomat, Chancellor Hyde, and indefatigable. Hold off giving Monck the bad news until I confirm him in his dukedom and gift him with a rich estate. I shall be eternally grateful to the general and intend to reward him generously."

The king strode over to another table littered with maps and deeds, where Digby, Earl of Bristol, sat preparing a list of all the properties owned by the Crown. "How are your charts coming along, George?" He picked up a paper. "Are these all the properties owned by the Crown in and around London?"

"Not *all*, Sire, but a good many of them."

"Then let's see—this Albemarle estate is worth nine thousand pounds and has a palatial house. I propose that Monck be made Duke of Albemarle." Charles returned to his seat at the other table. "Prepare a warrant to that effect, Chancellor."

"You asked me to remind you of Newcastle, Sire," Jermyn said.

"Odds fish, yes! My old governor has arrived in

London and I've summoned him to Whitehall tomorrow to thank him for his great sacrifices. The earl will now be made Duke of Newcastle and I can use one of his lesser titles to honor his son, Henry, and elevate him in the peerage. I thought *Marquis of Mansfield* would be suitable."

"All their estates were confiscated," Hyde reminded the king.

"Yes, Nottingham, Bolsover, and Welbeck shall be restored to them immediately," Charles declared.

Jermyn cleared his throat and rustled a parchment.

"What is it, Henry?" Charles asked impatiently.

"Strange, but this deed says Bolsover is owned by Eglinton."

Charles looked at the deed. "God Almighty, more complications! Apparently, the castle was confiscated and given to a Parliamentarian, who in turn sold it to Eglinton. If his heir has proof of purchase, he's every right it be confirmed."

"A contretemps," Edward Hyde murmured.

"A nightmare!" Charles corrected. He went to the door and summoned his personal page, Will Chiffinch. "I want you to find Captain Montgomery, commander of my guard, and bring him to me."

The page found Montgomery in the armory, where his guardsmen were being outfitted with new swords and scabbards. He asked his first lieutenant to take over and followed Will Chiffinch.

Charles greeted him informally. "Greysteel, questions have arisen about property holdings, which I hope you can answer."

"If you refer to Bolsover Castle, Sire, I learned from

my father's will that he purchased it for five thousand pounds from Cromwell's General Fleetwood."

"So you have proof of purchase?"

"I do, Sire."

"This presents a dilemma. Newcastle is returned and I've summoned him to Whitehall tomorrow to honor him for his great sacrifices to the Stuart cause, and to restore his estates." The king stared pointedly from beneath dark brows. "It occurs to me that if you were wedded to Newcastle's daughter, *as you solemnly pledged to do,* Bolsover would be back in the Cavendish family and there would be no problem. Am I correct?"

"Yes and no, Sire."

Charles, who had always found Greysteel exceedingly forthright with him, realized that the personal matter would benefit from privacy. "Excuse us, gentlemen." He opened the door to a small antechamber and beckoned Montgomery inside.

"Short of kidnapping the lady and forcing her to my will, I have done everything in my power to make Velvet my wife."

"She refuses?" His brows drew together. "On what grounds?"

"On the eve of our wedding she discovered I was acting as agent to Monck. Her loyalty to you, Sire, brands me as a dishonorable traitor in her eyes."

"Odds fish, why haven't you disabused her of such nonsense?"

"Primarily because it was true, but also because Velvet shouldn't need explanations. She should have put her trust in me as you did, Sire."

Charles hooted with laughter. "You don't know much about women—God help you! Females will ride over us roughshod if we allow it. You are well aware that Velvet is a little minx. You must never again allow her to gain the upper hand." Charles clapped him on the back. "I will speak with the lady. Your bachelor days are over. You can be wed in Whitehall's chapel."

Greysteel didn't want Velvet to marry him because she'd been ordered by the king, but realized he could hardly argue with his Sovereign. Instead, he bowed to the king's will.

Velvet read the note bearing the Royal Stuart coat of arms that had just been delivered to her. She found her father in the Bishopsgate library and was vastly relieved that Margaret was not with him. "Father, I'm summoned to Whitehall tomorrow."

"His Majesty wishes you to dine with us?" he asked.

"It says nothing about dining. I'm summoned to an audience at eleven. Strange I should accompany you and not Margaret."

"Nay, His Majesty wishes to honor me and is extending the honor to my children. No doubt Henry also has been invited."

"Please don't tell Margaret I'm to accompany you. I don't wish to antagonize her, Father."

"Margaret and Christian have their plans all set for tomorrow. They are off to visit Her Majesty. Queen Henrietta Maria has taken up residence at St. James's Palace."

Velvet shuddered involuntarily. The queen was a cold, dominant, devoutly religious woman, whom Velvet had avoided whenever she visited Minette at

Saint-Germain. *How lucky I am to be going to Whitehall instead!*

When the Earl of Newcastle arrived with his daughter at Whitehall Palace, Prodgers, one of the king's gentlemen-ushers, greeted them. Shortly thereafter, the king himself appeared with his favorite spaniels in tow. Velvet smiled radiantly, dropped a curtsy and bent to pet the dogs.

Charles embraced his old governor with warm affection. "Welcome home, William. None will ever stand higher in my esteem. On a personal level, you were like a father to me. As well, the selfless sacrifices you made for the Stuarts were above and beyond duty's call and can never be fully repaid."

"Your Majesty, my greatest honor is to serve you."

"I have invited Henry to join us for a private lunch, but before we dine, William, I would appreciate your advice on some horses I'm considering for the royal stables. I value your equestrian knowledge above that of all other men."

Newcastle beamed. "With the greatest pleasure, Sire."

The king glanced at Velvet. "Mistress Cavendish, could I impose upon your kindness to take the dogs outside? The corridor beyond that door leads to the rose garden. I will join you momentarily."

"Of course," she said breathlessly. *Charles wants to see me alone!* "Come along, boys." She opened the door and the dogs trotted after her.

"William, I have a new bay I want you to see—huge fellow by the name of Rowley. One of the few mounts I own able to carry my weight effortlessly. Prodgers will show you where he's stabled. I just want a private word with your daughter, and then I shall hasten to catch up with you."

The spaniels frolicked across the lawn in a game of nip and tumble. Velvet strolled along a bed of roses, cultivated for their intense color and heady fragrance. When Charles's tall figure emerged from the palace, her pulse began to race.

He strode toward her with purpose and used the name she disliked. "Lady Elizabeth, when I invited you to join our Court, I took it you understood it would be as a married lady."

"But, Charles—"

"You may address me as Sire."

Velvet gasped. She had forgotten he was a mercurial Gemini, ofttimes capable of great warmth and intimacy, yet equally capable of turning icily formal. "Marriage is impossible, Sire."

"Not impossible by any means. I understand that Lord Montgomery has proposed to you and you have willfully refused."

"He betrayed you, Sire. Montgomery was an agent of Monck's. They corresponded secretly. You are harboring a traitor!"

"You know nothing of the matter, nor should you, since it was secret. Montgomery was my go-between with Monck. He risked his life a dozen times crossing the Channel over the last year."

Velvet's hand flew to her throat. "I had no idea, Sire."

"I believe you owe the earl an abject apology."

"Earl?" *I didn't know that Greysteel's father had died.*

"You had best beg his pardon if you wish to become

the Countess of Eglinton." Amusement returned to the king's eyes. "Montgomery legally owns your Castle of Bolsover. To get it back in your family, you will have to marry him and hope he deeds it to you as a wedding gift."

Charles plucked a dark red rose and presented it with a gallant bow. "It would please me if you'd wed without further delay. You will make an enchanting countess, Velvet."

She stared speechlessly as he called the dogs and left the garden. Her thoughts were in total disarray, her emotions were in chaos, her poise had shattered, and her tranquility vanished. She had no idea how long she stayed in the rose garden, but presently it came to her that though her father and brother were invited to dine privately with Charles, she was not included.

Deep in thought, Velvet wandered through the rambling conglomeration of Whitehall buildings that were spread over twenty acres. The liveried servants paid her little heed and no porter or guard challenged her right to be there. She found herself at the King Street Gates and saw the merchants' stands set up outside the walls. This reminded Velvet that she had no money to pay for either food or transportation, so she made her way back to her father's carriage. The driver helped her inside and she sat in the corner, trying to decide upon the best course of action to take regarding Greysteel Montgomery.

She had been sitting there for almost two hours when her father returned. He was bursting with happy news and regaled Velvet with the details of his visit with King Charles. He pointed to the blue ribbon on his chest.

"His Gracious Majesty decorated me with the Order of the Garter for services rendered to the Stuart cause. As well, he is honoring me with a dukedom!"

"Congratulations, Father." Velvet was truly happy for him.

"That's not all. His Gracious Majesty honored your brother, Henry, by making him Marquis of Mansfield. We Cavendishes are truly basking in the monarch's favor."

"Truly," Velvet murmured. It was clear that she was utterly out of favor with *His Gracious Majesty* and would remain so until she made amends to Greysteel Montgomery.

"King Charles assured me that Nottingham Castle and Welbeck Abbey would be restored to us by an act of Parliament."

Velvet caught her breath. He said naught of Bolsover. Likely Charles had deliberately not mentioned that castle. Bolsover's return to the Cavendish family would depend entirely upon her. "Father, did the king say anything about my marriage?"

"Yes, he anticipates that it will take place forthwith. Montgomery has come into his earldom, Velvet, so it would be an advantageous match. You are getting no younger, my dear."

His words still stung when they arrived back at Bishopsgate. She deliberately pushed away all thoughts of her predicament, telling herself that at bedtime, when she could retire to the privacy of her own chamber, she would decide what she must do.

At dinner, the dowager graciously allowed Newcastle to describe every detail of his meeting with the king, while his wife, Margaret, basked in his reflected glory. Everyone at the table admired the duke's Order of the Garter. Velvet noticed there was one exception. Young Lord Cav's face was sullen, his eyes covetous as he stared at the medal. *He's already heir to an earldom, but that isn't good enough for the selfish lecher!*

"How was your visit with the queen?" Velvet asked Christian.

"I was never more shocked in my life at Queen Henrietta Maria's appearance. All those years of deprivation have certainly taken their toll."

Margaret interjected, "It was Her Highness's own choice to live on such a Spartan scale, sacrificing servants and carriages so the money could be used to restore her son to the throne."

"Yes, most admirable I'm sure, but now, instead of relishing every moment of Charles's restoration, she is obsessed with revenge. I fully understand her desire to punish all who were guilty of the regicide of her husband, but you cannot put to death the entire population of Parliamentarians."

"Charles certainly has his work cut out for him. The murderers of his father will be put on trial for treason and after that, he will make sure that all traces of the Cromwell regime are expunged," Newcastle assured them.

Christian, determined to change the subject, smiled at Velvet. "How was your day, darling?"

She hesitated only a moment. "I . . . I met King Charles's spaniels and had a most informative tour of Whitehall." She put down her napkin and arose from the table. "If you will all excuse me, I must put the finishing touches on the gown I'm going to wear to the Palmers' entertainment tomorrow night."

Alone in her chamber, Velvet sat down and delved into all that had happened between Greysteel and herself. Her thoughts carried her back to Roehampton, all those long months ago, and how happy they had been. She truly believed she had fallen head over heels in love with him, and their days and nights had been perfect. Then she had seen the Parliamentarian uniform in his wardrobe and found the letters in his desk that had branded him an agent of Monck's and a traitor to her beloved Charles Stuart.

When she confronted him and accused him, why had he not denied his perfidy? Why had he let her believe he had betrayed Charles and everything the king was striving to attain? She suspected now that Greysteel Montgomery was too proud to offer denials, or try to explain himself, especially to a woman. She tried to put herself in his place, and realized what an insult her accusations must have been to him, especially when he was risking his life to aid Charles's restoration to the throne.

It began to dawn on her that without the risks he had taken, probably Charles Stuart would not yet be King of England. The self-righteous words she'd flung at him at their last encounter came back to her: *How dare you? How dare you show your traitorous face at the king's reception?* Greysteel's reply had been, *King Charles is my friend, Velvet, just as he is yours.*

Velvet blushed. *I didn't give him a chance to explain anything. I must apologize for the dreadful things I said to him and beg him to forgive me.* Feeling contrite, she penned a brief note asking if she could come to see him. She lifted her pen. *Charles made it plain that he expects us to marry!* She decided against mentioning it in the letter. She sealed it quickly and would have it delivered first thing in the morning.

Charles's words about Bolsover came back to her: *To get it back in your family you will have to marry him and hope he deeds it to you as a wedding gift.* "How the devil can Greysteel Montgomery be the legal owner of our castle? It cannot be true, and yet the king is convinced of it." She bit her lip. "The devil will have to show me proof before I'm convinced of it!"

Velvet realized she was on her high horse again. *What if he does have proof? Worse, what if he has no desire to marry me?*

Filled with doubts and uncertainty, she went to bed and tossed and turned for more than two hours before she fell asleep. Then just before dawn, when she began to dream, she found herself standing between the two tall, dark men, beseeching them, but both turned their backs on her and walked away.

Chapter Fifteen

*W*earing her prettiest green silk gown adorned with silver ribbon, Velvet sat across from Christian as the coach carried them to the Palmers' house in King Street. She had waited all day for a reply to the message she'd sent Montgomery, and was both disappointed and annoyed that her wait had been in vain. *Hell and furies, the dominant devil is punishing me and making me wait for an answer. No doubt it is his way of bringing me to heel!* She was unaware that he had written to the dowager countess instead, informing her that he would be attending the Palmers' entertainment. He'd asked Christian to accompany Velvet, but not divulge that he would be there.

"If you were a married lady, darling, you would be free to go wherever you fancied, without the inconvenience of dragging me along as chaperone."

"I'm sorry, Christian. I enjoy your company and forget that sometimes you may not wish to be dragged out in the evening." She remembered the king's admonition. "I understand the Royal Court prefers that its ladies be married rather than unwed."

"Maidens were the fashion at Elizabeth's Court, but that was a century ago and times have changed." Christian glanced out the window. "King Charles will marry soon, and his Queen's Court will be made up of married ladies from the nobility, such as the Countess of Suffolk."

Velvet sighed. She had always loved Charles, and when she was a child, she had believed that he would marry her. Still, the thought of being one of his queen's ladies was most desirable. "Now that you have explained, I understand why the Royal Court prefers that its ladies be married." *I would be the Countess of Eglinton now, if only there hadn't been that dreadful misunderstanding between Montgomery and me.* A frisson of desire made her quiver and she quickly dismissed him from her thoughts before the aching longing overwhelmed her.

"There's Whitehall. King Street is close by. I believe the Palmers' mansion is quite impressive."

As they stepped from their carriage, they joined other guests who were attending tonight's entertainment. Liveried footmen opened the front doors, and they were greeted in the reception hall by their host and hostess, Roger and Barbara Palmer.

Three great chambers were open for their guests' entertainment. The large drawing room with its brilliantly lit chandeliers served as a ballroom where musicians provided dance music. Next to that was a banquet room, its tables set in the French buffet style with sumptuous food, rich confections and imported wine. Finally, there was a cardroom, where gambling of every sort was encouraged. Of course, this room was packed with fun-loving courtiers, and money was won and lost at the speed of lightning.

To Velvet's relief, Christian Cavendish seemed to know many of the guests and was able to introduce her to them. She met the Countess of Shrewsbury, the Countess of Maitland, Lady Anne Carnegie and Lady Elizabeth Hamilton. Velvet tried to remember that Lady Hamilton was a duchess, and Bess, Countess of Maitland, was married to the king's Scottish friend John Lauderdale.

Charles Stuart and Greysteel Montgomery left Whitehall together. The Palmers' house on King Street was within walking distance and both were looking forward to a most enjoyable evening. "I trust you remembered the bauble?"

"I did, Sire." Montgomery handed him a small jewel box. At the king's behest, he'd procured the gift from his goldsmith. Greysteel was one of the few people who knew Charles and Barbara Palmer were having an intimate liaison.

The king lifted the lid and saw the sparkle of the diamond brooch. "Very pretty. I believe a beautiful woman should be indulged. Do you have a jewel for your lady?"

"I do not, Sire. Your advice was to never again allow her to gain the upper hand. I do, however, have a wedding ring."

Charles cast a sardonic glance at his friend. "You have no need of a bauble when you have a castle to dangle before her."

Montgomery kept a wise silence. He believed that a woman could be indulged too much.

"Did you make arrangements at the chapel?"

"I did, Sire."

When they arrived at the Palmer residence, the majordomo announced, "His Majesty King Charles II," and word quickly spread throughout the rooms that the king had come.

The hosts came forward to greet him. Roger bowed and Barbara sank into a graceful curtsy as the king swept off his hat. When he kissed the lady's hand, they smiled into each other's eyes with anticipation.

"Charles is here!" Velvet felt excitement rush through her.

Christian set down her empty glass, raised her fan and murmured, "I expected as much. The Palmers are so ambitious they traveled to Holland to curry favor the moment they learned the king was being restored."

Velvet glanced at the table filled with fantastic desserts. "You think self-interest prompts this lavish hospitality?"

"Of course. But there is no shame in ambition. The king is shrewd enough to know that everyone in his circle will look to increase his . . . or *her* own fortune."

Music from the ballroom drifted to Velvet. "Do you think His Majesty will dance?" she asked breathlessly.

"If he does, I'm sure he will partner you, darling. You go to the ballroom and I shall proceed to the cardroom. It's a long time since I've enjoyed a good game of primero."

Velvet left the supper room and followed the music. At the entrance to the drawing room she saw Buckingham talking with someone with his back toward her. She stopped walking. She knew instantly that the broad shoulders belonged to Montgomery. She drew in a swift breath. *I had no idea he would be here!* Her hand went to her hair to make sure her curls were in place. Her ears thudded with her own heartbeat. Wildly, she wondered why he always had such a profound physical effect upon her.

Suddenly, Velvet was filled with anger. *When I accused you, why didn't you confide in me? Why did you allow me to make a bloody fool of myself, not once, but each time we met?*

Montgomery left Buckingham, turned and walked toward her.

She moved to meet him and snapped her fan closed. "You devil!" she hissed.

"Not one more word, Velvet." His face was dark and dangerous. He held out his arm and his intense grey eyes compelled her to place her hand on his sleeve. Too late, she remembered that she had meant to humbly apologize and ask his forgiveness. Why did the sight of him make her furious? Why did he bring out the worst in her?

"Where is the dowager?" he demanded.

She glared at him and remained silent, since he'd forbidden her to say one more word to him.

He imprisoned her hand beneath his and took her into the gaming room. He led her to the table where the dowager was sitting, and spoke quietly. "Good evening, Lady Cavendish." As Montgomery kissed her hand, he pressed a note into it. "Velvet and I are leaving, with your permission, of course. You mustn't worry—I'll take good care of her."

"You're captain of the King's Guard—of course you

shall." She saw Velvet's tightly controlled anger and rolled her eyes.

On their way to the front door they encountered Charles laughing at something his hostess was saying, and stopped to take their leave. Montgomery knew that the king would not require his services tonight; he would remain with Barbara until dawn.

Velvet curtsied. "Good evening, Sire." She looked at Barbara and smiled with tight lips. "Thank you for your lovely invitation, Mrs. Palmer."

The king hid his amusement. "Going so soon?"

Montgomery bowed. "By your leave, Sire."

As a footman brought Velvet's wrap, Barbara looked up at Charles. "Lud, I thought they'd give us a fireworks display."

"The sparks will fly all right, but Montgomery will make sure they are not for public consumption."

Outside, Montgomery led her past the carriages and Velvet had to quicken her steps to keep up with his long strides. She wanted to demand where he was taking her, but clamped her lips shut and remained stubbornly silent. *I'll be damned if I'll speak to the dominant devil.*

He took her through the Whitehall gates and nodded to the guard. When they entered the building, they passed other guards, who allowed them to pass unchallenged. They climbed a staircase that led to the second floor and Velvet guessed that he was taking her to his private quarters. She shivered with anticipation, knowing they would soon be alone together.

He opened the unlocked door and ushered her into a handsomely furnished suite of rooms where his manservant had just finished lighting the candles in the wall sconces. "Thank you, Thomas." After the servant departed, Montgomery took out a key and locked the door.

Velvet stood silently, her simmering anger her only defense against the irresistible attraction he aroused in her.

He removed his plumed hat, unbuckled his sword and laid them atop an oak chest. Then he turned to her and said, "So, let's have it. I now grant you permission to speak."

His words raised her anger from a simmer to a boil. She was so infuriated that she was momentarily speechless.

With a perfectly straight face, he prompted her, "You wish to apologize for all your unfounded, unworthy suspicions and beg me to forgive you. Let's hear it, Velvet."

She flew at him with clenched fists and smote him on the chest. "You arrogant monster! I hate, loathe and detest you!" She might as well have been battering the stones of Whitehall for all the impact her blows had on him.

He gazed down at her. "You are beautiful in your passion. The opposite of love is not hate, Velvet. It is indifference." His mouth curved. "You are far from indifferent, sweetheart."

"I am not your sweetheart!"

His smile reached his eyes. "Shall I show you that you are?"

She realized he was about to kiss her, and knew she would be lost if he did. Desperate to stop him, she voiced her thoughts. "Why did you allow me to make a fool of myself? When I accused you, why didn't you confide in me?"

Confide in a woman? The thought was incredible to him. His words were slightly more diplomatic. "Confide secret information that might put you in danger, and jeopardize the entire mission?" He took her wrap and led her to a chair. "It was imperative that I keep negotiations between George Monck and Charles Stuart confidential or the king would never have been restored to the throne." His face softened and he slipped to his knees before her. "You should have trusted me, Velvet."

Her anger began to melt in spite of her resolve.

He took her hands. "Wasn't making a fool of yourself a small price to pay to have Charles crowned king?"

Now he was patronizing her, and she would take her revenge. "Oh, yes! I would pay any price, make any sacrifice, for Charles." She said his name with adoration.

Montgomery's face fell, as if she'd touched an old wound.

She felt satisfaction that she had the power to make him jealous. She laughed, her eyes sparkling with triumph. "I too can be a devil if you want to play games, Greysteel Montgomery."

Somewhat relieved, he joined in her laughter. "You are an imp of Satan, Velvet Cavendish."

Filled with confidence, she licked her lips. "Didn't you bring me up here to ask me to become Velvet Montgomery?"

Will she wed me to secure her position at Court? "Let me think. . . . Do I want you for wife or mistress?"

Her confidence faltered. They had already been lovers; what need did he have to marry her? She thought fleetingly of Bolsover, of the Elizabethan manor at Roehampton, of her position at the Royal Court and lastly about having Greysteel Montgomery for her husband. She wanted all of them and feared she was in danger of having none. Her saucy tongue came to her rescue and saved her from revealing her vulnerability.

"More to the point," she drawled, "do I want you for husband or lover?"

"Only you can answer that, Velvet. I am sure you were taught the fine points to look for in a prized stud. Do you wish to inspect me?" He stripped off his coat and began to unbutton his shirt.

Her pulse began to race, and her blood heated. "There is no need for that. I've already experienced you as a lover."

"And did I measure up, my lady?" he asked insolently, determined not to let her have the upper hand.

She blushed hotly and lowered her lashes. "Why are you treating me like a strumpet?"

Relenting, he gathered her into his arms. "Velvet, you could never be a strumpet! You are my sweetheart." He dipped his head and feathered kisses into the bright curls at her temple.

She clung to him, desperately relieved that he had only been teasing her. *He is mad in love with me.* Confidence surged through her. *I have stolen his heart.* "Christian said that you are captain of the King's Guard. Is it true?"

He smiled ruefully. "When Charles asked me, I felt duty bound to accept, at least until I've recruited an adequate number and whipped them into shape. Then I'll consider turning command over to a successor. I have considerable property and business of my own to look after."

"I'm sorry about your father, Greysteel."

His arms tightened possessively. "Now that I'm an earl, I will need a wife. Will you marry me, Velvet?"

She smiled a secret smile. *I knew he brought me here tonight to ask me to marry him.* "Yes! I would love to become Velvet Montgomery." She stood on tiptoe and offered her lips without reserve. He kissed her so thoroughly it made her dizzy.

"Velvet Montgomery, Countess of Eglinton," he whispered against her lips, "the most beautiful lady at Court."

"I can't believe I'm marrying an earl." She gazed up into his eyes, mesmerized by their compelling intensity. The very air seemed filled with magic and she felt as if she were floating in a sea of happiness. Then suddenly she remembered that he owned Bolsover Castle and some of the magic dissolved. Charles's words came back to her: *To get it back in your family you will have to marry him and hope he deeds it to you as a wedding gift.*

Velvet didn't dare mention it for fear that Greysteel would suspect that was the reason she had agreed to marry him. Bolsover threatened to be a huge bone of contention between them unless she approached it delicately.

I'll have to have him eating out of my hand before I can persuade him to bestow such a gift upon me.

Velvet thought of her great-grandmother Bess, who had been able to get anything she wanted from any man breathing. *She used her sensuality ferociously, and I must do the same.*

She pressed her soft body against his hardness. Her tempting fingers began to finish the job of unbuttoning his shirt, and then her hands slipped inside to caress the slabs of muscle on his wide chest. "Why don't you show me the bedchamber?"

"You have bludgeoned me into submission," he teased. "Your hands are formidable weapons, my love. First they beat me; then they seduce me." He picked her up and carried her into the adjoining room. Then he allowed her body to slide down his until her feet touched the floor beside the wide curtained bed. He encouraged her to remove his shirt and groaned as she kissed his flat bronze nipple, then worried it with her teeth.

Velvet ached to have him undress her. She wanted him to worship her body with kisses. Desire coiled inside her, making her belly taut with need. She lifted her mouth to his, inviting his tongue to plunder her. When he plunged inside she moaned and writhed against him.

Greysteel undid the silver ribbons and unfastened her bodice. He cupped her breasts with his palms, teasing her nipples with his thumbs. Then he dipped his head and sucked the tiny fruit into his mouth as if it were a ripe cherry.

Velvet arched her breast into his hot mouth, panting with arousal. "Take me to bed," she whispered breathlessly.

He raised his head and his compelling grey eyes looked directly into hers. "You shock me, mistress."

Seductively, she laughed up at him, convinced he

was teasing her, and vowed to tease him back unmercifully.

He removed his hands from her lush breasts, closed the bodice of her gown and began to fasten the silver ribbons.

She swayed toward him. "What are you doing?"

He steadied her, then picked up his shirt and proceeded to put it on. "I have no intention of taking you to bed until we are married, Velvet."

Her eyes flashed dangerously. "You bedded me before!"

"Aye, and after I let you have your way with me, you suddenly changed your mind and spurned me. I have more good sense than to let that happen again."

She opened her mouth to refute such an outrageous accusation, but before she could speak, his mouth took possession of hers in a demanding kiss. She melted against him, yielding her will to his. He had warned her long ago that he would be in control, and she realized she wanted him no other way.

"Come." He led her into the other chamber, donned his coat and buckled on his sword.

Her heart and her body cried out in protest. She whispered, "Greysteel, I don't want to go back to Bishopsgate."

His grey eyes gleamed with victory. "I'm not taking you back to Bishopsgate, my sweetheart. I'm taking you down to the chapel so we can be married. I have no intention of letting you escape again."

"Tonight? Are you sure we can be married tonight?"

"Very sure." He grinned. "I've made the arrangements."

"You devil!" She ran to the mirror, intent on restoring order to her disheveled hair and gown.

He came up behind her and slipped his arms around her.

"Velvet, you look radiant and lovely, as always."

"I'm going to be a countess. I have to look perfect!"

Chapter Sixteen

*V*elvet's eyes were drawn to the beautiful statues of angels that stood guard in the Queen's Chapel at Whitehall. Greysteel led her to the altar draped in cloth of gold, and the Anglican priest who officiated at the king's services stepped forward.

"Holy matrimony is not to be taken unadvisedly, lightly or wantonly," he admonished, "but reverently, discreetly, advisedly, soberly and in the fear of God.

"Matrimony was ordained for the hallowing of the union betwixt man and woman; for the procreation of children to be brought up in the fear and nurture of the Lord; and for the mutual society, help and comfort that the one ought to have of the other, in both prosperity and adversity.

"Robert Greysteel Montgomery, wilt thou have this woman to thy wedded wife, to live together after God's ordinance in the holy estate of matrimony? Wilt thou love her, comfort her, honor and keep her, in sickness and in health, forsaking all other, keep thee only unto her, so long as ye both shall live?"

"I will." His voice rumbled like thunder around the chapel.

"Elizabeth Cavendish, wilt thou have this man to thy wedded husband, to live together after God's ordinance in the holy estate of matrimony? Wilt thou obey him, and serve him, love, honor and keep him, in sickness and in health, forsaking all other, keep thee only unto him, so long as ye both shall live?"

Velvet raised her eyes to the angel whose face resembled her mother's. *Montgomery is noble and strong. I vow he will protect you and always keep you safe, my darling.*

"I will." Her voice was tremulous. *I'm lying. . . . I know I won't always obey him.*

Greysteel heard her promise. *Will you truly love me, Velvet?*

The priest did not ask who gave her to be married. Earlier, Montgomery had produced the legal betrothal signed by Newcastle.

They held hands and gave each other their troth for better, for worse; for richer, for poorer; in sickness and in health; to love and to cherish; till death did they part.

Then, magically, Greysteel slipped a tiny gold ring on her finger. "With this ring I thee wed, with my body I thee honor, and with all my worldly goods I thee endow, in the name of the Father, and of the Son, and of the Holy Ghost. Amen."

Velvet did not deceive herself. Montgomery's properties were all in his name. Bolsover Castle was his unless and until he made her a gift of it.

"Forasmuch as Robert and Elizabeth have consented together in holy wedlock, I pronounce that they be man and wife together."

Greysteel placed a chaste kiss on her forehead, and the priest led the way to the vestry, where the newly-weds signed the register. A man and a woman stood waiting to sign as witnesses. Velvet recognized the man as Greysteel's servant, Thomas.

The woman curtsied. "Congratulations, yer lord-ship."

Greysteel smiled down at Velvet. "This lady is one of Whitehall's incomparable cooks, who befriended me when I first came to London. As always her service is invaluable."

Velvet thanked her and Thomas. Then Greysteel seized her hand and whisked her away, back up to their own suite of rooms. She became breathless climbing the stairs at the pace he set, so he swept her into his arms and carried her up the final flight. He didn't set her feet down until he had carried her across their threshold. Then he firmly locked the door and removed his coat and his sword.

Suddenly, she felt shy, and when her husband took her into his arms, she blushed profusely. "I feel all prim and proper—I don't know what has come over me."

"That's easily explained. When I married you, I turned a precocious, saucy baggage into a lady . . . *Lady Montgomery*."

Her shyness vanished instantly. She moved against him, tempting his manhood. "I'll let you decide. Do you want me to act like a wife or a mistress tonight, *Lord Montgomery?*"

He cupped her bottom and squeezed. "Both . . .

tonight and every night. Variety is the spice of life. Do you want me to make love as your husband or your lover?"

She licked her lips, pretending it was a difficult choice. "Let's start with the earl. . . . I've never had an earl before."

Greysteel didn't give her time to ache to be undressed. He began the ritual immediately. "This will always be my favorite gown. I must remove it before I ruin it."

As he removed each garment, he kissed every inch of satiny skin that the denuding revealed. Finally, she was naked except for her stockings and pretty silver garters. He picked her up and sat her down on the edge of the bed so that she could watch him strip off his clothes, while he told her in sensual detail the intimate things he intended.

She reveled in her husband's wide shoulders and well-muscled chest with its pelt of black hair. His height and darkness resembled the king's, but his face, now hard with desire, had a predatory, dangerous look that inflamed her senses.

Slowly, he pushed her down on the bed and spread her beautiful red gold hair across the pillow. He paid homage to her naked flesh by making love to her with his eyes. His intense gaze lingered on her mouth, then swept to her luscious breasts. His lips curved as he watched her nipples ruche with arousal. His glance trailed down her belly and came to rest on her mons. "Your saucy curls, set off by the silver ribbons of your garters, look like flames. Are you afire for me, Velvet? Do you burn as I do, my lovely?"

He came over her, kneeling on the bed, straddling

her hips with his hard-muscled legs, and then he captured her mouth and ravished it. Heat leaped between them as he kissed and licked and tasted every inch of her smooth, alabaster skin from her throat to her belly, now taut with arousal. He unfastened her garters, pushed down her stockings and set his hot mouth to the soft flesh on the insides of her thighs.

Her desire spiraled higher as she remembered how he had once made love to her with his mouth. She arched up from the bed, inviting his hungry mouth to devour her. When it came, the thrust of his rough tongue was far more erotic than she anticipated and she wanted to scream with excitement as he lifted her slim legs onto his shoulders. She threaded her fingers through his long, black locks, holding him captive at her woman's center. Then she began to cry out his name in pure, unadulterated pleasure. "Greysteel! Greysteel!"

She wanted the exquisite sensation to last forever, but soon she began to throb and moan as her pulsations began and she climaxed with delicious liquid tremors. She thought he would come over her and capture her mouth, but he surprised her by turning her over so that she lay facedown on the bed.

He lifted her hair and set his lips to the sensitive nape of her neck. Then in a tantalizing descent he trailed kisses down the length of her spine. By the time his lips touched her bottom, he was well aware that he had aroused her again. When he slid his tongue into the cleft of her bum cheeks, she began to writhe and he knew he could wait no longer for his own release. He raised her bottom and slid into her scalding woman's center from behind, sheathing his cock to the hilt.

The pleasure was so intense, she arched her bum and grabbed fistfuls of the sheet. They both cried out as they spent together and his white-hot seed erupted like a firestorm. They lay together for long silent minutes as the dark, erotic passion that had taken possession of them subsided. She loved the smell of his man-scented skin and the weight of his body on hers. She felt boneless from the release he'd given her.

He rolled her so that she lay supine between his thighs, and bent to kiss her lips until they felt bee-stung. She gazed up at him in wonder. "My God, the earl was a revelation!"

"Nobility has its privileges." He nuzzled her neck and cuddled her against him, loving the feel of her body, now soft with surfeit. He nibbled her ear and whispered, "The earl has made your husband jealous. When will it be his turn?"

Though she felt boneless, she could not resist teasing him. "My husband will have to wait while I pleasure a certain impatient captain of the guard."

Greysteel reached up and closed the curtains about the bed. "I want no witnesses to this military exercise. I must warn you I give no quarter and will accept only unconditional surrender."

Velvet groped him in the darkness. "My pleasure, Captain."

An hour later, when his bride fell asleep in his arms, Greysteel Montgomery held her possessively. He had never felt as happy and content in his life before. He gazed down at her for a long time, and then finally closed his eyes. His mouth curved with deep satisfaction. *She is my angel love.*

When Velvet awoke at dawn, her husband was

propped on one elbow, gazing down at her with possessive grey eyes. She smiled and stretched with delicious languor. His lovemaking had made her feel worshipped, like a goddess, imbued with power over him. She reached up to trace the dark shadow along his unshaven jaw and thrilled when he took her hand, dropped a kiss into her palm, then closed her fingers over it to keep it captive. She fancied that in this intimate moment he could deny her nothing.

She chose her words to elicit his response. "Greysteel, we were married so quickly, I have no wedding gift for you."

"Nay, traditionally it is the groom who gives his bride a morning gift. What would you like, sweetheart?"

She traced his lips with her fingertips and whispered softly, "Would you give me Bolsover Castle, my dearest lord?"

"No." He threw back the covers and quit the bed. A pain sliced through his heart. *You fool! She wed you for Bolsover.*

He had convinced himself that she loved him. Now he knew she had married him for all the wrong reasons—to gain Bolsover, to please Charles and to live at Court. He was a besotted fool!

Velvet was stunned. Her eyes fastened on his naked back as he walked away from her. She thought she couldn't possibly have heard him right. She drew her knees beneath her and sat up, holding the sheet to her breasts. "Greysteel, what did you say?"

He took a clean shirt from the drawer and came back to the bed. "I said *no*, Velvet."

Her eyes flashed and the sheet fell away. "Why the devil not?" she demanded imperiously.

"If I gave you the castle, you would turn around and give it back to your family."

"Of course I would. It belongs to my father!"

"No, Velvet, it belongs to me." His glance was drawn to her lovely breasts, which rose and fell with her agitation.

She grabbed the sheet and pulled it up to conceal them from his avid gaze. "You avaricious swine!"

His mouth quirked. "Very pretty language for a bride to her new husband. You think to beguile me with such sweet talk?"

"You devil! Your self-interest is appalling."

"It is your lack of self-interest that appalls me, Velvet."

"What do you mean?" she demanded.

"Your father will have Nottingham Castle restored to him along with his many other vast property holdings. His wife, Margaret, is to be made a duchess. Your brother, Henry, Marquis of Mansfield, will get Welbeck Abbey. The Cavendish family is now reaping its rewards from the king."

"The rewards are justified!"

"Of course they are," he agreed. "You are a member of the Cavendish family, far more deserving than Margaret. Where is your reward, Velvet? What will you get?"

She stared at him, hearing his words, and began to comprehend.

"If your besotted bridegroom gifted you with the castle and in your blind devotion you handed the deed over to your father, do you think he'd be generous enough to say, 'Bolsover is yours, Velvet'? If he wanted to, do you think Margaret would let him?"

She lowered her lashes. "I don't know," she murmured.

"You do know." He sat down on the bed and placed his fingers beneath her chin. "Look at me, Velvet." When she raised reluctant lashes, he said, "Bolsover Castle is *ours*: yours and mine. I intend to deed it to our firstborn child."

She could not help but be happy that Greysteel had such foresight. She hadn't given much thought to her future children, but it was apparent that he had. She was thankful that he had a good head for business, but she was a little dismayed that his head ruled his heart. *I knew from the beginning that he was a man who liked to be in control. In my conceit I believed I could make him lose control whenever I wanted, and wrap him around my fingers to do my bidding.*

Velvet smiled a secret smile. *I shall simply have to try harder.* Her great-grandmother's journal provided enough advice to enslave any man breathing. Subtle denial alternated with overt carnal lust, blowing cool, then hot, could bring a male to his knees. She deliberately let the sheet fall from her breasts. *Watch out, Greysteel. First I'll steal your heart, and then your soul.*

He reached down and lifted the sheet up to her chin. "Cuddle up and go back to sleep, sweetheart. Just because I must arise at an ungodly hour doesn't mean you have to. Thomas will bring your breakfast in an hour or so." He took his clothes to the dressing room.

There were not many about at this early hour, but as Montgomery passed the rear staircase that led to the king's private chambers, he encountered Charles returning from his nocturnal disport.

"From the look of satisfaction on your face, I take it you persuaded the lady to accept your proposal?"

"I did, Sire. We were married in the chapel last night."

"You sly devil! You deprived your king of witnessing your nuptials. But don't think you have cheated the Court of its entertainment. We shall celebrate with a wedding banquet tonight and follow it with a traditional bedding."

Montgomery groaned. "Velvet would not welcome a bedding."

Charles laughed. "I warrant she welcomed the one you gave her last night. Velvet is a saucy little wench, ready for a mischievous romp at the drop of a hat. You've had your fun and games; indulge me."

As if you haven't indulged in fun and games all night!
"Thank you, Sire. A wedding banquet is most generous."

In the early afternoon, the dowager arrived. She brought along Emma and all Velvet's clothes. The coachman carried in a huge trunk and went down to fetch another.

"A beautiful blushing bride and none there to witness it."

"How did you know?" Velvet was amazed that news had traveled so quickly to Bishopsgate.

"The impetuous earl slipped me a note last night. I came as early as I thought decent for a newlywed, since you had only one gown. A fashionable wardrobe is paramount for a Court lady."

"Thank you for packing all my things, Emma. We have a very spacious dressing room with two double wardrobes."

"I hope there are shelves for all your creams and cosmetics. It might be big enough to accommodate your garments, darling, but where on earth will Montgomery put his?" Christian teased.

"Speak of the devil!" Velvet declared as the door was thrown open and Greysteel carried in a trunk and the dowager's coachman wheeled in another.

"Who would have guessed the devil's bride came with so much baggage?" He lifted Velvet off her feet and branded her with a possessive kiss. Then he gave Christian a grateful smile. "Emma, the countess needs your services. Are you willing to come and live at Court?"

Emma bobbed him a curtsy. "More than willing, my lord."

"Good. I'll speak with the chamberlain and ask him to accommodate you with a cozy room close by. The king and Court are feting us with a wedding banquet tonight, so I'll leave you to your unpacking."

"Oh, how lovely!" Excitement bubbled up in Velvet. She would be the center of attention. "Christian, you must stay."

When Emma busied herself in the dressing room, Velvet drew the dowager to a comfortable chair and lowered her voice. "There's something I must tell you. The late Earl of Eglinton purchased Bolsover Castle and willed it to his son. The king told me I could get it back for my family when I married Montgomery. But Greysteel refuses."

"You asked him to give it back to your family?"

"I asked him to give it to *me*, but he refused on the grounds that I would turn around and give it to my father."

"Well, thank God you have a man with enough determination to save you from yourself. You are a Cavendish, Velvet. Once you get your hands on a piece of property, you must keep it for your children. Because you are female, your family would deprive you of your fair share."

"I don't think they would. Perhaps Father intended to leave me Bolsover in his will," she said wistfully.

"Not likely. I learned my lesson when my husband died. I inherited only because there were debts. When I paid them off I made sure from that day forward I controlled the purse strings."

"When Greysteel said Bolsover was ours, and that he would deed it to our child, I did see the wisdom of that, but what on earth will I say to Father?"

"I warrant the implacable earl will take care of Newcastle. A pity really, darling. Standing up to your father would give you invaluable experience in standing up to your husband."

Velvet's eyes glittered with amusement. "You are wicked!"

"Don't despair, darling. Wickedness can be learned."

As the newlyweds entered the Banqueting Room a loud cheer rang out from the crowd. When Velvet saw how many fashionably dressed ladies were present, she was thankful she'd chosen the peacock blue gown that contrasted so strikingly with her red gold curls. Barbara and Roger Palmer were there, along with all the guests who had been at their entertainment. As well, there were numerous courtiers she had not yet

met and many of the King's Guard Montgomery commanded.

As Greysteel led her to the head table to take their
places of honor at Charles's side, everyone they passed
offered congratulations. She tried to curtsy to the king,
but Charles would have none of it and took her hand
instead. "It gives me the greatest pleasure in the world
to present to you the newest and loveliest member of
my Court, Velvet Montgomery, Countess of Eglinton.
Greysteel, you are a very lucky man."

The applause was deafening and when Montgomery placed a proprietary arm about his new bride
and moved her out of the king's reach, everyone
laughed and shouted approval.

The food served was sumptuous and the wine
flowed freely, prompting dozens of toasts, to which
the groom gallantly responded. As the hour advanced
and the toasts became lewd and licentious, Montgomery's pithy rejoinders showed that he could hold
his own against all tormentors.

The courtiers moved to the Presence Chamber and
as the dancing began, Greysteel took Velvet's hand to
lead her out.

"By the Divine Right of Kings, I claim the honor of
being the lady's first partner," Charles declared loftily.

Velvet stood between the two tall men, looking
from one dark face to the other, feeling like the prize at
a cockfight.

Silence stretched between the trio for a full minute.
"By the Divine Right of Montgomery, I grant you the
honor, Sire." Greysteel bestowed his wife's hand on
the king, successfully masking his reluctance with a
smile.

Montgomery made sure he partnered Velvet in the next dance, but after that his guardsmen monopolized her to such a degree that he had no choice but to accept it with good-natured grace.

Suddenly, Velvet found herself flanked by Barbara and Christian and tried to make sense of their urgent whispers.

"A bedding . . . I don't understand."

"Hurry, darling, unless you wish to be stripped naked here in the Presence Chamber."

Holding hands, the three females made a dash for the exit, as determined courtiers plucked the bowknots and *galants* from Velvet's gown. The music and laughter grew fainter as they ascended the staircase to the newlyweds' second-floor apartment.

Barbara helped her undress while Christian went to the wardrobe to select a suitable chamber robe. As Velvet slipped her arms into the loose white silk garment, the dowager explained, "A bedding is an ancient tradition that has come down through the centuries. Such delightfully risqué customs were abolished during Cromwell's dreary years."

Barbara licked her lips. "Isn't the bride supposed to be naked and waiting in bed for the groom?"

"That was in medieval times. The bride's body was displayed to show that she was virgin pure and free from blemish."

"I don't believe I was ever virgin pure," Barbara drawled.

Christian turned back the covers. "Slip into bed, darling. I hear them coming."

Velvet's eyes widened with alarm as the bedchamber suddenly filled with courtiers, some of whom were falling-down drunk. Half a dozen, including the king, his brother James, Buckingham and the Scottish Lauderdale, carried aloft a stark-naked Montgomery and deposited him on the wide bed next to his wife. As the ladies of the Court pushed and shoved to get a better view of the virile groom, the gentlemen shouted lascivious suggestions about the various ways to copulate.

Buckingham bowed. "I hereby declare fornication, drunkenness and debauchery back in favor at the King's Court."

"Would ye like me tae show ye how tae fuck her, laddie?" Lauderdale's shock of red hair was standing on end.

"Stand back, you wild Highlander—I claim the first kiss." Charles elbowed his Scots friend aside.

"You're all too late. I initiated her long ago," an insolent voice drawled.

Velvet looked up into the leering face of young Lord Cav and began to tremble.

"The boy is flown with wine—get him out of here before I'm forced to draw my sword." Greysteel could feel his wife's shivers and decided to put a quick end to the bawdy entertainment. His eyes looked directly into the king's and signaled that Velvet had endured enough.

Charles held up his all-powerful hands and began to usher the revelers from the chamber. "Out, everyone! Montgomery's weapon is formidable. He's promised to sheath it the moment we leave."

Greysteel jumped off the bed and helped herd them through the door. Then he threw the heavy bolt across.

"Are they all gone?"

He heard the apprehension in her voice and returned quickly. He put out the lights, climbed in beside her and gathered her into his arms. In spite of the precocious facade she sometimes affected, he knew she was shaken by the men's overt coarseness.

He stroked her back to calm her, enjoying the feel of the slippery silk against his rough hand. He knew if he removed the night rail immediately, she would feel too vulnerable, and wisely decided to hold her fast and safe. *Perhaps she will learn to love me.* In the darkness his mouth curved with tenderness. He silently thanked the gods that Velvet was a gently bred lady.

Chapter Seventeen

Charles thanked the gods that Barbara had the lush body of a courtesan and the morals of a strumpet. He was a big man with a large sexual appetite, and his new mistress matched him in carnality, satisfying his lust with wanton abandon.

After draining him of his raging desire and quenching the fire that snaked through his groin, Barbara lay sprawled on top of him in the dominant position she relished. She gazed down at him with slumberous eyes, her luxuriant breasts pressed against his broad chest, and licked her lips with satisfaction.

"I rather like the royal bed. It's majestic and generous, just like you, Charles." Barbara had left Whitehall through the front entrance and reentered at the rear, where Prodgers had guided her up the back stairs to the king's private chambers.

He smiled drowsily. "I'm glad you feel comfortable here."

She rubbed her mons against his cock. "I'm always comfortable in bed with you—our bodies were made for each other. But Charles, I'm not always comfortable at Court."

Not really wanting to talk, he murmured, "Why is that?"

"Every other female at Court has a title. I have to curtsy to *Lady Muck* and bend the knee to *Baroness Big-nose*. Even the bride tonight just became a countess. It makes me feel like a commoner!"

You are a commoner. He hid his amusement and pulled her close. "There is nothing common about you, Barbara."

She pulled away from him and pouted her lips. "When they look down their noses at me, it is an insult to you, Charles. They wouldn't be able to do that if you elevated me."

He squeezed her bottom cheeks, stirred against her and leered wickedly. "I'll elevate you, my love."

"I'm serious, Charles. If I were truly your love, you would give me a noble title. One befitting the king's chosen lady."

If it were up to him, Charles would willingly reward her favors with a title or anything else she fancied, but he knew that Chancellor Hyde would strenuously object to raising the king's mistress to the peerage. On the other hand, he did not wish to lose this woman whose explicit sexual appetite matched his own. "I'll look into it, Barbara," he temporized, and made a mental note to buy her some spectacular diamonds to appease her inevitable disappointment.

Velvet stood on tiptoe to kiss her husband, who had just donned the new guard's uniform he'd been instrumental in designing. "You look very sober and commanding in blue."

"That was the idea. I fought tooth and nail against red. His Majesty's Royal Guardsmen are not merely for decoration, to be trotted out for display purposes at parades."

"Your military men are unsuited to the ballroom. I trust they ride better than they dance. May I come down later and look at the horses you've chosen?"

"By all means. I invited your father to come and give us his expert advice this morning. It may assuage his distress at the loss of Bolsover."

Velvet bit her lip. "When he didn't come to the wedding banquet last night, I feared he had learned about the castle and was outraged."

"I'm sure he'll be gratified to know his daughter will be mistress of Bolsover and will pass it down to his grandchild."

She secretly cherished a hope that her father had intended her to have Bolsover Castle someday. If not when she married, then as her Cavendish inheritance in his will. "Perhaps he won't be angry."

"If he is, he'll get over it—after I explain matters."

His words were implacable as always, and at the thought of a confrontation, her knees suddenly felt like wet linen.

Her maid knocked on the door and Greysteel opened it. "Are you happy with your room, Emma?"

"Yes, thank you, my lord. It's the largest chamber I've ever had. I'm just down the corridor next to Thomas."

Before Greysteel left the chamber, his glance roamed appreciatively over Velvet's revealing white silk robe. "She's coming down to the stables this morning. Don't let her wear anything provocative."

Greysteel knew Charles had a deep love and abiding interest in horses, so he fully expected him to be present when the final selection of mounts was made for his troop of Royal Guards, who were fast becoming known as "The Blues." He also knew that the king would expect him to smooth over any thorny difficulties with Velvet's father before Charles came on the scene.

When Newcastle arrived, Montgomery shook his hand. "I'd like to clear the air, my lord. It came as a surprise when I inherited the title deed to Bolsover. When I married your daughter, I pledged to hold it in trust for our child. In exchange I relinquish any claim to the considerable dowry agreed upon at our betrothal."

Newcastle vented his chagrin over the loss of his castle, and Montgomery countered every protest. By the time His Majesty arrived, the roiling waters had been calmed and the two nobles, now related by marriage, had settled their differences.

The focus of the conversation now turned to horses and both Charles and Greysteel showed great deference to Newcastle's equine expertise. Though both had been horsemen all their lives, they agreed that William Cavendish's superior knowledge made him England's leading authority. On his advice, since the horses were all showy animals of uniform size and color, the mounts were selected on the basis of health and temperament.

The guards were busy saddling up in preparation

for a test gallop when Montgomery spied Velvet in the stable yard. "Here comes the bride," he murmured to Newcastle, and the two men went outside to meet her.

She was wearing a long-skirted, buttoned-up coat over a matching blue riding skirt. The sophisticated, military style lent her an air of confidence.

She looks stunning! Greysteel, sensing her apprehension at meeting her father, squeezed her hand, then kissed it. "The duke and I have come to a mutual understanding regarding Bolsover."

Greatly relieved, Velvet smiled at her father and went into his arms. She stiffened as he quickly withdrew his arms and said grudgingly, "I always intended that Bolsover Castle would go to my son, and that Henry would pass it down to his son."

She stared at her father. The deep hurt of rejection washed over her. *The thought of giving me the castle never once entered his head.*

"However, since Montgomery holds the title deed, we have agreed that it shall be passed down to your son. In return, your husband relinquishes all claim to your dowry."

Velvet's glance swept over her father. He had used the word *son* three times, with nary a mention of a daughter. Her hurt was replaced by anger. She looked at her husband and raised her chin defiantly. "Does he really?" she drawled insolently. "How very civilized that the two of you have settled my affairs without even consulting me."

"Velvet—" Montgomery's stern voice warned.

She totally ignored the warning. "The Earl of Eglinton may relinquish all claim to my dowry, but I certainly do not! Twenty thousand pounds, wasn't it?

Now that I'm a lady of the Court, I shall need a little spending money. Don't delay—after all I'm not getting any younger."

Newcastle glared at Montgomery. "This is what I get for indulging her every whim when she was a child. I don't envy you the taming of her."

She smiled sweetly at her father. "When the earl and I are in residence, you must come and visit us at Bolsover. You and your lovely wife, Margaret, are welcome anytime." She picked up her skirt, sauntered into the stable and curtsied to the king. "Your Majesty, I have come to admire your Royal Horse Guards."

Charles swept off his hat. "And my Royal Horse Guards will doubtlessly return the favor, my beauty."

That night in the privacy of their apartment, Greysteel slipped an arm about his wife. "I'm very proud of the way you put our interests before those of your family, Velvet. It took a great deal of courage to assert yourself over Bolsover."

She basked in her husband's approval.

"I was taken aback, however, when you demanded your dowry after your father and I had settled the matter."

"That's because you were born under the sign of Aries. You enjoy being the leader who must be in control of everything."

He gazed down at her. "No, it is because I am a *man*, who does not enjoy a woman riding roughshod over his decisions."

She stood on her tiptoes and kissed him playfully. "I am a sore trial. Even my father does not envy you the taming of me."

"I relish the task. Bending you to my Arian will brings me endless pleasure." He branded her with demanding kisses until she clung to him. "Next time, don't flout my wishes in public."

The newlyweds' passion for each other soon doused the sparks that could have ignited into a blazing argument. The mating dance of domination and submission slaked all their needs.

Velvet quickly became a favorite of the Court. The Countess of Eglinton was beautiful, vivacious and stylish. These were not the qualities, however, that made her stand out at the Royal Stuart Court. Most courtiers were promiscuous, following in the footsteps of an amoral, pleasure-loving king, but Velvet Montgomery was the exception.

Men were drawn to her by the undercurrent of eroticism that surrounded her. This stemmed from the sense that she was a female who was *owned* by her husband. She was a fully grown woman to whom only her husband had access. They imagined that she became a sexual being only in private with her overwhelmingly masculine husband and she therefore represented an irresistible challenge.

The Duke of Ormonde arrived and brought with him the Portuguese ambassador, Francisco de Mello, who came offering Charles the hand of the King of Portugal's daughter.

Serious negotiations began immediately. The King of England pushed relentlessly for everything he could get and in early July, Mello sailed home with the offer of a contract. Catherine of Braganza could become Charles Stuart's queen in return for trading privileges with Portugal's colonies and a dowry of a third of a million pounds in cash.

All summer the King of England applied himself diligently. The multitude of tasks that he accomplished would have felled a less energetic man, but Charles was capable of intense concentration and hard work.

He charged the regicides with treason and brought them to trial, then passed an Act of Indemnity to pardon lesser figures who had sided with the Parliamentarians. He rewarded those who had helped restore him to the throne. He decommissioned and disbanded the Roundhead army, but kept his promise to pay their wage arrears. He set to work building a strong navy. Charles knew that shipping was the vital key to a nation's wealth.

Though he did not shy from duty, at the same time, it could not be denied that Charles Stuart enjoyed his pleasures and indulged them constantly. The king was easygoing and his good nature endeared him to everyone.

Velvet, along with many other Court ladies, was watching a tennis match between James Butler, Duke of Ormonde, and the king. "His Majesty usually wins, but your father is a worthy opponent, Mary. I hope you are enjoying your stay at Court."

Mary Butler, only fifteen, was in awe of the elegant countess who had befriended her. "Lady Montgomery, your hair is so beautiful. I wish I could have curls like yours."

"You must call me Velvet and you *can* have curls like mine. Come and visit me, and my woman, Emma, and I will show you how easy it is to fashion them. I know your father was on a mission to find a bride for His Majesty. Has he succeeded, Mary?"

Mary blushed. "Father would never discuss the king's affairs with me, my lady."

Velvet laughed at her choice of words. It hadn't taken her long to realize that Charles was having an affair with Barbara Palmer, especially since that lady flaunted her intimate relationship with the monarch. "And rightly so, Mary. Everyone's engaged in a guessing game, but we'll simply have to wait and see." Velvet smiled a secret smile. *I'll ask him!*

When the tennis match was over and the opponents had won two games apiece, Velvet fell in beside Charles as he made his way back to the palace, and his gentlemen in attendance fell back to give them privacy.

"Good afternoon, my beauty, did you enjoy watching the match?"

"Indeed. His Grace of Ormonde is a worthy challenger."

"Does Montgomery play? I warrant he'd make a great opponent."

"Certainly he plays. He's very good at games," she teased. "Whether tennis is one of them, I have no idea."

"Spoken like a besotted bride."

"Speaking of brides, Sire, wouldn't you like me to consult my astrology books and give you a personality sketch of a certain lady who shall remain nameless?"

"Velvet, you are curious as a monkey!" He considered her offer. "Give me time to bathe and change. Then bring your astrology books and we'll have a chat."

*   *   *

An hour later, when Velvet knocked on the door to the king's private apartments, she was ushered inside by a Gentleman of the Bedchamber who led her through to an inner room. The king sat at a desk piled with documents; his spaniels lay at his feet.

Charles rose immediately and the dogs came forward to sniff her skirts. "Velvet, do make yourself comfortable."

"I'm disturbing you, Sire."

"That's a good thing. My work is never done."

She found a comfortable chair and the dogs plopped at her feet. Charles went back to his desk. "I'm signing warrants that grant noble titles to those who served my cause. Edward Montagu, head of the Admiralty, is to be Earl of Sandwich."

"He will escort your bride to England on one of his ships."

"They are *my* ships." His eyes filled with amusement. "You are tenacious as a terrier. Do you believe in astrology?"

"I do, Sire. I told you years ago that it was written in your stars that you would become king and you believed me! If you will give me the lady's birthday, I will tell you her personality traits."

He frowned. "I know the year—now, let's see." He consulted a small notebook on his desk. "November twenty-fifth."

Velvet's eyes sparkled. "She's a Sagittarian, like me!"

Charles threw up his hands in mock alarm. "Heaven help me! Precocious, bold, tenacious, and curious as a monkey—"

"Oh, no, Sire. Those are the qualities of a December

Sagittarian. Those born in late November have a sweet nature. They are usually timid and straitlaced, with no hint of a naughty streak. They are forgiving, adore animals, hate confrontation and would never deliberately cause another distress."

"You make her sound like a saint. How could she be happy with a sinner like me?"

"She would be happy, Sire. All Sagittarians love deeply."

"Velvet, you are manipulating me, revealing qualities you think will appeal, and concealing negative traits."

She dimpled, and then confessed, "All born under the sign of the Archer are stubborn, blunt, and have eccentric opinions."

"Such as believing in astrology," he teased. "Give me a personality sketch for someone born in early November."

"Scorpions are ambitious, demanding and dangerous because of intense feelings of passion or hatred. They have few morals and a fierce determination, and cannot help stinging with their venomous barbs. They love to intimidate and cause turbulence."

Charles thought of Barbara. "Perhaps there is something to this astrology business after all."

The pair became engrossed in the subject and Velvet provided Charles with personality sketches of his siblings.

"My mother is an extremely dominant woman. When she realized that I couldn't be bullied, she focused on my youngest brother. I've always had a soft spot for Henry and been very protective of him. She tried her damnedest to convert him to Catholicism and when I forbade it and removed him from her influence, she vowed never to speak to him again. She's so vindictive, she still hasn't spoken to him."

They moved on to Charles's best friend, Buckingham, who was an Aquarian. As they laughed and talked they forgot about time and the dinner hour passed without notice. Finally, it was Prodgers, a master of discretion, who interrupted the tête-à-tête and reminded His Majesty that the hour grew late.

Greysteel came off duty and changed from his uniform. He thought nothing of Velvet's absence until the dinner hour approached. Since they always dined together, either in the privacy of their chambers or in Whitehall's Presence Chamber, he began to wonder where she was and questioned Emma.

"I saw her when she returned from watching His Majesty play tennis. She left again but didn't say where she was going."

Greysteel waited another thirty minutes, then went along to ask Thomas if he'd seen her. When the answer was no, he assumed she had joined some friends and they would likely be waiting for him to dine with them downstairs. He walked briskly from the west wing and as he passed the staircase that led to the Royal Apartments, the guard on duty saluted him.

He saluted back. "Has His Majesty gone down to dine yet?"

The young guardsman flushed. "No, Captain." He opened his mouth, shut it again and looked away.

"Is something amiss, Fenton?"

"No, Captain Montgomery." His flush deepened. "His Majesty is entertaining a lady."

"You must be more discreet about the king's private

affairs, Fenton, or you'll find yourself moved to outside duty."

"Yes, Captain," he replied awkwardly.

At that moment, Velvet swept down the private staircase. Her face lit up at the sight of her husband. "Greysteel! How did you know where to find me? We lost all track of time. The king invited me to sup with him, but I thanked him with all my heart and excused myself. I knew you would be waiting for me."

Greysteel quickly glanced at Fenton and it took all his control to maintain a calm facade. He wanted to say something that would obliterate any suspicion of his wife's impropriety, but knew anything he said would fuel the fire. He clamped his tongue between his teeth and took Velvet's hand. He knew he must crush his own suspicions before he crushed her fingers.

After dinner the chamber was cleared for dancing. Velvet loved to dance and Greysteel always accompanied her. His dominant presence kept the Court wolves from stepping over the line. He watched her dance with George Digby, Earl of Bristol, who was a good-looking man, but considered safe because he was fifty. Greysteel started across the room to rescue her when Charles and Buckingham arrived.

The music stopped and Greysteel watched as they engaged his wife in conversation. The charming, fashionable Buckingham was holding forth in his usual dazzling way as Charles and Velvet stood enthralled, hanging on to the charismatic Aquarian's every word. Suddenly they looked at each other and began to laugh. Charles doubled over and tears ran down Velvet's face.

As Greysteel joined them, Buckingham looked at him and smoothed his elegant, pointed beard. "They share some devilishly amusing secret to which you and I are not privy."

"Never fear—I shall beat it out of her." Montgomery wasn't sure he was jesting.

Chapter Eighteen

"*I* beguiled the king into revealing the name of the princess he is considering for his bride."

"*Beguiled?*" Greysteel had not yet joined Velvet in bed.

She ignored the dangerous edge in his voice. "She is Catherine of Braganza, the King of Portugal's daughter. Since we are the same age and both Sagittarians we are sure to become friends. I'd like to be one of the queen's ladies-in-waiting."

"These things do not happen overnight. We may not be at Court by the time Charles takes a wife." He saw that she wasn't really listening. Her beautiful head was filled with plans. Some of his jealousy dissipated. *Perhaps Velvet's infatuation with Charles will end once Queen Catherine comes to Court.*

Greysteel got into bed and pulled her into his arms. He had a driving need to brand her as his woman and obliterate Charles from her heart.

Barbara waited until Charles was sated. He had not yet withdrawn after spilling his seed but lay content and sleepy, enjoying the feel of her generous body pressed against his.

"I have a secret I must tell you, Charles."

Though he smiled, his eyes remained closed.

"We are having a baby."

He opened his eyes and saw that she was watching his reaction from beneath half-closed lids. "Don't be afraid, darling."

"Why should I be afraid?" she demanded. "I'm proud to be carrying the king's child!"

"Softly, Barbara. You are a married lady. There'll be no scandal unless you shout it from the rooftops."

She climbed off him and knelt on the bed. "What d'you mean? That everyone will assume Palmer is the father? I haven't slept with him since we met. Don't you dare deny this child!"

His voice became low and soothing. "Of course I won't deny it—to you. If we know, what does it matter what others think? It is far better to be discreet in these matters."

Her eyes narrowed; her voice became shrill. "Far better for *you*! So, it's true! You are negotiating for a foreign bride and don't want them to know you have fathered a royal bastard!"

Charles sat up and swung his feet to the floor, weary of her tumultuous arguing. "Barbara, you know I must marry."

"You'll cast me aside for a sallow-faced foreigner instead of marrying me!" She burst into passionate tears.

He hung on to his temper and gathered her in his arms. "You know that's impossible, darling; you forget you have a husband. Come. Dry your tears. I swear on my life I won't abandon you."

She sniffed and dried her face. "You promised me a title, but it's a long time coming. Anyone would think Chancellor Hyde rules this kingdom! A title is paramount now. The mother of your son must belong to the nobility. 'Tis the only way I'll be able to hold up my head."

The following week a gala entertainment was held in the Presence Chamber to celebrate the birthday of Henry, Duke of Gloucester. Montgomery gifted the king's youngest brother with a sword. Velvet, remembering how heartlessly his own mother treated him, stood on tiptoe to give Henry a birthday kiss, then presented him with an astrology scroll. It listed in glowing detail the admirable qualities of one born under the sign of Cancer the Crab, such as his warmth, humor and ability to put others at ease. She had deliberately left out the moody sensitivity and tendency to withdraw into his shell at the least hint of censure. "Many happy returns of the day, Your Highness."

"Lady Montgomery, since I am twenty, does that not call for twenty kisses? Sorry, Greysteel, I didn't mean you to hear that. I will be most happy to settle for a dance, my lady."

"It will give me the greatest pleasure in the world, Your Highness." She gave him her hand and he led her onto the floor.

When the gavotte was over, Gloucester returned her to Montgomery, who partnered her in a courante, her favorite dance. After that, she left him to his own devices. She knew he preferred talking with the men to dancing with the ladies.

Velvet greeted Barbara. "You are absolutely glow-

ing tonight. Isn't it exciting that the theatres are opening again? I've never seen a play, but I'm certainly
looking forward to it."

Barbara was wearing her new diamond necklace to
help hold up her head. "When His Majesty granted a
patent to Killigrew to form the King's Players, he stip-
ulated that henceforth only women be allowed to play
women's roles."

"Charles considers actresses such harmless de-
lights." Buckingham deliberately pricked Barbara with
his barb.

She jabbed him with her fan in retaliation. "Velvet,
have you met my dear friend Lady Arlington? Her
husband, Henry Bennet, has just been named secretary
of state."

As the two ladies exchanged pleasantries, Barbara
smiled at Buckingham and wafted her fan toward a
liveried footman. "Would you be a darling, George,
and get me a glass of that new champagne wine? I'm
told it's excellent for settling a belly that's in a delicate
condition." She smiled archly at Lady Arlington,
knowing she would spread the word to the Court.

Velvet opened her fan and lowered her lashes. *If
Barbara is having a child, who is the father?*

"Good evening, Lady Montgomery. Your gown is so
pretty."

Velvet turned to see Mary Butler, and introduced
the Duke of Ormonde's young daughter to Barbara.
From the tail of her eye Velvet saw Lord Cav approaching and she stiffened.

He ignored Velvet and bowed before Mary Butler.
"May I partner you in the dance, Lady Mary?"

She blushed. "It would be my pleasure, Lord Cavendish."

"Hell and furies," Velvet muttered as he led the girl away.

"Your kinsman is exceedingly handsome," Barbara drawled.

"He's dissolute!" Velvet hissed.

"Really? Lucky Lady Mary."

"She's only fifteen," Velvet protested.

Barbara sipped her champagne. "Lucky Lord Cav."

When the dance was over, Velvet approached Will Cavendish and voiced her disapproval. "Mary Butler is an innocent maiden."

"I wouldn't be interested otherwise," he declared.

"I won't allow you to corrupt her."

"My intentions are honorable. She is a duke's daughter."

"Marriage?" Velvet gasped, imagining how utterly miserable young Mary's life would become, married to this lecherous lout.

His cold blue eyes glittered with malice. "You wed for rank and property. Don't begrudge me, you two-faced little bitch."

Velvet was outraged at his accusation. "I shall have a word with her father about you."

"If I see you speak to the Duke of Ormonde, I shall spread it about the Court that you shared my bed. If you utter one word against me, I will make you rue the day," he threatened.

As she watched him saunter away, fury and frustration made her tremble. Her first instinct was to go to her husband. Greysteel would protect her against all threats from any source. With a sinking heart, she realized she couldn't tell him, lest he believe the lies. Then Greysteel might kill the lout. Her glance swept the chamber until she located her husband. He was conversing with none other than the Duke of Ormonde and Velvet knew if she joined them, the vindictive swine would retaliate.

During the next hour, Cavendish partnered Mary Butler three times and Velvet's apprehension for the young girl mounted. She accepted a glass of champagne and sipped it to quell her fears and frustration. By the time she drained the glass, her courage had returned. *I'll be damned if I'll allow Lord Bloody Cav to thwart me!*

Velvet slowly traversed the chamber until she reached the side of King Charles, who was standing just inside the ornate doors. She went down into a graceful curtsy before him. Charles bowed gallantly and raised her fingers to his lips. She stood on tiptoe and, using her fan to shield her words from those close by, whispered her concern for Mary Butler.

His smile was sardonic as he bent to murmur, "And how do you know young Cavendish is a notorious womanizer?"

"He tried to ravish me, Sire!"

Unknown to Velvet, two pairs of eyes watched her every move. The first pair belonged to Will Cavendish, who immediately suspected that he was the subject of her furtive conversation with the king. A thirst for revenge almost choked him.

The second pair of eyes belonged to Montgomery, who immediately suspected secret dalliance was the reason for the hurried whispers. Jealousy almost choked him.

Charles took Velvet's hand and led her through the doors, where they could be more private. "I'm honored you confided in me, Velvet. Your protective instinct toward the young lady is commendable. I'll drop Ormonde a word to the wise."

"Thank you, Sire. You have put my fears to rest."

"I was looking for Barbara. I suspect she's in the gaming room." He bowed. "By your leave, my lady."

She sighed at his gallantry and returned to the chamber. When she saw Greysteel talking with the king's brothers, James and Henry, she joined them. They were discussing the pools that the king had ordered dug in St. James's Park.

"The ponds will all be connected like a chain when they are finished," James explained to his younger brother, Gloucester.

"But won't they become stagnant?" Henry asked.

"No, they'll be fed by the Thames and flow continually so they can be stocked with fish," Greysteel explained.

Henry saw Velvet and lost interest in the fishponds. "Lady Montgomery, your humble servant. I cannot believe you are without a partner for the next dance."

"My wife is about to retire." Montgomery's tone was implacable.

Velvet couldn't believe her husband's rudeness. She gave the young prince an enchanting smile. "I hope you had a happy birthday, Your Highness."

"Promise you will allow me to partner you tomorrow night?"

"It will give me the greatest pleasure in the world, Your Highness." She swept Henry and James a curtsy.

Before she could say good night, Greysteel nodded

to the king's brothers, clamped his fingers around her wrist and took her from the chamber.

"What the devil is the matter with you?" She glanced at his face and saw that it had a dark, closed look.

He didn't speak until they were in their own rooms. He released her wrist, paced across the chamber, then turned and glared at her. "Is there no end to your conquests, madam?"

A bubble of laughter escaped her lips. "Gloucester?" It was preposterous. A virile man like Montgomery could not be jealous of the king's young brother. There was only one male in the world who could arouse his jealousy. *Oh, God, he saw me whispering with Charles!*

"It seems you have a *flagrant fondness* for Stuarts."

"If you are referring to His Majesty, he asked me if I'd seen Barbara and I took him next door to the gaming room," she improvised quickly. "He is obsessed with her."

"Barbara's a whore," he said with contempt.

"There is no shame in being mistress to the king."

"Why? Because a royal whore sets a higher price on her sexual favors?"

"Barbara is having a child. I warrant it's the king's, since she's proud as a peacock."

"A peahen," he corrected as his anger toward Velvet began to evaporate. "Perhaps I'll take you away from Court for a while."

"Greysteel, you know how much I adore Roehampton, but please let's not go just yet. The theatres are about to open and I'm simply dying to attend the play!"

"I'll take you to the theatre early next week," he promised.

"Thank you, darling." Velvet knew the storm clouds had almost dispersed. She was learning to handle her dominant husband, born under the sign of the Ram. Instead of flying at him, accusing him of spying on her and being possessive as a dog with a bone, she soothed him with soft words. All she had to do now was take him to bed. She shivered with anticipation.

Velvet was too wise to try to make love to Greysteel. He was too dominant to take the passive role, even in lovemaking. Especially in lovemaking. He took the lead in the mating dance and she followed. He was the seducer; she, the one seduced. Greysteel was the conqueror; Velvet yielded to all his demands.

Much later, when her frenzied cries had quieted and his fierce needs had been satisfied, she drifted into sleep, safe and warm against his powerful body. Velvet began to dream:

She was climbing the staircase that led to the king's private chambers. She knew he was waiting for her, but somehow she had forgotten about time and now she was late. She tucked her astrology book beneath her arm and began to hurry. Though she climbed higher and higher, the steps went on and on and she began to fear that she would never reach him. It grew dark and the panic inside engulfed her. All of a sudden her hand reached out and touched a door. It opened and there was the king, bathed in a silvery light that flooded the darkness.

"Charles!" She felt his powerful arms about her and pressed her face against his heart.

Greysteel went rigid and looked down at his sleeping wife in horror. It was obvious she dreamed she was in Charles's arms. He withdrew from her stiffly, but she didn't awaken.

The king pulled away from her and turned toward two other women who stood behind him. One was Barbara with a baby in her arms. The other was his queen, wearing a golden crown. "I have no time for you, Velvet. We can no longer be friends."

As he abandoned her, her cry was heartrending. "Charles!"

Greysteel quit the bed. He bit down on a foul oath and left the chamber. He paced across the sitting room, fighting the urge to smash something. He kicked a chair savagely and the leather split open and the stuffing spewed out. His eye fell on a pair of decanters. He pushed aside the wine and reached for the whiskey. He dismissed the idea of using a glass; his vengeful hand would crush it to smithereens. He carried the decanter to the window and stared out into the night with unseeing eyes as he lifted the whiskey to his mouth and tipped it up.

His guts roiled and burned with red-hot fury, yet he welcomed it, clung to it, for once it subsided, the pain would begin. His iron will kept his thoughts at bay while he concentrated on swallowing, yet he knew they were there, slithering like serpents waiting to sink in their fangs and poison his mind.

He stood at the window long after the decanter was empty. Finally, he went into the dressing room and stretched out on the daybed. His arm lay across his eyes as if he were attempting to keep out visions that would threaten his sanity.

Insistent thoughts gradually penetrated through his defensive shield. In the deep recesses of his brain he

knew that the king had not lain with Velvet; to Charles
she was a childhood friend. Why, then, did he have
this raging jealousy? Greysteel knew the answer, had
always known it. Tonight he would face it squarely.

Since the day of their betrothal Velvet had compared him unfavorably with Charles Stuart. When she
was a child, she had become infatuated by a prince,
and over the years of their mutual exile, her every
wish, every dream, had been focused on Charles becoming King of England. He had become an obses-
sion, overshadowing everything and everyone else.

Though Greysteel had coerced her to wed him, he
knew that Velvet did not regret the marriage. Not only
was she proud to be the wife of the Earl of Eglinton;
she was highly attracted to him physically. But she did
not *love* him. Even worse than that, she imagined herself in love with Charles. Greysteel knew he could not
go on this way. He had far too much masculine pride
to tolerate being anything but first and always in Velvet's heart and soul. If she was not willing to give him
everything, then perversely Greysteel wanted nothing.

In the morning when Velvet awoke, her husband
had already left. She had slept later than usual and the
corners of her mouth lifted in a smile. Greysteel, always considerate, had been careful not to disturb her.

Christian came to Whitehall to join her for lunch,
and then the two of them were going shopping at the
New Exchange in the Strand. "I'm looking forward to
our excursion. I haven't been into London for weeks,"
Velvet declared.

"Oh, darling, you won't recognize the town. Everything has been transformed. Of course the cobble-
stoned streets are still lined with decaying buildings

that have stood rotting for centuries, but now there is a tavern on every corner called the King's Head or the King's Cock—oh, no, that was a brothel."

Velvet laughed at her droll wit. "No more religious fanatics preaching hellfire and brimstone?"

"I swear the same men stand on the same corners, but instead of trying to convert you with a religious treatise, they are trying to corrupt you with perverted poems, a penny a page!"

"I cannot wait to be corrupted. Lead on."

"Oh you must take a mask, darling. They are all the rage. Makes everyone suspect you are going to an assignation. No self-respecting female would be caught dead without one."

"I only have a black sequined butterfly mask. It's more suitable for evening wear."

"It will be perfect. The fashions are outrageous. You'll need a mask to hide your blushes."

As the dowager's carriage made its torturously slow way along the overcrowded Strand, Velvet was entranced at the changes she saw. People laughed, jostled each other, exchanged pithy insults and then laughed again. The street scenes that once had seemed painted in drab black and white were now ablaze with color, from the fantastic shop signs to the vivid garments of the males and females who paraded about.

Inside the Exchange, the stalls had been transformed. Everything imaginable was being offered, imported from foreign ports across the sea. Christian was in seventh heaven buying satin slippers and kid boots. "I must have these pattens. They lift your feet above the sewage that runs in the kennels."

When Velvet looked skeptical, Christian explained

with a straight face, "For if I take up streetwalking, darling."

Velvet purchased French perfume and lace stockings as finespun as cobwebs. She bought a new mask, some ostrich feathers dyed in brilliant shades and a frilly parasol.

Back at Whitehall, she stepped from the carriage and thanked Christian for a lovely afternoon. "I had a marvelous time. We must do this again soon."

"Good-bye, darling. Kiss your handsome husband for me."

Velvet rushed upstairs and put away her purchases. She had time only to wash her hands and face and change her gown. Then she hurried downstairs to join her husband for dinner.

She spotted his tall figure across the chamber, and as she walked toward him she noticed that he did not greet her with a smile; in fact he turned to walk away. She hurried to close the distance between them. Then a voice she detested spoke her name. "Lady Montgomery." She turned to face Lord Cav.

"I hope you enjoyed the play this afternoon. I envied you your vantage from His Majesty's royal box that put you closer to the stage than the rest of us."

"You are mistaken. I was not at the theatre, and certainly not with His Majesty," she said coolly.

Cavendish glanced at Montgomery, then back at Velvet. "Ah, I see," he drawled. "Forgive me. I am mistaken. The lady in the butterfly mask was not you after all."

Velvet gasped. She knew exactly what the swine was doing. This was retaliation for last night.

Greysteel calmly took hold of the young lord's lace

cravat and smashed his other fist into his face. Cav went flying into a table before he lay stretched out on the floor. Montgomery turned on his heel and left the room.

Chapter Nineteen

*V*elvet stood aghast, rooted to the spot, as a couple of young courtiers helped Cavendish to his feet and handed him a linen napkin to stem the blood from his nose. The voice level in the dining hall had risen to a pitch over the incident and she felt everyone's eyes upon her. She saw two ladies whispering behind their hands and feared the gossipmongers would have a feast.

Embarrassed down to her fingertips, she lowered her lashes, raised her chin and with quiet dignity left the chamber. Velvet returned to her own apartment. She expected to find Greysteel there, but instead she found Emma.

"I could scream! Lord Bloody Cav just blatantly lied to my husband. He told Greysteel that I was at the theatre with Charles this afternoon . . . hinting at an assignation!"

"What did Lord Montgomery say?"

"He knocked him down. Everyone's talking about it."

Emma clasped her hands together. "I knew something must be dreadfully wrong between you when he spoke to me this morning."

"What do you mean? What did he say?"

"He asked me if I would mind moving my things into your dressing room."

Velvet looked puzzled. "Has someone taken your chamber?"

"Yes." Emma hesitated. "Lord Montgomery has taken it."

Velvet went through to the large dressing room and opened her husband's wardrobe. His clothes were gone and Emma's hung in their place. She went pale and experienced a sinking feeling. "When did all this happen?"

"This afternoon while you were gone, my love."

Anger rose up in her. *How dare he move out of our apartment without a word to me!* Velvet marched down to the end of the corridor and banged loudly on Emma's chamber door. When there was no answer she turned the knob and found it locked. *You devil!* She kicked the door, hurt her toes and limped back.

Emma threw her a worried glance. "Did you have any supper?"

"I'm not hungry." Velvet sat down to rub her toes and stared at the chair that had been split open.

"I'll fetch some wine." Emma left with the empty decanter.

Velvet's thoughts chased each other like quicksilver. *He was gone when I woke up this morning. We made love last night; nothing was wrong.* Then she remembered how angry he had been after he'd seen her whispering with Charles. Her thoughts flew back to the previous week when he'd seen her coming from the king's private chambers. *Did the guard tell him I was with Charles? Was Greysteel waiting for me?* She wondered how long he had been standing at the bottom of the private staircase. For every minute he waited, his jealous suspicions probably multiplied. *My God, does he believe I was at the theatre with Charles this afternoon?*

Emma returned with the wine and poured her a glass of golden Rhenish. Velvet drank it and poured herself another. "I'll never be able to show my face again, after what happened tonight. Montgomery is mad with jealousy."

"Mayhap you could go to Roehampton for a few days."

"I've done nothing wrong! Why should I run away?"

"But if you can't show your face, my love—"

"Hell and furies! Men sow all the trouble in our lives and leave women to reap it! Fighting and brawling is all they know. Yet I warrant a man wouldn't hide in his room. I shall go downstairs and brazen it out. Help me change my gown."

Velvet arrived in the Presence Chamber wearing a silver tissue creation with small black bows leading from her tiny waist to the low-cut neckline. She had pinned black ostrich feathers into her red gold curls, and a black silk beauty spot sat at the corner of her mouth.

She paused at the entrance and languidly wafted her large fan as she decided who to join that would garner her the most attention. She saw Lord and Lady Arlington laughing with Barbara and Buckingham and knew she'd found her mark.

George held up his hand in mock alarm. "Pray tell

me I will not suffer anatomical indignities if I speak to you, my lady."

The others laughed that he had dared to touch on the subject.

"Intercourse with me is not without risk, my lord."

Arlington guffawed. "Touché! Top that one, George."

Barbara touched her belly and said archly, "Risking intercourse can have its rewards."

George shuddered. "And its anatomical indignities."

Everyone laughed, including Barbara. "I swear you are the most inconsiderate brute alive, George."

The Duke of Lauderdale and Anna Marie Shrewsbury joined them. "We're on our way to the gaming room and need a laugh before we get plucked like partridges. What's so funny?" she asked.

"We were laughing at you, Anna Marie," Buckingham drawled. "Now we'll have to find another butt for our jests."

Lauderdale winked. "Any of you lasses fancy a plucking?"

"I'm always game," Barbara murmured suggestively.

"Then stick a feather up yer arse and start crowing." The coarse Scot laughed at his own joke.

"Don't encourage her; Barbara never stops crowing," Buckingham said. "Shall we all have a game of bassette?"

Velvet felt a twinge of panic. "I'm not good at cards."

"Och, lassie, I'll tutor ye." Lauderdale took her hand.

"Thank you, Your Grace." *The wine has made me reckless.*

He squeezed her hand. "Call me Johnnie."

They all made their way to a round card table with a few empty seats. Velvet drew in her breath at the sight of her husband. She had never seen him gamble before.

Since Court was a place of loosest morals but strictest manners, Montgomery nodded politely to his wife. Henry Jermyn, who sat next to him, immediately offered Velvet his chair.

Velvet wanted to hurt Greysteel, as he had hurt her. "Pray don't disturb yourself, m'lord. The honeymoon is over. We lead separate lives, as Court fashion dictates for married couples."

As they all took seats, Montgomery threw in his cards and stood up. "I won't take advantage. I only play to win."

King Charles strolled into the room. He knew that his presence would keep Barbara from wagering recklessly and losing his money. He stopped to talk with Montgomery.

Greysteel knew Charles would have heard about the punch he'd thrown. "I've been thinking of withdrawing from Court, Sire."

"We won't permit it. Who would teach young pups their manners? You pledged to stay until after my coronation."

"Any leads yet on the missing royal regalia?"

"The search is futile. Melted down to fill some Roundhead general's coffers, I warrant. New crowns and scepters are being ordered. I'm having a saddle, worked with gold and jewels, made for the horse of state."

Buckingham, tired of cards and the company, joined them. "You will look like King Solomon, Sire."

Montgomery grinned. "Dazzling pageantry will assert the triumph of the monarchy."

"Speaking of horses, I know you both share my interest in racing. Newmarket was the Mecca for horse races in my father's time and will be again with my support. I've decided to go for a couple of weeks in autumn. I'm negotiating with the Earl of Suffolk to buy Audley End. The Jacobean mansion is large enough for the entire Court and there's enough land for a breeding farm. Nothing like horses for relaxation."

"Racing is the sport of kings." Buckingham glanced over at Barbara. "Though some might disagree."

Charles followed his glance. "Next weekend there is a race meet much closer to home, at Epsom Downs, Surrey. I've decided Montgomery and I will attend. It will show our ladies that they do not lead us around by the nose. Won't you join us, George?"

"If my dearest wife gives her permission," Buckingham said with a straight face.

"May I offer the hospitality of my house at Roehampton, Sire? 'Tis only a few miles from Epsom."

"Excellent. We'll celebrate *before* the races in case we lose. I'll have food, wine and other things sent for our enjoyment. With your permission, I shall invite Lauderdale." Charles walked over to the gaming table and stood behind Barbara to watch the play.

George lowered his voice. "My cousin has decided to withhold her favors until he agrees to ennoble her. I wonder which one will give in first?"

Montgomery frowned. "In a battle of the sexes, the king should reign supreme."

"Only in chess, my friend, not in bed."

Though it was most convenient to have Emma on hand to do her hair and entertain the ladies of the Court when they gathered in Velvet's chambers to sample the face creams and cosmetics that she and her woman concocted, she found sleeping alone more than inconvenient. After sharing a bed with Greysteel Montgomery, she found sleeping alone almost impossible. She lay awake, hour after hour, as her body ached to be fulfilled. Her skin became so sensitive, the touch of the sheet against her flesh made her want to scream. Yet it wasn't just the sex she missed. She longed to be held, safe in his powerful, protective arms.

In the evenings the Montgomerys often attended the same Court functions. They were unfailingly polite to each other in company but never spoke or even met in private. Their actions mirrored those of every other married couple at Whitehall and caused little comment.

In the afternoons Velvet, along with the other ladies of the Court, went into London to shop, to have their fortunes read or to attend a performance at the playhouse. Greysteel of course had not kept his promise to take her to the theatre, so she pretended it was of no consequence and went without him. She attended with the dowager countess, and also accepted an invitation to join His Majesty, Barbara Palmer and Anna Marie Shrewsbury in the royal box.

That night in the Presence Chamber Barbara remarked, "The king has attended every performance this week. The play holds him in thrall. The novelty will soon wear off."

"Are you speaking of the novelty of the saucy actresses singing titillating ditties, or the novelty of the dancers baring their pretty legs?" Buckingham asked blandly.

"The costumes were rather revealing, but the girls on the stage were all exceedingly pretty," Velvet conceded wistfully.

"Common as muck," Barbara sniffed. "Promiscuous trollops—half a crown would lay one down."

"We all have our price," George drawled.

Barbara's eyes narrowed. "What's that supposed to mean?"

George shrugged negligently. "If the shoe fits, cousin—"

"The bloody shoe certainly fits you to a tee. You held on to your vast fortune by marrying the daughter of Fairfax, the Roundhead general who got your land."

Velvet was shocked. Men were all devious swine, especially when it came to landholdings and estates.

"Dr. Fraser could give you something for your distemper."

"The Court physician who cured your pox, George?"

Velvet wished with all her heart they would stop fighting. Witty rejoinders were one thing; vicious slurs were another.

"Is it any wonder His Majesty is escaping to Epsom this weekend? Two days free of *demands* will be a welcome respite."

Barbara yawned in his face and took Velvet's arm. "Excuse us, George. We need a welcome respite *now*."

"It's very warm in here. Would you like some fresh air?" Velvet asked as they walked away from Buckingham.

"Yes, let's get some wine and go out on the balcony." George's barb about her *demands* had found its mark. She wondered if Charles had said something about her, and George was giving her a subtle warning. *I refused to sleep with him, so he has no reason to stay in London. Perhaps I should relent.*

They carried their wine out onto the balcony and sat down on a stone bench. "When you want something from Montgomery, what d'you find most effective, vinegar or honey?"

"Sometimes neither is effective. He likes to be in control." Velvet immediately wished she hadn't confided such an intimate thing to Barbara.

"Yes . . . yield a little and allow him to think he's in control. That's very clever." Barbara drained her glass. "Lud, it's even hot out here, and the river stinks tonight. I have an idea. Why don't we take my carriage and drive to Epsom on Saturday? The country seems an inviting alternative to London."

Velvet agreed. "We could visit my house in Roehampton."

Charles Stuart and Greysteel Montgomery, astride their favorite mounts, set out from Whitehall late Friday afternoon. A coach followed them, carrying the king's body servant, one groom and a footman who was in charge of the food hampers and cases of wine.

"I thank you for your generosity, Sire," Montgomery said, "but I warrant there's enough food and drink to feed a battalion."

"Buckingham and Lauderdale appointed themselves in charge of entertainment for tonight. Lord only knows how many they'll bring. I suspect George has a surprise up his sleeve."

"Foolish me to think cards and dice would suffice. They seem an odd pair of conspirators with such disparate tastes. I can't wait to see the results of their collaboration."

They arrived at Roehampton in less than an hour and when Mr. Clegg emerged from the stables and realized that the king accompanied Lord Montgomery, he was struck dumb.

"His Majesty has brought a groom, Alfred, so let him take care of the carriage horses. We're off to Epsom races tomorrow."

Greysteel took Charles up to the house. "This Elizabethan manor is charming. How did you acquire the place?"

"I bought it from the Dowager Countess of Devonshire."

"Odds fish, that family never relinquishes an acre once they get their hands on it. Yet you have managed to collect two of their properties. I assumed the animosity between you and Lord Cav was over a lady. Now I see it's Roehampton."

Montgomery shrugged. "I fear it is both, Sire."

Bertha Clegg met them at the door. She recognized the king immediately and sank into a reverent curtsy. She simpered like a young girl when he gallantly kissed her hand.

Montgomery gave the king his own master bedchamber that had a view of the gardens and lake, and took his own things to a chamber at the front of the house that overlooked the driveway. Bertha followed him into the room, and began to wring her hands. "You mustn't worry about anything, Mrs. Clegg. His Majesty has his own body servant, who will make up the bed with the king's royal linen. A footman is on his way to the kitchens with a dozen food hampers. Come downstairs with me now and tell him where you want everything."

Within the hour, Buckingham and Lauderdale rode in, accompanied by a huge berlin coach. When they opened its doors, half a dozen pretty girls, wearing scanty costumes, spilled out. The still country air was stirred by excited laughter and nervous giggles as the females were ushered into the manor's great hall.

"I bring you these lovely singers and dancers from the Drury Lane Theatre," Buckingham said with a flourish. "We lured them with an invitation to perform privately for their royal patron. But as you see, ladies, that was a blatant lie. This gentleman only resembles His Majesty. His real name is Mr. King."

The actresses squealed and made elaborate curtsies. Since Charles had been at the theatre every afternoon for a week, they recognized him immediately.

"Well done, Mr. Duke, Mr. Scot." His usual saturnine look vanished. "Would you lovely ladies introduce yourselves?"

A chorus of "Meg," "Moll," "Nan," "Kitty" and "Dolly" issued forth.

Charles held up his hand as he gazed with appreciation at a fair-haired creature with long legs. "This ravishing gamine is Rachel Rose. Your dancing enchants me, mistress."

"Thank you, Mr. King."

Everyone in the room laughed, except Montgomery. The corners of Charles's mouth lifted. "Would someone get Mr. Grey a drink? It might whet his appetite for a little levity."

Montgomery threw up his hands and banished the thunderous look from his brow. "Clearly, I am outnumbered."

"Ma appetite's ravenous. Let the fun an' games begin!" The red-haired Scot's accent thickened noticeably as he sat down and pulled one of the females onto his knee.

"I know you are all eager, but before you perform the acts you do best, could we have a song?" Buckingham asked wickedly.

Soon the great hall was filled with laughter as the young women sang the naughty ditties that were delighting London audiences and the men joined in the chorus of "Cuckolds All Awry," "The Battle Of The Sexes" and "The Virgin's Lament."

When Rachel Rose re-created the dance she did on the stage, kicking and twirling to reveal her long, lithe legs, Moll chanted:

> She's got a trick to handle his prick,
> But will never lay hands on his scepter!

The next four hours were spent eating, drinking, singing and laughing. Occasionally, Mr. Duke or Mr. Scot would disappear with one or sometimes two of the ladies to presumably indulge other appetites, but

Mr. King and Mr. Grey were content to look and listen. At midnight the nymphs were helped into their coach and sent on their way, each richer by five gold crowns. Rachel Rose, however, remained behind.

"We bid you good night, gentlemen." The king took Rachel by the hand and led her upstairs for a command performance.

Montgomery picked up half a dozen empty bottles and took them to the kitchen. "Mrs. Clegg, I told you to retire hours ago."

"I couldn't leave you with a mess, yer lordship."

"My friends are not as considerate. Off you go, Bertha. The king's servants and I will clean it up."

"Your matched team of white carriage horses is magnificent, Barbara. Wherever did you find them?" Velvet asked as her friend's coach rolled smoothly along the Richmond Road.

"They were a gift from the king. Because of their unique color, all Londoners recognize my coach and make way for me."

"We are making very good time. I believe the Epsom races don't begin until afternoon."

"That will allow us to spend an hour at Roehampton. I shall need to use the garderobe. I pee at the drop of a hat, these days." She took out her hand mirror. "I'd also like to freshen up my toilet so that I look my ravishing best."

Velvet had chosen an eye-catching outfit that complemented her bright hair. She wanted to stand out from the crowd and make sure that Montgomery noticed her. The emerald green jacket was tight fitted. Her voluminous skirt was rustling taffeta and she brought a wide-brimmed hat, decorated with ostrich feathers and green ribbon, to shade her delicate complexion from the sun.

The carriage stopped and the driver asked for directions.

"It's about a mile farther. To your right, you'll see a long driveway that leads to the manor," Velvet instructed.

In a few minutes the carriage slowed, then turned. Velvet gazed with appreciation at the rolling pastures. "Here we are. I love this place. I always feel that it welcomes me."

Montgomery arose early, as he did every day of his life. Though he knew Charles was an early riser, often taking a brisk walk through St. James's Park at sunrise, he realized that the king would stay abed this morning.

Greysteel shaved and completed his ablutions quickly, so that the bathing room was free for the others to use. He returned to his chamber to dress and heard the king's servants moving about in the room next to his.

He was relieved that last night's entertainment was over and done, and looked forward with anticipation to the races on Epsom Downs. Horses were a passion of his. *I hope the weather stays fine.* He crossed to the window to look for clouds.

Montgomery's brows drew together as he saw a carriage coming up the long drive. *Who the hell is this?* he wondered with annoyance. *If we'd wanted others, we'd have invited them.* Suddenly, his eyes widened as he recognized the white horses. A foul curse dropped

from his lips as he strode from the room and entered
the one next door without knocking. He spoke to the
king's body servants. "Good, you're dressed. His
Majesty will need your services immediately." He directed them into the room he'd just vacated and
crossed the hall to the master bedchamber.

Montgomery gave the door a perfunctory tap, but
didn't wait for an invitation. He was relieved to see
that the king's eyes were open, though the female in
bed beside him was sound asleep. "Sire, Barbara's
here! Her coach is on the driveway. Someone must
have told her you were staying here."

Charles threw back the covers. "Odds fish, she'll go
mad! Have you ever heard one of Barbara's tirades?"

"I'll take your place here, Sire. Your gentlemen
await you in the chamber across the hall." He hastily
gathered the king's garments and thrust them at
Charles. "Don't forget these."

As the door closed behind the king, the female in
the bed stretched, yawned and opened her eyes.

"Good morning, Mistress Rose. An early storm
threatens. I pray you go back to sleep until it has
passed."

Chapter Twenty

Velvet opened the front door and led the way into Roehampton's great hall. "We don't have a staff of servants, just a housekeeper." As she glanced about, she received an impression that something was different. The furniture and cushions seemed out of place and a strange scent lingered in the air.

"Do make yourself at home, Barbara." She set her hat on a hall table and opened a mullioned window. Then she raised her eyes and stared at the oak beams overhead that were creaking. She listened intently and thought she heard muffled sounds.

Barbara heard them too. "There is someone up there, unless you have a ghost."

"It must be Mrs. Clegg." Velvet went to the foot of the stairs. "Bertha," she called softly, and went up to investigate. When she arrived in the upper hall, she saw that all six bedchamber doors were closed. She thought it strange, since they usually stood ajar when the rooms were unoccupied. She turned the knob on her own chamber door and it swung silently open.

She stared at the tableau before her in disbelief. Her

husband was standing silently beside their bed. A naked female with disheveled blond curls lay amid the tumbled covers. "Dear God," Velvet murmured as she recognized the dancer from the theatre. As if she were in a trance, Velvet stepped back from the scene and quietly closed the door. Stunned, like a bird flown into a wall, she slowly descended the staircase.

Barbara, intent upon adjusting her garters, didn't look up. "Was it a burglar, ransacking the place?"

Velvet didn't even hear the footsteps behind her.

The king descended the stairs in stocking feet, wearing a lace shirt and breeches. "Not a burglar, but definitely a knave."

"Charles!" Barbara cried with delight.

"To what do I owe this pleasure, my dearest lady?"

"I missed you so much, I decided to surprise you and attend the races. I hadn't the least idea you would be at Roehampton."

Charles bowed gallantly to Velvet and saw her bloodless lips. "Lady Montgomery, I shall be forever in your debt for the generous hospitality of Roehampton."

Velvet stood rigid as a pillar of salt, feeling faint, but willing her legs not to collapse, as the king's body servant came downstairs carrying Charles's coat and sword. The footman followed with the king's red-heeled shoes. "I shall see about breakfast, Sire." Both servants headed to the kitchen.

Charles took Barbara in his arms and kissed her. "This is splendid. We shall all attend the races together."

Velvet flinched as she heard footsteps on the stairs.

It was Buckingham, elegantly groomed as always. "Ladies adore surprises; gentlemen abhor them."

"I see no gentlemen," Velvet said coldly, and went outside.

"The little bride's wit is as sharp as her tongue. I wonder what has upset her?" The situation vastly amused Buckingham.

Barbara laughed. "Obviously you, George. Not everyone can abide the sight of you this early in the day."

Lauderdale lumbered down the stairs, unkempt as always.

"Speaking of sights," Buckingham drawled.

Charles and Barbara laughed. George joined in, though he was laughing *at* them rather than *with* them.

Velvet put one foot in front of the other and found herself at the stables. *If I'd come here first, I'd have seen their horses and been warned.* An inner voice argued. *You're wrong! Nothing could have warned you for what you found.*

She went into Raven's stall and leaned her forehead against the animal's warm neck. Her eyes flooded with unshed tears. *Don't cry! Don't you dare cry!*

"He doesn't love me anymore."

Mayhap he never loved you.

"Then why did he marry me?"

It was the king's wish, not Montgomery's. The thought was a revelation. An icy hand gripped her heart. Because Greysteel owned Bolsover Castle, Charles had ordered him to marry her so that technically it would be back in the Cavendish family and there would be no breach between her father and the king.

Velvet didn't know what to do. She wanted to saddle Raven and ride back to London, but running away would be the coward's way out. Timidity and panic were contemptible signs of weakness. Far better to summon her bravado, take a horsewhip, march upstairs and have a knock-down, drag-out fight with the unfaithful bastard. She'd create a scene they'd never forget.

A lump rose in her throat that almost choked her. *If I did that, they would all know that Greysteel has broken my heart.*

Her pride took precedence. Defiance and audacity came to her rescue. She would show Montgomery and the rest of them just how indifferent she was to marriage. Her cavalier attitude would demonstrate that faithfulness and wedding vows meant less than nothing to her.

She lifted her skirts and wiped her nose on her petticoat. "How fortunate that I came to Roehampton today. What a pathetic creature I would be if I'd been kept in ignorance."

By the time she returned to the house, her husband had joined the other men and they were eating breakfast. "Oh, please don't get up, gentlemen. Good manners go by the board in the country." She avoided looking at Montgomery, but could feel his eyes on her.

"I'm having a second breakfast, since I'm eating for two," Barbara declared.

"Won't you join us, my dear?" Charles invited.

She shook her head. "But don't let me stop you from indulging your appetites." Everyone but Barbara understood Velvet's exquisite sarcasm.

She went into the kitchen and found Mrs. Clegg piling slices of gammon ham on a platter. "Good morning, Bertha."

"Oh, my lady, I never thought I'd be cooking for His Majesty the King. Imagine the shock I had last night."

Velvet poured herself wine and put some water in it. "Imagine the shock I had this morning!" She refilled her glass.

"I'll put everything back to rights as soon as everyone has left," Mrs. Clegg promised.

If only you could. Velvet drained the second glass of wine. "I want you to burn the sheets on my bed." *Burn the bed! Burn bloody Roehampton!*

With a careless smile on her lips, Velvet conjured a false air of gaiety that got her through the day. She laughed, jested and made audacious remarks that kept everyone entertained, save Montgomery. She made wagers on the races that became more reckless with each passing hour, and ironically, her wildest bets won her the most money.

The crowds of spectators on the Downs made way for the royal party. Not only did they gaze in awe at the king, but they also stared agog at the two beautiful females, wearing resplendent wide-brimmed hats, who accompanied him.

Velvet tucked her arm into Lauderdale's and cajoled, "Come on, Johnnie, show them you're not a tightfisted Scot and wager some of your gold. I'll pick you a winner!"

Barbara was in her glory. On top of the excessive amount of attention from the crowds, she also had Charles's adoration. Nevertheless, she was loath to lose money. "Lady M., you have the Devil's own luck."

Velvet laughed. "The *M* stands for *moneybags*, I assume?"

"The lady knows a thing or two about horses," Charles said.

"And about horses' arses," Velvet murmured to Lauderdale.

"Speakin' of Buckingham, where is the laddie?"

"He's over yonder, talking to some jockeys. He's either seeking inside information or an assignation. You decide!"

Johnnie clapped Greysteel on the back. "Yer lass is priceless—I'm havin' such a guid time I may not give her back."

"I may not take her back," Montgomery threatened.

Velvet laughed and tucked back a wayward curl that escaped her hat. "You may not get the chance."

The Epsom races did not end until the last afternoon light had faded from the sky. The ladies were helped back into their carriage, and the day was declared a success.

Barbara kicked off her shoes and put her feet up on the opposite seat. "Lud, I'm exhausted. You may count your winnings, but I intend to sleep on the ride back to Whitehall. I warrant His Majesty won't give me any rest tonight."

Velvet sank back against the squabs. She removed her smile and closed her eyes.

Late that night, alone in his chamber at Whitehall, Greysteel Montgomery mulled over the events of the weekend. He had averted disaster from Charles, at great cost to himself. He had a wry sense of humor and clearly saw the strong element of comic farce that had unfolded, but there was nothing amusing about the look he'd seen on Velvet's face when she had opened their bedroom door.

He was convinced that he had done the right thing, the only thing under the circumstances, and knew if he had it to do over, he'd make the same decision to shield the king from Barbara's vengeful wrath. He was Charles's friend; he had no choice.

Velvet should trust me! Her lack of trust in him was what had caused all the trouble between them from the beginning. Greysteel's resolve wavered. Velvet had walked into their room and found him with another woman. What other possible conclusion could she have come to under the circumstances? He was tempted to go to her and explain what had really happened.

She left me on the eve of our wedding and it took the king's intervention to make her change her mind. Deep down inside of him that still rankled.

She has no faith in me and never has had. Not only did that anger him; it also mauled his pride that his wife was always ready to believe the worst about him. He stubbornly refused to admit that he had given her just cause.

Once more his resolve wavered. With all his heart he wanted a loving relationship with Velvet. He knew that his military training made him view things in stark black and white, but perhaps where Velvet was concerned he might have to be more reasonable and accept some grey areas if there was ever to be peace between them.

If Velvet loved me, she would trust me. He knew he had put his finger on the heart of the matter. Velvet did not *love* him. It filled him with hopelessness and made him feel bereft.

Because she was his wife, he had been confident that he could teach her to love him. But now he feared that love wasn't something that could be taught. It had nothing to do with the mind, or the body for that matter. Love sprang from the heart, the soul and the spirit. It needed room to blossom and flourish. He had been far too possessive of her. Love couldn't be forced. It must come from her, a gift given freely. Montgomery vowed to be patient.

Velvet was sure she had never felt this lonely before. Prior to the Epsom races, she had hoped that Greysteel would get over his suspicious jealousy and move back into their apartment, but the infidelity she had witnessed at Roehampton had torn their marriage asunder. She felt betrayed and angry, but underneath, she also felt unloved and insecure. With a wounded heart she decided that the separation would be permanent, but each day they were apart, she became more fragile and vulnerable.

In August, when Christian visited, Velvet did not mention her marital problems, but let the dowager do the talking.

"My grandson is about to become engaged. His parents are extremely gratified at the great match."

"Who is the lady?" Velvet asked with apprehension.

"Mary Butler, the daughter of the Duke of Ormonde. She is a great heiress. He owns Kilkenny Castle and vast landholdings in Ireland, as well as the valuable property here in England that the king bestowed upon him for his years of loyal service."

"Mary is barely fifteen!" Velvet protested with dismay.

"What has that to do with anything? I was wed at twelve. Ormonde must be over the moon. My grandson is heir to the wealthiest dukedom in the kingdom."

"But riches don't bring love and happiness!"

"Marriage seldom brings love and happiness, darling, but it's far easier to tolerate if you are well compensated. I have decided to let my son have his inheritance of all the Devonshire estates—Chatsworth, Latimers, Leicester Abbey, Ampthill and Hardwick. He'll pass a couple of them along to young Lord Cav and his bride. So you see, there is no need to feel sorry for Lady Mary Butler."

"No, of course not," Velvet said faintly. She was loath to vilify Will Cavendish to his grandmother. "What will *you* do?"

"I shall retain Bishopsgate and enjoy my old age without having the responsibility of all those properties. Devonshire, of course, has his own stewards, so Mr. Burke will no longer be in charge of overseeing them."

"What will Mr. Burke do?"

"Your husband has been after Mr. Burke since he bought Roehampton. Then when he inherited Bolsover, he asked him again. Out of loyalty, Mr. Burke stayed with me, but now he's going to be Montgomery's head steward. Didn't Greysteel tell you, darling?"

"He . . . he seldom discusses business affairs with me."

"That's not wise, darling. When men control the wealth, women have to go begging whenever they need money. You should tell him you want a say in things. Surely you have him wrapped around your little finger by now?"

"Oh, yes. I lead him around by the nose."

"Better to lead him by the prick, darling. Have you learned nothing from your friend Barbara?" She stood up. "Well, I'm off to my sitting with Lely. I wish I'd had my portrait painted when I was your age. Now I'm a wrinkled old prune."

"Barbara is having her portrait done by Lely. He's all the rage with the Court ladies. Perhaps I should have mine done."

"It's an absolute must, darling, before your figure is ruined by babies. It would be a lovely surprise for your husband. Why don't you come with me now and make an appointment?"

A short time later, they alighted from the carriage in Pall Mall, where Lely had his studio. Velvet's hopes were dashed when she learned there was a long waiting list for the artist's services and he was booked up for a full year. An artist named Beale was recommended. Beale was a friend of Lely's who also had a studio in Pall Mall.

"Velvet, while I'm having my sitting, why don't you go along and take a look at Beale's work? He's sure to have a portrait gallery to display his paintings."

Lely's assistant took Lady Montgomery to a studio that was close by, and introduced her to Charles Beale, who led her into a room where three full-length portraits were displayed on easels.

Velvet was extremely impressed by the colors and exquisite detail. "You are a magnificent artist, Mr. Beale. This portrait of George Savile is so lifelike. . . . I've seen Lord Halifax at Court."

"Thank you, but I am not the artist, my lady. My wife, Mary Beale, is the paintress. I just do the accounts."

"Why, I think that's absolutely marvelous! Her work is every bit as good as Lely's. Do you think she would be able to paint my portrait, Mr. Beale?"

"It would be an honor, Lady Montgomery. It's not easy for a female artist to become established. If you would sit for Mary, perhaps other ladies of the Court would follow suit. Would you like to come through and meet her?"

Velvet followed him and he introduced her to a young woman holding a baby. "Dear heart, this is Lady Montgomery from Whitehall, who would like you to paint her portrait." He took the baby from her. "I'll leave you to have a chat."

"You'll have to forgive my husband. He's so proud of me and tries to extol me as a great artist."

"But you *are* a great artist. I'm amazed that he allows you to do this without feeling threatened by your talent. Most men like to be in control."

"I couldn't do it without my husband's help. He does all the accounts, prepares my canvases, sometimes even mixes my paint and doesn't mind looking after the baby."

"He's a man in a million, Mary. Tell me how it all began."

Mary told her she had been born in the village of Barrow in Suffolk and that her father was a clergyman who dabbled in oils. She'd painted as long as she could remember. Then Kathryn, Lady Barrow, had become her patroness and paid for her lessons. The village was close to Newmarket, and she painted portraits of people who came to the races. She met the great artist Lely, who was commissioned by the nobles in the area, and he encouraged her to come to London and open a studio. After she married Charles Beale, her husband pushed her to take the chance.

"I'm doing a self-portrait. Would you like to see it?" Mary uncovered a canvas that stood on an easel.

Velvet was stunned. It was a painting of Mary and her baby and both were nude. "Oh, it takes my breath away!"

"I should have done the self-portrait before I had a child," Mary said, laughing. "My figure has thickened."

"Oh, no, you look absolutely beautiful." *I want to be painted naked. But it would be too shocking—I couldn't do it. Don't be such a bloody coward!* Suddenly, Velvet felt reckless. She knew an overwhelming need to be audacious and defiant.

"Mary, would you be willing to paint a nude portrait of me?"

"Of course, my lady. Do you want me to come to Whitehall?"

"Oh, no, I'll have my sittings here at your studio."

"Very good. Let's work out a schedule."

When Velvet went outside, she leaned against the wall, convulsed with laughter. She lifted her chin and said aloud, "Top this one, Barbara Palmer!"

Chapter Twenty-one

Velvet's facade of gaiety as she moved about the Court did nothing for her reputation. Now that gossip was rife that the Montgomerys kept separate chambers, her behavior had become devil-may-care and her laughter had become brittle.

At the archery butts, she challenged Bess Lauderdale and Anna Marie Shrewsbury to a contest. "Five guineas says I can hit a bull's-eye before either of you." After many wild arrows and numerous lost wagers, Velvet was ready to move on to another diversion. The three women strolled past the cockpit and slowed as they arrived at the tennis court.

Velvet spied Mary Butler watching her father, Ormonde, play tennis. She desperately wanted to warn the young heiress about Will Cavendish. "Hello, Lady Mary. I hope you've been well."

Lady Mary raised her chin defiantly. "I've been very well, thank you. I am engaged to be married to Lord Cavendish."

"Mary, you are so young. I urge you to take your time. Don't rush into marriage."

"You are just jealous! I know all about your affair with Cav, but I assure you it is over. He has pledged his love to me and I trust him with all my heart." She turned away from the women.

Velvet gasped. Anna Marie and Bess exchanged smug glances. "He's filled her head full of lies because I spurned his advances," Velvet assured them.

"There isn't a man breathing can be trusted," Bess declared.

Velvet had the decency to flush. Bess's husband, Johnnie, had given her his undivided attention at the Epsom races.

That night, Velvet had a vivid dream. Lady Mary was in it, steadfastly declaring her devotion to Will Cavendish. *I trust him with all my heart.* Bess Lauderdale scorned, *What a fool! There isn't a man breathing can be trusted. Tell her what Montgomery did to you, Velvet!*

She was back at Roehampton, floating in the lake. Greysteel held her hands and took her deeper and deeper into the water. *Trust me, Velvet. Trust me to keep you safe.* The scene changed and she stood outside their bedchamber. She turned the knob and the door swung silently open. She stared at the tableau before her in disbelief. Her husband was standing silently beside their bed, his intense grey eyes staring directly into hers. *Trust me, Velvet! If you loved me, you would trust me!*

Velvet awoke and stared at the empty place beside her in the bed. *I did trust you and you betrayed me!* She curled over into a ball and began to cry. She turned her face into the pillow so that Emma would not hear her from the other room.

*   *   *

The next evening, Velvet joined Barbara in the gaming room. "I'm sick to death of this place. We do the same thing every evening with the same people. I'm ready to scream."

"You're right. We need a diversion. Buckingham is attending a private party tonight at Suffolk House. Why don't we go?"

"Won't His Majesty miss you?"

"I sincerely hope so. I make myself available far too often, and what thanks do I get? Today, the king signed a contract that will make Catherine of Braganza his queen. He dragged his heels until Portugal offered England the cities of Tangier and Bombay and suddenly, miraculously the price is right!"

Velvet remembered how Charles had told her he could not afford the luxury of love when he married.

"Yet he can't sign a warrant to make me a countess!" Barbara was working herself into a fury. "Come on, let's go."

Suffolk House was next door to Whitehall, so it didn't take them long to get there. After half an hour, Barbara cornered her cousin. "George, this is without doubt the dullest affair I've ever attended. Why the devil did you come?"

"I thought it good manners to come and congratulate the Countess of Suffolk. The king has asked her to be a Lady of the Queen's Bedchamber."

Barbara's face seemed to freeze for a moment. "What a coincidence! I too am to be a Lady of the Bedchamber." She opened her fan. "Lud, it's close in here. Lady Montgomery and I fancy going to that new gaming hell in Tothill Street."

He bowed to Velvet. "I am always ready and willing to corrupt a lady, providing she doesn't fear her lord's wrath."

Velvet laughed recklessly. "I'm trembling with terror!"

The next day, Velvet bought herself a small carriage. She was sick and tired of relying on others for transportation and it also gave her a sense of freedom. She could now travel wherever she wished without obtaining her husband's approval.

Velvet went to Mary Beale's studio in Pall Mall for her first sitting. She had to overcome her innate modesty in the small dressing room where she removed her clothes and put on a loose robe, but when she emerged, Mary assured her of complete privacy and put her at ease. "My lady, you have the loveliest skin I've ever seen. It is like flawless alabaster."

"Thank you; with my hair color I'm lucky not to be freckled."

They discussed various poses and Velvet chose to be painted as Venus, reclining upon a couch with a graceful scallop shell at her feet, and her red gold curls cascading over one delicate shoulder.

Later that week, Barbara Palmer threw a party at her King Street residence, but did not invite His Majesty.

"I hear you lost a small fortune last night in Tothill Street." Anna Marie Shrewsbury was piqued. "Next time you go carousing until all hours, I expect to be invited."

Bess Lauderdale overheard the conversation. "Why don't we ladies of the Court form a *Cabal,* as the king has done? We could all be Barbara's advisers."

Velvet laughed. "I doubt I could advise, but I'd be willing to aid and abet."

"Sounds amusing. We need two more. . . . Let's include Buckingham's wife, just to annoy the smug devil, and how about Elizabeth Hamilton? She's always ready for a lark."

Before the party was over, the six sin seekers made a pact to visit all the fashionable and risqué establishments that had opened to cater to Londoners' newfound taste for vice. Many of the gaming clubs provided entertainment. Bawdy skits, racy songs or scantily clad dancers were used to lure in gamblers.

The female cabal left Whitehall each night at eleven and for a fortnight made the rounds of establishments from the Haymarket to the seedier sections of the city, including Cheapside.

Velvet, wearing her new mask, followed the other women into a soot-blackened building on Ludgate Hill. It wasn't until she was inside that she learned it was a brothel that had opened a gaming room as a sideline. The madam, who wore a fantastic spangled gown and purple wig, greeted them. She led them to the cardroom, where each table had a dealer who was similarly clad.

"This is a queer sort of place," Anna Marie murmured.

"Queer indeed," Barbara drawled.

Bess Lauderdale slapped her thigh and roared with laughter.

Velvet's glance moved slowly about the room from table to table as the cards were being dealt. Then she leaned over to Barbara. "I suspect some of these women are men."

"Only some?" Barbara and Bess were shaking with laughter. "They cater to all tastes here."

"I'm not sure I should be here." Buckingham's wife looked extremely nervous.

"Don't pretend to be shocked. It was your husband who recommended this place. Surely you've caught George wearing your gowns? There, now, even Velvet is laughing at that one. Have some wine. Relax and enjoy yourselves, ladies."

At midnight, a curtain was drawn back to reveal a stage. The show presented was a lurid affair of dancers with painted bodies, writhing about in erotic positions and simulated sex acts. Though it was deliberately prurient, Velvet was repelled rather than aroused because the men coupled with other males, and the women did likewise.

After the show, Barbara and Bess paid to go on what was billed as an "observation tour," while the other members of the cabal chose to be satisfied with a game of dice. When the pair returned they described the things they'd seen the prostitutes and their customers doing as they'd watched through peepholes.

Velvet shuddered. She felt unclean, and decided on the spot that she would spend no more nights indulging in such shallow and mindless pursuits.

When they left the building it was after two o'clock and a low rumble of thunder threatened in the distance. Barbara signaled her coachman, but as they stood waiting, a carriage pulled up to the curb, and a tall, dark figure stepped out.

Montgomery, garbed in black from head to foot, held the door open. "Get in," he ordered Velvet.

Go to hell! She didn't dare say it aloud. His tone was

so implacable, his stance so intimidating, she obeyed and climbed into the carriage.

Montgomery followed her, slammed the door behind them and sat down on the opposite seat. The vehicle lurched on its way so quickly, Velvet was thrown back against the leather squabs. She righted herself and sat in stiff silence in the darkness.

Suddenly, a flash of lightning lit up the interior of the cab and she saw his intense grey eyes riveted upon her. Her impulse was to babble an excuse. She bit down on her tongue, and stubbornly refused to take the defensive role.

As the silence stretched between them, the air was charged with electrifying tension. Velvet felt the hair on the nape of her neck stand on end, and a prickle of fear ran down her spine.

When the carriage pulled up at Whitehall Palace, Velvet opened the door and jumped out quickly. She raced up two flights of stairs, hoping to reach their apartment before he did. She didn't look back. She didn't need to; she could hear his measured, relentless footsteps closing the distance behind her.

Velvet opened the door, confident that Emma would be there. When she turned up the lamps and found the rooms empty, she knew that he had planned this encounter, making sure she would be alone and at his mercy.

He locked the door and she was shocked that he still had a key to her chambers. When he turned to face her she saw his savage, black fury, barely contained. He had been stalking her and she felt like his snared prey. The room trapped her, imprisoning her, alone with her captor, and there was no escape.

"If you act like a whore, I will treat you as one. But you are *my* whore, Velvet—never forget it!"

"How many whores do you need?" she cried, her outrage momentarily overcoming her fear.

He stripped off his coat. "Only one at a time."

She wanted to run, but the only retreat open to her was the bedroom. With sheer bravado she challenged, "How dare you follow me and spy on me after what you did at Roehampton?"

"I dare anything, madam, as you are about to learn." He snatched off her cloak and flung it aside.

Her breasts, half exposed in the low-cut gown, rose and fell with her agitation. She saw his powerful hand reach out. "Don't touch me!" she cried.

His hand did not hesitate. He lifted off her mask. Then his fingers gripped her shoulder, forced her into the bedroom and led her to the mirror. "I want you to see what you look like."

She stared at herself, seeing the disheveled hair, the glittering green eyes, the painted face, the indecent gown.

"You were once sweet and innocent as an angel. Now you are hell-bent on destroying your reputation and turning yourself into a strumpet." His mouth set. "Let me help you."

"Don't touch me. Don't you dare touch me," she hissed.

For answer, he thrust two strong brown hands into the neck of her gown and viciously tore it to the hem. "I'll do more than touch you. I'll teach you who is master here."

She watched in horror as his insolent glance roamed

over her naked flesh, and lust turned his dark face into a devil's mask. She knew he was going to ravish her.

"Get into bed." A thunderbolt crashed overhead.

"If you do this thing, I will hate you forever, Montgomery!"

The muscle in his jaw flexed. "Since you deny me love or trust, I will gladly settle for hate." He reached for her with cruel, possessive hands.

Velvet screamed. "Look at yourself!" She pointed wildly to the mirror. "Just look at yourself."

He glanced at the glass. A flash of lightning illuminated their reflection and he was shocked at what it revealed. He saw a six-foot male manhandling a fragile female. Her skin was as delicate as porcelain and his cruel fingers were bruising her. He had thought he was demonstrating his strength, but saw that he was exposing his weakness. He remembered that he had raped her once in a dream, and was horrified at how close he had come to defiling her in reality. He released her immediately.

Velvet saw his remorse and sensed the danger was past. Now that he was no longer a threat, she could not resist wounding him. "You are mad with jealousy, yet think nothing of betraying me with another. Then you swoop down on me like a raptor, ready to devour me. Your lust repels me, Montgomery!"

He closed his eyes and held up his hands. "Let's stop hurting each other, Velvet."

She swooped down and picked up her torn petticoat and held it like a shield to cover herself.

"The king and some of the Court are going to Audley End, in Essex. I have to accompany him. Come with me, Velvet."

Up went her chin. "I wouldn't be caught dead with you. Why don't you take your little dancing whore, or any other *lady* of your acquaintance who fancies a fucking?"

His face hardened. "I just might."

On the first day of September, the king, along with a large retinue, departed Whitehall to travel to Audley End, the vast country estate he had purchased. It was about forty miles from London and the journey could be accomplished in one day. Newmarket, the famous racing town, was approximately fifteen miles farther north and an easy ride by saddle horse.

Servants and baggage carts had left Whitehall the previous day. Charles and some of his nobles chose to ride, while their wives traveled by carriage. Montgomery and a dozen of the King's Guard accompanied the royal party.

At lunchtime Velvet came upon Barbara in the Presence Chamber. "The place is empty. We are the only ones here."

"Yes, I watched the cavalcade ride through the King Street Gate and past my house this morning. His Majesty begged me to go, but until he agrees to give me a title, I refuse to be at his beck and call. As well, I'm almost in my fifth month and a long bumpy carriage ride didn't appeal. I decided to come and see who was conspicuous by their absence."

"Buckingham, Lauderdale, Shrewsbury and their respective wives have obviously rushed off to Audley End."

"Their wives' presence won't stop them from the game of bed hopping. The rumor mills have it that certain *noble* ladies have been invited to accommodate the men."

"There isn't a man breathing can be trusted," Velvet spit.

"Montgomery was riding with the Countess of Falmouth."

"Isn't she Charles Berkeley's wife?" Velvet asked.

"Yes. She's notoriously promiscuous. Aren't you worried about letting Montgomery go without you?"

Her words were like knives twisting in Velvet's heart, yet she was loath to let Barbara see her pain. She knew Barbara enjoyed being spiteful, and decided two could play that game. "Gossip has it that the Countess of Falmouth is eager to lie with His Majesty."

Barbara's eyes narrowed. "Perhaps I should have gone."

Velvet felt contrite. She didn't want her friend's heart to hurt the way hers did. "I was just teasing you, Barbara."

"Don't waste your pity on me. Save it for yourself!"

After Barbara left, Velvet realized she was feeling sorry for herself. *Surely there is nothing more pitiful!* She went upstairs and told Emma to pack. "This place is empty as a mausoleum. I'll be damned if I'll sit around here moping for a sennight. We shall go to Roehampton."

"Oh, how lovely. I'll be able to gather mallows, tansy and vervain so we can make more face creams."

When they arrived at Roehampton, Velvet showed off her pair of matched carriage horses to Alfred. "This is Ned, my driver from Whitehall. He can't wait to taste Mrs. Clegg's cooking."

Alfred grinned. "It's pheasant fer dinner tonight,

my lady. The woods are overrun with game now it's September."

The two women walked up to the house. Bertha came rushing from the kitchen when she heard Velvet's voice. "Welcome home, Lady Montgomery. Hello, Emma, it's good to see you again."

"Hello, Mrs. Clegg. I'll just take these bags upstairs."

Bertha dried her hands. "I'll go up an' plenish yer chamber."

"No, please don't," Velvet said quickly. "I haven't decided which room I'll use, yet." She glanced about the great hall and was relieved to see that everything was in its rightful place and welcoming as it had always been. She knew that upstairs would be another matter. She feared she would never be able to enter the master bedchamber again because of the painful images it would invoke.

"My lady." Bertha hesitated. "I know ye told me to burn the sheets, but I couldn't bring myself to do it. They bore the king's royal crest, so I washed and ironed them and put them away with some sprigs of lavender."

"The king's crest?" Velvet puzzled.

"His Majesty's body servant brought his own linen, and of course Lord Montgomery insisted the king use your master bedchamber—"

"Thank you, Bertha, I don't wish to be reminded." *Greysteel used the master bedchamber. I saw him with my own eyes!*

"Sorry, ma'am. I'll go and see to my game birds."

Velvet walked to the window and gazed out with unseeing eyes as her memory relived the morning she and Barbara had arrived. She remembered the look of surprise on Greysteel's face when he saw her, yet Charles was not surprised to see Barbara. *Someone saw her carriage and alerted the king.*

"Oh, no!" Velvet's hand went up to her mouth. "Of course Greysteel put Charles in the master bedchamber. When he saw Barbara's carriage, he switched places with the king. It was Charles who spent the night with the pretty dancing girl!" She pictured the events in her mind's eye, and suddenly everything made perfect sense.

Velvet, weak with relief, sat down on the padded window seat. At the same time, she was overcome with remorse at the accusation she'd hurled at her husband.

The damnable part is that it's not the first time I've refused to trust him. "Hell and furies, why didn't he deny it?" She remembered the dream she'd had and knew the answer. *Trust me, Velvet! If you loved me, you would trust me!*

"Do I love you, Greysteel?" Velvet wished with all her heart that she had gone to Audley End with him. *It's not too late; I can go tomorrow.* Velvet bit her lip. Perhaps it was too late. She recalled her exact words to him when he invited her: *I wouldn't be caught dead with you. Why don't you take your little dancing whore, or any other lady of your acquaintance who fancies a fucking?*

She remembered his answer: *I just might.*

"What if I went rushing up to Audley End and found him with the Countess of Falmouth?" She knew it would break her heart all over again.

That night as she lay abed in the master chamber, she gave silent thanks that Greysteel had not betrayed her with another. She loved this room that had always been so welcoming and made her feel safe, especially when she had slept in his arms.

She awoke at dawn and knew she had been dreaming of him. She looked at the empty place beside her and felt she could not bear to go on this way. If she didn't make things right between them, she feared she might be sleeping alone for the rest of her life. "I'm going to Audley End."

What if you find him with the Countess of Falmouth?

"I don't give a damn! I'll fight her for him!"

Chapter Twenty-two

As the small carriage crossed from Hertford into Essex in the late afternoon, Velvet's anticipation at her reunion with Greysteel was tempered by her fear of finding him with another woman. It had been easy to convince herself that she loved him; the fact totally escaped her that she still did not trust him.

Velvet had seen the look of disappointment on Emma's face this morning when she had announced her plans, and was glad she had not dragged her away from Roehampton. "I can manage alone, Emma. I know you'd rather spend a few days drying herbs and concocting face cream than rushing up to Audley End. Besides, I could easily return tomorrow if things don't work out."

It was evening when the carriage turned in at the magnificent country estate, ablaze with light. In size, it reminded her of the Cavendish castles she had lived in as a child.

"Ned, I shall leave my bag in the carriage until I am assigned a room." With all her heart she hoped it would be her husband's chamber, but she was completely unsure of her welcome.

The guard on the front door recognized her and welcomed her into the large reception chamber. A footman wearing royal livery informed her that she was just in time for dinner and he directed her to the immense dining room. She allowed him to take her cloak and with head held high, but hesitation in her heart, she entered the room.

The cacophony of voices over and above the clatter of dishes and cutlery did not cease until the king got to his feet. Then a hush fell across the room. "Lady Montgomery! We are delighted that you changed your mind and have decided to join us. There is always room at my table for a reigning Court beauty. You may come and sit between Ormonde and me."

Velvet flushed as the Duke of Ormonde stood, gave her his seat and beckoned a footman to bring him another chair. Since his daughter, Lady Mary, now despised her, she feared that Ormonde would not welcome her as a dinner partner. *Oh, God, I should not have come!*

"I heartily recommend the partridge," Ormonde said with a smile. "It tastes almost as good as the game in Ireland."

Charles winked at her. "Ah, high praise indeed if it compares with anything from the *old sod.*"

With relief Velvet realized that Ormonde was not ostracizing her. "I have never been to Ireland, Your Grace. But I can understand your pride in a civilization that is more ancient than that of England."

The king gave her a hearty buzz on the cheek. "Velvet, I swear you've kissed the Blarney stone. No wonder I adore you."

She felt eyes upon her and glanced over to the next table. She wanted to sink through the floor when she looked straight into the intense grey gaze of her husband. She licked dry lips and was about to gift him with a smile when she saw that his dinner partner was the slim, blond Countess of Falmouth. Her heart sank like a stone and she quickly lowered her lashes to hide her pain. She realized that both the king and Ormonde were bantering with her, but hadn't the least notion what either one had said. She smiled at Charles and turned to the duke. "I understand you were born in county Kilkenny, Your Grace."

Charles saluted him with his wine. "Indeed he was. *Ormonde* is a far more ancient title than *Stuart*, if truth be told."

"We are a very select group," he told Velvet with a grin. "You'll notice His Majesty has created many English nobles recently, but there's been a dearth of Irish titles handed out."

"That's true." Charles gazed thoughtfully into his wineglass. "You know, my dear, this talk of Irish titles has given me food for thought." He covered her hand with his large one. "You are an inspiration."

Velvet had not been following the conversation. Instead she had been surreptitiously looking about the dining room for Charles Berkeley and had come to the painful conclusion that the Earl of Falmouth had not come to Audley End. Velvet put down her knife and fork. Another mouthful would choke her. The footman removed her plate and she refused dessert. Instead, she picked up her wineglass and drained it to give her courage.

"Montgomery and I are going to a breeding farm tomorrow. You must join us. You have a good eye for horseflesh." The king stood up and it was the signal that released the other diners from their seats. "Speak of the devil, here comes your husband to remind me that I have monopolized you long enough."

"Good evening, my lord," Velvet murmured.

Montgomery offered his arm. "Allow me to show you the house."

"Can the Countess of Falmouth spare you?" Velvet regretted the words as soon as they slipped out. She knew that the invitation to show her the house was so they could move away from others and speak privately. She placed her hand on his arm.

"Do you have a room yet?" he inquired carefully.

She shot him a quick glance, trying to read his expression. "No, I . . . no." She shook her head. "My bag is in the carriage."

"We shall retrieve it together." He led her through the east wing of Audley End and they emerged into a courtyard, well lit by iron lanterns and occupied by two dozen empty carriages.

Outside, they stopped walking and turned to face each other. Alone, there was no longer a need to pretend politeness, no room for any pretense at all. "Why did you come?" he asked plainly.

"I came to apologize. When I saw you with that girl at Roehampton, I assumed the worst. I was sure you had betrayed me by sleeping with her in our bed. Now I believe it was Charles who spent the night with her.

I cannot take back the things I said. I can only ask you to forgive me for saying them."

She was so contrite, he had to fight the urge to take her in his arms. "I never worry about the things you say, Velvet. My concern is the way you think of me. You don't trust me."

"When you invited me to Audley End, I wish with all my heart I had said yes. Instead, I pushed you into the arms of that Falmouth woman, and I have no one to blame but myself!"

He shook his head. "Velvet, you still don't trust me."

"She's not here with you, sharing your room?"

"Come and see for yourself."

They located her carriage and Montgomery extracted her bag. They walked together back to the house and he led the way to his chamber on the second floor of the east wing. He unlocked the door, set her bag down and watched as her glance swept about the room, seeking evidence of a woman's presence.

When she caught him watching her, she laughed guiltily. "I was ready to scratch out her eyes."

"Poor lady. She is out of favor with everyone."

They both looked at Velvet's bag sitting by the door and it was an awkward moment.

Will he ask me to stay with him? She held her breath.

I am longing for you, Velvet, but if you stay here tonight, it will shatter my resolve. I vowed I would have all or nothing. I want your love, but tonight I am dangerously close to settling for your passion.

By design, she was wearing her green gown with its silvery ribbons. The one she had been wearing when they married.

She's wearing my favorite dress. It makes her look love-lier and even more vulnerable than she did the night we wed.

"Greysteel . . ."

"Velvet, won't you put your things in the wardrobe?"

"Yes, I will!" Her words came out in a rush of relief.

"Would you like me to ring for a bath for you?"

"Oh, that is so thoughtful. Thank you, Greysteel."

In truth he had suggested the bath as a delaying tactic. He wanted to snatch her up and take her to bed immediately. His body was in a fever to make love, to touch and taste her, and smell the unique scent of her flesh, but he realized he would be much too possessive and demanding if he laid hands on her now. It would be far better for him if he could be a little detached.

By the time Velvet had unpacked and brushed out her hair, the bath he had ordered for her arrived. A footman carried in a large slipper bath, and a pair of house servants followed and filled the tub with buckets of hot water.

Greysteel took a chair beside the fire, his long legs stretched out before him. As Velvet undressed, she was acutely aware of her husband's eyes upon her. She had forgotten how much pleasure it gave her, and drew it out. She carried her precious gown to the wardrobe and hung it up. Then she slowly crossed the room, sat down on the bed and removed her pretty high-heeled shoes. She drew off her garters and stockings. "Charles invited me to go with you tomorrow."

All his attention was focused on her legs and he was only vaguely aware of what she said. "Mmm."

Velvet removed her petticoat and busk and was surprised that he remained in his chair, half a room away.

She stood up and gracefully stepped into the water. She looked at him through lowered lashes and saw that he still had not moved. She slipped down into the water. "May I have my soap from the dresser?"

He swore silently. *So much for vowing to keep my distance.* He handed her the scented tablet and sat on the bed to observe and enjoy her ablutions. Though his fingers ached to dip below the water, he restrained himself with difficulty. When Velvet was finished bathing, however, his hands refused to obey his will. They lifted the towel of their own accord, enfolded her and lifted her into his lap. As he patted her dry, he marveled anew at the flawless beauty of her delicate skin. Velvet. The name she had chosen for herself as a child was perfect for the woman she had become.

She slipped from his arms, donned a silk robe and pulled the bell cord. Then she sat down before the fire and waited for the servants to come and remove the bath. "What did you mean before when you said the Countess of Falmouth was out of favor?"

Greysteel drew closer and leaned his arm on the mantel. For some perverse reason he did not feel inclined to keep the king's secrets from his wife. "His Majesty invited her. After only one night he found that they did not suit and regretted the invitation. He longs for Barbara. None other can satisfy him."

Charles asked you to take her off his hands. If I hadn't arrived tonight, would you have done so? "Poor lady, indeed," she murmured. *Dear God, will I ever learn to trust him?*

When the servants came, he opened the door and gave them each a coin for their trouble. When they left, he locked the door.

Velvet felt suddenly shy and a little wistful that he seemed in no hurry to make love to her. She glanced at the bed, wondering if she should remain where she was, since Greysteel liked to be the one in control.

He fought the urge to pick her up and carry her to bed. Velvet had often chided him about his Arian control and he feared his overt possessiveness disturbed her. He decided to undress and go to bed, allowing her to choose if and when she would join him. He removed his coat, then his shirt, and sat down on the edge of the bed to take off his shoes.

From beneath her lashes she watched his every move. When he removed his shirt, a hunger to be held in his powerful arms rose up in her. She wanted him to press her soft breasts against the slabs of muscle in his chest, so that she could lift her arms about his neck and bury her lips against his throat.

She was irresistibly drawn to him, and without conscious thought she left the chair and walked a direct path to the bed. She stood before him and reached out to remove the leather thong that bound his black hair. It fell across his shoulders in dark, abundant waves and his virile, male beauty made her dizzy.

His fingers unfastened her silk robe and he worshipped her naked breasts and belly with his eyes before he allowed his greedy hands to cup and stroke her warm, rosy flesh. Now he was in a hurry, and quickly stripped off his breeches and hose. He opened his legs and pulled her close to stand between his muscled thighs. His palms moved over her round bottom and his fingers dipped into the tempting cleft between her bum cheeks.

She slid her arms about his neck, buried her lips

against his throat and rubbed her mons against his throbbing erection. She knew it was an invitation he would not refuse, and gasped with pleasure as he pressed her forward and thrust his cock into her hot, honeyed sheath, making her contract upon him and then pulsate. He drove in and up and the fierce pleasure was so intense she bit him to stop from screaming, but as his strong fingers tightened on her bum, her cries of passion urged him to plunge deeper, faster and harder. Suddenly they went rigid together for a long, drawn-out moment and then she felt his burst of white-hot seed erupt like a surging wave that engulfed all her senses.

He picked her up and lifted her into bed, then lay down beside her and gathered her into his embrace.

"I missed you, Greysteel," she whispered against his lips.

Lord God, not one-hundredth as much as I missed you. He kissed her gently, softly, now that their urgency had been quenched. He warned himself not to let his thirst to possess her body and soul consume him. His kisses were slow and lingering, rather than rough and demanding. He threaded his fingers into her curls, marveling at their silken texture, taking time to enjoy the feel and the scent of her hair. Though he had sworn to control his intensity and possessiveness, he soon became feverishly aroused again. Perhaps if he used his mouth to talk rather than kiss, he could curb his fierce desire.

"Will you come with me tomorrow? I want to buy some horses for Bolsover. I'd like to start breeding my own horses and believe Bolsover Castle would be ideal. I have enough sheep at Montgomery Hall. What do you think, Velvet?"

He had never discussed business affairs with her before and she was flattered. "I think it's a sound idea. My father bred horses there, and I know enough that sheep and horses shouldn't be raised on the same land. Is that why you wanted Mr. Burke?"

"Yes, I intend to make him head steward at Bolsover. After the coronation, I expect to spend a great deal of time there. I'd like you to come with me, Velvet."

Montgomery was asking her, not ordering her, and she was so thrilled that she arched against him, combed her fingers through his long, black lovelocks and set her mouth against his. It effectively put an end to his talk, and his kisses began in earnest. In spite of Greysteel's best intentions, his lovemaking became demanding and possessive.

The next day, the king, a few of his male friends and his brother Henry visited the Chesterford breeding farm. Velvet, mounted on a palfrey, was the only female and as she rode between Greysteel and Charles, it reminded all three of the day they had ridden together at Nottingham Castle.

Greysteel saw the easy companionship that his wife and the king shared, and he wondered if Charles would always be his rival for Velvet's love. He might be able to accept it, so long as he came first and received the lion's share of her devotion.

The king was interested in purchasing a couple of horses that he could race at Newmarket. He and

Henry went off to conduct some speed trials with the trainers.

Montgomery was more interested in broodmares, bloodlines, heats and studs. With Velvet's input he purchased six mares, four of which were already in foal. "I don't think I'll spend the money on a stud just yet. Perhaps my stallion, Falcon, can serve the mares." He grinned at Velvet. "The king simply takes what he wants and the Chancellor of the Exchequer pays for it. I have to fork over my money today, even though I'm not ready to take delivery yet."

Their time at Audley End sped by quickly. Their days were spent at the Newmarket races, or visiting horse farms. Their nights were spent together as they became adept at eluding the evening entertainments the rest of the company enjoyed.

Though originally Charles had planned to stay at his new country mansion for a fortnight, and though he had enjoyed himself immensely, by the tenth day he couldn't wait to return to London. He and Prince Henry, attended by Montgomery, rode at the head of the cavalcade and managed to arrive hours before those traveling by carriage.

Charles and Henry were greeted by their brother James, whom the king had named high admiral of England. "I trust all is well, James, and we were not invaded while I was gone?"

James laughed. "Nay, though there are many foreign merchant ships in the Pool of London."

Charles clapped Henry on the back. "This lucky knave won far more than I at Newmarket. He'll likely want to join you in your carousing tonight."

"Not me. I'm off to the ships to buy a Spanish leather saddle and perhaps some fine French fashions."

"You are in danger of becoming a dandy, my lad." Charles had a great affection for his young brother, who had known no luxuries until recently.

Charles left them and went straight to his cabinet. He took out a map and spread it across his desk. Then he sent his page, Will Chiffinch, to fetch Arlington, his secretary of state.

When Henry Bennet arrived, he soon learned that the king did not wish to indulge in small talk about Newmarket.

"Henry, correct me if I'm wrong, but I believe the lord chancellor's power does not extend to Ireland."

"You are absolutely right, Your Majesty."

"Good. I want you to prepare a warrant for Mr. Roger Palmer to be Baron of Limerick and Earl of Castlemaine . . . and let me have it tomorrow."

Arlington couldn't wait to share the news with his wife, and Lady Arlington immediately dispatched a note to her friend Barbara, in King Street.

An hour later, Prodgers greeted the lady, who was wearing a mask and a voluminous cloak. He escorted her up the back stairs to the king's private chambers and tapped on the door. It was opened without delay to admit His Majesty's *maîtresse en titre*.

Barbara plucked off her mask and flew into the king's welcoming arms. "Charles, I don't know how I endured your absence. It felt like you were gone a twelvemonth. I was wicked to refuse your invitation to Audley End and can only plead my belly. Will you forgive me for being cruel to you?"

"Don't I always, my love?" Charles kissed her pouting lips and brushed the dark red tendrils from her temples. His seeking hands slipped inside her cloak and caressed her voluptuous curves. "You grow lovelier each time I see you."

"I grow bigger, at any rate," she murmured.

"As do I." He pressed his erection against her soft belly. "I ordered supper up here. Come and share it with me." He removed her cloak and led her to a comfortable couch.

Barbara kicked off her shoes. "Lud, that's better."

Charles lifted her legs onto the couch so that she could recline more comfortably. He captured a foot and began to rub it, and then he massaged the other one.

Barbara sighed with pleasure. "Your hands work magic."

They shared a light supper, and Charles took delight in feeding her succulent morsels of lobster and prawns. The way she licked his fingers was a potent aphrodisiac to him. His anticipation of her joyous reaction to the gift he was ready to bestow upon her grew apace with his lust.

Barbara gave no hint that she knew about the title. She did not wish to spoil his pleasure when he told her.

Charles made short work of stripping off his garments, but lingered over undressing Barbara. She wore French silk undergarments especially designed to arouse a sensualist like Charles Stuart. He enjoyed the foreplay as much as coitus.

He carried her to the royal bed and exulted in the generous way she opened to him, giving all, holding back nothing. Charles did a masterful job of masking his cynicism. He knew full well that Lady Arlington would waste no time informing Barbara that she was about to become a countess. He smiled sardonically and took satisfaction from the knowledge that they were well matched in both passion and guile.

Chapter Twenty-three

Who Velvet's carriage arrived back at Whitehall, the hour was late and she was travel weary. She opened the door to her apartment and was happily surprised to find Greysteel there.

"Emma is at Roehampton," she said breathlessly, hoping that knowledge would induce him to stay.

The corners of his eyes crinkled. "Good. I won't have to send her down the hall tonight." He took her bag and set it down in the dressing room. "Are you hungry? The king and I arrived hours ago, so I've already eaten."

"To be truthful, all I want is my bed."

He saw the faint violet shadows beneath her eyes. "You've had a long day." He poured them wine. "Here, drink this. You'll be asleep before your head touches the pillows."

Greysteel helped her undress and lifted her into bed. Then he disrobed and hung his clothes in the wardrobe. He put out all the lights, climbed in beside her and gathered her to him.

"I always forget how small you are, until we lie in bed together." He feathered kisses along her brow.

"When I was a child, they called me a throwback. A little fish that's not worth keeping."

He smiled into the darkness. "Frizzy Lizzy, my imp of Satan." He raised her chin and kissed her.

"You taste of wine," she murmured happily.

"And you taste of wine and woman, a delicious combination."

Velvet felt so warm and safe cuddled against him that she soon succumbed to peaceful slumber.

Greysteel lay a long time, savoring the way she clung to him in sleep. The last time they had shared this bed, she had dreamed of Charles and called out his name. He pushed the thought away, confident that she would not do so tonight. Finally, he drifted to the edge of sleep. *Perhaps you are starting to love me, Velvet.*

In the morning, when she awoke, Greysteel was not beside her, but he had left her something on his pillow. Velvet picked up the crackling document and her eyes flooded with tears. *He has signed the deed to Roehampton over to me because he knows how much I love the Elizabethan manor.* "It's the loveliest gift I've ever received in my life!"

Barbara Palmer is to be Countess of Castlemaine. The news swept through the Court like wildfire. The king's mistress absolutely glowed as she reveled in the attention and newfound respect accorded a titled lady. Now, of course, she wanted chambers at Whitehall, and set about persuading Charles.

Velvet went to Pall Mall for another sitting of her portrait. She decided it would be a gift for Greysteel. It might shock him at first, but he cherished her flawless skin to such a degree, she believed he would grow to treasure the painting.

"I want to thank you for recommending my work." Mary Beale meticulously mixed the warm cream-toned oil paint she used to re-create Velvet's flesh. "Your kinsman Lord Cavendish has commissioned me to do a portrait of his future bride."

"I cannot take credit for that. His grandmother the Dowager Countess of Devonshire must have recommended you."

"Painting ladies of the Royal Court is such a feather in my cap. It will establish me in London's art world."

"Barbara Palmer is to receive a title. I'm sure she will want a portrait of herself as Countess of Castlemaine. Lely did her last one, but I'll suggest she come to you this time."

When Velvet arrived back at Whitehall, she changed her clothes and went down to the Presence Chamber, where Greysteel joined her for dinner.

"Young Henry collapsed in the stables this morning. He was eager to try out a new Spanish leather saddle, and went down like a stone. He was hot as fire when I got him to his feet."

"How awful! He was in good health at Newmarket."

"Here comes Charles." He left Velvet's side and went to greet the king. "Good evening, Sire. I hope Henry is better."

"No, I'm afraid he isn't. Dr. Fraser says he has a quartan fever. Must have picked the damn thing up from a foreign ship."

Barbara and Buckingham joined the king, and

Greysteel returned to Velvet and told her what he had said.

"Charles will be very concerned. He's always been like a father to Henry. The queen hasn't spoken to the boy in years. She should be ashamed of herself," Velvet declared.

The following day they learned that Prince Henry was covered with red papules and smallpox was feared. He was ordered to be isolated with only Dr. Fraser and the king in attendance. Charles had suffered a mild dose as a child and was immune.

The Countess of Castlemaine was conspicuous by her absence, and indeed many of the courtiers made excuses to leave Whitehall. By nightfall, Prince Henry's papules had turned into pea-sized blisters and smallpox was confirmed.

Charles was at his young brother's bedside all night, fighting to cool his fever, calm his delirium and clean up his vomit. His efforts, as well as his prayers, were all in vain. Henry, Duke of Gloucester, died before midnight, September 13. The king was distraught. The Court was in deepest mourning.

Velvet cried herself to sleep, comforted by Greysteel's arms. Never again would young Henry compliment her, dance with her or beat her in a card game. "The saddest part is that death has claimed him at such a tender age and only a few months after Charles was restored to the throne. It is so tragic."

The entire Court and half of London attended the Duke of Gloucester's funeral. Since it was out of the question to celebrate a coronation when England was in mourning, the king and his council made the decision to postpone it until spring.

"Barbara is absolutely delighted that the coronation will be celebrated at the end of April. She says her child is due to be delivered in February and she'll have her figure back by then. She can't wait to be on the front row," Velvet said with scorn.

Greysteel broached the subject that had been foremost in his mind for a few days. "I'm going to ask Charles for a leave from the King's Guard. My first lieutenant can competently take over as captain of the Blues. Now that the coronation has been postponed, it gives us the opportunity to take our horses to Bolsover and spend some time there. Mr. Burke is now free to take up his stewardship at the castle."

Velvet stared at him as if he had lost his senses.

"Is something amiss, sweetheart?" Greysteel was trying his best to be less controlling by telling Velvet before he approached Charles, rather than after the fact.

"I cannot go to Bolsover."

Greysteel searched her face, seeking an answer. "Why not?"

"I cannot desert Charles. He is in despair over Henry."

Greysteel stiffened. "Charles has his family and Barbara to comfort him."

"Barbara is utterly selfish and thinks of none but herself! You do not comprehend the devastation of losing one so young."

Greysteel thought of all the brave young soldiers who had died under his command; some had breathed their last in his arms or while he was tending their wounds. He would never tell Velvet of such horrors. "He will carry the sorrow forever."

"I am his devoted friend. I must try to ease his sorrow."

He rubbed the back of his neck to ease the tension that was building inside him. "I don't have to leave immediately—I can wait a week, or even longer, if that will help, Velvet."

"No, I cannot leave him. It is absolutely out of the question. Charles is withdrawing to Hampton Court Palace to grieve in private. I cannot go to Bolsover. . . . I'm going to Hampton Court."

Greysteel bit down on a curse. He had asked Velvet to choose between him and the king, and as he had always dreaded, she had chosen Charles. *She's still in love with him. . . . She feels his pain as if it were her own.*

"Very well—the choice is yours." His voice was curt, his mouth hard and set. Greysteel knew he could insist that she accompany him, but where would that get him? Certainly not to first place in her affections.

He withdrew immediately and went to the king's private chambers, seeking an audience. A Gentleman of the Bedchamber asked him to wait in the anteroom. In a short time he was ushered inside to Charles. The king, dressed all in black, his saturnine face haggard, looked pleased to see him.

"Montgomery, you are just the man I need. I have a mission for you, if you would be so kind as to oblige me."

"Anything, Sire. I and my guardsmen are at your command."

"My sister Mary is on her way from The Hague. I sent her a dispatch about Henry and she insisted upon coming. If you would meet her at Dover and safeguard her journey to London, it would relieve my anxiety."

"I'll make preparations immediately, Sire. Do you know how many will be in her party?"

"Not precisely. Mary will be bringing her ladies-in-waiting, but I believe she will leave her son, William, with his attendants in The Hague." Charles threw Greysteel a sardonic look. "She has an agenda, of course. She wants the house of Orange reestablished as the leading political family in the Netherlands and seeks my support to have William made captain general of the Dutch Republic." Charles heaved a weary sigh. "Everyone wants something."

Montgomery gave a rueful laugh. "I am no exception, Sire."

"There are no exceptions. What do you desire?"

"When I return, I would like a leave from my captaincy to go north and attend to my properties."

"I grant you leave, Montgomery." Charles searched his face. "I hope it won't be permanent, but that choice is yours."

"Thank you, Sire."

Greysteel returned to their apartment and found Velvet packing for Hampton Court. "His Majesty has asked me to go to Dover to escort his sister Mary to London."

"I'm so glad she is coming. She must be devastated, but brother and sister will be a great comfort to each other."

"This afternoon I intend to take Mr. Burke to Roehampton. Though the property is yours, it will benefit from the services of a steward. I shall bring Emma back."

His words were formal and brief, as if he were speaking to a stranger, and Velvet was well aware that Greysteel was still angry at her refusal to leave Charles and go running off to Bolsover. His attitude was totally unreasonable to begin with, but now that he wasn't going to the castle, his anger should have been rendered moot. But she knew it was not; her husband had withdrawn from her and already she could feel the distance between them. "Thank you," she said with equal coolness.

At Hampton Court, Velvet and Emma shared a suite of rooms. The formal gardens of the palace were calming and restful to the spirit, and the pair spent as much time as they could outdoors enjoying the late September sunshine. All too soon the cold winds of October would sweep in, stripping the leaves from the magnificent copper beech trees and withering the spectacular blooms of the autumn flowers.

The Countess of Castlemaine came to visit Charles, but she did not remain for more than a couple of days. The king required no entertainment, no music and no gambling, only solitude and long walks with his dogs for quiet reflection. Each day he attended a morning and an evening service in the chapel.

Barbara rolled her eyes at Velvet. "This place is enough to bring on a bout of melancholy, not dispel one. I have decided to return to London. If I leave, can Charles be far behind?"

During the course of the following week, Velvet and Charles often met by accident in the gardens and walked together. One day Emma went to enjoy the Elizabethan knot garden and Velvet decided to explore the maze. She saw a pair of spaniels race past her and knew Charles was about somewhere. When she arrived at the center of the maze, she found him sitting on a bench. "Would you like to be alone, Sire?"

"A king is always alone, Velvet, no matter the company." He smiled sadly. "I pray you come and sit with me."

"I believe that is true of all of us, Sire, not just kings." She sat down and looked up at him. "It is the human condition."

"I never thought of it that way. Perhaps you are right."

"Each of us must face loss alone . . . come to terms with it, and finally accept it."

"The loss of Henry seems particularly difficult."

"That is because of the injustice involved. He was so young, cut down before his prime, and just when you were in a position to give him everything, his life was taken away."

"And mine was spared."

"You feel guilty, but that will pass," Velvet assured him. "When my mother died in France, it was the injustice that was so heart scalding. She had sacrificed everything and lived in exile so many years. If only she could have lived until you were restored to the throne. She could have come home to her beloved country, returned to her homes that she cherished. When I came home without her, I felt guilty. But I finally realized that I was not to blame, and I have let go of the guilt."

"You are very wise for one so young."

"Not really. I still resent my father. Instead of my mother, it was another wife my father brought back to England. It is Margaret who will enjoy my mother's cherished homes. I feel that he betrayed my mother, and he betrayed me. As a result I find it extremely difficult to put my trust in a man."

"I put my trust in Montgomery and he has never failed me."

"I was not speaking of my husband."

"Were you not, Velvet?" he asked quizzically.

She quickly changed the subject. "If you talk to Henry, it will seem like he is still with you and it will ease your loss."

"Perhaps the spirits of those we love are always with us. You are a dear friend, Velvet. I hope you will befriend Catherine of Braganza when she comes to be my queen. I am sure she will feel lost and lonely at first."

"Of course I will be her friend." *We both know Barbara will resent her and try to make her life miserable.*

"I feel much better. Life is so short—we should seize our happiness with both hands. Shall we go forth?"

They stood up and began to make their way through the maze. They made a wrong turn and then another until they were lost.

Charles raised his eyes heavenward. "Henry, lead us from the wilderness."

A young hare leaped into their path from beneath the clipped yews. It saw them and sprinted away to the left. Laughing like children, they followed it and successfully made their way from the maze and back to the palace.

A few days later, Charles and the close friends who had spent time with him at Hampton Court returned to Whitehall.

Velvet went for another sitting with Mary Beale.

"Your portrait is almost finished, Lady Montgomery. I hope you are pleased with it."

"You have an amazing talent, Mary. You have made me look beautiful." Instead of making her happy, the painting made her feel sad. She had intended it as a surprise gift for Greysteel, but another rift had opened between them and she had no idea if it could be mended.

"You *are* beautiful. That is why I painted you as Venus!"

The goddess of love . . . how ironic. I wish with all my heart that my husband loved me. Instead he wants to possess me, own me, body and soul. He is madly jealous and resentful of my affection for Charles.

"You need not come for another sitting, my lady. I can finish the background and the border without you. You may come and see the final result next week."

"Thank you for all your work and patience." Velvet sighed. All the pleasure had gone out of having her portrait painted.

*   *   *

At Dover Castle, Montgomery addressed the dozen
Royal Guardsmen he had brought to escort the king's
sister back to London. They had arrived a fortnight
ago and still there was no sign of the lady.

"I just spoke with the captain of the Dutch merchantman that put into port this morning. He confirms
that when he left The Hague, Mary's ship was vict-
ualed and ready to make the voyage across the Channel. Unfortunately, the only thing the vessel lacked
was the lady herself and her maids of honor," he said
dryly.

"October gales could delay her departure further,
Captain."

"Aye, let us hope the lady realizes that November
weather will be even worse." Montgomery tried to
school himself to patience, though it was no easy task.
He hated being in a position where he had no control.
*I wanted to get my mares to Bolsover before the end of Oc-
tober, but royal ladies have a will of their own.* He thought
of Velvet. It seemed that *all* bloody ladies had a will of
their own.

"You may consider the next two days as leave from
duty. When you report back on Wednesday, try not to
be too hungover."

Montgomery found that cooling his heels in Dover
gave him too much time to think. Whenever thoughts
of Hampton Court Palace tried to intrude, he ruth-
lessly pushed them away. They always came back to
taunt him, however. The intimate setting was romantic, a place where the whole world could be shut out, a
palace with a haunting history of love, liaisons and intrigue.

Montgomery rode out to the chalk cliffs each day with a telescope from the castle. He gazed out to sea, sighting ships and identifying their flags. The lonely, windswept cliffs of Dover, however, were conducive to introspection, so instead, he began to visit the foreign vessels that docked in the port, examining their cargoes and seeking out treasures from far-off exotic lands.

Amazing what exotic treasures can be found in Pall Mall. Young Lord Cav glanced at the bill Charles Beale handed him, and then settled the account and added a bonus. "My cousin Velvet asked me to pick up her portrait. She couldn't trust such a delicate errand to a footman, you understand," Cavendish said with a knowing leer.

"Thank you, my lord. Your betrothed, Lady Mary, may have her first sitting tomorrow at eleven, if that is convenient."

Cav picked up the painting that had been carefully crated and wrapped with brown paper. "Most convenient, Mr. Beale."

Will Cavendish returned to Whitehall and asked his driver to carry the crate up to his chambers. When he was alone, he removed the painting, set it against the wall and stepped back so that he could appreciate the subject it portrayed.

His eyes narrowed as he looked at Velvet's naked image. *She certainly is an exquisite piece of flesh.* As he traced his fingertips up her long limbs and touched the red gold curls between her legs, his cock hardened and began to throb.

Little bitch! I'd like nothing better than to give you a good fucking, but you'd go running to that dark brute you married, and I'd end up in the Thames with a saber slash across my throat. Cavendish smiled. *I'll settle for something else I've always desired.* He put the painting back into its crate, and then he sat down at his desk to compose a letter.

Velvet was lonely. Though the Presence Chamber was filled tonight with the ladies and gentlemen of the Court who were her friends, the shallow existence of the Whitehall courtiers had begun to pall. Surely there was more to life than shopping, attending the theatre and losing money at cards.

She bit her lip and admitted that it was Greysteel's absence that was making her lonely and restless. When the devil would he be back from Dover, and once he returned, would he be willing to overlook their differences and try to make a success of their marriage? She stiffened as she saw Will Cavendish approach.

"What the devil do you want?" she snapped.

Young Lord Cav bowed politely, handed her an envelope and went to join his future bride.

Velvet tore open the envelope and read the note inside:

I have your Venus portrait in my possession. I will happily exchange it for the deed to Roehampton. If you do not cooperate, the naked lady will be placed in the hands of one so high it will cause a shocking scandal that will rock the Court.

Velvet gasped and crumpled the letter in her fist. The walls of the Presence Chamber suddenly came together, and the floor seemed to come up and hit her in the face. Her legs turned to water and Velvet collapsed in a faint.

Chapter Twenty-four

"*O*h, my dear! Lady Montgomery . . . do let me help you." The Countess of Suffolk lifted Velvet to her feet, sat her down in a chair and began to fan her as other ladies gathered round. Some were concerned, others merely curious, but all came to the same conclusion: The Countess of Eglinton was with child!

"Thank you," Velvet murmured, trying to catch her breath and compose herself before the semicircle of females. Relief washed over her that she was still clutching the note in her fist. *No one must learn of its contents.*

"Here, Velvet, have some wine." Anna Marie Shrewsbury offered her a glass of golden Rhenish.

"No, no, perhaps she shouldn't have wine if she's in a delicate condition," Lady Suffolk advised.

"I'm not . . ." Velvet thought better of denying it or suspicion might fall on the letter she held. "I'm not thirsty. Perhaps I'd better go upstairs and lie down."

"I shall escort you to your apartment," Lady Suffolk offered.

Buckingham glanced archly at Barbara. "Egad, your

condition must be catching. Perhaps I should keep my distance from you."

Barbara tossed her hair. "I'm simply setting the fashion now that I'm a countess, George."

Upstairs, Velvet sat down before the fire and with shaking fingers read the letter once again. "How the devil does that filthy swine know that I own the deed to Roehampton?" She began to piece things together and realized that she had told Christian Cavendish of Greysteel's gift to her when they had attended Henry's funeral. She cursed Lord Cav under her breath, and then she cursed herself for leaving her portrait at the Pall Mall studio after it was finished.

"The whoreson is blackmailing me!" She jumped up quickly, paced across the chamber and was swept with a wave of nausea. Velvet sat down quickly and covered her mouth with her hand. *Well, one thing is certain—the lecherous pig will never get his hands on Roehampton so long as there is breath in my body!*

She read the note once more and flung it into the fire, watching with glittering eyes as the flames devoured it. Velvet tasted fear. How wickedly impulsive she had been to have her portrait painted as a naked Venus. Now her sins would catch up with her, for she had no doubt that Cavendish would do as he threatened and cause a shocking scandal.

As Velvet sat gazing hopelessly into the fire, she remembered the lessons that had been drilled into her as a child. *Never show fear; it is a contemptible sign of weakness. Timidity, anxiety, alarm and panic are other names for cowardice! Pride must always take precedence over fright.*

Emma opened the door and hurried in. "Whatever

happened, my love? Lady Suffolk's maid told me that you fainted in the Presence Chamber."

"Don't be alarmed, Emma. I'm feeling much better now." On the inside she was riddled with fear, but the face she presented to her woman was calm and collected. She stood and went into the dressing room.

"What are you doing? You should rest, my dear child."

"I am going to wash my face and brush my hair. Then I am going back downstairs."

"If you are hungry, I can fetch you a tray."

"Thank you, no, Emma. I am hungry—ravenous in fact." *I am going to make a meal out of Lord Bloody Cav and lick my lips over the bastard!* Velvet selected an ostrich feather fan from the wardrobe and swept from the room.

Downstairs, she stalked through the chambers like a predator hunting its prey. She finally spotted him in the ballroom, dancing attendance on Mary Butler.

Velvet approached him directly, without hesitation. She knew that at all costs she must present a bold facade.

"Your attempt at blackmail is pathetic. You will get Roehampton over my dead body!" She wafted her fan with the assurance of a royal empress. "As for my naked portrait, you may display it in the Presence Chamber for all to admire." Her smile was a bold challenge. "Do your *worst*, my lord."

Velvet didn't sleep well that night. She wished she knew some way to get her portrait from Lord Cav's clutches, and worried hour after hour of what the consequences of her bravado would be. She fell asleep just before dawn and had a nightmare.

When she awoke, the sun was high and Emma was tiptoeing about so that she wouldn't disturb her. Velvet threw back the covers and set her feet to the floor. The moment she sat up, she vomited. "Oh, dear, I had no warning."

"That is how morning sickness takes you, my love."

Velvet's eyes went wide. "Do you really think I could be having a baby, Emma?"

"Of course you are. You fainted last night, and now your morning sickness confirms it."

Velvet counted on her fingers the days since the last time she had bled. "Emma, I think you are right! Oh, this is marvelous . . . a baby of my very own to love and cherish. I cannot believe my good fortune!" Her joy swept away her worry about Will Cavendish and put the paltry matter of her naked portrait into perspective.

Emma began to clean up the mess. "No more jumping out of bed like a cricket. You must lie quietly for a few minutes after you open your eyes in the morning."

"I'll clean it up, Emma. You shouldn't have to do it."

"What nonsense. You cleaned up after me when I was seasick coming from France. Now I can return the favor."

"Thank you. Oh, I'm so happy, Emma. . . . My heart is singing!"

"You need to nibble on dry toast and sip some ginger wine. I shall go to the kitchen and get some, if you'll be all right?"

"I'm perfectly all right. In fact, I'm euphoric!"

When Emma departed, Velvet went to the mirror

and put her hand on her belly. "Flat as a fluke," she muttered, but when she looked at her face, it was wreathed in smiles, and joy shone from her eyes. She immediately thought of Greysteel and wondered what his reaction would be.

"He'll be proud as a peacock." Velvet was thankful that she had married Greysteel Montgomery. He would be a perfect father. She thought fleetingly of the coolness that had developed between them before he departed, but quickly dismissed it. Her momentous news would heal their silly rift and draw them closer than they had ever been.

The following day, she again experienced morning nausea. This time, however, by moving slowly and sipping watered ginger wine, she found it soon passed off.

Velvet decided to visit her dear friend Christian at Bishopsgate and share her wonderful news. She decided too that she would mention the despicable actions of the dowager's grandson. Perhaps Christian could help get her portrait back.

As her driver, Ned, was harnessing her carriage horses, one of the king's Royal Guards rode into the stables.

"Fenton, are you back from Dover?" Velvet asked hopefully.

"Aye, Lady Montgomery. The captain sent me to deliver a message to His Majesty."

"You are alone, then? My husband isn't with you?" Velvet could not hide her disappointment.

"No, ma'am. The good news is that Princess Mary and her entourage have landed safely in Dover." Fenton bent closer so he wouldn't be overheard. "Captain

Montgomery will do his best to herd the gaggle of ladies as quickly as he can."

Velvet laughed. "I can see the relief on your face that you were not chosen to ride herd. It will take four or five days."

"Yes, ma'am—at least, ma'am."

"My dearest child, that is the most wonderful news I've heard since I learned Montgomery carried you off and married you." Christian rang for tea. "When your husband came to collect Mr. Burke last month, he never mentioned a word."

"Greysteel doesn't know! It happened when we were at Audley End, so I'm only about two months. I can't wait to tell him. You knew that he went to Dover to escort Princess Mary to London? Her ship has finally arrived, so he will be back in a few days."

"Yes, the queen is looking forward to Mary's visit. You are absolutely blooming, darling. Has anyone at Whitehall guessed your secret?"

"I believe the entire Court knew before I did. I fainted one night and everyone immediately assumed I was *enceinte*."

"What a dramatic way to announce you were carrying Eglinton's heir. Let's hope it knocked Castlemaine from the center of attention for once."

Velvet laughed. "Barbara is my friend."

"All the more reason to rub salt in her wounds whenever you get the chance, especially when you are the one who has inflicted the wounds. She must seethe with jealousy every time she looks at your flawless complexion, darling."

"Ah, that reminds me. I have brought you some of your favorite face cream."

"Thank you so much, darling. I have a flagrant fondness for your miracle cream. My skin used to be chafed and red as a lobster before you concocted your luscious face cream. You must try it on your belly—I trow it would prevent stretch marks."

"Stretch marks?" Velvet puzzled.

"Darling, you are such an innocent. Babies ruin your figure, especially large ones such as your husband is likely to father. Henrietta Maria and I used olive oil. It didn't help the queen much. She was such a tiny thing, and carrying Charles stretched her belly out of all proportion."

"I refuse to let that spoil the pleasure I am taking in this baby. It's a price I'm willing to pay."

Christian rolled her eyes. "The things we do for love."

Velvet sipped her tea slowly, and nibbled on a biscuit. "Did you by any chance tell your grandson, Cav, that Greysteel had deeded Roehampton to me?"

"I believe I did, darling. He asked me if I thought Montgomery would be interested in selling the Elizabethan manor to him. I told him your husband had signed it over to you as a gift and that you loved the place so much, there was no chance you would sell it. Did I guess right?"

"Yes . . . I would never sell it. But Cav didn't offer to buy Roehampton; he tried to get it by blackmailing me."

"Blackmail? Whatever are you talking about, darling?"

"It's a long story." Velvet sighed.

"Well, I have all day and vow to keep you prisoner until you confess all the delicious details."

Christian listened avidly as Velvet told her about asking Mary Beale to paint her in the nude, and by the time the tale was finished, the dowager was agog.

"You actually told him to display it in the Presence Chamber for all to admire? Darling, how I wish I had been there to witness your triumphant declaration!"

"It was all bravado—I was a quivering jelly on the inside! I'm afraid I said it in front of his fiancée, Mary Butler. She may refuse the match."

"Mary Butler is a child of fifteen and has no say in anything whatsoever. Ormonde will see that the match is brought off. The Devonshire fortune is the largest in England," Christian said dismissively. "My grandson always did lust after you. So now he has the nude Venus and you would like to get it back?"

"I thought it a total calamity that brought everything crashing down around me. Then I found out I was having a child and suddenly the portrait's importance in the grand scheme of things has become almost insignificant."

"Men are so venal, especially Cavendish men. This can actually work in our favor, if we stoop to their tactics. Naturally, I wouldn't hesitate to blackmail my grandson."

"Do you think it would work, Christian?"

"All I have to do is threaten to withhold my signature on a couple of documents pertaining to his inheritance, and voilà, your portrait is miraculously returned. When I come to visit Princess Mary, I shall issue the young lecher an ultimatum."

"I shall be forever in your debt."

"Yes, you will have to name me godmother to your babe."

"Thank you, Christian. That will be a great honor." Velvet set her teacup down. "I wish it were Minette who was visiting—we were such close friends. I've never met Princess Mary."

"It will be interesting to watch the byplay between Mary and Henry Jermyn," the dowager said with a coy look.

"The Earl of Saint Albans? Really?"

"Really! Gossip had them secretly wedded at one point, but Henrietta Maria stoutly denied that to me. Mary was a widow at nineteen, so who could blame her for taking a lover?"

"You amaze me. You know all the Court intrigue."

"Yes, one of the advantages of being a confidante of the queen. Old women indulge in endless gossip." Christian leaned forward confidentially. "One of Princess Mary's ladies is Anne Hyde, the chancellor's daughter. I have it on good authority that she is in love with Charles's brother James."

"The Duke of York has a reputation as a rake, I'm afraid."

Christian's laugh trilled out merrily. "Velvet, you never cease to amaze me. There is no greater rake in England than Charles Stuart, yet your infatuation for him blinds you to his blatant lechery. In your eyes, the king can do no wrong."

Velvet blushed as she thought about the long-legged dancer Charles had amused himself with at Roehampton. She thought of the fair Countess of Falmouth and the very pregnant Barbara Palmer. "No, I'm not blind to it any longer and his lax morals have cured me of my infatuation, but he will always be my friend, no matter how many mistresses he keeps."

"That is most creditable, darling. You will make a wonderful mother, Velvet."

Montgomery had never been so glad to see the smoke and church spires of London in his life. Princess Mary and her entourage of maids of honor traveled at a snail's pace, no matter how organized the captain and his King's Guard had been.

Unloading the ship from The Hague had taken two full days because the ladies had brought their horses as well as a mountain of baggage that included beds and furnishings. Princess Mary had stayed abed for forty-eight hours to recover from mal de mer. In addition to carriages, Montgomery had had to hire baggage carts, dray animals and drivers. With great efficiency he had sent a man ahead to reserve accommodation in Canterbury for their first stop after Dover Castle. This was a scant fifteen miles, yet he was greatly irritated to realize the royal party would not cover that reasonable distance.

Montgomery curbed his impatience and made alternate arrangements for the ladies. On the second day, his planning was more realistic and he sent a man to reserve lodgings only ten miles hence. The captain, however, had reckoned without the rain. Princess Mary adamantly refused to travel anywhere until the sun came out.

This is England, woman! Greysteel kept his tongue between his teeth, while he silently cursed royal ladies, their addled attendants and every other spoiled female on earth.

By the fourth day Montgomery had a damned good idea why shrewd Charles Stuart had not come himself to meet his sister. He thought with affectionate longing of the young men he had commanded in the army. Under horrendous conditions they had never complained, never bemoaned their lot, never been peevish or spiteful or thankless as were these pampered bitches.

On the sixth day he offered up a prayer of thanks that Velvet was an angel to live with, compared with these women. If his wife ever behaved as they did, he would take her over his knee and tan her arse, which was exactly what this lot needed.

It was day eight before they reached Southwark and prepared to pass over London Bridge. Montgomery dispatched one of his men to alert His Majesty that they would arrive at Whitehall sometime before dark. He scribbled a note to Charles, telling him the number of ladies as well as a tally of the baggage wagons, and advised that it would take at least two dozen servants to unload everything.

As it turned out, Beatrice, one of Princess Mary's ladies, began to feel poorly, and Mary herself developed a headache from the raucous sounds of London traffic. As a result they urged Montgomery to make all speed for Whitehall and the entourage arrived at five in the early evening.

While the baggage carts trundled into the courtyard, and the ladies' horses were taken to the stables, the carriages they were riding in stopped at Whitehall Palace's main entrance. The weather had turned bitter cold and the ladies, all proclaiming they were freezing, pulled their voluminous fur capes close as they stepped from their coaches.

King Charles, James, Edward Hyde, Henry Jermyn and the ever present Buckingham were there to greet the royal party. Montgomery dismounted and escorted Princess Mary to her brother. He waited while Charles embraced his sister, in case the king had further instructions for him.

His Majesty conveyed his gratitude with a speaking look and murmured, "I deeply appreciate this service you have done me. I am well aware it was a thankless task, Montgomery. I now grant you leave to be about your own affairs, but I shall miss you."

"Thank you, Sire."

Montgomery and his guards proceeded to Whitehall's vast stables to tend to their mounts. The Blues took great pride in their horses and never left the grooming, feeding and watering to the stablemen.

Charles greeted all his sister's attendants graciously. His easy charm was in complete contrast with Mary's personality. She was cool, aloof and haughty, as she thought befitted her station, and the king had no illusions that she felt much affection for either him or the other members of her family. He watched with melancholy eyes as Chancellor Edward Hyde and his daughter, Anne, had a touching reunion.

"Mary, my dear, an entire wing has been prepared for you and your ladies. I want you to be happy here and if there is aught we can do to make you more comfortable, please let us know. I took the liberty of arranging a formal reception to welcome you tomorrow night, assuming you would wish to rest this first evening at Whitehall."

"I have a fierce migraine and I am frozen to the bone. I ask that your servants set up my bed immediately."

"My dear, the beds are all aired and awaiting you."

"I insist on my own bed and feather mattresses, Charles. I would never sleep otherwise."

"It shall be as you wish, Mary. Apartments have also been readied for you at St. James's Palace, where Mother resides. The building is not so ancient and dilapidated as Whitehall. You may reside at either palace or alternate to suit yourself."

"How is Mother? Riddled with guilt over Henry, I imagine."

"One would imagine so, though she shows no trace of it. Ah, here we are. This entire floor is yours, to ensure privacy."

It was close to seven by the time Montgomery tended his horse and then supervised the unloading of the baggage wagons. He could have left it to the palace servants, but he wanted them to know which carts held Princess Mary's bed and baggage and the items she would demand immediately. Though he was glad his duty was over and done, his temper was still somewhat testy. He decided tomorrow would be soon enough to turn his guards over to their new captain and thank them for their loyal service.

He had brought a small gift for Charles that the king could experiment with in his laboratory. From a vessel in Dover he had obtained a canister of sodium nitrate known as saltpeter and another of potassium nitrate known as gunpowder. Greysteel carried the gift up to the king's private rooms and gave it to Prodgers.

"This is something I picked up for His Majesty to use in his laboratory. I got it off a ship from China."

"Thank you, Lord Montgomery. That was most thoughtful. His Majesty will be most pleased." Prodgers cleared his throat. "There is a matter I wanted to see you about, if you have a moment, my lord?"

"Of course, Prodgers."

"From time to time, ladies of the Court often send gifts to His Majesty. They give them to Will Chiffinch, who in turn passes them to me for presentation to the king."

Montgomery listened patiently, wishing he'd get to the point.

"Chiffinch passed along to me a portrait of Lady Montgomery, which I haven't.yet presented to His Majesty."

Montgomery's mouth set. He'd no knowledge of Velvet having her portrait painted, but if she wished Charles to have it, it didn't surprise him. "Is there a problem?"

"The matter is a delicate one, my lord. If you would come into the anteroom for a moment?"

Montgomery looked at the crate Prodgers indicated.

"Take a look at the portrait, my lord."

Greysteel began to lift the painting from the crate. "Judas Iscariot!" Velvet's naked likeness smiled at him seductively and he quickly shoved it back into the crate. "Who the hellfire has seen this besides you, Prodgers?" he demanded.

"Will Chiffinch gave me the crate, but I have no idea if he looked inside."

"I shall relieve you of your problem immediately."
He lifted the crate with hands that wanted to smash it
to smithereens.

Montgomery unlocked the chamber that used to belong to Emma, carried the painting inside and then
locked the door. Before he even removed his coat or his
sword, he opened the crate, lifted out the portrait and
stood it against the wall.

Without doubt it was one of the loveliest, most
provocative paintings he had ever seen. Velvet's flawless, porcelain flesh looked as if it would be warm and
alive to the touch. Her red gold hair looked as if it
would curl possessively about his fingers if he
brushed them across the shining waves.

An explosive combination of fury and jealousy rose
up in him. "The little bitch!" His fists clenched. "That
unfaithful, wanton little bitch!"

Chapter Twenty-five

The door flew open with such force it crashed against the wall.

"Greysteel!" Velvet, who had been sitting to put on her shoes, jumped up from the chair. Her pulse began to race at the sight of him. "I'm happy you're back. I missed you so much."

She saw his clenched fists and his thunderous brow. She sensed that something had upset him, but could not wait to share her joyous news. "I'm going to have a baby."

His eyes narrowed dangerously. "Who's the father?"

His words pierced her heart like three steel-tipped arrows. She staggered a little and, to steady herself, quickly placed her hand on the back of the chair. Her other hand went to her belly to protect her babe. Then her chin went up defiantly, and her eyes glittered emerald green.

"Charles, of course! What woman wouldn't want the king to be the father of her child?"

Montgomery stood staring at her. Raw pain tore

through his gut, and he fought the violence that rose up in his brain. His fists clenched tighter in an effort to control himself and his gorge rose with contempt. "Prodgers gave me your wanton portrait—it's in Emma's chamber."

He's seen the naked painting! "You don't understand."

His lips curled back and bared his teeth like a snarling wolf. "No, *you* don't understand. I am no complaisant Roger Palmer. The marriage is over, Lizzy. It's finished!"

Velvet stared at the door for a full minute after he left. She felt nauseated and, as if she were in a trance, walked over to the small refectory table to pour some ginger wine. Suddenly she picked up the decanter and hurled it at the door. It shattered into crystal shards and the wine splashed the ceiling.

"I hate you, Greysteel Montgomery!"

An hour later, Emma opened the door and as she entered, broken glass crunched beneath the soles of her shoes. "What on earth is that?" She hurried to light the candles and saw Velvet in the big chair. "Why are you sitting in the dark?"

"I . . . I was . . . contemplating."

"Are you unwell, my love? Did you drop a glass?"

"No, I deliberately threw the bloody thing!" Actually, she had not been contemplating. She had been sitting, thinking nothing, feeling nothing, with every sense numbed. Now she came out of her trance. "Come with me, Emma."

A mystified Emma followed Velvet down the corridor to the private chamber she used to occupy. The door was locked, but Emma had a key.

Velvet saw the crate immediately. "Help me carry

this." The two women each lifted an end and took it to the Montgomerys' apartment. "Thank you, Emma." She sat down in the chair, knowing she should be immensely relieved that the naked Venus was back in her possession, yet the thought that went through her mind was, *What does it matter now?*

As Emma carefully picked up the glass shards, Velvet sat deep in thought. *He said Prodgers gave him the portrait. That swine Cavendish must have asked Prodgers to give it to Charles. Because I wouldn't give in to his blackmail and let him have Roehampton, the whoreson carried out his threat.*

"Did you know that Princess Mary and her ladies have arrived? Have you seen Lord Montgomery yet?"

"Yes, I've seen the jealous bastard. Why do you think I hurled the bloody decanter? He thinks Charles is the father of my baby!"

"Who on earth would tell him such a wicked lie?"

"I did!"

Emma stared, aghast. "Perhaps you should lie down, my love."

"You think I've gone *mad*, when in reality I'm *mad as hell!*"

"Who are you mad at?"

"Men! I hate every last one of them," she vowed.

"Now, I know you don't hate King Charles. In fact, you should feel sorry for His Majesty. The servants tell me Princess Mary is demanding and thankless."

"He's a man. I'll be damned if I'll waste pity on the male of the species. All men are created evil!"

"You are angry at your husband," Emma guessed.

"No, I'm not. I'm completely indifferent toward

him. My marriage is over. I'm finished with Montgomery forever."

Emma did not dare contradict her when she was in this mood. "Did you have any supper, my love?"

"I don't remember."

"I'll go down and get you a tray."

"Please, just fetch me some more ginger wine, Emma. It truly does settle my nausea. I was wicked to waste it."

I don't need Greysteel Montgomery. I don't need any husband, she thought as she sat alone. *It isn't a tragedy that the marriage is over. It's merely a provocation I shall overcome, like an oyster takes an irritating grain of sand and makes it into a pearl.* Her inner voice mocked her. *Things are so simple when they are theoretical.*

Velvet moved over to the couch and laid her head against a pillow as she watched the flames in the fire. An old superstition said that when the flames burned blue, the Devil was present. *Old Nick is here tonight.*

When Emma returned, bringing fruit and biscuits along with the ginger wine, she found Velvet asleep. She decided against disturbing her, believing sleep would do her a world of good. Emma quietly retired to the daybed in the dressing room.

Just before midnight, Velvet awoke. She was disoriented for a moment before she realized where she was. Then the episode with her husband came full-blown into her consciousness.

"I hate you, Greysteel Montgomery!" she hissed aloud.

She sat up and looked at the dying embers of the fire. Not only did she feel lonely; she felt completely alone. Her hand slipped to her belly. *We are not alone.*

The angels will watch over us. Velvet felt strangely compelled to go down to the chapel and say a prayer for her baby. She thought of the angel statue that resembled her mother and knew she must seek her out.

She closed her chamber door quietly and shivered. The hallway was cold, but she had decided to forgo getting a cloak because it would have disturbed Emma. With quiet, slow, but determined steps, Velvet made her way through the labyrinth of Whitehall to the Queen's Chapel.

The corridor outside the chapel was shrouded in darkness and Velvet hurried inside toward the lights that were always kept burning. A couple, standing at the altar with the same Anglican priest who had solemnized her marriage, jumped apart guiltily.

"Who is she?" the lady at the altar cried.

Velvet knew immediately that the couple were being wed in a midnight ceremony. Moreover she recognized the bridegroom as James Stuart, the king's brother.

"It is Lady Montgomery, a friend," James told his bride.

"I . . . I am so sorry. . . . I didn't mean to intrude." She clearly saw that the bride was *enceinte.* Her pregnancy looked to be as far along as Barbara's. Christian had told her that Anne Hyde, the chancellor's daughter, was in love with James.

A tall, dark man stepped from the shadows and she saw that it was King Charles. "Come to me, Velvet," he said quietly. He waited until she stood beside him, then signaled the priest to continue. When the marriage was solemnized, Charles said, "We will act as witnesses to make it legal and binding."

Velvet put her signature beside that of Charles Stuart and curtsied deeply to Anne, the new Duchess of York.

The newlyweds departed quickly and quietly and the priest disappeared. Charles towered above her, looking down with melancholy eyes. "It must be kept secret for a little while. When it leaks out, as it inevitably will, we will say that they were secretly wed in Breda, last November, for obvious reasons. My dearest Velvet, I trust we may rely upon your discretion?"

"You may, Your Majesty," she pledged. She raised her eyes to the angel. *Please, watch over my babe and keep him safe.*

Charles led her from the chapel and along the corridor that took them from the ancient wing. The king spoke to one of his Royal Guards who stood duty. "If you would escort Lady Montgomery to her chambers, we would deeply appreciate it." Charles swept off his hat and bowed. "Good night, my dear."

At her door, she thanked the guard and wondered fleetingly if he would tell Montgomery that she had been with Charles at one in the morning. *What does it matter? The damage has been done.*

Velvet undressed quietly in the dark and slipped into bed. She couldn't get the picture of Anne Hyde's face out of her mind. The young woman, who was her own age, had been pale as death. *For five months she must have been racked with fear and anxiety. How frightening it must be to find you are carrying a child when you are unwed.* Velvet pictured the young woman trying to hide her pregnancy beneath loose garments and flowing capes. She felt infinitely sorry for Anne. She doubted that James Stuart would make a good husband, for all he was a royal prince. It was, nevertheless, a blessing that he had married the lady; otherwise the scandal for the chancellor's daughter would be horrendous.

The following morning Velvet awoke when Emma drew back the curtains in her bedchamber. "I fell asleep on the couch," Velvet said.

"Yes. I didn't disturb you. I knew if you awoke later, you would go to bed. I brought fruit and biscuits for you."

"Thank you so much." Velvet was relieved that Emma had no idea she had left her chambers last night. She was the keeper of a royal secret and she had vowed to keep her mouth shut.

She sipped her ginger wine, nibbled on the biscuits and enjoyed a pear and some plums. When she was certain her tummy would behave itself, she took her bath and dressed.

Midday, Thomas knocked on the door and she invited him in.

"If it is convenient, my lady, I must get his lordship's garments and personal articles from your apartment. Lord Montgomery has asked me to pack all his belongings."

"It is perfectly convenient, Thomas. How soon does he plan to leave Whitehall?"

Thomas gave her an odd look as if she should know these things better than he. "Tomorrow, I believe, ma'am."

"Montgomery has asked His Majesty for leave. Have you any idea how long he plans to be away?"

Thomas cleared his throat. "Well, I believe he will travel first to Roehampton. Then he and Mr. Burke are to take delivery of some horses at Newmarket and take them to Bolsover Castle. After that, his lordship intends to go home to Worksop, Nottingham, and then visit all his other northern properties. He mentioned returning for the coronation."

"But that's not until April!" *I'll be ready to have my baby!*

"No, ma'am . . . I mean, yes, ma'am."

Let him go and good riddance. "You'll find his things in the dressing room, Thomas." *I hate you, Greysteel Montgomery!*

That night, Velvet took pains to look her best for Princess Mary's reception. She had never met the king's eldest sister, but from all the accounts she'd heard, she didn't expect to become friends with her. On the other hand, Velvet decided she would speak to Anne and let her know the bride had an ally.

"Mary holds her royal nose high so she won't have to breathe the same air as the rest of us," Barbara commented to Velvet. "The bitch snubbed me. Seems that the rank of countess is beneath her. I shall have to ask Charles to make me a duchess!"

Buckingham looked his cousin directly in the eye. "Even the wicked get worse than they deserve in this world."

"Talking about yourself again, George?" Barbara smiled smugly. "That Anne Hyde is as plain as a pikestaff and her figure is rather lumpy to boot," Barbara said spitefully. It was common knowledge that she hated the chancellor, Edward Hyde, who made no secret of his total and complete disapproval of her.

"She is a clever young lady, Barbara; do not underestimate her," Buckingham advised. "Quite witty too, a rare talent that attracts the male of the species."

"I'm an expert on what attracts the male of the species, George—I'd say it's more tit than wit!"

Velvet laughed. "I wonder if my friend Christian Cavendish is here tonight. Have either of you seen the dowager countess?"

"Probably run off with Montgomery," Buckingham drawled. "Both seem to be missing tonight."

"Christian is too shrewd to saddle herself with a man," Velvet declared blithely.

"He's only been back a day and already there appears to be trouble in paradise," Buckingham declared.

"Never taunt a mother-to-be, George," Barbara warned. "Every one of us has the unpredictable temper of a tigress. I'm off to separate the siblings—I believe Charles has kissed Mary's arse quite long enough."

Velvet watched the pair as they approached the king and his sister. They were ever a team. Buckingham would occupy Mary so that Barbara could monopolize Charles.

Velvet made her way to Mary's maids of honor and smiled warmly at Anne Hyde.

"Good evening, Lady Montgomery. I believe it was your husband who gave us safe escort from Dover. I wanted to thank him, but I don't see him here tonight."

She saw that Anne still looked pale and the haunted

look she'd had last night had not yet vanished. Anne gave Velvet an anxious glance that seemed to plead for her friendship. "Please call me Velvet. My husband cannot be here, but I welcome you and hope you will be happy here in London."

Anne murmured, "I feel rather faint, but I don't want anyone to notice."

"Here, take my fan. I just found out that I'm having a baby, and I fainted right here in the Presence Chamber not long ago. Shall we go and find some seats?"

Anne tucked her arm through Velvet's and the two ladies strolled over to some gilt chairs. Before Anne had a chance to sit, she drew in a quick gasp of air as if she was in pain. She looked down in horror as bright spots of red appeared on the folds of her blue gown. "I must go upstairs—please help me?"

Velvet immediately shielded her from those close by and led her newfound friend to the door. She put her arm about Anne as they ascended the stairs and then hurried to the bride's chamber. She helped Anne onto the bed and raised her feet by propping pillows beneath them.

Anne clutched Velvet's hand. "You mustn't tell anyone."

"You need help. I must get the doctor." She went out into the hallway where royal maids were moving in and out of the chambers that accommodated Mary and her ladies.

One of the chambermaids approached her. "Is that another lady who has fallen ill with fever?"

"Another?" Velvet asked sharply.

"Lady Beatrice is delirious. The doctor is attending her."

"Dr. Fraser is here?" Velvet's heart raced with hope.

"Yes, my lady. He's in this chamber with Lady Beatrice."

Velvet tapped on the door but didn't wait for an invitation. She opened it and hurried into the room. The doctor was washing his hands, while his nursing assistant tried to give the patient a fever potion.

"Lady Montgomery, what is amiss?"

"Dr. Fraser, you are needed immediately. Please follow me."

"Ods blood, don't tell me it's more fever!"

Velvet shook her head and put her finger to her lips. "Come." After they entered Anne's room, she carefully shut the door.

Dr. Fraser immediately surmised what was happening. "Help me to undress her." Between them, they removed most of Anne's garments. "Mistress Hyde, Anne, my dear, are you in pain?"

"I had one tearing pain, but that's all—it has passed."

"You have lost blood, but your contractions have stopped." He glanced at Velvet with guarded speculation.

"It's all right, Dr. Fraser. I know."

"There is only a slight chance that we can save the child." He asked carefully, "Am I right in my assumption that you are unwed, my lady?"

"Certainly not," Velvet blurted. "Anne is the Princess of Wales. She and James were secretly wed in Breda last November."

Dr. Fraser blanched. James was heir to the throne, which made Anne's child next in line. "You must remain in bed with your legs and feet elevated. I will give you a sleeping aid because rest is the only thing that may avert a miscarriage. I will arrange for a nurse to sit with you tonight and instruct her to call me immediately if aught untoward happens. Lady Montgomery, will you stay until the nurse comes?"

"Of course, Doctor."

When he left, Velvet moved to the bed. "Are you comfortable?"

"The sleeping draft tasted horrible, but other than that I have little discomfort."

Velvet squeezed Anne's hand and found it chapped and red. "Tomorrow I will bring you some cream that will heal your skin. Would you like me to tell your husband?"

Anne looked horrified at the suggestion. "No, please, no. Oh, God, I hope we can keep all this from my father."

Velvet pictured the straitlaced and honorable Chancellor Hyde and shuddered. All his moral tenets would be compromised by the foolish actions of his daughter. By the time the nurse arrived, Anne had drifted into a light sleep and Velvet left. She returned to the Presence Chamber and found that Princess Mary was again monopolizing Charles, telling him in minute detail about the excruciating pain of the migraine headache that kept returning.

Barbara had taken herself off to the supper room, but Buckingham had not yet deserted the king. Velvet placed her hand on George's arm and gave him a speaking look.

Intuitive as always, Buckingham addressed Mary. "I do believe that Henry Jermyn has a remedy for migraine." He offered Mary his arm. "Shall we consult him?"

Jermyn, for the sake of discretion, was keeping his distance from the royal lady.

Velvet stood on tiptoe and whispered to Charles, "Sire, the bride is in danger of grave misfortune."

His brows came together in an anxious frown. "What?"

She shook her head and placed a finger to her lips. She watched him leave and felt sorry for him. *I shall go up to bed; otherwise I will be the one explaining to Barbara why Charles deserted her.*

As Velvet lay abed with her emotions in turmoil, sleep eluded her. Everything that had happened focused all her thoughts on her own baby. Though her belly was still flat, she placed protective hands over her child and vowed to take every precaution to keep him safe. *I could be having a baby girl.* She tried to picture such a child and could not. She had no trouble, however, imagining a son who looked exactly like Greysteel Montgomery. Velvet prayed for Anne and the child she was carrying. *If I lost my baby, it would break my heart.*

When Velvet awoke the next day, her morning sickness had vanished. She looked from her window and saw that it was snowing. Everything had turned white overnight and the world looked fresh and clean and bright in spite of the fact that Montgomery had probably already left her, alone at Whitehall.

She banished thoughts of self-pity by thinking of poor Anne's plight. She breakfasted with Emma, but never mentioned anything about last night. She went to her shelf of jars and pots, selected a cream that contained glycerin and calamint, and went to visit Anne. When she arrived, a maidservant opened the door. Velvet approached the bed and saw that Anne was in a deep sleep. She had no idea how much the royal servant knew, so did not question the woman. "When she awakens, would you tell her that Lady Montgomery brought her some hand cream? Thank you."

Out in the hall were half a dozen servants carrying fresh bed linen. "How is Lady Beatrice this morning?"

"She must be better, my lady. Princess Mary and all her maids of honor moved to St. James's Palace."

Velvet was astonished. "When did they go?"

"I don't rightly know, my lady. When I came on duty this morning, they were already gone."

That's strange! They must have moved in the night. On the way back to her own apartment, she passed the staircase that led to the king's private apartments. She was curious as a cat about what had happened, but knew she could not knock on Charles's door with her questions. She nodded to the guard and walked on. Then she heard someone behind her and turned.

"Dr. Fraser. I've just come from Anne's chamber and found her sleeping. Has the danger passed?"

Fraser's face was set in grim lines and he looked extremely worried. "Danger?"

"The child," Velvet prompted.

"There was no child," he said shortly. Then he hesitated and said more kindly, "There *is* no child."

"I see, Doctor."

"The lady is resting comfortably."

"I understand that Beatrice, the lady who was delirious with fever, moved to St. James's Palace."

Dr. Fraser sagged visibly. "She was moved because her fever could be contagious to Anne. Just a precaution, my lady."

"But why would Princess Mary move to St. James's if the fever is contagious?"

Fraser looked as if he had just been caught out in a lie. "I am following His Majesty's orders, Lady Montgomery."

"Forgive me, Doctor. I understand you must exercise discretion." Velvet, walking along beside Fraser, decided to change the subject. "I am going to have a baby, Doctor."

"Congratulations, my dear. When is the happy event to be?"

"Probably in late April or early May. I was suffering from morning sickness, but it seems to have passed."

Fraser hesitated, as if he wanted to say something, but didn't quite know how to put the matter. "Lady Montgomery . . . Velvet, promise me you will stay away from St. James's Palace. I don't want you exposed to the contagion."

"Thank you, Doctor. I promise I will stay away from there."

At lunchtime, Velvet mingled with the ladies of the Court, determined to keep her ears open for any gossip. During the meal she spoke with Anna Marie Shrewsbury, Lady Arlington and Bess Maitland. They spoke in disparaging whispers of how haughty and arrogant Princess Mary acted, but no one seemed aware that she had moved from Whitehall to St. James's.

In the afternoon, Velvet donned her fur cloak and went for a walk in the snow. Her footsteps led her to St. James's Park. As she stood staring up at the windows of the palace, it finally dawned on her that the king's sister would not have been moved away from Whitehall unless she too had come down with fever.

This time, Velvet did not hesitate. She went straight to the king's private apartments and knocked on the door. There was no answer so she knocked more insistently. Prodgers came to the door and told her that His Majesty did not wish to be disturbed.

Velvet pushed past him and opened the door of the antechamber, with Prodgers on her heels.

"I'm sorry, Sire. Lady Montgomery could not be dissuaded."

"It's all right, Prodgers," Charles said wearily.

Velvet stood before Charles, trying to control her agitation. "Anne lost her child in the night."

Charles's melancholy eyes sought hers. He nodded. "Yes."

"That's not all, is it?" she asked apprehensively.

He shook his head sadly. "No, that's not all, Velvet."

"Princess Mary and her ladies were moved in the night because they have come down with fever."

"Just a precaution, my dear."

"They were moved from Whitehall and put in isolation."

"We cannot risk infecting the Court, Velvet."

"Infecting them with what?"

The king did not reply.

"Damn you, Charles, tell me!"

"It is smallpox. Again."

"Oh, sweet Jesus, no!" Her heart contracted. "My husband traveled with them for at least eight days. He has no idea he has been exposed to smallpox!"

Chapter Twenty-six

"Can't you wait until morning?" Emma asked anxiously.

"Absolutely not! Greysteel more than likely has already left Roehampton and is on his way to Newmarket. I don't have an hour to lose . . . nay, not a minute." Velvet was hastily packing a bag with her warmest clothes when a knock came on the door. She opened it quickly and told the page she had summoned to find Ned, her driver, and have him harness her carriage.

"It's going dark, and it is still snowing," Emma declared. "It is not safe to go tonight."

"Emma, you don't really think I'm worried about my safety, do you? My husband's *life* may be in danger."

"I'll pack my bag," Emma said with resignation.

"You will do no such thing. If Greysteel has been infected with smallpox, he will be contagious. There will be enough people at Roehampton to worry about, without adding you." Velvet bit her lip. "I do thank you sincerely, Emma, for your generous offer, but it's best that I go alone."

"But you won't be alone, will you, my love? What about your babe?"

"Please don't burden me with guilt. I love Greysteel with all my heart and soul. He must come first."

"I'm sure all your worry is for naught. Lord Montgomery is young and strong. I've never known him to get sick."

"I hope and pray that you are right, but I remember that Prince Henry was young and strong, yet he died horribly." *I mustn't tell Emma, but I have a premonition that is driving me.*

She slipped a couple of jars of cream made from cowslips and cucumber into her bags and then sat down to pull on her fur-lined boots. When Ned arrived he picked up her bags and Emma put on her cloak to come down with her. Velvet eyed the crated portrait, apprehensive that if she left it unattended, it might again fall into the wrong hands.

"Help me carry this, Emma. I'm taking it with me."

Ned put her bags inside the carriage and the two women lifted in the wooden crate. Emma enfolded her. "You are very brave."

"No, I'm not, Emma. I'm more afraid than I have ever been in my life before. Take care of yourself."

As the carriage rolled along, Velvet was thankful that Roehampton was only a few miles from London, and yet tonight it seemed a long journey. Once they left the city and were out on the open road, the east wind was fierce, blowing the snow almost horizontally and making the visibility extremely poor.

Velvet huddled in a corner, pulling her fur cloak

close about her and stamping her feet in an effort to keep them warm. Her breath formed white vapor clouds and she worried that Ned might not be dressed adequately. She also hoped that the horses didn't feel as cold as she did. She prayed that her husband and Mr. Burke had not yet left Roehampton. If they had, she knew she could go no farther tonight.

Finally the carriage slowed and stopped, but she knew they hadn't arrived at the manor yet, because Ned had not turned in at the driveway. She was about to open the door when Ned did it for her.

"I cannot find the opening to the drive, my lady. It's hereabouts somewhere. You sit tight while I have a gander."

In a few minutes, Velvet felt the carriage lurch forward and she guessed he had found it. But no sooner did it turn than it stopped dead. She tried to open the door, but a drift of snow prevented her. Then Ned cleared away the snow and managed to get it open.

"The coach is stuck, I'm afraid. I'll walk up to the house and get help, my lady, if you'll sit tight."

"No, I will not sit tight. We'll leave the carriage and baggage here and unharness the horses. We cannot leave them here in the cold. Help me get out."

Velvet stood in snow up to her knees. "I'll unfasten this one, if you can go around and get the harness off the other."

The breath from the horses rose in white vaporous clouds as they moved restlessly between the carriage shafts. It took a lot of struggling to get the leather tracers off the animals, and Velvet soothed them with soft, reassuring words.

When they were finally free, Ned urged, "Why

don't you get on your horse's back, my lady, and I'll lead them both?"

"You could ride the other one, Ned."

"Nay, I know how to drive, but I'm not much of a rider." He gave Velvet a boost up onto the carriage horse and they began to slowly plod their way to the manor through the blinding snow. It took them the better part of an hour before they reached the stables. Velvet was weak with relief to see that Greysteel's horse was in its stall. She trusted Ned to feed the animals and give them a good rubdown.

"Come up to the house when you are done, but go around to the back kitchen door. I'll tell Mrs. Clegg to expect you. She will feed you and plenish a room for you, but please keep away from Lord Montgomery. When he went to meet Princess Mary's ship at Dover, he was exposed to smallpox."

"Is the rumor true, then, that His Majesty's sister has the smallpox?"

"Yes, Ned. The king himself told me."

Velvet, tired and wet, had used up almost all of her strength. She took a deep breath, pulled her cloak tightly about her throat and stepped back out into the elements, determined to battle her way to the house.

Greysteel sat alone in front of the fire, contemplating locking up for the night. Mr. Burke had retired to bed an hour ago. Mrs. Clegg was still puttering about in her kitchen, but Montgomery hesitated to urge her to retire to her own quarters with Alfred, because the kitchen was her domain and she truly enjoyed being the controlling proprietor without interference.

The snowstorm had prevented him and Mr. Burke

from setting out on their journey north. *If the temperature rises a couple of degrees, the snow will turn to rain and wash away all the drifts that have accumulated. It's just as well we didn't leave today—this damnable headache won't let go.* He rubbed his temples and contemplated getting up from his comfortable chair.

A thud at the front door brought him out of his lethargy. Greysteel stood and strode through the great hall, wondering who the devil could be arriving. The door opened and what looked like an animal fell across the threshold. Montgomery saw fiery tendrils of hair and realized it was his wife bundled up in fur.

"Velvet! What the hell are you doing here?" He helped her to her feet and glared at her with angry consternation.

"My hands and feet feel frozen," she said through blue lips.

"You are wet through! Come to the kitchen—you need something to warm you up."

Velvet held up an imperative hand. "You stay here! I'll go myself." She pulled off wet gloves and dropped them. As she moved toward the kitchen, she unfastened her cloak and let it fall to the floor. She saw Greysteel move toward her. "Stay!"

Greysteel stopped. *She's commanding me like I'm a bloody dog.* He raised his voice so it would carry into the kitchen. "What the hell is going on, Velvet?" He could hear the voices of Bertha and his wife, but could not discern their words. He moved closer so he could hear.

"I'll heat this barley broth, and warm some bread too. There'll be plenty for Ned when he comes," Bertha said.

"I want you to give him a room near yours. I don't want him upstairs near the master bedchamber, and I don't want you or Alfred up there either. Do you understand, Mrs. Clegg?"

"Yes, my lady. I hope yer precautions are all for naught."

"So do I, Bertha. I hope it with all my heart."

Greysteel puzzled why precautions were necessary, but the thoughts brought pain to his head.

"Take this mug of broth and be careful you don't burn yourself. Let me put a drop of whiskey in it . . . there."

"Thank you. I'll take it with me while I talk to Greysteel."

He moved back from the kitchen door, but when Velvet saw him, she glared so sternly, he retreated back to the sitting room. She followed and they each took chairs before the fire.

As he looked at her, his mind conjured her beautiful naked portrait, and he remembered her cruel words about carrying the king's child. *She was lying to me— please, God, she was lying!*

"Greysteel, Princess Mary has come down with smallpox."

He saw her hands tremble and the broth almost spilled. "Holy God, she must have contracted it from the ship. That's how Henry caught it, you know." He knelt to remove her boots. "Charles must be consumed with worry."

"At least one of her ladies has it, possibly more. You were in close contact with her for almost ten days. You too may have been infected."

He jumped back from her. "You must be mad to

come here and risk exposing yourself. You should have just sent a message!" He moved away from her across the room. "You are putting your child in unnecessary danger too, Velvet."

"Danger, yes, but absolutely not unnecessarily. If you fall ill, I shall be here to nurse you."

"No, you will not. As soon as you have warmed yourself, you are getting back in your carriage and returning to London."

She smiled wanly. "My carriage is stuck in the snow at the end of the drive. Ned and I had to unharness the horses and bring them to the stables."

"You struggled through this storm to get to me?" Greysteel was incredulous. What she'd done had taken a great deal of courage, tenacity and love too, if he wasn't mistaken.

"How are you feeling? Do you have a headache or backache?"

"No, nothing like that," he lied. "I never felt better."

"Thank God! To be on the safe side, you must keep your distance from Mr. Burke and the Cleggs."

"And *you*, Velvet, for Christ's sake!" He brushed his hair back from his forehead with an impatient hand. "What about the King's Guards who also traveled with Mary—have any fallen ill?"

"I don't honestly know; I didn't wait to find out." She took a deep breath. "I think I should go up to bed. I'm exhausted."

"You take the master bedchamber and I'll use one of the guest rooms. Put your boots near the hearth. After you go up, I'll put the guard in front of the fire down here."

Velvet put her boots to dry. "I want *you* to sleep in

the master bedchamber tonight. If you are in a guest room and you do get sick, it will be an added burden for me to move you."

"We'll do it your way, if it makes you feel better."

"Thank you, Greysteel. Good night."

"It is I who thank you, Velvet. What you have done is so selfless and I know how much courage it took."

"It's not courage, Greysteel." Her voice dropped to a whisper. "It's love."

He could not hear the last word, but he knew what he wanted it to be. *I love you with all my heart and soul, Velvet.* "Good night . . . get some rest and we'll talk in the morning."

He watched her leave; then he returned to the fireplace and set the protective guard in front of the fire before he sat down. *Mary Stuart mustn't die! Charles must not lose both a brother and a sister to smallpox in such a short time. Fate couldn't be that cruel!*

Yet Montgomery knew that Fate could be that cruel. More than anything in the world he wanted Velvet to return to London, but Fate had stepped in and disabled her coach. He willed the contagion to leave him untouched; at the same time he pressed his hands to the staggering pain in his head.

"I have to face up to it. The possibility I've caught smallpox is very real." He forced himself to get up from the chair and go up to bed, for as Velvet had pointed out, she didn't need the extra burden of moving him.

When he reached the top of the stairs, he thought about awakening Mr. Burke. They could lock Velvet in her room to try to keep her safe. He heard a noise in the master bedchamber that distracted his thoughts.

When he opened the door, he saw that a log in the fireplace had fallen to ash, and he suddenly shivered from
the coldness of the room. He replenished the fire before it went out entirely, and then he undressed slowly
and crawled into bed.

Velvet opened her eyes and for a moment wondered where she was. Then she remembered. She was
at Roehampton, where she had fallen into an exhausted sleep in one of the guest bedchambers. She
was no longer tired and slipped from the bed to look
out the window. The moon was still fairly high, rather
than low on the horizon and this told her that it wasn't
yet morning. She guessed that she had slept deeply for
about four hours.

She felt chilled in her petticoat and sat on the bed to
pull on her stockings. Then she put on her green velvet gown. Silently she gave thanks that she had
reached the manor without incident and that Greysteel
was well. Then she said a prayer for Charles and asked
God to give him strength.

She lit a brace of candles and wrote a note for Mr.
Burke, telling him about Princess Mary's smallpox and
her husband's exposure to the contagion. She gave the
steward strict instructions to keep his distance from
Montgomery. Then moving slowly, with as little noise
as possible, she left her chamber, walked down the hall
to Mr. Burke's room and slipped the note beneath his
door.

Velvet felt invisible threads drawing her to
Greysteel. She tried to resist their pull and told herself
that she should not disturb his sleep. When she got to
her own door, however, she could not go through it.

She gave in to her instincts and went down the hall to the master chamber.

She turned the knob quietly and held her breath, hoping the door wouldn't creak. She slipped inside and moved toward the bed. There was no sound, no movement, and she assumed he was asleep. Then she saw him. The moonlight showed that he lay naked and his eyes were open.

She reached out and placed her hand over his. Its burning heat alarmed her. "Greysteel!" She felt his forehead and knew he had a raging fever.

Velvet lit all the candles in the room and came back to the bed. His pewter eyes glittered feverishly; his face and neck were flushed a dull red. His lips were dry and cracked.

"Water," he murmured indistinctly.

She rushed to the washstand and poured some water from the jug into a cup. She lifted his head and tipped the water toward his dry lips. She watched him drink avidly and when he would take no more, she eased his head back down onto the pillow.

Velvet poured the rest of the water from the jug into a bowl. She took it to the bed with a sponge and a towel, and then she bathed his face, neck, chest and arms. She did it over and over in an effort to cool him down. Fear gripped her, but she knew that so long as her hands were busy, it would help to keep her devastating thoughts at bay.

She drew in a swift breath when she heard a knock at the door. She crossed the room and asked who was there.

"It's Mr. Burke, my lady. I read your note. . . . I hope

you are wrong about Lord Montgomery catching the contagion."

"I am afraid I'm not wrong, Mr. Burke. He has a raging fever. For safety's sake, I want you to move to the servants' wing. I've exposed myself to Greysteel and I wish to remain the only one at Roehampton who is exposed. I'll do the nursing, but there will be lots of other things you can do."

"I'm so sorry, Lady Montgomery. I'll do whatever you ask."

"As soon as it stops snowing, you can retrieve my luggage from the carriage. It got stuck at the end of the drive. You and Ned, my coach driver, can help Mr. Clegg to keep us supplied with wood for all the fires. I'll need water to bathe my husband and something for him to drink . . . water and whatever else you think best. I know how staunch you are, Mr. Burke. Your presence is a great comfort to me."

"Thank you, my lady."

"Don't come to the door again. Leave the stuff I need at the top of the stairs, and you can leave me a note too, if there is something you want to tell me."

"Is there anything you need right away?"

"Yes, you can fetch an empty bucket and some fresh drinking water, thank you."

Velvet pulled a chair to the bed and sat down. She had no idea if her husband could understand her, but she knew she must talk to him, mostly for her own sake. "I know how ill you feel, Greysteel, yet you refuse to moan. Let it out—I'm sure it will make you feel better, my love."

He moved his head on the pillow so that he could see her, but he uttered no sound.

"It's almost dawn. The wind has dropped and the snow is not falling as thickly. Once it stops and the sun comes up to sparkle on the soft blanket of white, I'm sure that Roehampton will look more beautiful than it ever has before. I love this old manor. It is the loveliest present I've ever had, or could ever have, and I thank you for it with all my heart, Greysteel."

"Water," he mumbled.

Velvet went into the hall. She found an empty wooden bucket and a fresh jug of drinking water. She carried a cup to the bed and again raised his head. He was burning hot to the touch and when he drank eagerly, she prayed it would lessen his fever.

A short time later she heard a noise in the hall and, when she went to investigate, found a bucket of warm water and a note. Mr. Burke told her that he had put borage leaves in the wash water that would turn it red. He also said that he was boiling some borage leaves and seeds, a common drink for fever.

When Velvet sponged her husband with the red-tinted, piquant-smelling water, she saw old scars on his torso that she'd never noticed before, and it reminded her that Greysteel had been a soldier most of his life, fighting to put Charles on the throne. "This is one battle you must win," she told him firmly.

By the time morning arrived, she saw that he had closed his eyes and he seemed to have fallen into a fitful sleep. An hour later she found her two bags and the wooden crate at the top of the stairs. "Thank heaven they left my portrait crated up!" She dragged it into the bedchamber, and went back for her bags.

The day went by in a blur. She changed her clothes

and put on a peach-colored gown. It was an impracti-
cal shade for nursing duty, but she chose it for her
beloved. She remembered eating food that had been
brought upstairs, but later could not recall what it was.
As twilight neared and Greysteel's fever had not broken, terror of the coming night gripped her.

She lifted his head so he could sip the borage drink,
but he turned his face away, and muttered incoher-
ently.

She fought her fear, feeling contempt for her
cowardice. She turned his face back to her and stared
intently into his fever-bright eyes. "Robert Greysteel
Montgomery, you are going to have to give your control over to me. I am in command tonight and you
must obey my orders. Do you hear me, Captain?"

"Cold," he murmured.

She pulled up his blankets and tucked them about
his neck and when her hands came in contact with his
skin, it scalded her. She tried to mask her alarm and
went to the fire to put on coal and wood to make it
blaze hotter. "Are you warmer now, love?"

He shivered and his teeth chattered. "So cold."

Velvet began to panic. *He's cold because he's going to
die!* She brought an extra blanket from the chest and
threw it over her husband, yet still he shivered. Instinct took over and told her what to do. She threw off
her clothes, slid beneath the covers and enfolded him
in her arms. Though he shivered, his naked flesh
against hers felt hot as fire. "The heat from my body
will seep into yours. . . . Feel it, Greysteel, feel the
heat!"

Gradually, his shivering stopped and he lay still as
death. She rubbed her cheek against his shoulder. Her

throat choked with tears. *If you die, this is the last time we will ever be able to sleep together.* She swallowed the lump and whispered, "I love you more than life. . . . Feel my love seep into you."

Chapter Twenty-seven

When Velvet woke, dawn was lighting the sky. She was immediately aware that she lay against Greysteel's back. She could feel wetness between their bodies and her heart lifted in hopes that his fever had broken. When she slid down the covers and peeled her body away from his, she saw to her horror that his back had a dozen large blisters filled with water and she had broken some of them.

She scrambled from the bed, hurried around to the other side and found him awake. "Can you understand what I say, love?" He closed his eyes once, and she took it to mean that he could. She saw his tongue come out to lick cracked lips, but his mouth had no moisture in it. She poured him a drink of bitter borage and water and held it to his lips. Miraculously, he drank it and she knew he had given his control over to her.

When she cupped his unshaven cheek, she found him still warm, but not raging hot. She sent up a swift prayer of thanks and then quickly donned her petticoat. She emptied the old wash water into the wooden bucket and filled the bowl with fresh. Before she began the sponge bath, she examined him all over to see how many smallpox vesicles had erupted. As well as the dozen on his back, he had at least another dozen scattered over his arms, legs and belly. Velvet decided to fudge the number. "Greysteel, you have maybe twenty pox on your body, but miraculously, you have none on your face."

When his mouth curved slightly, she knew he had understood. She sponged his front first, moving slowly so that she would not break any more blisters, and then she washed his back, which was the worst. She put a clean linen case on the pillow and urged him to lie on his stomach. Again she emptied the dirty water into the bucket and carried it to the fireplace.

She scooped up all the ashes from the hearth and put them in the bucket too and carried it to the top of the stairs. Along with fresh water, Mr. Burke had left her another note.

I've seen outbreaks of smallpox. At first the blisters are filled with a watery fluid, and the fever subsides. Very shortly, though, they fill up with pus and the fever returns along with delirium. Prepare yourself for this dangerous stage.

She heard someone at the bottom of the stairs and shouted, "Lord Montgomery has about twenty-six pox at the watery stage."

Mr. Burke called back, "Once they turn into pustules, they take at least five days before they start to dry up, if—"

He didn't finish the sentence, but Velvet knew he had been about to say, "If he lives that long."

"Thank you. Is anyone else showing symptoms?"

"No, my lady, but if you start with a headache, I want you to promise me that you won't hide it from me."

"I promise, Mr. Burke."

Velvet returned to the bedchamber, dispirited at the thought of Greysteel's fever returning. She knelt at the hearth and lit a new fire with paper and kindling. *How provident that I learned how to light a fire when I lived in Saint-Germain.* She smiled sadly as she remembered the difficult times in exile, but realized that she was a better person because of the lessons hardship had taught her. She thought back to her childhood and laughed. *Oh, Lizzy, you were so spoiled!*

She washed her hands and face, quickly ran the brush over her hair and donned the peach-colored gown. Then she returned to the chair beside the bed.

"Thank you," Greysteel murmured.

She smiled into his eyes. "You may not talk—only listen. You have to save your strength."

"I love you, Velvet."

Tears sprang to her eyes. He had never told her that before. *Perhaps he mistakes love for gratitude.* "I love you, Greysteel. I'm sorry, but by tonight you will have your fever back. You have always been a warrior and I want you to fight the coming battle with all your might. You are not alone. I am here with you and if we join our forces, we will be victorious!"

"You are my shield, my buckler," he murmured. His eyes closed and he drifted off to sleep.

Velvet used this time to break her fast. She ate the

food that had been left at the top of the stairs. She set down the empty platter and took the wine back to the bedchamber.

By nightfall, the vesicles on Greysteel's body had filled with pus, and his temperature soared. She sponged him over and over with cooling water, but in spite of her efforts he became delirious. He threw off his covers and began to rave. It was all about death and dying and Velvet realized he was speaking of the young soldiers who had served under him. He ranted about surrendering them to General Monck.

The revelations tore at her heart. "You surrendered control to save their lives!"

He sat up and grabbed her arms. "He never loved her! She died for me. . . . I'll see her at last."

Velvet did not pull away. She guessed he was speaking of his mother. "No, Greysteel! I need you here. Our child needs his father. You must fight *Death*; it is our enemy!"

His grip tightened. "You'll leave me."

"No, no, I won't. I'll stay here with you," she vowed.

"You love Charles. . . . You'll go to Charles."

"I promise on my soul I will not go to Charles. I will stay with you forever. I love *you*, Greysteel. . . . I *need* you!"

"Velvet?"

"Yes, it's *Velvet*," she assured him.

Gradually, his desperate hold on her slackened and he fell back to the bed. His raving stopped and though he did not close his eyes, his restless movements quieted.

Is he leaving me? The thought terrified her so much

she poured herself some wine to give her courage for what might come. She drained the glass and then she lay down beside him and took his hand. She put her other hand on her belly and gained a little comfort from knowing that all three of them were together and touching. "I'm here, love. I won't leave you."

The next thing she knew, it was morning, and Velvet realized that she had slept. She jumped up in alarm and rushed to the other side of the bed to see if her husband was still alive. As she bent close, his eyes opened and she heaved a sigh that the crazy light had gone out of them. His fever was coming down, his senses were returning to him, and she dared to hope that the crisis had passed.

I shouldn't have had that damned wine. My head is throbbing!

"You are going to live, Greysteel! The danger is over. You are going to recover from smallpox!" She didn't know if it was true, but she wanted him to hear it and believe it.

At St. James's Palace, King Charles knelt in prayer at his sister's bedside, while a priest administered the last rites.

"She's gone, Sire." Dr. Fraser placed his hand on Charles's shoulder. "Her suffering is over."

Charles got wearily to his feet. *Disease and Death play no favorites. A princess has no more sway than a page.* "Thank you, Dr. Fraser, I know you did all that was humanly possible. Her husband died from smallpox, you know, and how ironic that I survived it when I was a boy, yet within weeks it has taken my brother and my sister."

"You had a *mild* dose of smallpox, as did I. All my nurses have survived the pox. It is no wonder that servants who are pockmarked are in high demand."

"How is Lady Beatrice?"

"I have hopes she will survive, but one of the Royal Guards who accompanied Princess Mary from Dover has come down with it. I hope Lord Montgomery wasn't infected."

Charles remembered the look of fear on Velvet's face when she learned it was virulent smallpox. "Pox plays no favorites."

Charles spoke to the priest. "Would you accompany me to my mother's apartments, Father? The queen will be inconsolable."

An hour later, the king returned to his own chambers at Whitehall. He had many difficult letters to write. The first and foremost would have to be to his late sister's son, William. *Is there a kind way to tell a boy who is not yet eleven that his mother has died?* Charles knew that there was not.

Though the king did not wish to become embroiled in a diplomatic squabble, he knew he would do his best to fulfill Mary's last request. He would write in support that William be made captain general of the Dutch Republic.

With a heavy sigh, he dipped his quill and wrote to his beloved sister Minette. It was the second time in as many months that he had had to inform her about a sibling's death. Charles sent up a silent prayer to keep his youngest sister safe from all things that might harm her, including her effeminate French husband, Philippe. *I'd love to invite Minette to visit England, but if she caught smallpox, the guilt would kill me.*

Charles wrote hurried notes to his brother James, who had taken himself off to Hampton Court, and to Barbara, who was also absent from Whitehall. *Both have excellent survival instincts!* He summoned Will Chiffinch and asked him to deliver the notes.

Before he forgot and other pressing matters took his time and attention, Charles wrote a letter to Velvet at Roehampton.

> *My dearest Velvet:*
> *It is with great sadness that I tell you my sister Mary has gone to her eternal rest. She must have picked up the virulent smallpox infection from the ship on which she sailed to England. To my great sorrow, sailing vessels cannot be thoroughly cleansed of these dreaded contagions.*
>
> *I have written to Minette with the sad news and hope you will write her also. I know a letter from you will greatly cheer her. Dr. Fraser has every hope that Mary's maid of honor Lady Beatrice will survive, and we are praying for her recovery.*
>
> *I most sincerely hope with all my heart that Greysteel escapes this pestilence. I will never forget the look of fear on your face for your husband when you learned that he had been in close contact with a victim of smallpox. It told me how deeply you love him. You should never have gone to Roehampton to warn him, risking the infection to yourself, but I know nothing in this world could have prevented you from going to him. I envy Montgomery your devotion, because I know I will never have so great a love.*
>
> *Please let me know that all is well with you. After my coronation, when Catherine comes from Portugal to be my wife and queen, I know I could have no more worthy Lady of the Bedchamber to serve her than you, Velvet.*

Whitehall is not the same without the Earl and Countess of Eglinton.
    Your devoted servant,
    Charles Rex

He sanded the letter, melted the wax and pressed his seal ring into it. Charles had never felt so alone in years. He went into the anteroom and spoke to Prodgers. "Would you see that a messenger takes this letter to Lady Montgomery at Roehampton?" He rubbed his hands together as if to rid them of something that clung. "I shall bathe and change my clothes. Then would you be good enough to find Buckingham for me? I don't wish to dine alone tonight."

Charles walked across to the window and looked out at London. The snow, which only days ago had made everything look pristine, had now turned to dirty slush. He knew and accepted that a pristine world was an illusion. Dirty slush was the reality.

Greysteel pushed the covers from his body and sat up. He looked down at his chest with critical eyes, assessing the crusted scabs that decorated his flesh. His hands went to his cheeks and forehead and he realized that Velvet had been telling him the truth: His face had escaped the scarring vesicles.

He swung his legs to the carpet beside her chair and reached out to gently touch his sleeping wife's hand. His fingers jerked back in alarm. *She's on fire!*

"Velvet—sweetheart—wake up!" It was then that he realized she was not asleep. Her lids were only half closed and beneath them her eyes were glazed with fever. "Christ's blood, I've given you the smallpox!"

He left the bedchamber, went to the head of the stairs and called down. "Mr. Burke!"

In a moment he heard Burke's joyous voice carry up the staircase. "My lord, you are going to recover!"

"Don't come up. Velvet is burning with fever. I'm going to get fresh sheets, then put her to bed. I'm weak as a bloody kitten, Burke—can you get me something to put in my stomach?"

"Right away, my lord. Your wife wouldn't listen—she insisted on nursing you herself."

"Yes, we both know she can be an imp of Satan."

"I'm so glad you understand. Do you fancy some ale?"

"I'd kill for a jug of ale. Can you brew me some borage for Velvet's fever?"

"We have some in the kitchen. It's so bitter, you refused to drink much of what we made for you."

"Leave it at the top of the stairs." Greysteel hurried to the linen press for clean sheets and towels, then returned to Velvet. He stripped the bed and remade it. Then he filled the washbowl with cool water and knelt before his wife.

He removed her clothing with gentle hands and his gut knotted when he saw how flushed her skin was beneath her garments. He sponged her face, arms, shoulders and breasts, over and over with the cool water, and then dabbed her dry with the towel. He touched his lips to her temple. "My angel love."

He picked her up tenderly and laid her on the bed naked. There was no way he was going to struggle putting on and taking off a nightgown. A sheet would do to cover her nakedness until she began to shiver.

When he heard noises in the hall, he went out to re-

trieve a kettle of stew, a jug of ale, and the decoction of
borage and water. *Thank God he brought stew and not
broth. I'll likely need all my strength to get that vile potion
into Velvet.*

Greysteel ate the food slowly. He didn't want to ag-
gravate his empty stomach. When he had eaten, he
quaffed the ale, relishing every mouthful. He set down
the empty tankard and focused his full attention on
Velvet.

"You asked me to give my control to you and
though it was difficult, I did it, sweetheart. You saved
my life, and now I am going to save yours. But I need
your help, Velvet—I cannot do it alone. Do you understand me?"

Her eyes, which were a dark glittering green,
sought his. Her fevered lips could form no words.

His big calloused hands raised her head and he
tipped the borage drink against her lips. When she
took a few sips, he praised her and encouraged her to
take more. He knew she still understood him. Later on,
when she became delirious, he knew, she would not.

"Velvet, my love, in the past I know you have had
trouble putting your trust in me. This time, however, I
am giving you no choice. You must trust me with your
entire mind, your heart and your soul when I tell you
that you *will* recover. I would never lie to you about
something this crucial."

May God forgive me!

He tipped the cup once more and was amazed that
she did not balk at the bitter potion. *Perhaps females are
better patients than males. This particular female has every
bit as much courage as a soldier.* The thought brought a
lump to his throat.

Greysteel sat beside her until she slept. Then he went to the mirror and examined his torso, twisting about and counting his smallpox scabs. *It's a miracle I survived!* He picked up a pot of the face cream Velvet had made and daubed a little on each of his sores. It was common belief that they were better off left open to the air, to dry, but his experience had taught him that wounds healed better if they were soaked until the scabs came off, and then kept moist with ointment. Firsthand knowledge had taught him that a moist environment sped healing and reduced scarring. He decided to experiment with his own pox, so that he could use the knowledge on Velvet, if she survived. He slipped on a shirt. *Take that thought out of the air immediately. She will survive!*

During the next three days, Velvet's survival became doubtful as her fever raged higher until she became delirious and then began to vomit.

She looked at him with terrified eyes. "Anne lost her baby and I'll lose mine! She was bleeding in the Presence Chamber and I tried to keep it hidden from everyone."

Greysteel made no sense of what she said. "You are not bleeding, darling, I promise you. Trust me, Velvet."

That night, Greysteel lay beside her on top of the bed. It helped him regain his strength, and Velvet seemed much calmer when he talked and murmured comforting, reassuring words to her. He held her hand tightly so she could not leave him.

In the morning, he saw that the water blisters had formed, and knew that for the time being, her fever would subside. Her vesicles rose up along the sides of her torso, rather than her back or front. She had a few on the insides of her arms and up underneath her armpits on the warmest parts of her body. She had one above her left breast, and the one that almost broke Greysteel's heart had formed on her right cheek.

Her skin was so perfect, without blemish. How could a loving God be this cruel? How could you do this to Velvet and leave my face unscathed? He quickly told himself that this did not matter; all that mattered was that she survive. *It makes no difference to me, but it will matter to Velvet.*

He knew the worst stage was still to come. When the vesicles filled with yellow pus, how would his beloved bear it? He knew that during the days of her fever, when she had eaten nothing, she had lost weight. He feared she would not be strong enough to endure this grave illness. They had already received one miracle when he survived smallpox; they would need divine intervention to be blessed by two. Greysteel had scant time to pray, however; Velvet needed a drink and a sponge bath.

Between sips, she asked fearfully, "My baby?"

"The baby is safe, love. Trust me, Velvet."

She finished the bitter borage. "It's *your* baby." Her whisper was intense.

"I know that, sweetheart." He began to bathe her. *I don't care if it's the bloody pope's baby. All I care about is you!* Greysteel sponged over the vesicles, rather than avoiding them, but he did it with infinite care.

"I want you to rest now and try to sleep. It will give you strength to fight what lies ahead."

She nodded and closed her eyes, content her baby was safe.

Greysteel's appetite was improving daily and he ate

his food at the stair head, where Mr. Burke had left it. He didn't want the smell of it to nauseate Velvet. She had vomited too much.

Today, a letter sat beside his jug of ale. He picked it up and saw that it was from Christian Cavendish to Velvet. He hurried back to the bedchamber, but found his wife asleep. He hesitated only a moment before he opened it. Even if she was lucid when she awoke, Velvet would ask him to read it to her.

He sat down in the chair beside her and opened the envelope.

> *Dearest Velvet:*
>
> *When I learned of Princess Mary's tragic death from smallpox, I hurried to Whitehall and learned from Emma that you had gone to Roehampton, to warn your husband that he had been exposed. I am extremely worried for you and Montgomery and beg that you immediately let me know that you are well.*
>
> *The contagion is spreading, I'm afraid. My grandson, William, came down with a mild dose, but unfortunately for him his once handsome face will be badly pockmarked. You will likely believe this is just punishment for stealing the portrait you were having painted for Greysteel. Using it to blackmail you into exchanging it for Roehampton was an evil deed for which he has now paid.*
>
> *Henrietta Maria is in deepest mourning for her daughter and I believe the queen is secretly suffering from guilt over the way she treated her son Henry. I warrant she now realizes that the estrangement can never be rectified. It's a lesson we should all heed; never let silly quarrels separate us from those we love.*
>
> *I feel great empathy for Charles. Ruling a kingdom does not protect him from tragedy and sorrow. Though*

*surrounded by both fawners and friends, I believe he is
the loneliest of men.*

*If I do not hear from you shortly, I shall come to Roe-
hampton to see for myself how you are faring.*

Fondest love,

Christian

Greysteel set aside the letter and approached the
crate in the corner of the chamber. He lifted out the
portrait and gazed at it with new eyes. *Velvet had this
painted for me! She is exquisite—far lovelier than Venus.
That bastard Cavendish was blackmailing her and she didn't
dare come to me.*

Montgomery's heart was heavy. With shame he relived the confrontation over the painting and how he
had closed his ears when she protested that he didn't
understand. He glanced over at his sleeping wife. *I
vow to make it up to her.*

Quietly, he carried the portrait over to the fireplace
and set it on the mantel. *She'll see it when she awakens.*
He changed his shirt and sat down beside his wife. "I
love you, Velvet," he whispered softly. *When you open
your eyes, I'm going to tell you just how much. I've waited
far too long to tell you how I cherish you.*

Another disturbing thought struck him. *I denied her
Bolsover Castle, the only thing she ever asked of me. I said I
wanted it for our children, but I also wanted it for myself, to
breed horses.* He searched for the deed in his strongbox
and signed it over to his wife. He immediately felt better.

Greysteel jerked awake. He had no idea how long
he'd been asleep, but the chamber was bathed in dark-

ness. Velvet was thrashing about and moaning piti-
fully. He quickly lit a branch of candles and set them
on the bedside table. He went rigid when he saw that
her blisters had turned into pustules. He knew she was
suffering and cursed heaven.

Desperately, he began to murmur comforting, calming words. "Lie quietly, my sweetheart. Breathe
deeply, slowly. Hold on to my hands and use my
strength to carry you through your pain. I love you,
Velvet; feel my love."

The sweat stood out on his brow as he knelt beside
her, clasping her burning hands. To his great relief, he
saw that his words were having an effect and she was
quieting. Finally, she lay still and her breathing
calmed. Then to his great horror, her breathing slowed
and finally stilled. "Stay with me," he ordered frantically, but he knew in his bones that Velvet had drawn
her last breath.

Chapter Twenty-eight

Greysteel let go of his wife's hands and pressed down on her chest as if he were working a pair of bellows to get air into her lungs. The vesicle on her breast burst open and the pus sprayed across his chin. "Breathe, Velvet, breathe!"

He lifted his hands to see if she was breathing on her own and cursed that she was not. Then he took the curse back and began to mutter a plea. "Christ, please help me. Don't take her from me. Give me strength and guide me."

A desperate idea came to him. Since she wasn't breathing for herself, he would simply have to do it for her. Without hesitation he lowered his head, covered her mouth with his and breathed into her mouth. He felt air on his cheek coming from her nostrils and realized it was his own. He firmly pinched her nose and breathed again. Once, twice, three times he blew air into her mouth before he felt her shudder. The pustule on her cheek erupted. Greysteel wiped the matter from his eye and resumed his mission with unwavering intent.

* * *

Velvet was in an unknown place that frightened her. It was quiet and then someone calling her name broke the stillness. She turned and saw a tall, dark figure beckoning to her, and she felt something was familiar. Had she had this dream before?

"Charles!" She felt weak with relief as she took a step toward him. Suddenly, she stopped. *That isn't the king beckoning to me; that is Death!*

"Greysteel! Greysteel! Where are you?" Velvet turned and saw another tall, dark figure that spoke her name.

"Velvet."

It was Greysteel. . . . She would know him anywhere. She realized what her mother had told her long ago was true: *He will always keep me safe.* Without hesitation Velvet went to her husband.

Greysteel had no idea how long he persisted, but slowly, miraculously, he realized that Velvet was breathing on her own. Her breaths were shallow, and he hung over her, ready to resume his labor of love. His eyes flooded with tears of relief as he realized he had succeeded in snatching her from Death.

He feared she still hovered on the brink, and clutched her hands to keep her from leaving again. "Stay with me, Velvet!"

For the next thirty hours, Montgomery did not dare to close his eyes as he watched over his beloved wife. Finally, sleep seduced him and he drifted off to a place that was rife with danger. He drew his sword and slew a score of dragons.

When he awoke the chamber was filled with daylight and he found Velvet watching him. His dark face lit with a smile and to his great joy she responded in kind. He immediately brought her a drink. All he had was ale, but she gulped it thirstily.

He went out to the stair head and called down. "Mr. Burke, Mrs. Clegg, I think Velvet is over the worst—I believe she's going to recover! Is everyone else all right?"

Burke came to the bottom of the stairs. "Thank God! All has been so silent up there, we feared the worst. How blessed we are that no one else at Roehampton has been infected."

"That's a relief. Best to keep your distance—I warrant Velvet is still contagious. Would you ask Bertha to make her some barley water? She needs something to give her strength."

"A letter has arrived for Lady Montgomery from His Majesty the King at Whitehall."

"When I go back into our bedchamber, bring it upstairs."

Greysteel returned to his wife and found that the ale had made her sleep. He took the opportunity to bathe and change his clothes, and then he went out to get fresh linen for her bed.

He picked up the letter from Charles and brought it back with the clean sheets. He sat down and pondered if he dare open and read his wife's personal correspondence.

Since he'd played the role of spy before and his conscience had recovered, he slit the red wax with his thumbnail. He knew that reading a letter from Charles to Velvet was playing with fire and he fully expected to get scorched.

As Montgomery read the letter, he felt Charles's

overwhelming sadness at losing both a brother and a sister. Somehow it didn't seem right that royalty was not immune to infectious diseases. He read the words that showed the king's concern for him.

> *I will never forget the look of fear on your face for your husband when you learned that he had been in close contact with a victim of smallpox. It told me how deeply you love him. You should never have gone to Roehampton to warn him, risking the infection to yourself, but I know nothing in this world could have prevented you from going to him. I envy Montgomery your devotion, because I know I will never have so great a love.*

Greysteel sat stunned. He was the one who had always envied Charles. The words revealed that the king and Velvet did not love each other, except as friends, and Montgomery felt shame at his suspicion. *I swear by Almighty God that I will never be jealous again.* He lowered his eyes and finished reading the letter.

Charles is right. He could have no more worthy Lady of the Bedchamber to serve Queen Catherine than Velvet.

Montgomery lit a candle and melted the wax seal so that she wouldn't know he had acted dishonorably and read her letter.

He put it on the bedside table along with the one from Christian. Greysteel felt as if a great weight had been lifted from his heart, and went out to the stair head.

"Mr. Burke, I'm starving to death. Would you ask Mrs. Clegg to cook me a rump steak?"

"I hear you, my lord," Bertha shouted. "If your appetite is restored, all must be well with your world."

"It is indeed, Bertha. I could eat an ox, tail an' all."

When he returned, Velvet roused and looked at him with large emerald eyes. She held her arms away from the sides of her body. "I hurt," she whispered.

"I know, love, but that's such an encouraging sign." *I feared you had gone beyond pain.* Greysteel grinned. "I'm going to bathe your scabs and matter with some borage water."

Velvet attempted a smile. "Scabs and matter . . . how amusing."

"If we don't laugh, sweetheart, we'll cry."

When Greysteel began to sponge her pustules that were now starting to crust over, he handled her so gently that she did feel like crying.

"I don't mean to upset you, Velvet, but I accidentally broke open one on your breast and the one on your cheek. I'd like to try an experiment and keep them moist and covered."

"Experiment on my face?" She smiled at his audacity.

He brought fresh water and cleansed her cheek. Then he dabbed the weeping sore with her face cream, cut a small square from a linen sheet and pressed it over the cream.

Velvet gazed up at her portrait. "I'll never look the same."

"You are far lovelier than the painting, you know."

"The eye of the beholder . . ."

He carefully sponged the sore on her breast, daubed it with cream and covered it with a square of linen. "Let's hope these stay put." He took away the dirty washbowl. "Now you are going to drink some barley water to put some spunk in you."

"Controlling swine," she murmured tenderly.

He grinned. "I wonder if there's an herb I could brew to control your tongue?"

"Hemlock."

He couldn't bring himself to smile at her deadly humor. He heard a noise on the landing and went out to find a jug of barley water and a fresh goblet.

Greysteel went about the procedure of getting the restorative drink inside her the quickest way he could. Some spilled onto the bedding and he was glad he'd had enough foresight to feed her before putting clean sheets on the bed.

By the time he finished his ministrations, he could see that his wife was exhausted. "Try and rest, love. I'll go and eat; hopefully, it will give me enough strength to keep the upper hand over you."

Montgomery was ravenous by the time his dinner tray was laid at the top of the stairs. He carried it into a guest bedchamber and devoured everything Bertha had cooked for him, including a jug of autumn ale. Food had never tasted better in his life and he knew his health was returning to normal.

That night, Greysteel lay on top of the bed next to Velvet and held her hand. She was restless and he had to fetch her drinks and help her use the chamber pot, but he was gratified to see that she did sleep for a few hours.

In the morning, he began all over again with her ablutions. Greysteel changed the small dressings on her breast and cheek and dreaded the moment when she would ask for a mirror. When she was clean and fed, he handed her a parchment. "Here is the morning gift you asked me for after we were married."

Velvet unfolded the deed to Bolsover Castle and saw that he had signed the ownership over to *Elizabeth Montgomery*. Her eyes searched his face and she saw that though it was a sacrifice, it was one he was eager to make. "Thank you, Greysteel."

"You have two letters. . . . I read the one from Christian."

I won't tell her that I also read the one from Charles. It would embarrass her—odds fish, it would embarrass both of us!

"Will you read it to me?"

"It contains sad news. Princess Mary has died."

"Oh, dear God . . . poor Charles."

Greysteel took the letter from the envelope and read:

> *Dearest Velvet:*
> *When I learned of Princess Mary's tragic death from smallpox, I hurried to Whitehall and learned from Emma that you had gone to Roehampton to warn your husband that he had been exposed. I am extremely worried for you and Montgomery and beg that you immediately let me know that you are well.*
> *The contagion is spreading, I'm afraid. My grandson, William, came down with a mild dose, but unfortunately for him his once handsome face will be badly pockmarked. You will likely believe this is just punishment for stealing the portrait you were having painted for Greysteel. Using it to blackmail you into exchanging it for Roehampton was an evil deed for which he has now paid.*

Greysteel raised his eyes from the letter and looked at Velvet. "You know I want to kill the whoreson, don't you?"

She shook her head. "It would hurt Christian too much."

His eyes went back to the letter and he continued reading.

Henrietta Maria is in deepest mourning for her daughter and I believe the queen is secretly suffering from guilt over the way she treated her son Henry. I warrant she now realizes that the estrangement can never be rectified. It's a lesson we should all heed; never let silly quarrels separate us from those we love.

Greysteel and Velvet exchanged a poignant glance.

I feel great empathy for Charles. Ruling a kingdom does not protect him from tragedy and sorrow. Though surrounded by both fawners and friends, I believe he is the loneliest of men.

Greysteel avoided looking at his wife and finished the letter.

If I do not hear from you shortly, I shall come to Roe-hampton to see for myself how you are faring. Fondest love, Christian.

"Will you write to her for me, darling?"

"As soon as I see that you are fully recovered."

"I refuse to expire . . . again," she added softly.

The light in his grey eyes was fierce. "You did take your last breath, Velvet."

"Yes . . . I know what it feels like to die."

"What *does* it feel like, love?"

"Frightening . . . so I decided to come back to

you. . . . I knew you would keep me safe." She twisted her wedding ring that now fitted so loosely, and it fell off in her hand. She looked down at the tiny circle of gold and noticed something inscribed on the inside. She held it up to the light and squinted her eyes so that she could read it. LOVED FOREVER.

Velvet's heart fluttered and her eyes widened. "Why did you never tell me that you loved me, Greysteel?"

"From the day we were betrothed, I believed you were in love with Charles. Now that I'm older and wiser, I realize that you love each other as friends."

"Devoted friends," Velvet teased.

"If you are ready to pour salt on my wounded heart, you must be feeling a little better. Here is a letter from your *devoted* friend. I shall give you privacy while you read it."

Alone, Velvet looked at the sealed letter in her hand. Though they had been friends since Charles was eight, this was the first time he had ever written to her. As she broke the seal and began to read, the pain Charles conveyed over the death of his sister dwarfed her distressing discomfort.

She came to the words

I will never forget the look of fear on your face for your husband when you learned that he had been in close contact with a victim of smallpox. It told me how deeply you love him.

And she read them a second time. When she came to the words *I envy Montgomery your devotion, because I know I will never have so great a love,* she read them three times.

Velvet suddenly became suspicious of Greysteel's words. " 'Older and wiser,' be damned," she murmured. "Perhaps you realized that Charles and I love each other as friends only after you read this letter." A hint of a smile touched her lips and she decided not to examine the seal too closely.

After a short time, she again focused on the letter.

After my coronation, when Catherine comes from Portugal to be my wife and queen, I know I could have no more worthy Lady of the Bedchamber to serve her than you, Velvet.

"That is true," she whispered.

Whitehall is not the same without the Earl and Countess of Eglinton.

Velvet sighed. "That is also true." The letter fell from her fingers as her mind drifted off, conjuring imaginary scenes.

Each and every day of the next week, Greysteel nursed his wife, washing her, tending the eruptions on her body, feeding her and showing her in every way how precious she was to him.

"My scabs and matter are healing." She raised her arm to reveal her armpit. "Some more crusts fell off in the night."

He took hold of her fingers, kissed them and

slanted a dark eyebrow at her. "Can you guess what I'm going to do to you when you are strong again?"

She rolled her eyes in anticipation. "Tell me."

His teasing look vanished. "I'm going to beat you to a jelly for putting your life in jeopardy!"

"Do you have a big stick?" she asked innocently.

"Big enough," he threatened. "Let me put more cream on your cheek." He peeled off the small square of linen and shook his head regretfully. "How the hell do you expect me to live with the knowledge that I infected you with smallpox?"

"Are these pangs of guilt you are suffering caused by the pockmark I'll have on my face?" she asked incredulously.

"It is a terrible price to pay for rushing here to warn me."

"Greysteel Montgomery, it is a mere trifle. If it's ugly, I shall wear a fashionable patch over it."

Her courageous nonchalance touched and amused him. "It will have to be a hell of a big patch."

"They have some outrageous ones at the Exchange in the Strand imported from Paris. I warrant a patch in the shape of a coach and horses will do the trick."

"You will be mistaken for a French courtesan," he teased.

"By you, I hope . . . and sooner rather than later," she invited.

He rubbed cream on her cheek and decided to leave it uncovered. Since a second scab had never formed, he had high expectations that the scar would not be unsightly. Since she had never asked for a mirror, Greysteel wondered if she was afraid to look at herself.

He forced himself to go to her dressing table and bring her a hand mirror.

Velvet took one look at her reflection and screamed.

"Sweetheart, it's not that bad."

"It's my *hair!* It's enough to frighten the ducks off the pond. Bloody hell, is it any wonder they used to call me Frizzy Lizzy? How can you bear to look at me?"

He grinned. "You've been naked for over a fortnight—I didn't notice your hair."

"I wanted to go downstairs tomorrow, but I'll have to wash my hair before anyone sees me looking like this. . . . I'm a countess."

"I'll get the bathing tub out. I'm not sure I'm strong enough to carry hot water for you, though," he teased.

"If you have a relapse, I'll put you to bed and do my utmost to restore your faculties." She licked her lips suggestively.

"You're starting to frighten me, Lizzy!"

"You devil! It's *Lady Lizzy,* and don't you forget it."

That night, after she had dried her hair before the fire, Velvet put down her brush and posed naked before her portrait. "What do you think?"

Greysteel stepped from the bath and toweled himself. He studied the painting, then cast a critical eye over his wife. "Well-ll . . . you've been very sick, you know," he said doubtfully.

She stared at his cock as it stood up and turned rigid. "Now there's an honest answer. I shall reward the tall fellow."

He strode toward her, picked her up with mock ferocity and carried her to their bed. With tender hands he laid her down and brushed the red gold tendrils from her face. "I love you so much, Velvet. We are miraculously lucky to have survived and to be together like this."

Her arms slid about his neck, which was now heavily pockmarked, and she lifted her mouth for his ravishing. *His long lovelocks will hide them; his splendid dark beauty is intact.* Her mind stopped forming thoughts as she reveled in the taste and the feel of his powerful body. Her fingers sought out his old battle scars when he made love to her. It thrilled her to know he had been a warrior.

When Greysteel kissed her breasts, he cherished the one that had been left pockmarked as much as he did the other—more than he did the other. It was a badge of her great courage.

Velvet shuddered. His unshaved chin prickled against her flesh and perversely it excited her because it added to his overt maleness and his dominance. By contrast she felt fragile and feminine and so sensually feline, she wanted to purr.

When Greysteel slid up inside her, he cried out as her scalding sheath gloved him, clinging possessively as she yielded to his hard demanding thrusts. Though he had intended to be gentle, his instincts told him that Velvet wanted to be taken with thunder and fury. She was his woman and he needed to brand her with his fierce love and adoration. Tenderness could wait until the afterglow.

Much later, with their bodies curled together, the lovers talked and whispered for hours, murmuring love words, making plans, rejoicing over their baby, declaring passionate vows and exchanging sacred promises. They ran the gamut of emotions from laughter to tears as they revealed their innermost fears and fancies to each other. They had both learned the hard way that being together was the only thing they truly needed to be happy.

The next morning, before they broke their fast, they went downstairs and ran outside like children escaping from the prison of the schoolroom. They visited their horses in the stable and when Velvet saw the pair of striped cats who lived there, she decided to give them names. "Let's call them *Scabs* and *Matter*. I have a flagrant fondness for scabs and matter."

"You have a predilection for peculiar names, my love."

"If someone called *Greysteel* is referring to the name *Velvet*, the wretch has no leg to stand on!"

He bowed. "Your witty point is taken. Let's go and eat breakfast before I faint from hunger."

"You need some boiled owl to toughen you up!"

"And you need your arse tanned to curb that saucy tongue."

"Tell the truth and shame the Devil, you love my tongue!"

"You are the rudest little girl I have ever encountered."

They went off into peals of laughter. Then, hands clasped, they entered the manor through the kitchen door.

They ate their breakfast at the kitchen table and insisted that Mrs. Clegg join them.

"Roehampton has spawned another love match," Bertha said. "It's the romantic Elizabethan atmosphere. . . . It's inevitable."

"We are going to have a baby." Velvet's face glowed.

"Congratulations! When is it to be, my lady?"

"Well, I hope he doesn't put in an appearance before May."

"So that you can attend the coronation?" Bertha asked.

"Good heavens, no! If he's born in April, I'll have *two* males under the sign of Aries trying to control me."

"And what if it's a female imp of Satan like yourself?" Greysteel demanded.

Velvet's face softened. "If it's a girl, I shall call her Paisley."

"My mother's name!" His heart melted with love. "You are so generous, Velvet."

"Nonsense, I just like beautiful names." She pushed back her chair. "Now, if you will both excuse me, I have to write a letter to a friend." She glanced wickedly at Greysteel. "A *devoted* friend!"

They left the kitchen and Greysteel watched her sit at the writing desk. "I shall give you some privacy, Lady Montgomery."

Velvet spent the next hour composing a letter to the king. Just as she was about to sand it, she heard a carriage on the driveway and ran to the window. "It's Christian," she called upstairs. "Didn't you answer her letter?"

"Of course, I did. I invited her to come and visit us."

The two women enjoyed their reunion, and Greysteel sat bemused, unable to get a word in edgewise, as the pair talked without seeming to take a breath.

"What will you wear to the coronation?" Christian asked.

"I'm not going to the coronation. I have more important things to do, like giving birth to the next Earl of Eglinton."

"Darling, you won't have your baby until the following month. King Charles will expect you both to be there."

"Charles is quite capable of receiving the Crown of England without us holding his hands. We have our own life to live. We are going to take our horses to Bolsover and spend Christmas there as well as the spring. We want our child to be born at the castle."

The dowager countess was taken aback. "You mean to say you don't intend to return to Whitehall until Catherine of Braganza becomes Charles's queen?"

"I don't intend to return at all, except for an occasional visit. I have just written to Charles, declining his invitation to be a Lady of the Bedchamber."

"Are you pulling my leg, Velvet?"

"No, I am perfectly serious. My mind is made up."

"How will you exist without the intrigue and gossip?"

"I shall rely on you for every salacious detail!"

"That reminds me . . . the latest rumor is that James, Duke of York, secretly wed Anne Hyde, and now wants a divorce!"

"The lecherous swine! 'Tis no rumor. I was there with the king when James and Anne were married in the chapel. I was also there when the poor lady suffered a miscarriage. Now that there's no child, the whoreson wants a divorce! I shall add a postscript to my letter to Charles that I will be a witness if he wants me to testify that they are legally wed!"

Montgomery sat stunned, listening to his wife. She was willing to give up her glamorous life at Court to be a wife and mother and allow him to fulfill his dream of breeding horses. Velvet was ready to return to Whitehall to right a wrong, but other than that, she was ready to kiss the Court good-bye.

Suddenly, she looked across the room and their eyes met in an intimate glance that aroused him instantly. He knew he was the luckiest man alive.

Velvet lowered her voice to Christian. "I'll be busy being a Lady of Montgomery's Bedchamber. The man is insatiable!"